Roses are red, violets are blue.

Only one woman could make NFL star Gideon Wells walk away from the Super Bowl: His Mama, "Queen" Elizabeth, the beautiful, strong black woman who adopted him and his two white brothers when they were just kids. So when Elizabeth develops a pressing health issue, Gideon doesn't hesitate to come home and run the flower shop she loves almost as much as her boys. But there's an unexpected complication in Queen Elizabeth's shop: and that complication looks really good in a gardener's apron and pruning gloves.

This mama's boy has a naughty side too.

Janelle Gold has always thought of herself as a geek, more into books than sports, preferring brains over brawn. So a gorgeous jock like Gideon Wells is not exactly the type she usually goes for. But there's something about the hot quarterback that makes Janelle think sometimes opposites do attract, and it's not just his dedication to his family, or the fact that he can hold his own in the flower shop. There's just something irresistible about a man who stops to smell the roses.

Books by Crystal B. Bright

Mama's Boys
The Look Of Love
Forget Me Not

Published by Kensington Publishing Corporation

Forget Me Not

Mama's Boys

Crystal B. Bright

LYRICAL PRESS
Kensington Publishing Corp.
www.kensingtonbooks.com

Lyrical Press books are published by
Kensington Publishing Corp. 119 West 40th Street New York, NY 10018

All Kensington titles, imprints, and distributed lines are available at special quantity discounts for bulk purchases for sales promotion, premiums, fund-raising, and educational or institutional use.

Special book excerpts or customized printings can also be created to fit specific needs. For details, write or phone the office of the Kensington Special Sales Manager:
Kensington Publishing Corp.
119 West 40th Street
New York, NY 10018
Attn. Special Sales Department. Phone: 1-800-221-2647.

Kensington and the K logo Reg. U.S. Pat. & TM Off.
LYRICAL PRESS Reg. U.S. Pat. & TM Off.
Lyrical Press and the L logo are trademarks of Kensington Publishing Corp.

First Electronic Edition: February 2016
eISBN-13: 978-1-61650-713-8
eISBN-10: 1-61650-713-6

First Print Edition: February 2016
ISBN-13: 978-1-61650-714-5
ISBN-10: 1-61650-714-4

Printed in the United States of America

This book is dedicated to my family and friends, who have always believed in me even when I didn't believe in myself. Thank you for blowing my head up when I needed it while keeping me grounded. Thank you to Lisa Adkins, who laughed at my lack of football knowledge, then helped me whenever I asked questions about it. Thank you to the love of my life, Jimmy. Thank you for sharing your football know-how, too. My characters went from being Mountain Lions to Wolves because of you. Your love and support means everything to me. I love you.

Author's Foreword

I have always had a soft spot for rough and tough men who are put into awkward situations. I think it brings out a vulnerable side to men...plus it can be a bit comical. Movies like "The Nanny", "The Tooth Fairy", and "The Game Plan" are examples of men put in strange situations but also make them endearing.

Because of that fish-out-of-water type of genre, I got the idea of having three brothers, all stars in their sports, put into a situation where they would have to run their mother's very feminine businesses. I also wanted to write a series about brothers. What's hotter than three sexy brothers?

I hope you all enjoy my story about the Wells brothers and the way they run a hair salon, a flower shop and a clothing boutique.

Enjoy!
Crystal***

Acknowledgements

Thank you to the professors at Old Dominion University and Seton Hill University who taught me a lot about crafting a great story. Thank you to Lyrical Press for taking a chance on an unusual series. Thank you to every author I have read. I learn from each and every one of you.

Chapter 1

Gideon Wells pressed his phone to his ear in a feeble attempt to drown out the shouts and chants of his teammates in the expansive locker room. The sounds brought him back to the first time he'd run with a football to the goalpost as a kid, trying to balance the big shoulder pads on his feeble frame. Time had changed him and his body, and ramped up his love of the sport.

He couldn't blame the men for their excitement. The Super Bowl only happened once a year for two teams. Gideon's Virginia Beach Wolves had made it. He hadn't stopped smiling since their last game. Every time he'd talked about his upcoming participation in the Super Bowl, his first and, hopefully, not his last time, his skin had felt like he had electric sparks dancing over it. He hadn't been able to think about anything else but this game.

Then the call from his mother had come a week ago with news that had made him feel like he had been doused in ice-cold water. Gideon's thoughts had split between his mother and his career, two aspects of his life that gave him purpose.

At the first ring, he paced the red-carpeted floor ringed in a black-and-gold border in honor of his team's colors. His mother had approved of him going to play for the Wolves, not because the team made Virginia Beach their home and he could still be close to his family, but because they wore her favorite colors. Recalling his mother's almost regal voice forced him to smile.

Gideon took a deep breath on the third ring. The great thing about being a Super Bowl team had to be the way people catered to them. This locker room in Pasadena, California had been repainted with their colors and had their emblem over each wall. The fresh-paint smell still lingered in their air. Between the paint and the new carpet, the place had a new feel even though the stadium itself had been around for decades.

In his white tights, he didn't want to think about the confining feeling constricting his legs and waist. The armbands he wore compressed his limbs from his wrists to the middle of his biceps.

The cleats on his shoes sank into the plush carpeting. He wanted to wait before suiting up with the full shoulder pads. He found it necessary to wear knee pads right now. He tugged on the side of one as he lifted his leg. At that point, he heard a click on the other line.

"Hey, Gid! Getting your mind right?"

Gideon smiled when he heard Gunnar answer the phone, until it hit him why his professional-athlete brother had had to stop his career to go back home. As a champion mixed martial artist, Gunnar understood what it took to get prepared. Gunnar had had an MMA championship fight right when their mother had gotten sick. Gideon had this game, this one life-changing, dream-come-true game.

Standing in an area between the chaotic locker room and the shower area, the quietest area there, he leaned against a nearby wall. "The mind is right. Hyped up to play, you know."

"I know. I get it." Gunnar kept his voice low and even, as though Gideon had planned on leaping from a plane without a parachute and Gunnar had to talk him out of the act.

The shorthand way of talking about their professions worked for Gideon. The same went for his younger brother, Thane, another professional athlete, who also understood the importance of pregame rituals.

"Congrats on your match. You took your opponent out in, what, ten minutes?" Gideon scratched the back of his head as he imagined his older brother's serious countenance cracking.

"Seven, but who's counting." Gunnar laughed.

The sound brought him back home, back to a time when the two of them used to wrestle until one submitted or they got tired, whichever came first. Only one thing would have truly transported him to his childhood home in Virginia Beach. If he could see his composed mother, not in a hospital, but in her beloved flower shop where he used to help her, he would feel better.

"Good luck today. I'm sure you're going to kick ass," Gunnar exclaimed.

"Gunnar Wells."

Gideon beamed as soon as he heard their mother in the background, the true reason for his call. Her calming voice and soothing nature always centered him. He could never figure out how he and his brothers had gotten so lucky to be adopted by a caring and compassionate woman.

He never saw himself and his African-American mother as being different. He saw himself as being Elizabeth Sommerville's son. Full flesh and blood. She never treated him or his brothers any differently.

"Sorry, Ma," Gunnar said to their mother. "Gid, I'm going to hand you over to Mom. I'll talk to you later. Love you."

"Love you, bro." Gideon looked toward the locker-room area. He spotted one of his wide receivers shrugging his shoulders and pointing to his wrist, pantomiming that Gideon would need to hurry up and get ready.

Gideon nodded and turned his back on his teammate to give his full concentration to his mother.

"Darling, how are you doing?" Elizabeth's words dripped with her trademark grace and elegance.

Gideon couldn't help but smile.

"I'm fine, Mom, except I have this little thing I'm doing later." He laughed.

"Cute." She laughed and then got silent for a moment before she spoke again. "Ah, my baby." She sighed.

"Thane's your baby."

"All of you are my babies. I worry about each and every one of you." Elizabeth sighed, the sound audible through the phone.

Gideon remembered the nights she'd stay up staring out the living room window during Gunnar's rebellious phase. She'd kept vigil by Thane's bed, a particularly sickly child who'd grew out of that as soon as he'd hit puberty and discovered the opposite sex. Gideon had recognized his mother being pulled in different directions and had been determined, even as a snot-nosed kid, to be the least of his mother's worries.

"I'm more concerned about you. How are you doing?" Elizabeth's struggles with her health plagued his thoughts.

"Don't worry about me. I'm doing okay. Gunnar and Eboni are taking great care of me."

Gideon blinked. "Eboni? Eboni Danielson? Really?" He remembered Gunnar had gotten on that Greyhound bus years ago right after he'd graduated high school, leaving Eboni, his high school sweetheart and professed love of his life, behind to pursue his mixed martial arts fighting dream. "Are they—"

"Together…for now." The lightness that filled his mother's voice became heavy by the end of her statement.

At least Gunnar had someone by his side. After this game, Gideon would be rushing back home to take care of his mother. He'd learned from her to put family first.

"I'm glad he's there for you. Right after the Super Bowl, I'll come home to be with you all when you have your surgery."

"Oh, darling, won't you have press to do and have sponsors to please?"

"Come on. You don't think I'll do any of that with you having heart surgery. Hell—"

Queen Elizabeth, as her friends so dubbed her, cleared her throat.

Gideon stood up straighter. He'd forgotten to keep his locker-room talk segregated to his teammates. "Excuse me. I mean, I'm fighting staying here instead of coming home now."

"Only playing in the Super Bowl has been your dream since I put a football in your tiny hands. Do you remember that?"

Remember it? He still kept that same dirty, deflated, misshapen football in his home. To tease his mother, he said, "I barely remember that thing."

"Again, you are so cute." Queen Elizabeth laughed a little but completed the light expression with a slight cough.

An uncomfortable ripple slithered over his gut and up to his heart, where it constricted it from pumping for a hot second. He couldn't let her feel his worry. He continued smiling to maintain the lightness in his tone.

"Some new magazines came into the salon," she said with a playful lilt to her tone.

Gideon heard the joy in his mother's voice. He ran his hand over his head, knowing she would bring up some aspect of his personal life as only the tabloids could capture. "Really? That's interesting."

"It sure is." Elizabeth cleared her throat.

"Whatever you do, don't say it." Gideon shook his head.

"Say what?"

"America's couple." Gideon bristled at the moniker the media had dubbed his brief relationship with actress Hilary Cox. He paced the floor, waiting for his mother's next statement.

"I must admit, you and that little blonde actress are cute together. Matching hair, both with blue eyes and great smiles. Bet you don't mind that I put braces on you when you were younger, huh?"

Gideon laughed, but he recalled those years. Girls hadn't given him a second look. He'd fought wannabe bullies every day on top of that. He hadn't needed Gunnar's help to win his fights back then. Gideon could be accommodating, but couldn't be called a pushover…well, except when it came to his mother.

"I wish you wouldn't read that trash. They're all full of lies." He moved closer to the shower area to get farther away from the noise.

"It's the only way I can find out about your private life. You talk to me every day but never share anything about the special women in your life. I'm your mother. You should tell me everything."

Gideon imagined that his mother stood in front of him, wagging her finger at him with its impeccable manicure and, of course, the nail painted fire-engine red. "Mom, I have to keep some things from you. I'm not a boy anymore."

Elizabeth made a disapproving noise from her throat. "I know. You and Gunnar are so quick to tell me that." She paused a moment before barreling on with their conversation. "Will you be bringing Hilary home with you? I would love to meet her."

Gideon swallowed before he answered. "We broke up."

His mother gasped. "Oh, sweetie. Why didn't you tell me?"

"I didn't think you would really care. We weren't together that long." Six months equated to a lifelong relationship in celebrity terms. For Gideon, it meant that the woman he'd spent time with wouldn't be the future Mrs. Gideon Wells or the mother of his children.

"What happened?" Elizabeth asked.

"The separation got to her. She would be off doing movies. I had games and training, plus living in Virginia and not California. It didn't work." He turned his back on the group. "Besides, my sucky love life has helped the team. I'm only concentrating on the team and how I play."

"You could have made it work if she was the right one."

Gideon knew a hint of truth existed in his mother's statement. As he thought about it, maybe he hadn't wanted a relationship with Hilary to work. With her, he'd felt more like an accessory, a great piece to have on her arm for red-carpet events. He'd gotten tired of hearing what a striking couple they made. Thinking about that label now had Gideon gritting his teeth.

"Honestly, that's not what I was going to ask you about." Elizabeth lowered her voice.

Gideon shook his head. He could only imagine what else his mother had read about him in those rags. "Spill it."

Elizabeth released a long exhale before she spoke. "Are you hurt?"

The question from his mother froze him to his spot. No way would one of those fashion magazines littering Queen Elizabeth's hair salon mention something like that. Gideon felt sure he kept his pains hidden. On instinct, he tugged on his knee pad again, which caused the joint to twinge. He placed his foot down to the floor and walked around to lessen the ache.

"I'm fine. Never better. Remember, I'm the one you never have to worry about."

Gideon recalled the nights of watching how Elizabeth had paced in their home as she'd waited to see if the police would bring Gunnar home or relay some tragic news to her. Thane had needed constant attention. Gideon hadn't wanted to add to her concern. He wouldn't be breaking that trend today.

Elizabeth cut into his thoughts. "I know. But if you are hurting, you know you can—"

"Don't get yourself worked up over nothing." Gideon took a breath before saying, "I apologize for interrupting you." The pain didn't hurt him enough to forget his manners. He glanced at the digital clock over the door. "And I don't have a lot of time."

"I know you have to go, baby. We're cheering for you from Virginia Beach. I love you." Elizabeth made a kissing sound over the phone.

"Love you, Mom. Be sure to tell Gunnar not to screw it up with Eboni again." One of the brothers had to be lucky in love. Gideon remembered how great Eboni had been with his older brother.

If Queen Elizabeth knew about Thane's penchant for loving and leaving women, she would pull the young player back home by his earlobe like she used to do when they'd misbehaved as children.

Gideon disconnected the call. Before he could resume with his team, he had one more quick call to make. He had to hear from Thane. He could go in this game with a clearer mind if he knew his entire family had his back. He knew he wouldn't hear from Hilary.

After the first ring, Gideon heard a click before he heard a voice.

"Gid! How the hell are you?" Thane's light voice seemed in conflict with the impression Gunnar had given of their brother.

Gunnar had told Gideon that each time he'd tried calling Thane, he hadn't gotten an answer. Gideon didn't know if Gunnar had exaggerated or if Gideon had gotten lucky with scoring a conversation with their youngest brother.

"Wound tight, Thane. But in a good way." Gideon shook out his free arm when he started to feel some tingling in it. He couldn't wait to start this game. It had been twenty-seven years in the making.

"I hear you. Thanks again for the tickets. With spring training coming up, I couldn't go. You understand, right?"

Gideon nodded. "I get it."

Like Gideon had his pro-football training, Thane had to prepare for his whole Major League Baseball season starting soon. Then Gideon heard a strange voice behind Thane. The tone and content of the statement didn't sound like any trainer Gideon had ever encountered.

"Come back over here, baby."

Gideon's shoulders tightened. Had his brother actually pushed him aside so he could lay up with some woman?

"Who's that?" Gideon balled his hand into a fist, stretching the tape across his knuckles.

"I'm not sure of her name yet, but believe me, she has the lungs of a cheerleader." Thane laughed.

Gideon found no amusement in it. Since Thane hadn't gone back home to help Gunnar with their mother, he would have thought his baby brother would have come to California to cheer him on his most important day ever.

"I got off the phone with Mom. She sounds good today." Gideon hoped his message got through to his younger brother.

"Yeah, I talked to her earlier. She told me she's having a Super Bowl party at her house." Thane laughed and then said something that sounded muffled.

Gideon assumed his attentions had been diverted by the stranger in his room.

"Didn't mean to interrupt your special day." Sarcasm dripped from every word Gideon uttered. "I'll talk to you later. Love you, man."

"Yeah, later." Thane disconnected the call.

Even at Thane's age, Gideon didn't remember being that self-centered. He had bigger things to worry about now. If his mother read in some magazine or saw on TV that he may be hurt, it wouldn't take long for his coaches to say something to him. It also meant he had to watch his back out on the field. The opposing team would love to take him out of the game, preferably on a stretcher.

Time. Gideon had to play in this one game. Then he could heal and move on with more training. Today, he would have to be faster against the other team. They'd probably be gunning for his leg to take him out of the sport, not only the game.

As he turned to go back into the main locker room, he ran into Dennis, the receiver who'd tried getting Gideon's attention earlier. Dennis had become like a third brother to Gideon. They had gone to University of North Carolina together. They'd been drafted together. They had even ended up on the same NFL team.

The big man with dreadlocks that went down to his shoulders smiled wide enough to express his happiness and the team's. "Come on, man. You ready?" He held up his hand to Gideon.

                    Crystal B. Bright

Gideon slapped his hand against Dennis's and pulled him in for a half hug. "We got this. Like back in the day as a Tar Heel."

"Were you talking to your mama?" Dennis paced as Gideon strolled to the main locker-room area.

Gideon nodded.

Dennis smiled harder and shook his head as he let out a low whistle. "Your fine-ass mama needs me in her life."

Gideon laughed. "Hey, watch your mouth when you talk about her."

"I hear you. I hear you." Dennis chuckled. "When we first met back in college, I used to think it was weird for a white dude to have a black mama. After meeting her, I wanted to marry that woman." He pounded Gideon on his shoulder with his fist. "I'd even let you call me Daddy."

Gideon pushed his friend's shoulder. "Oh, you have jokes, right?" He shook his head. "Sorry. Mom doesn't go for young men. She said they remind her too much of her sons."

"Fine. Be sure to tell her I said hi." Dennis lowered his head to Gideon and in a hushed tone asked, "I know this is part of the QB duty, but can I do the rally speech?"

The electric current that had been flowing through Gideon's body defused with Dennis's request. Long before the first hair had sprouted on his upper lip or down below his belt, he'd dreamed of being the quarterback in the Super Bowl and being able to bring his team to a win. Part of that dream included giving the speech to his team that would inspire them to annihilate the opposing team. He couldn't give up any part of his dream, even to his friend, even if that friend had played as quarterback in college.

He stared at Dennis for a moment. "It's the Super Bowl, Den. It's my first one."

"Yeah, mine too." He leaned in and lowered his voice. "Remember back in the day, you and I would do this kind of thing together all the time."

Gideon nodded. "I remember. And I know you want to make MVP. I get it." He pointed to himself with his thumb. "I'm responsible for this team."

"That's cool." Disappointment laced Dennis's statement. "Make sure you keep throwing me the ball, okay? I'll make sure to get it in the end zone every time." In Dennis's dramatic fashion, he took a big step to the side to illustrate his point.

"Maybe for the new season we can share the motivation duties. The guys are already hyped up. We need to go into this game in control." Gideon wanted to set a tone for his team. Acting out of control would kill their synergy.

Dennis's smile softened. Gideon saw his shoulders slump under the shoulder pads.

Gideon turned away from his disappointed friend and glanced into the bustling locker room. Dennis didn't understand the importance of leading a team in the Super Bowl, not merely playing in the game. Gideon had to be the puppet master. If a play failed, it would be on him. He couldn't let his team down, not today.

"Sure. You're the boss." Dennis offered his neon smile again.

"I promise I won't let you all down." Gideon wrapped his arm around Dennis's shoulders as they headed toward the team.

"Hey, now that you and Hil are over and this is our last game of the season, are you going to try and hit up that cheerleader?" Dennis winked and licked his lips.

Gideon didn't have to guess which cheerleader his friend wanted him to hit up as he called it. Brittany or Tiffany or Brandy. Something with an E sound at the end of her name. The bouncy, bubbly brunette had made it known she wanted Gideon. At practices where cheerleaders weren't needed, she popped up and managed to run into him. When he worked out at the team gym, she would be waiting for him outside. One time after practice, as he'd soaked in an ice bath, she'd shown up in her bikini ready to join him.

Gideon had never liked a desperate woman. This cheerleader reeked of neediness.

"Man, I don't want any part of her." Gideon shook his head. "For one, it's against the rules. Players can't date the She-Wolves."

"During the season." Dennis pounded his fist on Gideon's shoulder. "After the season…"

"I still don't want her." Gideon shook his head. "But you, you have at her. Be sure you treat her right." No matter what Gideon did, his mama's words always crept into his mind and out of his mouth.

"She only has eyes for you, brother. Bet you five big ones that when you come out of the tunnel, she'll run into you."

Gideon snickered. "No way. The cheerleaders know not to interfere with our entrances, especially for this game."

Dennis held up his large hand with his long digits splayed. "Five big ones."

Gideon nodded. "You're on." He glanced at the team. "Hey, everyone! Listen up!" He waited until the team members stopped their actions and moved around him and Dennis.

He couldn't keep his mind on what he would have to do in these next few hours while he knew his mother would have to have heart surgery soon. The phone call home to talk to his mother and his brothers hadn't calmed his nerves. His team didn't need to know about his worry.

"Friends," Gideon began, "we didn't get to this position by luck." He strolled around the locker room, making sure to look each one of his teammates in their eyes. "We got here with heart. We got here because we're all dedicated. We trained our asses off. We ran drills until we dropped. Hell, I think even Thumper put on a clean jock one time." He pointed to the large lineman standing behind the group.

"Nope!" Thumper responded and moved in closer to the group to share his stench.

"Damn, dude! Get the hell back." Stephen, a running back, covered his nose and waved his hand in front of his face. "Offensive lineman is right. Your smell is brutal."

Gideon and his teammates laughed but also made space around Thumper. Since training camp, Thumper had convinced himself that wearing the same cup and jock strap without washing the duo kept him in high playing form. As a result, he reeked. Coaches had to keep him away from the press and charity events.

Not Gideon. It didn't escape his attention that as quarterback, he'd become the face of the team. The press ate up his boy-next-door look, as one magazine described him.

He could care less about his appearance or what the female fans thought of him. He had a job to do, a game to play, a chance to be taken seriously as an athlete.

"To win, we're going to have to remember our training." Gideon didn't raise his voice, a trait he'd learned from his mother. If spoken with conviction, people will listen. "We're going to remember how we got here. We're going to play like this could be the very last time we will ever play this sport we love again." Gideon peered over his teammates' heads when he saw the locker-room door opening. He focused on his team. "Play hard, men. Play with integrity. Win for Virginia."

"Do it for the Gipper, man?" Dennis asked and then laughed.

Gideon smiled. "I don't know what your girl's name is now."

The group of men around them laughed.

Dennis put his hand on Gideon's shoulder and pulled him back. "I got this."

"Got what?" Gideon felt his eyebrows knit together as he watched his friend move to the center of the room.

"We are Wolves!" Dennis shouted the encouraging words in the middle of the crowded locker room. He illustrated his exclamation by howling like a wolf, something their fans did on a regular basis for the team.

Gideon shook his head. He should have known Dennis would kick up the guys into a frenzy. He would have to be that calming voice of reason, even if his insides screamed along with Dennis.

The team, dressed in their standard red-black-and-gold uniforms, cheered while pumping their fists in the air.

"Fuck 'Sharknado'! We all know a shark can't beat a wolf, am I right?"

The team laughed and cheered at the same time.

"The Maui Sharks are going down!" Dennis raised his fists in the air.

Gideon put his hand on Dennis's chest and faced him. "That's enough." As the quarterback, he had to be the leader. He had to set the mood for how the team played during this important game.

"Okay, guys. Huddle up." Coach Brick, who must have walked into the locker-room area, waved his hands in the air signal the men to come together. "Christ, I can't wait until this game is done so that you can take a damn bath, Thumper."

The team laughed again.

"I bathe. It's my jock that's fragrant." The big man cupped his crotch and grinned through his big, bushy red beard.

"Serious time, guys. Don't think about this being the Super Bowl. Think about this as the game of your lives. Like Gid said, you've all trained for this. Stay smart. Stay sharp. Think two steps ahead of the other team. We can win this together. All in." Brick put his hand palm down in the center of the circle.

The team put their hands on top of his.

Without prompting, the team shouted in unison, "Wolves rule!" Then they howled, leaning their heads back to project to the ceiling.

"Line up in the tunnel." Brick pointed to the doorway.

The team all filtered out in a line with Gideon bringing up the rear. He picked up his shoulder pads and secured them onto his shoulders. One more thing he had to carry. He grabbed the collar portion of the weighted plastic protection to occupy his hands until he got onto the field.

"Uh, hold on, Gid." Brick put a hand on Gideon's chest.

Gideon peered down at his coach's hand and took a step back as the rest of his team filed out of the room.

His coach epitomized his name. The former Hall of Famer stood about a foot shorter than Gideon's six-foot-three height. His width nearly matched his height, and looking at the man from behind, it didn't look like he had a neck. Topped off with his crew-cut hair, his coach looked like a pale brick.

Seeing the coach accelerated Gideon's heartbeat. Gideon already had a hard time corralling his feelings about living out his dream at such a young age. Too bad he knew why he had arrived. His left knee throbbed as though it wanted to give its two cents about his situation.

"How are you feeling? You know all the plays?" Brick's expression became somber.

Gideon tapped his temple. "Got them all. And I studied the Sharks' previous games. They rely on their size to steamroll over their competition. It won't happen to us."

"And you're doing okay?" His coach scanned Gideon from head to toe, purposefully stopping at Gideon's knee area.

To refute his coach's assumption, Gideon paced in his spot as he kept his gaze on Brick's eyes. He couldn't be seen as weak. No way could he miss this game.

"I've got a lot of pent-up energy. I can't wait to get on the field." Gideon pointed to the door to give his coach a hint to end this conversation.

"Okay. You got it." Brick pointed to Gideon. "You know if you have any problems, you can tell me. We have Joshua waiting in the wings to fill in as quarterback. Push comes to shove, we can use Dennis."

Gideon shook his head. "Why are you talking to me about contingency plans like I'm not going to play?"

Determination filled Gideon's head and heart. He wouldn't get himself to this point without seeing this game to the end.

Brick held up his hand to Gideon. "You're right. If there's nothing for anyone to worry about, I won't press the issue."

"Good." He tried walking by Brick when the coach put his hand on Gideon's shoulder.

"Did you get the shot?"

Gideon didn't know what bothered him more, the fact that his coach knew Gideon had problems with his knee or the fact that he wanted him to push his body until he broke. He couldn't put all the blame on Brick's nonplussed reaction. Gideon had made it clear he would need to be dragged off the field for him to miss this game.

Gideon dropped his gaze and shook his head. "I don't need it." He wanted to do this win on his own head of steam, without chemical assistance.

Brick held up his electronic tablet. "The team doctor said—"

"He said they didn't find anything wrong with my knee, not on the X-rays, not in the physical exam. Nothing." He stared into his coach's eyes when he spoke. "But I'm sure the doctor wrote down I mentioned my knee had been bothering me. I took a hard hit the last game."

"That was two weeks ago." Brick scratched his head under his Wolves baseball cap.

Gideon didn't need a reminder. He'd worked his knee out harder, trying to strengthen it for the game. His big mouth had gotten him in trouble. "I'm fine. I was fine through training. I was fine for our last game. I'm going to get us that championship." Speaking with conviction had to help him now.

Brick stared at him for a moment. "Lord knows, I want this championship. It's been fifteen years since I led a team to a Super Bowl win. I want you to bring that home to me." He pointed in Gideon's face. "One time. Mess up once, and I'm pulling you. Got that?"

"I wouldn't have it any other way." Gideon smiled to assure his coach. "And sorry for interrupting you earlier. I'm passionate about playing. I can't get this far only to be benched."

"Understood. But know that if I know, the other guys know." He patted Gideon. "Watch yourself."

Gideon nodded. "Understood." He grabbed his jersey from his assigned locker. He slipped it over his head but kept his cell phone. Win or lose, the first people he wanted to talk to after the game would be his family.

"Play hard, son." Brick patted Gideon on his back.

Gideon grabbed his helmet and ran out of the locker room. He reached the rest of his team at the end of the hall. Through the double doors, he heard the full stadium of fans screaming. He listened to the stadium announcer.

"Introducing the Virginia Beach Wolves!"

The double doors opened. Fireworks shot off, white and blue sparklers erupting on either side of the doors. The screams and howls from the crowd blanketed the entire place until it sounded like late night in the middle of a rain forest. When Gideon looked into the stands, he saw a mixture of fans wearing the colors of his team and fans wearing the Sharks' traditional blue and gold colors. In his mind, more fans wore his team's colors.

The She-Wolves cheerleaders jumped around, waving their pompoms as the team rushed through the hallway.

"And the quarterback for the Wolves, Gideon Wells!" the announcer exclaimed.

Gideon ran from the hallway. Before he could join his team, one cheerleader jumped in front of him. He managed to catch her before he knocked her down.

"Whoa. Easy there." Gideon set her back on her feet.

"Sorry, Gideon." She wrapped her arms around his neck after the collision and didn't act ready to release him.

Gideon gazed at her and recognized her as the cheerleader who had been running into him during practices and team events. Through the padding and his gloves, he couldn't feel her body, despite her best efforts to wriggle herself against him.

Even if dating cheerleaders hadn't been against the rules, Gideon wouldn't have gone for this woman anyway. He had to pry her arms from around his neck before he could keep going.

He met up with the team on the sidelines.

Dennis leaned over to Gideon. "Pay up." Then he released a big belly laugh.

"I knew she was crazy. Who does that before a Super Bowl?" Gideon shook his head.

Before the National Anthem could be sung, Dennis elbowed Gideon in his side. When Gideon looked at him, Dennis asked, "For real, are you good?'"

Gideon dropped his gaze to the ground before answering. "Yeah. Why?"

"The streets are talking, man." Dennis shuffled in his spot before he spoke again. "You hurt?"

"Don't worry about me." Gideon gazed around to see if anyone could hear him. Nowadays, everyone had cameras and microphones everywhere.

"You want us to run the 300?"

Like the movie the name came from, Gideon and Dennis called the method to protect the quarterback 300 because they liked the strategy of funneling the opposing team toward the quarterback in smaller doses to handle them better.

Gideon shook his head. "Stick to my plays. Don't deviate."

"Whatever you say, man." Dennis nodded. "As usual, you want to do things your way, right? Got it."

Gideon ignored Dennis's sly remark. Dennis had never had to be the glue to keep things from falling apart—families, friends, businesses. Gideon managed to hold everyone together. No one ever had to worry about him.

After the coin toss, the game started. Gideon got in a zone like he always did during a game. As long as he could see Dennis, he could get the ball to him. They worked like a machine.

As expected, the team looked out for Gideon, keeping the Sharks' huge defensive line from crushing him. The Hawaiian team had brute force. They couldn't account for the Wolves' speed and Gideon's tactical game play.

Before halftime, Gideon threw a pass to Dennis. He watched the ball barely spiraling in the air before his friend caught it and hauled ass down the field. Gideon didn't expect to be hit from the side, sweeping his legs from under him as he crashed to the ground. The reserve of air he had in his lungs expelled from his body, leaving him limp and gasping.

Gideon heard a crack in his knee before crashing to the ground, but he could still move it. Good. That meant it couldn't be broken. He brought his foot close to his body to prop up his aching joint.

He gripped a handful of grass as he lay on his back like a hapless turtle. Touching the blades of grass helped him slow down his breathing, to focus on the here and now. In his reclined position, he attempted to catch his breath as he gazed up at the sky starting to get a dusky-pink appearance. Even though no one stood around him, it felt like that 300-pound lineman sat on his chest.

Get up, Gid. Christ, stand up. Don't let people worry about you. Get. The. Hell. Up.

Gideon sat up in time to peer up at the scoreboard. Dennis must have made the touchdown. His team led by six points, but he couldn't get excited. Not yet. He had watched and participated in plenty of games that had been turned around after halftime.

As soon as Gideon stood, he knew his knee had taken far too much abuse from the hit. After the field goal had been made, he walked off the field without limping or wincing, a feat considering how bad the joint felt.

Dennis managed to catch up to him as they funneled their way back down the hall. "You good?"

Gideon kept his gaze straight. "Those are some big guys, huh?" He smiled before turning to his friend. "I need a quick ice pack and I'll be good."

"Are you sure? I mean, we can get—"

"Drop it." Gideon didn't mean to snap at his buddy, but a lot rode on this game. "I apologize, man. It's the game."

Dennis put his big hand on top of Gideon's helmet. "Get out of your head and get into the game. Keep getting the ball to me and all will go great."

Despite getting the team to the Super Bowl, he knew all too well that owners and coaches liked cutting players with too many injuries. He'd come too far to get dropped now.

During the halftime show, Gideon found a quiet corner of the locker room and put an ice pack on his knee. He sat back, closed his eyes, and envisioned winning this game with his team. Once they did that, he could go home.

Going to see his mother consumed his thoughts. If he could see her, he would be happy. He would have to make sure she got through her surgery. Then he could worry about himself.

The last minute of the game tested Gideon. His knee throbbed each time he crouched down to get the ball. The Sharks got their second wind, and they seemed bound and determined to take out Gideon. Each play, they jumped on him harder and faster.

Gideon didn't complain much, but it started wearing on him. The last few seconds of the game, Gideon pulled his team together.

He glanced at Dennis before he spoke. "Last run, fellas. We can do this."

"The last twenty seconds, and they're up five points." Dennis pointed up. "Give me the ball. Once you get it in my hands, we've won the Super Bowl, baby!" He pounded Gideon on his back.

Relying on Dennis didn't suit Gideon. He wanted to go in this game playing it to the very end. "Give me a 300."

"What? That's crazy. You're going to run that play now when—"

"Watch my back." No time for apologies. Gideon broke from the pack to resume his spot.

He spied the goal line. He needed to do more. After looking off to the sideline, he watched his other teammates staring at him like a savior. He saw panic and disbelief in each of their faces.

Gideon called the play. The center hiked the ball to him. The taut ball slid into his awaiting hands. Gideon watched Dennis faking out one of the larger Sharks players to coast down the field, but he never turned around to Gideon. Without seeing Dennis's eyes, he couldn't chance throwing the ball to him and expect him to receive it. Instead of throwing the ball, Gideon took off down the field around the outside where his team managed to corral the Sharks players and keep them in the center.

Gideon charged toward the goal line. He gripped the ball as though it contained the cure to whatever ailed his mother. He chomped down on the black mouth guard as he pushed his body to incredible limits. No one from the opposing team blocked his path. In the goal area, he saw Dennis jumping up and down and waving his hands. Too late.

Gideon kept running. From the side, he caught the image of an opposing team player catching up to him. Mustering every bit of strength he had, Gideon took a big leap over the player as soon as the man attempted to tackle him.

When Gideon landed with a crunch, his bones and muscles ached. He peered over and saw he had made it over the goal line. He couldn't help but laugh out of sheer joy. His knee didn't share in his happiness. He'd made it.

Dennis stood over him. "That was a dick move, man." He hesitated before putting his hand out to him. Gideon accepted it.

"Looking out for the team." Gideon walked alongside Dennis.

"No, you weren't." Dennis jogged ahead.

Gideon didn't see his move as one to slight anyone. He wanted to see his team win. After their successful field goal kick and time running out, they did win. Colorful streamers, confetti and tickertape filled the arena. The team jumped around after dousing Brick with a cooler full of a bright orange drink.

Dennis, although he celebrated with his team, kept his distance from Gideon. In the loud arena, the silence from his friend drowned out everything else. He would have to get Dennis alone to tell him why he did what he did.

He had to call his mother and Gunnar first. He had to hear their voices. After getting his cell phone, he called his mother's house.

"Queen's not here," Victor Dabu, one of his mother's trusted employees at her flower shop, said. "She's at the hospital."

Gideon covered his free ear with his hand to make sure he had heard what Victor said. "What? Did you say hospital?"

"Yes. She's fine."

Gideon breathed a sigh of relief. He imagined that his last play may have caused her to have a heart attack. He glanced at Dennis, who now busied himself doing an interview with a popular female sports journalist.

"Why is she at the hospital?" Gideon hated shouting over the crowd, but he had to have this conversation.

"Gunnar was shot. He's in surgery now."

The sounds of the crowd faded away. For a moment, the movement around Gideon slowed down. Shot. His brother had been shot.

"Hey, son, the president would like a word with you." Coach Brick held up the phone to Gideon.

"I can't. I got to go home and see my mother." Gideon ran from the sidelines and tried making his way through the throngs of people now on the field.

Gideon didn't care how it sounded. He knew he had to make it home before he lost his family.

Chapter 2

"Ugh, turn that off." Janelle Gold moved a large glass vase filled with bright red roses that sat by the front door of her flower shop, Flowers Galore, next to the front counter. "That's why I got into flowers and plants, to stay away from meathead jocks who can't tell the difference between a tulip and a rose." To illustrate her point, Janelle held a yellow tulip in one hand and a rose in the other.

She took a deep breath, inhaling the fragrant scents swirling in the air. Besides the smells, Janelle fell in love with the vibrant colors all around her. Reds, blues, yellows, oranges, greens. Beauty in every place she looked. Every day felt like she had fallen into a Monet painting that she never wanted to escape. Too bad her bank could be the turpentine that might erase her from her dreams whether she wanted out or not.

"Come on, Janelle. It's the Super Bowl. I mainly watch for the commercials anyway. They're hilarious." Penny, one of Janelle's employees and a friend since elementary school, stayed glued to the TV as she watched the Virginia Beach Wolves celebrating. "Look at that. Our home team won! Isn't that exciting?"

"Not really." Janelle locked the front door. "So a local team won. It won't get customers in the store." She pulled a dozen roses with baby's breath from a vase and wrapped it in green paper so that the flowers trumpeted from the large open end.

"Maybe if you'd done like I asked and made a Wolves bouquet filled with red, yellow, and black roses." Penny shrugged.

Janelle cocked her head. "Black roses?"

"I would have added dye to their water or spray painted them."

Janelle laughed and shook her head.

Penny continued. "The point is, I made a suggestion and as usual, you turned it down."

"I wouldn't have turned down your suggestion if it was a good one."

Penny screwed up her face and stuck out her tongue before staring at the TV screen.

Janelle shouldn't have even bothered opening up and staying late on a Sunday, Super Bowl Sunday no less. No one wanted flowers then. No, her time would be in a couple of weeks when Valentine's Day rolled around. She'd already gotten some orders in by phone and e-mail.

Although she didn't want her friend Elizabeth Sommerville to be sick, she'd thought with Elizabeth being out of commission for a while, perhaps sales at Flowers Galore would go up a little. They hadn't.

Janelle needed her business to turn around if she had any chance of making it. She'd only had Flowers Galore open for less than two years. Opening it up so close to Pick 'N Clip, Elizabeth's business, hadn't seemed like a wise thing to do, but the cost to lease the space had been right. The location worked for her.

As soon as she'd opened her doors, Elizabeth had come over, introduced herself and bought a bouquet of roses. Janelle never forgot how supportive Elizabeth had been, then and now. Elizabeth had become an unexpected mentor.

"You know I love seeing those men in their tights." Janelle's sassy friend grunted a sound of approval through her nose. "High and tight." She lifted her hands and curved her fingers as though she could grab one of the guys' backsides through the TV screen. "You could bite one."

"No, *you* can do that." Janelle had found all through school that guys hadn't gravitated to girls who loved learning.

The jocks had thought calling her a brainiac and nerd had hurt her feelings. She didn't care about them. They might get million-dollar contracts, but Janelle knew in a few years they would bust up their bodies or lose the rest of their mediocre brain cells. Janelle would have her business and be doing something she loved, tending to her plants.

"You don't find these guys hot?" Penny twirled her newly dyed red hair around her finger.

Janelle's pale friend licked her lips. At one point, Janelle thought she'd caught Penny sliding her fingertips down the screen as though stroking a potential lover. Janelle shook her head.

"Athletes are blessed with great hand-eye coordination and halfway decent bodies." Janelle tapped her finger against her temple. "The brain. That's the sexiest organ."

"You are such a nerd." Penny shook her head.

"Thank you." Janelle bowed her head and smiled as though her friend had given her a compliment.

"Let high school go. You're a hot business owner." Penny stopped and scanned Janelle from head to toe. "Strike that. You're a business owner."

"Hey!" Janelle picked a rose stem from her bouquet and threw it at Penny. "Not nice."

"Look at you. Yes, it's February, but you're in a million layers of clothes."

Janelle turned and stared at her reflection in the front door glass. Her long cardigan sweater went almost down to her knees. The pockets on either side looked like they drooped down out of exhaustion. She loaded her pockets with shears, rubber bands, pens, and tags.

Under her cardigan, she wore a black turtleneck sweater and jeans. She had to be comfortable in what she did, although she always wondered how Queen Elizabeth could work in a full skirt suit, high heels, and a face full of flawless makeup.

Janelle didn't need a mirror to see she didn't wear anything on her face. Applying tinted lip balm had been her only beautifying product. Her sneakers squeaked over the brown tiled floor.

She ran her hand over her naturally curly hair that she had styled back from her face with a hair clip on top of her head. Shortly after starting college, Janelle had stopped putting chemical relaxers in her hair to allow the natural texture to come through finally. Back then, she'd done it because of low funds. Now other African-American women adopted the look to be trendy.

"What I wear is appropriate for where we work. No one is looking at me to be some fashionista." She held her hands up like a game-show beauty. "People come here to see these flowers and plants. They're the stars." She exhaled as she gazed around her business. "Come on. Let's go home."

Penny leaned forward to turn off the small flat-screen TV that sat behind the counter when she stopped. Local news broke to talk about a shooting not far from Janelle's business.

"Police are on the lookout for a suspect who broke in and shot an employee at Press 'N Curl, a hair salon in Virginia Beach." The news anchor spoke slowly, making sure to emphasize certain words in a dramatic fashion. "The victim is none other than MMA champion Gunnar Wells."

"Holy shit." Penny covered her mouth.

Penny could best be described as dramatic. Their differences in their races didn't matter. Back then, their tastes in boys matched. Now Penny kept up her admiration for the jocks, but Janelle had decided to expand her horizons and go for a well-rounded man with goals and ambition.

"Isn't that horrible?" Penny shook her head. "What's the world coming to?"

"Desperate times call for desperate measures, I suppose." Janelle went behind the counter to retrieve her coat and purse. "It's a shame though. Press 'N Curl is one of Queen Elizabeth's businesses. She owns, like, three or four of them."

"Okay, so what in the world is a champion MMA fighter"—Penny glanced at the screen again—"a fine one at that, doing in Queen's business? Don't tell me he's there getting his hair done."

Janelle laughed. "Wouldn't that be a hoot? He would never live that down." She wiped under her eyes. When the idea that a man had been shot registered to her again, she sobered to the situation. "Seriously, I hope he's okay."

"Any tips on this crime, please contact Virginia Beach police. Now we'll return you to the Super Bowl, already in progress."

The screen switched back over to the game, or rather, the end of the game. The Virginia Beach Wolves celebrated. Colorful streamers filled the screen, and screams filled the inside of Janelle's store.

Janelle didn't care to look at the screen until she heard a woman attempting to interview the team's quarterback.

"Gideon! Gideon! Congratulations on the win. I understand the president is on the phone for you." The savvy African-American journalist managed to get her microphone up to Gideon's face.

Janelle finally glanced at the screen. She froze. The football player, covered in sweat with his blond hair stuck to his face, kept her hypnotized to the screen with his incredible blue eyes. No one's look had rendered her immobile since her days in high school.

Janelle stared at him some more, then scanned the banner across the bottom of the screen that displayed his name.

Janelle swallowed hard. She couldn't help but drop her gaze down his body to his crotch. Penny would have called Janelle a hypocrite if she knew Janelle checked out this man.

"I can't. I got to go home and see my mother." The player darted off screen and attempted to make his way through the sea of people.

"That was nice, right?" Janelle put on her coat and pulled her purse strap on her shoulder.

Nice? Yes. Janelle felt a strange tickling sensation going through her body. Since Gideon Wells played for the Virginia Beach Wolves, did that mean he lived in town? Would he be coming home to Virginia Beach?

She shook her head. What was she thinking? He could come back home and she would never see him in person. No way would this multimillion-dollar athlete have some little house in the same neighborhood she lived. No, he probably lived at the Oceanfront area with one of those big, fancy houses people like her only dreamed about having.

"Dude has the opportunity to talk to the president of the United States, and he bolts to see his mama? I don't know. Sounds like a straight-up mama's boy to me." Penny turned the TV off and grabbed her things.

"Hey, these are your kind of men, right?" Janelle brought her hands up and curved her fingers like Penny had done earlier. "High and tight." Then she picked up the bouquet she'd made.

"Yeah, but they have to be a little more macho than that." Penny shook her head. "Hey, that guy's name was Gideon Wells."

Janelle shook her head as she opened the front door for them to leave. "So?"

"I wonder if he's related to that guy that got shot, Gunnar Wells."

Janelle cocked her head. "What's the chance that an MMA fighter and an NFL football player are related and from Virginia Beach? I don't see that happening."

Penny shrugged. "You never know. Now if that guy was rushing home because of his brother, that would be a different story."

"Oh, then he would be dateable?" Janelle walked to her car.

"Maybe. It depends."

Janelle shook her head. "See you in the morning."

"Bright and early." Penny blew her a kiss before ducking into her car.

As soon as Penny drove away, Janelle sat in her car and stared at her business. She cranked up the heat to not freeze to death as she stared at small storefront that sat in the middle of a shopping strip. An accountant's office and an ice-cream parlor flanked either side of her place, which had a pink, green, and white sign at the top.

As she stared at her baby, Janelle recalled the very first day she'd opened. She and Penny had taken pictures of the place before the first customer, well, Queen Elizabeth, had arrived.

She glanced over at the stack of mail she'd left on the passenger seat. At the top sat a notice from the bank. Janelle had opened the first notice a couple of months ago that had stated she had missed her November payment. Last month's notice had detailed how delinquent she'd become in paying her lease for the store. She had no desires to get yelled at again. To hide the bad news, she tossed her bouquet on top of them.

Janelle had kept this information from Penny, hoping to turn things around. As long as she kept her employees paid, she would be okay. Janelle needed a miracle. Something had to go her way for once.

She arrived at her small one-bedroom apartment near the Oceanfront area of Virginia Beach. With barely being able to take home a salary, she couldn't afford one of those new, ritzy apartments being thrown up near the strip. Maybe one day…

She closed her car door, making sure to leave her mail sitting on the passenger seat. No use bringing the bad news into her home. She did grab her bouquet. As though the slamming door signaled him, her downstairs neighbor, Buddy Harrison, appeared at his door.

Janelle smiled as soon as she saw him. "Good evening, Mr. Harrison." As soon as she arrived at his door, he reached out and held her hand.

"You are as lovely as the flowers you sell."

The elderly man reminded Janelle so much of her grandfather. His weathered, mahogany skin made a perfect backdrop to his shocking white ring of hair around his bald head and his white teeth, his own, he proudly proclaimed.

"You are so sweet." Janelle patted the back of Buddy's hand.

"You and my youngest son would make pretty babies."

Janelle slipped her hand out of Buddy's. "Too bad all your sons are married."

Mr. Harrison made a disapproving grunting sound deep in his throat. "His wife is not good for him. Always spending his money, and she doesn't work." He smiled as he looked at Janelle. "You. You would be good for him. You got your own business and you're cute."

Janelle laughed. "How could I not love a glowing endorsement like that? I'm fine working and tending to my plants. Romance can wait."

"Not right now. Valentine's Day is right around the corner." Buddy registered his excitement by doing a slight dance.

At least romance hadn't died for this senior citizen. Janelle hoped to be so lucky to have a man who would be that romantic from the start and for the years they would be together.

She brought up the bouquet she'd made. "For you to give to Mrs. Harrison." She knew the duo didn't leave their apartment much.

From what Althea Harrison told her, their children lived in other states and didn't come home often. Buddy treated Janelle like one of his own, often asking her to join him and Althea for dinner or trying to give her money. Being too proud, Janelle never took the money. She would always accept their gracious hospitality.

"You are spoiling me and her." Buddy waved his hand in the direction of his apartment. "That woman is trying to kill me. Always trying to get me to eat right and exercise."

Janelle leaned forward to whisper to him, "Call me crazy, but it sounds like she wants you around for a little bit longer."

"No. She's killing me. I'm telling you. If she asks you for extra flowers, don't bring them. They'll be for my grave." Even Buddy couldn't hold back his laughter.

"Shut that door! It's cold out there." Althea's raspy voice held enough power to be heard all the way outside.

It didn't take long for the woman to sidle up behind her husband. As soon as she saw Janelle, her face lit up like a neon sign. Janelle always imagined that Althea's complexion had probably looked like honey gold in her heyday. Now her ashen skin looked well-worn. Wrinkles creased her cheeks and forehead. When she smiled, more complementing lines shot out from the corners of her eyes.

"She brought these for you." Buddy handed his wife the bouquet. "I told her that you are as mean as a snake and didn't deserve them."

"You know you like me mean." She accepted the bouquet and nudged her husband's side with her elbow.

"You are right about that." He chortled and gave her a kiss on her cheek.

"Janelle, come on in and get you some hot cocoa and cookies." Althea tapped her husband on his shoulder. "Stand back and let the baby in."

"She can get by me. Are you calling me fat?" Buddy threw his shoulders back as he looked down at his wife. Although he tried looking hard with his bottom lip poked out and his potbelly protruding proudly, he couldn't keep up the hard expression. A smile broke on his face before his wife spoke.

"I have more of you to love." In her pink bedroom slippers with blue flowers embroidered in them, she shuffled up to her husband and gave him the sweetest kiss on his lips.

To see the duo together gave Janelle a front-row seat to her possible future. She would love to marry a man, have children, and be with him for years.

'Til death do us part.

"Thanks for the invite, but I'm beat." Janelle took a step back. "Maybe another time."

"Don't be a stranger. You come down and visit whenever you'd like." Buddy winked at her, but it came off as a fatherly wink than anything else.

"Leave the girl alone. She has a business to run." Althea tugged on Buddy's tattered blue robe.

"I'm not telling her to close up shop and move in. I said if she needs anything to come see us." Buddy shook his head. "You have a good night, dear."

"You do the same. Good night, Mrs. Harrison." Janelle waved as she started to climb the stairs.

"Good night. See you tomorrow."

Buddy closed and locked his door. As soon as Janelle hit the second-floor landing, she wasted no time unlocking her door and getting into her apartment. The warmth inside enveloped her.

Home sweet home.

She hung her coat in the closet and headed to her bedroom. When she flicked on the light to her bedroom, Janelle hesitated in the doorway. Her bed that she'd made that morning remained untouched. As she stared at it, she realized once again that she lived alone. She had no one. She had great neighbors and a super best friend who also worked for her, yet she lived her life alone. If something happened to her, who would help her? No, what she really wanted to know is who would love her?

Janelle padded to her bed and sat on the edge. Devoting her time to her studies, working, and her shop left her little time to date. She had dated some in college. She'd even had a boyfriend during her senior year, one she'd thought would have been her future Buddy to her Althea.

A day after graduation, and after a night of passion at the Cavalier Hotel down at the Oceanfront, he told her in no uncertain terms that he had bigger plans in life outside of Virginia, and the plans didn't include her.

Although Janelle didn't want to cry over a jerk like that, the tears came anyway. Having Penny by her side and hearing her detail the horrible things she wanted to do to him had allowed Janelle to get over him.

Having him dump her the way he did gave Janelle some perspective. She had to keep her eyes on the prize. Once she established her business into a successful venture, she could go out and date again.

Janelle stepped into the bathroom next door to her bedroom and started running hot water into the tub. Soaking for a bit before going to bed would help her relax. As the water ran, she took her time undressing.

Her mind wandered to thoughts about her younger, more awkward self, the gangly teenager who'd found solace in books and botany rather than boys. With Ida for a mother, Janelle had had no chance of becoming the wallflower she'd wanted to be.

"Go out. Meet boys. Hell, pretend like you're going to do something wrong," Ida would tell Janelle during her impressionable teen years.

Not great advice coming from a mother. Ida couldn't be classified as a typical parent. Janelle would never admit her mother had nailed that one bit of instruction. Attending a dance had her doing a lot of firsts. First time going to a dance, first time she didn't get teased for being a loner and hugging the wall, and her first real, sensual kiss.

As though feeling that soul-stirring sensual expression again, Janelle touched her lips. The tips of her fingers danced over them lightly before she nipped the tip of her middle finger with her teeth. He'd done that to her, teased her by grazing his teeth over her bottom lip and then taking a taste.

Even now, Janelle's knees quivered as they had done so many years ago. At the time, it had felt as though the kiss had lasted for twenty years. She remembered everything about the surprising lip-lock…except for the identity of the mystery boy who looked more like a man. She remembered how he'd towered over her and the way he'd placed his large hand next to her face.

Afterward, he pulled away from her. In the darkened corner, she only remembered his eyes, those piercing blue eyes that had mesmerized. Could that boy have been Gideon Wells?

Janelle shook her head. No way in the world could the mystery kisser from her youth be the same Super Bowl winning quarterback. Besides, what young man would kiss a young woman like that without introduction or permission or even a follow-up question or statement? A commotion had happened on the dance floor, and as fast as he had grabbed her and let his intentions known, he'd disappeared into the crowd. Janelle had taken that moment to make her exit. Until today, she hadn't known who had rocked her world so many years ago.

Who was she kidding? She still couldn't be sure. She couldn't rely on her memories about his eyes.

Curiosity killed her. Janelle opened her laptop next to her bed and did a search for Gideon Wells. She didn't want to read the stories, especially the ones about his dating life. She wanted to see his picture.

A catalogue of pictures appeared. She scrolled through each of them until she stopped at one of his advertisements promoting eating spinach. Like the cartoon character, Popeye, Gideon held up a can of spinach and carried a menacing expression. The company's tag line appeared underneath a shirtless Gideon. *Spinach is good for everybody.*

Janelle scanned his broad shoulders down to his lean, long arms to his incredible chest. When she got to his abdomen, her search ended. She now understood the term six-pack abs. She licked her lips. Like Penny had early, Janelle stroked the screen as though she could feel every bulge in his biceps.

"What the hell am I doing?" She snatched her hand back.

Gideon Wells was now a hometown hero. He looked good enough to lick from his head to his toes. He would be coming home soon. That didn't mean she would see him in person. Even if she did, so what?

No use dwelling on the past. Janelle had bigger fish to fry. Her personal life could wait. She had a business to save.

Chapter 3

Gideon took a red-eye flight from California to Virginia. Passengers, shocked to see the Super Bowl-winning quarterback on their flight, congratulated him on the plane and as he went through the airport. Manners his mama had taught him kept him from snapping at these people and demanding they give him his space.

After such a big high of winning the game of his life, his dream, it had all come crashing down as soon as Victor had told him about Gunnar. Gideon's good knee bounced as he sat in first class on the last leg of his flight from Colorado to Virginia.

He couldn't wait to land, not so that he could get to his family, but so he could at least call them. Not being able to use his cell phone right now killed him.

"Would you like something to drink, Mr. Wells?" The cordial flight attendant with sandy-blond hair smiled at him as she kept her stare directly into his eyes.

"No, thank you." Gideon couldn't think about food or anything else until he could see Gunnar and know he would be fine.

First, his mother, and now this. Queen Elizabeth always told him and his brothers, *"God never gives you more than you can handle."* Right now, Gideon felt tested.

A passenger walked by him to get to the lavatory. Since he sat in the aisle seat and took up a lot of space in his area, Gideon shifted his legs to allow the woman to get by him.

A light dinging sound rang before the captain spoke. "We're about twenty minutes from landing in Norfolk. We ask that all passengers return to their seats and fasten their seat belts."

Gideon hadn't taken off his seat belt the entire flight. His mind raced with thoughts about his brother. Would Gunnar be able to walk after this?

Did the shooter shoot his brother in the head? Had his mother been there when all of this went down?

Gideon braced his elbows on his knees and rested his forehead on his hands. He took deep breaths, hoping to slow down his raging heartbeat. Hearing the hum of the plane's engines helped him concentrate on something other than his negative thoughts. Without warning, he felt a hand on his shoulder that caressed him down to the middle of his back.

Gideon lifted his head and turned. The woman who had gone to the bathroom swayed back and forth as she headed to her seat. She didn't look back to him. He took her touch to be an accident. Although he hadn't felt any turbulence, there must have been some. He did see her looking unsteady on her feet.

When the plane landed, Gideon wasted no time getting off as soon as he could and headed to the baggage-claim area. He shifted in his spot as he waited for his one suitcase to show. Since hearing about his brother, he hadn't felt any pains in his knee, a feat considering what he'd put himself through last night.

Gideon looked at his watch. He'd crossed over into Monday. Nine in the morning. No wonder the airport bustled. He had hoped to miss the big crowds when he came into town. At the first sighting of him, he knew it wouldn't take the local media long to follow him around and ask him probing questions he didn't want to answer.

Time slipped by so quickly. The waiting area around the baggage carousel filled with the passengers from his flight…he assumed. He had been too consumed with his own thoughts to even notice anyone else.

The red twirling light on top of the carousel lit up and spun as an annoying beeping sound honked before the scales of the carousel shifted and moved. Gideon kept one eye on the bags and the other on his phone. He called his mother's cell phone first, knowing the woman would be awake and with Gunnar no matter the time.

"Gideon," Elizabeth whispered. "What are you doing calling so early? Shouldn't you be resting?"

"Hey, Ma." He took from her whisper that she must be in the hospital room with Gunnar. Knowing that eased some of his fears. "I'm in town."

"What?"

Gideon had to blink when his mother raised her voice. She never did that. She continued. "Why are you here? I thought you were in California."

"I called after the game. I got Victor. He told me about Gunnar. Is he okay? Didn't mean that. I know he's not okay. He made it, right? You're with him, aren't you?" Gideon couldn't stop his babbling, but every question he'd thought of on his way back home came rushing out of his mouth.

"Gunnar is resting. He got shot in the stomach." Elizabeth's voice hitched.

"Oh, God." Gideon spotted his red suitcase. He grabbed it with one hand and pulled it off the conveyor belt. "Who did this? Did they catch him?" He went out the door to the front of the airport. A row of cabs sat off to the side. He got in the first one.

"No. The police tried asking Gunnar some questions when he got here, but he was pretty out of it. The wound is what they call a through and through, whatever that means."

"Means it went right through him." Bastard. Gideon gritted his teeth as he thought about the agony his brother must be feeling.

"Right. It did come out the other side. He got shot in his stomach on the side. It went through his intestines. He's going to make it, but he'll be here for a few days." His mother sighed. "Eboni is here with me."

"I'm coming there."

"No, son." This time his mother's voice sounded firm. "You've had a rough enough day yourself with your game and all. You should be out celebrating, not dealing with all this." His mother paused. "Oh, no."

"What?" Gideon sat up taller in the backseat of the cab.

"There's no one at the house to let you in. Shay is in the apartment over the garage behind the house, but I don't want you to wake her."

The name Shay didn't sound familiar to Gideon. He assumed if Elizabeth had allowed her to stay in that apartment, she must be someone special to her.

"Don't worry about that, Mom. I had planned on staying at my house." As much as he loved his mother, Gideon valued his privacy more.

"Oh, no, you're not. You're staying with me like old times."

Gideon imagined the stately, gorgeous African-American woman wearing one of her many designer outfits and stomping her stiletto-heeled foot. The thought of his mother standing in a hospital room dressed to the nines had him smiling.

"Mom, I've been to your house since you've remodeled. You've changed all of our old rooms into something else. I think my old room is your shoe room now."

"No, yours is the exercise room. But there is a futon in it, dear."

Gideon waited a beat before continuing. "You've got someone else staying with you. And I'm betting Gunnar will be recovering at your house. You have your hands full right now. I'm going to stay at my home. When Gunnar is discharged, I'll have him stay with me. You should stay with me. I have an in-law suite that's connected to the house, and it's on the lower level so you don't have to climb stairs."

"No, son. I'm your mother. I take care of you, not the other way around. For tonight, or rather today, you can stay at your house. Then I want you back at my house, understand?"

Gideon forgot how tough his mother could be. "We'll talk about it. For now, I'll get a couple of hours of sleep, and then I'll come to the hospital, okay?"

Elizabeth sighed. Knowing she got some relief with his news unknotted his shoulders.

"I can't wait to see you again. I'm so glad you're home. I wished it could have been under better circumstances."

"You and me both." Gideon hadn't even waited long enough to see who made MVP. He'd missed the full celebration.

"I'm proud of you, Gideon. Not because of the game. You put family first."

A warm feeling washed over Gideon. Only his mother could weaken him like this. No one else. "Of course. You taught me well."

"By the way, have you cut your hair? I don't want to see you coming here looking like a hippie." Elizabeth tsked over the phone. "Gunnar finally cut his off. I want you to do the same."

Gideon had grown his hair out as a personal style choice. He knew his mother would have a problem with it. Good thing she owned a hair salon. If he decided to make that drastic cut, he could do it at her business. He didn't feel the need to conform yet.

"Oh, wow, Mom, I can't hear you. The phone is breaking up." Gideon made a screeching sound with his voice. He had to pull the phone away from his face to keep from laughing.

"Gideon Nathaniel Wells, don't you hang up this phone without answering my question."

This time Gideon did hear what sounded like his mother stomping her foot on a tile floor.

"I think we're losing connection. I'll talk to you later. Love you."

"Love you, you rascal. You and your brothers are going to be the death of me."

Gideon smiled as he disconnected the call. Elizabeth would hate his hair. No doubt about it. She would love them being together as a family. Too bad Thane wouldn't be here. It would be like old times.

On the cab ride to his home, Gideon thought about the game. He hadn't forgotten the virtual daggers his friend had thrown at him after his final play. Dennis didn't understand. Gideon couldn't fail. He couldn't let his team fail. Because of what he'd done, they'd won. That should be all that mattered.

When his cell phone rang, Gideon looked at the screen first to see the caller. Would his mother be calling to go for a second round of arguing about his hair?

No, as soon as he saw *Coach Brick* across the top of the screen, he clicked Ignore and shoved it back into his jacket pocket. Coach would want to yell at him for several things right now—leaving the game, his bum knee, the cheerleader. Too many issues to think about as he approached his home.

Gideon arrived at the security guard to his beachfront sanctuary. His huge five-bedroom, four-bathroom house could have held a large family. As a teenager, he used to proclaim how one day he would have a house like he and his brothers had seen riding their bikes up and down the Oceanfront boardwalk. He had planned on getting married and filling the house with children. Plus, the place afforded him a little bit of privacy.

When the cab stopped at the guard station, Gideon popped his head out the back window to address the guard. "Hi. Would you mind opening the gate? I live here."

The guard screwed up her lips as though preparing to argue with him. As soon as her stare met his, she stopped. Her mouth dropped open. "You're Gideon Wells of the Wolves! I can't believe you're here. I saw you play." The young woman pointed to a TV screen in her little shack. "You were great, especially that last play."

Too bad not everyone would think that last play had been perfect. Gideon would have to call Dennis. No way would he allow this to mess up their decade-long friendship.

Gideon gave her a slight smile. "Thanks."

"I'm new here." She craned her body outside of the guard window and presented her hand to him. "My name is Pearl. Nice to meet you."

He shook her hand. Although small, he felt calluses across her palm. A part of him respected her implied work ethic. "Do you need to see my ID?" Gideon reached into his pocket for his wallet.

"No, sir." The thin Asian woman with shaggy brown hair started typing on her computer. "I recognize you."

"I appreciate that."

"I can't believe you're home so soon after the Super Bowl." She winked at Gideon.

"Had a family emergency." Gideon shrugged and started to lean back into the cab.

"I hope everything is all right."

Gideon hoped so. The guard opened the gate for the cab driver after issuing him a temporary pass.

Weariness caught up with Gideon the longer he sat in the cab. He yawned more than once before getting to his house. He needed to get some sleep and rest his knee for a bit. Now that he moved around, it started to throb.

Gideon paid the driver and took his bag into his big, empty house. "Hello!" he shouted if only to hear the echo reverberating back at him.

The inside looked the same. The same colorful Spanish tile floors greeted him. His oversize, custom-made furniture decorated the rooms. Having furniture made that fit his height and stature had been another perk of getting paid the ridiculous amount of money he'd been given to throw a ball and get pummeled by buildings posing as men.

He peered down the hall to the kitchen area. With it being morning, light streamed through the windows. The all-white kitchen looked clean. Although the small bag of peanuts on the plane hadn't satisfied his hunger, Gideon didn't feel like eating right now.

He looked straight ahead through the patio doors that led to his backyard area. His in-ground pool remained covered, and on top of that cover sat a layer of blinding-white snow. February in Virginia. He had to love it.

Gideon set his house alarm and started to drag his body and suitcase upstairs to his bedroom. Thankfully, the maid service kept his house cleaned. He knew he would come home to a bed with fresh sheets.

The first step he made on the bottom landing step shot a painful reminder to his brain of what he'd put his body through last night. The excruciating pain crumbled him to the floor until he had to take a seat on the step for a moment.

"Damn it!" He grasped his knee over his jeans.

Through the denim, he felt the tight bindings he'd used to wrap around his knee to keep it steady and stave off some of the discomfort. Too bad it hadn't worked. Not this time.

Gideon rubbed his knee. "One more day, and then I'll get it looked at. I need more time."

He took a couple of deep breaths before standing and taking the stairs with ease and careful precision as to not aggravate his knee further. Had Dennis been here, he would have given Gideon the I-told-you-so speech for not having an elevator installed in his home. At the time he had his house built, the contractor had asked Gideon if he wanted an elevator. Gideon had turned down the offer flat without further argument. Honestly, he liked his house, but he hated being in a gated community. With rabid fans, he found it to be a necessity.

He breathed a sigh of relief once he got to his bedroom.

He flicked on the light in his bedroom and released a curse. His heart felt like it rocketed up to his head and pounded out of control until the steady beat filled his ears.

"Hi, Gideon." The perky cheerleader he'd been trying to avoid sat up on her knees in his bed…naked. "Welcome home."

Gideon took a deep breath before speaking; otherwise this young woman would hear a string of profanities that would make his mother blush. He also made sure to keep his stare directly on this woman's eyes.

Scanning down at her body would only get him in trouble. Breaking up with a starlet had managed to get him out of the media's eye. He didn't need to go back with some new controversy.

"How did you get into my home?" Gideon stood by the bedroom door.

The way he felt, if he had moved in closer to this nut job, he would grab her and remove her from his house. Gideon had no plans of putting his hands on this woman. He held his cell phone and crossed his arms to keep it hidden.

"Actually it was a lot easier than I thought it would be." She moved to the edge of the bed. "I was going to sit at the guard shack until you showed up and ask you to invite me up." She hugged her body, which pushed her augmented breasts together.

Again, Gideon wouldn't peer down. Nothing good could come from him looking at her like he wanted her.

She continued and smiled as though she had done a great thing. "I was on the same flight as you. Did you feel me touching your shoulder?"

So that strange touch hadn't been on accident. As Gideon thought about the connection, a shiver ran through his body. He had been stepped on during a game by an opposing team member. He'd even been spat on in his face through his face guard. This cheerleader's touch made him want to crawl out of his skin.

"Right when the plane landed, I went straight to your house."

"How did you know where I live?" he asked.

"A girl's got to have her secrets." She winked. "Maybe later I'll tell you so we can laugh about it."

Gideon's blood boiled with each treacherous word she spoke. Not only had she violated his personal space, she'd somehow managed to get his personal information.

"I didn't have to wait for a bag because I came here with the clothes on my back. There was a male guard at the gate. I told him I was a She-Wolf and here to see you. It helps that we had that personal interaction at the Super Bowl." She swung her legs back and forth. "Did you like that? I liked touching you."

Gideon remained quiet. He had to hear her full story first before he took action.

When Gideon didn't answer, the cheerleader's smile started to fade and she continued with her tale. "He let me in and called your house. Your cleaning staff was here so they let me in." She raised her hands in the air. "Tah dah. That was smart of me, right? Do you know any other woman who would do this much for you?" She snaked her tongue over her red, bee-stung-looking lips.

Nothing about this plastic woman appealed to Gideon. She didn't seem real. The more she smiled, the more he saw her as a mannequin that had come to life. This one, though, had sought refuge in his home, in his bed. He couldn't have that.

Gideon never wanted to be one of those athletes that bought a big, ostentatious house because they made millions of dollars. Once he'd seen the security measures taken for the area, he'd decided to buy in this subdivision. With this intrusion, he had to think twice about his decision.

Gideon started counting in his head to lessen his anger. He took a deep breath before he said, "One hundred." Then he glared at her. Counting in his head hadn't eased his frustration as he had hoped. Regardless of what she did, he had to treat her like a lady. His mother would never forgive him if he did anything less. "For one thing, I don't even know your name."

"It's—"

Although Gideon's mother had taught him not to interrupt people, he had to stop this one. "I don't want to know it. I want you to get dressed and get out of my home before I call the police."

The smile started melting down her face before she firmed it up again. "You are such a kidder. That's what I like about you."

"Lady, you don't even know me. You've seen me play. I probably said hi to you once or twice, and now you're stalking me."

"I am not. I love you, Gideon. I love watching you play. I love how you are with your friends. I don't even care that your mother is black. I think it's cool. It's like the reverse *Blind Side*."

Gideon blinked. "You know what? Sit right there." He brought his phone to his face. "It'll make it easier for the cops to get you."

The cheerleader hopped out of bed and snatched her clothes from the floor. "Loser!" She put on her tight T-shirt. "I can't believe you're letting all this go out the door."

"I'm not. I told you that you can stay right there until the police get here." After the first ring, Gideon heard a click.

"Nine-one-one. What's your emergency?" the dispatcher asked in a canned fashion.

"Yes, I got home and found an intruder in my house." Gideon kept his stare on the She-Wolf to make sure she didn't do anything else foolish. He had no idea if she had a gun or a knife or any type of weapon. How far would she go to get him?

She growled as she slipped on her skirt. "Bastard! Are you really on the phone with the cops?"

"Ma'am, do you hear her? She's in my bedroom." Again, Gideon kept his glare on this intruder. He spouted his address to the operator.

"Yes, sir. We'll get officers to the scene."

Gideon heard the woman typing as she spoke to him.

Dennis would have probably loved these antics. Gideon found nothing amusing about it. He felt violated and like he'd lost some control.

The cheerleader slipped on a pair of boots and then snatched her purse from the floor. So the woman wore no underwear? Okay, part of that did appeal to Gideon, but nonetheless, she'd crossed several lines. Don't encroach on his space and never, ever talk about his family.

She started to make her way to the bedroom door to leave when she stopped. She turned toward Gideon and strolled toward him.

Gideon stood firmly in his spot as he pointed to the door. He'd seen careers of other athletes crumble from one stupid move. No way would this one opportunist make him step out of his character. He wouldn't lay a hand on her.

"I'm leaving. I need to get this." The cheerleader reached around his shoulder and removed a small cell phone from behind the picture of his family on the middle bookshelf. She pushed a button on it before slipping it in her purse.

"You were taping this?" The longer Gideon stood in front of her, the more it felt like lava coursed through his veins. His eyes and the back of his neck felt hot. He couldn't stop balling his hands into fists. If he didn't calm himself down, he would snap his phone in two.

"It would have been so intense. Me, you, and your Super Bowl ring." She gazed down at his hand. "Oh, guess you don't have it yet."

Gideon spoke to the dispatcher. "Please send someone right away. She's about to leave and I'm definitely pressing charges." He gave a description of her outfit to the dispatcher while the She-Wolf continued growling at him. With the call over, he glared at the stranger in his home. "I'm calling the Wolves' head office to get you removed from the team and banned from getting anywhere close to us. I don't ever want to see you again."

The tiny terror stomped down the marble steps to the door. She opened it, triggering Gideon's alarm. She didn't even turn around to acknowledge him. He closed the door, locked it again, and then disabled the alarm. As expected, his cell phone rang.

First, his alarm company called him. Gideon explained what he'd found when he'd gotten home.

"We'll send police to make sure she leaves the premises," the alarm company representative said.

"I've already contacted the police. They're sending someone over now." Gideon didn't want to go that route, but she'd given him no choice.

Then Pearl from the front gate called him. "I got a report your alarm went off. Forget the code, Mr. Wells?"

"No. The guard before you allowed a stranger to come to my home and gain entrance with the cleaning staff here. I don't appreciate that, and I will be reporting that to management." As he thought about it, he would also have to call his cleaning company and complain about them letting this woman into his home. They had no right to open his door to a stranger.

"Oh, shit. I mean, I'm so sorry, sir. That shouldn't have happened. I'll call my boss right now and connect you to him."

Gideon shook his head. "Later. I'll talk to the police, and then I need some sleep." He disconnected the call.

The police arrived within two minutes.

"The woman who was here left." Gideon pointed down his driveway. "I want to make sure you get her before she gets away."

"She won't, Mr. Wells." The officer took a step into Gideon's home. "The first unit saw her walking down the road and they apprehended her. I'm here to take your statement." He pulled out a notepad. "By the way, great game last night. Still can't believe you're here so soon."

Gideon couldn't believe everything he'd had to deal with within a twenty-four-hour period. Could he get a break?

After completing a police report, taking a couple of pictures with the officers and signing some autographs, the police left. Too bad now Gideon couldn't sleep. He needed to rest to think clearly.

He lumbered up to his room after making sure he secured the downstairs and strolled into his large yet empty bedroom. When he crossed the threshold, he peered over to the bookshelf where the cheerleader had hidden her phone. If she'd hidden her phone, what else had she done? Had she bugged his room with some other recording device?

"Damn." Gideon retreated to a spare bedroom.

With each step to the other bedroom, he gritted his teeth. His home should be his sanctuary. Now he felt like a guest. Never again would he allow a woman or anyone else to derail him. He wanted to keep his focus on his family, the reason for his trip back home.

Chapter 4

Janelle's mother, Ida, could only be tolerated in small doses. Conducting her conversation with Ida by phone allowed Janelle an easy out when her mother got on her nerves. She rolled her eyes again, probably the fourth time during their chat, as she drove to her shop and listened to her mother give her advice on how to live her life…again.

"What you need to do is get you a rich man to pay your bills and get you out of this mess," Ida said.

Janelle had made the mistake of not updating her address with her bank before they sent out a notification about her delinquent status. He mother had seen it and now felt she had every right to comment on Janelle's personal affairs.

"Mom, I was able to get the loan on my own. I had the business idea on my own. I developed the business plan on my own. I don't need a rich man to bail me out. As usual, I'll figure out how to get myself out of this mess."

"You mean without me, right?" Bitterness laced Ida's words.

Janelle squeezed her eyes shut for a quick moment to collect her thoughts. "I have a plan to get Flowers Galore more customers."

"Really? How's that?" As usual, doubt filled her mother's voice.

"There's a flower competition. I'll enter and win." Janelle smiled as she thought about the plant she'd been cultivating for months.

"How much do you get for first place?"

"I don't know. 350 dollars, I think." Janelle believed she'd seen that amount on the application, but she hadn't paid a lot of attention to it.

She knew what winning the prestigious Virginia Flower Show contest would draw true flower and plant admirers to her store. She would be taken seriously in her field. The new perception would give her publicity. Then she would be able to see the payoff. It had to work. She had no other options except close the store.

"So wait. Winning this contest won't get you enough money to pay off your bills? Sounds like a waste of time." Ida pushed a disapproving grunt through the phone.

"I wouldn't expect you to understand, Mom. Your plan for me is to find a rich guy. Coming from you, that advice is surprising. It's not like you're hooked up with Warren Buffet." Janelle didn't mean to hit her mother with a low blow, but Ida had been shooting down her dreams for as long as Janelle could remember.

"So you think your one and only boyfriend makes you some sort of expert? Men need to be used. They have no problem in using women, now do they?"

Janelle shook her head. Some traits she didn't want to inherit from her mother. She'd already gotten her height, lithe body, and her huge backside. Janelle wouldn't take on her hatred of men.

"You gave me your advice. I'm telling you what I'm going to do. As always, thanks for the support." Janelle disconnected the call before their discussion ended up as it always did, in an argument.

Janelle pulled up to the store and parked in her usual spot at the farthest corner of the lot. She wanted to leave plenty of space for potential customers. She unlocked the door and scanned the contents of her place.

"I need a miracle." Janelle went behind the counter and stowed her purse and coat.

Before Penny showed up for work, Janelle went to the back room where she kept her baby. With all the lights on and in a heated glass cabinet, sat her swamp hibiscus. She opened the door long enough to check the moistness of the murky, muddy water she had the plant's roots in. Out of habit, she took a sniff from one of the closed buds. The fragrant aroma soothed her. This would be her ticket.

Janelle stroked one of the leaves. For its unappealing name, the petal tickled the pads of her fingers. This would be her salvation. She closed the cabinet door and checked the thermostat to make sure it remained at the right temperature. Everything had to be perfect.

Until something great happened, she would continue to work hard until…well, until the bank forced her to stop what she loved in this space.

* * * *

After a few hours of restless sleep and a long, hot bath, Gideon changed into something comfortable, got into his garage-kept car and sped down to the hospital. He didn't drive anything fancy or special. As a matter of fact, he'd picked this crossover vehicle because it resembled a station wagon. He liked the wholesome feel he got from being in something that looked like his mother would drive.

What was he thinking? His mother had owned a Cadillac, and now had a small Mini Cooper. She could never be described as typical…thank God.

Gideon got to the hospital and approached the information desk. "I need to see Gunnar Wells."

The older woman at the desk peered up at him over her wire-rimmed silver glasses. "Are you family? We've had a lot of fans up here looking to see the man."

"Yes. I'm his brother." He took out his Virginia state driver's license and handed it to her, thankful that she didn't know him as the Gideon Wells.

She handed his license back to him and then took his picture for his temporary visitor's pass. She handed him the sticker. "Wear this while visiting him. He's on the fifth floor in room 522." She smiled.

"Thanks." Before leaving the counter, he affixed the sticker to his shirt, not his jacket. He planned on being there for a while.

"Mr. Wells?"

Gideon turned back to the woman.

"Great game yesterday." She gave him a thumbs-up sign.

His heartbeat slowed as he smiled back to her. For a brief moment, he had only been Gunnar Wells's brother and no one else.

He loved being a football player. Yet he could never appreciate the notoriety that came with being a star quarterback.

Gideon got up to the floor and strolled down the hallway in search of Gunnar's room. A couple of the nurses gasped as he made his way to the correct room. To lessen the excitement that could be generated with his presence, he didn't acknowledge any of their whispers or looks. He kept his head up and continued walking until he finally came across the room.

With the door closed, Gideon knocked first before entering. His heart stopped for a moment when he saw his older brother, his hero. For all of Gideon's life, Gunnar Wells had seemed invincible.

As children, Gunnar had been the one to protect him and Thane against their abusive biological mother and horrible foster families. Once they'd gotten with Queen Elizabeth, Gunnar had squared off against their adoptive mother's former husband. Gunnar seemed destined to fight for the rest of his life. Seeing him now made Gideon think someone had taken out Superman.

Gunnar appeared to be sleeping. The big man's head had been elevated in the bed. IVs had been hooked to his arm. A constant beeping greeted Gideon as he stepped inside and closed the door behind himself. Although the lights in the room had been extinguished, the opened blinds allowed the room to be illuminated in sunlight.

Gideon peered at the whiteboard across from him. He read Gunnar's doctor's name and the name of the attending nurse and nurse care partner taking care of him today. On the scale of his pain, Gunnar had listed it as a one, which meant for a normal human being, it would rank as a ten.

Gunnar never wanted to admit his pain or that he needed help, something Gideon understood. The throbbing in his knee hadn't stopped at all since arriving in Virginia. He would have to see someone about it soon.

Gideon stood at the side of the bed and put his hand on Gunnar's shoulder. He didn't expect his brother's eyes to flutter open, but it sure made Gideon smile when he saw Gunnar looking alert.

"Hey, man. How are you doing?" Gideon patted Gunnar's shoulder.

"Been better." Gunnar smirked. "Oh, shit."

Gideon's eyes widened. "What?" He searched for the nurse call button in case his brother needed medical assistance right away.

"I missed your game."

Gideon exhaled. "Don't worry about it. You're all that matters." He pulled up a chair next to him. "So what happened?"

Gunnar reached for a cup on a raised tray that had a bendy straw inside. He took a long sip before answering. "I got a message on my phone that the alarm was going off at the salon. I went down there, expecting to meet with the police. No one was there yet. I went inside—"

Gideon groaned and leaned back. "You should have waited for the cops."

Gunnar rolled his eyes. "Now you sound like Mom."

"She's right. Look at you."

Gunnar peered down. "I have seen better days, huh?"

"You think? You could have been killed." Gideon grabbed Gunnar's hand and held it. "Do you know who did this to you?" He balled his hand into a fist.

Gunnar shook his head. "Take that thought out of your head, man. We're not about that life anymore. Let the police handle this."

Gideon hadn't gotten tied up with gangs like Gunnar, but he had no problem defending his family. If it required that he use his fists, he would do it. Gunnar must have recognized the intent behind his eyes and in his question.

"With everything going on with Mom, and Thane being"—Gideon looked at Gunnar and at the same time they said—"Thane."

Gideon laughed along with Gunnar. At least the shooting hadn't taken away Gunnar's sense of humor.

Gideon became serious again as he talked to his oldest sibling. "I can't lose you. Family is all we have."

"I know." Gunnar nodded. "That's why you need to take care of Mom's flower shop. Victor's done a great job, but he's been there alone."

"Done." Gideon ran his hand over his hair, which caused Gunnar to look up.

"You know Mom is going to hate that." He pointed up.

Gideon smiled. "Yeah, she already warned me that a lecture is coming. I am ready for a change." He rubbed his hand over Gunnar's newly shorn head. "I see you got a new look. What's up with that?"

"It was time for me to grow up, stop hiding, you know?"

Gideon knew all too well about his brother's once-troubled past and his former mistakes. He'd seen the No Equal gang tattoo when Gunnar had gotten it done. Even back then, Gideon had called him an idiot and told him how great they had it with Queen Elizabeth. Until their mother had proved herself by putting herself in harm's way, Gunnar hadn't embraced their charmed lives.

"Mom told me that you and Eboni are together."

Gunnar didn't smile. He beamed. Everything on his face lit up like he'd won the lottery. His pale skin held some color now. He pressed a button on a controller on his bed to raise his head a bit more.

"Since we're alone, I can tell you this. I bought her a ring." Gunnar nodded. "Doing it right this time. I can't let more time pass between us."

Gideon stood as fast as he could with his bum knee and embraced his brother. "Congratulations."

"Yeah, I had planned on proposing after your game but, well, you know." Gunnar shrugged. "She's perfect, man."

Gideon sat down. "She was pretty special back in the day. I remember thinking how great she was to hang with you after all the stuff you had gone through with the drugs and the fighting and that gang. She never left your side."

"I know." Gunnar got quiet for a moment before looking at the window across the room.

Gideon peered down to give his brother a moment. He hadn't seen him get emotional about much. Eboni really must have gotten to his heart more than before.

Gunnar wiped his eyes and sniffed before he continued talking. "What about you? Did you tell Mom that you and Hilary are over?"

Gideon nodded. "Told her yesterday before the game. She was disappointed, but what can I say? It wasn't meant to be."

"You have bigger fish to fry."

"I know, like making sure you're okay. Watching out for Pick 'N Clip. And—"

"Your knee."

Gideon stared at his brother.

"Sorry for cutting you off, but you know I'm right." Gunnar stared at him.

Gideon returned the look and tried not to blink. "I'm fine."

Gunnar tilted his head. "Dude, if I recognized that you're hurting, you know Mom will know. She knows everything."

"That she does." Gideon laughed.

The phone in the room rang.

"It's been mainly the media." Gunnar waved his hand dismissively.

Gideon had no problem telling off a nosy reporter. He answered phone that rested at the head of Gunnar's bed. "Yeah?"

"Gunnar?"

Gideon recognized the voice but needed to hear a bit more. "This isn't Gunnar. What can I help you with?"

"Is Queen Elizabeth there? This is Victor. I need to talk to someone about the store."

Gideon relaxed back into his chair. "Hey, Victor. This is Gideon."

"Oh, thank God. You're in town." Victor exhaled. "I need some help with some the business. Queen was way better at this than me."

"I'll come down there." Gideon stood. The pain didn't register to him this time as he thought about the store and his duty to his family.

"Good. Good. I'll see you later."

Gideon disconnected the call. "Victor needs help already. I hate to leave you so soon after getting here. I was hoping to see Mom and Eboni."

"Hopefully, I won't be here for very long." Gunnar smiled like he wanted to reassure Gideon.

"If you want to stay with me at my house, you can. You know I have plenty of room." Gideon embraced his brother.

"I know. But you know how Mom is. At least for now, I'll stay with her." He waved at Gideon as he walked out of the room.

He got into the elevator and made it down to the lobby. As he stepped out of the elevator, he saw Eboni going into a different one. He had to smile at her dedication to Gunnar. His brother had better treat her right this time.

Gideon walked through the lobby and went by the gift shop, where he noticed someone familiar. He walked into the store and stood behind a woman he recognized. As she admired a display of freshly cut flowers, he watched her touching a petal and smelling an open bud. He took a deep breath and caught her distinctive flowery scent. Even among the various bouquets for sale, her aroma brought Gideon back to his days of sitting at the kitchen table and inhaling every bit of food his mother produced and then some.

"Are you going to stand there or are you going to hug your mother?" Elizabeth said without turning around.

"How do you do that?" Gideon laughed.

Elizabeth turned and embraced Gideon. "Don't you boys know that you can never get anything by me?"

As soon as he embraced Queen Elizabeth, Gideon felt like he had arrived home. His shoulders relaxed. His breathing slowed. Even the throbbing in his knee subsided. She made everything right.

"I'm learning. I saw Gunnar. I was going to stay but Victor called and said he needs some help."

"Oh, no. I can go."

Gideon shook his head. "No, you stay with Gunnar. Besides, I have a feeling he's about to do something special."

Queen Elizabeth cocked her head. "Do something special? What is he going to do? Walk on water?"

Gideon shrugged. "He might. You did raise us to be the best at whatever we do."

She gave him a playful slap on his arm. "You're cute. Good luck at the store, honey. If you need help, I have a friend who also owns a flower shop nearby. Her name is Janelle Gold. She owns Flowers Galore. Hold on." She opened her purse and retrieved a business card from inside. "Here's her information. See her if Victor can't help you."

Gideon blinked. "So the competition helps you? That's like me asking Peyton Manning for tips. Doesn't happen."

Queen placed her hand against Gideon's cheek. "Florists are way different than football players, darling."

Gideon laughed again. "You are right about that. I'll check out the store and hopefully will be back soon."

"Good. If not, be sure you come by the house for dinner tonight." She kissed Gideon on his cheek.

He wanted to spend more time with Gunnar and his mother, but duty called. He would handle it and get back as quickly as he could.

"Oh, and once you get done at the store, make an appointment with a doctor about your knee." His mother smiled and crossed her arms over her chest. The silk purse that hung from a gold chain dangled from her arm.

Gideon remained quiet. He smiled and almost laughed off her assumption about his health. To stall for time, he said, "Mom, I got checked out by the team's doctor. I'm fi—"

"Don't lie to me. I apologize for interrupting." She pointed down. "I know you haven't developed a strut in your walk after twenty years. What's going on with your leg?"

Gideon glanced over to the cashier area. When he noticed a couple of customers looking at him and whispering, he kept a cool head while talking to his mother.

"I love you, Mom. I'll try to be by your house later for dinner." He kissed her forehead.

"Love you, baby." She patted his shoulder. "Remember to go see Janelle if you need anything, understand?"

Gideon nodded. He would have to school his mother on having public conversations about him. He had seen too many real and fake stories about him in the press. For once, he wanted to control his image.

As though on autopilot, Gideon got to Pick 'N Clip in record time. He parked in the back like he used to when he'd worked alongside Queen Elizabeth. Once he got out of the car, he realized very quickly that he no longer had keys to access the store from the locked back door. After his mother made him and his brothers sign power of attorney forms for her business, she'd tried giving him a set of keys to the store. Believing that holding the keys meant something bad would happen to Elizabeth, Gideon had refused. Now he would have to get that extra set while he stayed in town.

"Damn." He circled the standalone store to get to the front door.

Nothing had changed about the place. Gideon's mother had a way of making every place, including all of her stores, feel like home. The front of the all-white store with a black shingled roof created a great frame for the black wrought-iron trellis that surrounded the front door. His mother had ivy creeping up each to give the place a garden appeal.

As soon as he opened the door, a fragrant bouquet greeted him. As he scanned the inside, he realized not much had changed in here either. Roses, daisies, and lilies remained housed in lit glass cases. Vases lined the shelves behind the bouquet-making counter. Streamers of different colored ribbon came off rolls on both sides of the counter. His sneakers squeaked over the brick-colored tile floor.

"Oh, great. You're here." Victor put his hand to his chest as he came from the back room.

Except for the sprigs of gray hair, Victor looked exactly the same. The diminutive Filipino man embraced Gideon before taking a step back.

"The shipment came in." Victor pointed to the storeroom.

Gideon glanced around but noticed that the glass cases and shelves still looked bare. "Did you have a good sales day or something? I don't see any merchandise."

"I received a shipment two days ago, and I put it all in the cases like usual. I didn't know the thermostat stopped working." Victor rushed over to one of the cases and opened a door. "Feel."

Gideon strolled over to him. He put his hand in the case to feel the temperature. Hot air surrounded his digits. "That's too hot."

"No shit." Victor covered his mouth. "Sorry. Didn't mean to curse in front of Queen's boy."

"Don't sweat it. I've heard worse in the locker rooms."

"I'm sure you have. I'm used to you being a little kid." Victor put his hand up to his waist to illustrate Gideon's height when he'd first started working with his mother at the store. "Anyway, I think one of the delivery drivers must have knocked the thermostat out of whack when they were putting away the merchandise. I didn't discover it had been messed up until today. Every flower and plant in the cases has open buds or worse." He went to a nearby trash can and picked up a long-stem rose.

It drooped down. To illustrate Victor's point, a petal fell from the bud.

"I can't sell any of these. Your mother has very high standards." He slammed the stem back into the bin. "What am I going to do?"

Gideon put his hands on Victor's shoulders. "First thing's first. Have you called an electrician or heating and cooling tech to fix the thermostat? No use restocking it if it still doesn't work."

Victor shook his head. "No. Your mother keeps this place in tip-top shape. Any maintenance she's done, she's kept me out of the loop." He pointed to her office. "There's only a few things in her office that I can touch. I don't go in the drawers." He shuddered and shook his head.

"I'll contact her to see who she uses."

Victor gripped Gideon's arm. "No, don't. If your mother finds out that I couldn't handle something like this, she'll freak out. She'll never trust me to run the store for her again."

Gideon cocked his head. "You can't believe that. You've worked for her for years. You're like family. She would understand."

He shook his head. "I let thousands of dollars' worth of merchandise get destroyed. I love Queen, and I know she loves me. But to let all that money go down the drain is something even I couldn't forgive."

Gideon found it hard to believe that his saint of a mother would be that irrational. Then again, Victor did have a flair for the dramatic.

"Okay, I'll go in the office and see if I can find a number for someone to fix it. If I can't, I'll find someone to do it. Can't be that hard." He patted Victor's shoulder. "Next, we'll need more plants and flowers."

"That's the other thing. I called the vendor. They won't be able to get us more flowers for two days. He said he may be able to bring something tomorrow, but it would be late." Victor ran to the front counter and held up some papers. "We have orders that have to be fulfilled today." His eyes widened as he stared at Gideon. "Maybe you can call them and tell them who you are—the great Gideon Wells, Super Bowl champion—and they'll make an exception."

Gideon counted in his head, a second time within twenty-four hours, before he addressed Queen Elizabeth's employee. "No. I don't work that way. You've been around my mother long enough to know that. We do things the right way every time."

Victor shrugged. "Suit yourself. In the meantime, we're out of everything, and one of Queen's biggest clients is expecting their order tomorrow."

"Let me see the orders. I'm sure there are plenty of greenhouses around that would be willing to help us out."

Victor shook his head. "You're going to have to make a miracle happen to get them to give up their stock. You know what time of year it is, right?"

Gideon slipped his hands in his pockets. A brief thought hit him to go to as many florists as he could to get what he needed. What his mother didn't know wouldn't hurt her. He had never betrayed her trust, and he wouldn't be starting now.

His fingers brushed over a card. He pulled it out and read it. "I think I have an idea. I'll be right back."

Chapter 5

Janelle decorated the front window of the store with vases filled with red roses and white baby's breath. Nothing said stereotypical Valentine 's Day bouquet like roses.

"Pretty." Penny nodded as she arranged the greeting cards on the rack by the counter. "Anyone ever tell you that you should do this for a living?"

Janelle snickered. "Maybe once or twice." She put her fists to her hips as she scanned the store. "I think we're ready."

"Ready for romance?" Penny sprayed the counter and wiped it down.

"Ready for more business. It's been a bit slow. I'm hoping now that football season is over, men will be more attentive to their wives and girlfriends and get some flowers." So that she didn't worry her friend, Janelle smiled.

Janelle heard the front door opening before she heard the bell over the door ringing. "Welcome to—" She stopped her standard greeting when she saw her other employee, Thelma, approaching her.

"Thelma, what are you doing here today? You know it's your day off." Janelle moved closer to the older woman.

When she caught Thelma's standoffish vibe from her sour expression and the way she kept her arms crossed over her chest, Janelle stopped."What's wrong? Your team didn't win last night or something?" She laughed.

When Thelma kept her stoic expression, Janelle stopped laughing.

"Can we talk?" Thelma glanced over at Penny. "In private."

"Uh, yeah. Of course." Janelle led her to her office.

With the two of them inside and the door closed, the space seemed so cramped. Janelle didn't keep a lot of items in her office, just a desk, her rolling swivel chair, a chair across from her, and a plant in the corner. Without a window, the office felt more like a closet sometimes.

"What did you want to tal—"

"I'm quitting, effective immediately." Thelma leaned back in her chair as though waiting for a fight.

Janelle felt her bottom jaw unhinge and nothing coming from her mouth. After Penny, Janelle had hired Thelma based on her years of experience working at the Norfolk Botanical Garden. She had a love of horticulture like Janelle did. Besides that, the older African-American woman reminded her of what a real mother should act like.

The nurturing woman would dispense good advice to her and treat her like a daughter. On occasion, Thelma would bring in plates of freshly baked cookies.

After collecting her thoughts, Janelle managed to muster enough strength to say one word. "Why?"

Thelma took in a deep breath through her wide nostrils and on the exhale said, "You're in trouble, baby. I'm going to go before I see this place get shut down."

Janelle shook her head. "What are you talking about? You're always paid and on time. I've never said—"

Thelma cut her off. "You're a great boss. One of the best I've ever worked for. When I retired and decided to do some fun part-time work, I knew I would love working here, and I have. You make it a joy to come here."

Janelle's throat started to tighten and her eyes stung from the impending tears. She never wanted to show weakness in front of anyone, let alone her employees. They looked to her to be a strong leader. How could she portray that if she cried at the drop of a hat?

Janelle clasped her hands together and sat them on her desk to give off the air of authority. "So again, why?"

She lowered her tone to almost a whisper despite the door being closed. "I saw the disconnection notice for the light bill, and I paid it."

Damn it. She wouldn't crack. She wouldn't break. Janelle ground her teeth together to harness her feelings. Bosses didn't weep in front of their employees.

She covered her eyes and lowered her head. Damn if she didn't feel defeated.

She didn't expect to feel an arm wrapped around her shoulders. She turned her face away from Thelma before she pushed her chair back to create a wedge between the two of them.

Janelle cleared her throat. "I'm so sorry you felt obligated to do that. I never wanted—"

"You don't owe me any excuses." Thelma's confused expression showed her bewilderment at Janelle's distant demeanor. "You've created a fine business." She retreated back to her chair. "When you get yourself turned around, and I know you will, call me if you're in need of more help."

Janelle nodded. "I'll take that into consideration." Talking like a boss would remind her of her position. She owned a business. She had employees, well, an employee under her. Without any money, she would lose it all.

"Thank you." Thelma smiled. "You run a beautiful flower shop."

Janelle tried smiling to show some level of control. "I wish you wouldn't go."

Thelma moved closer to the door. "I'll say good-bye to Penny." She shook her head. "She's good people but horny as a devil."

That assessment made Janelle laugh. "You are right about that. She's been that way for as long as I've known her." She straightened herself up and brought the serious countenance back to her face. "You leaving might make her worry. I don't want her fearing she may lose her job." Janelle put her fists to her hips.

"I'll tell her that I've decided to retire for real this time. If she doesn't know about the problems, she doesn't have to know." Thelma opened the door. "Thanks for hiring this old lady."

"Thanks for working for me. You made this a better place." Janelle took a couple of deep breaths.

"No." Thelma pointed to Janelle. "You make this place. It has Janelle Gold all over it. Now go make your mark. I'll be rooting for you."

Janelle fought the urge to put her arm around the shorter woman and, instead, patted her shoulder and walked her out to the main store.

"Penny, you be good to Janelle." Thelma walked toward Penny with her arms outstretched. "I've decided to retire for good this time."

"What? You're leaving?" Penny hugged Thelma. "Who's going to bring in hot cookies?"

"Maybe you can learn to bake." Janelle tried hiding the frustration in her voice, but she knew it crept out anyway.

Penny shivered as though Janelle had suggested she bake with severed kitten heads.

"Don't be a stranger." Janelle waved to Thelma as she walked out of the store.

She wanted to break down and cry, but business owners didn't do that.

Janelle turned her back on the front door and faced Penny. "It's a big loss for the store, but we'll manage."

Penny nodded. "Yeah. I'll miss her though."

Janelle would also. Not only would she miss the woman, with her leaving it became clear she had a failing business. She couldn't take another loss.

"Oh, wow." Penny's eyes became wide as she stared at Janelle, or rather something behind her.

"What?"

The door opened again before Janelle heard the bell over it ringing.

"Welcome to—" She stopped her introduction again as soon as she came face to chest to a wall of a man.

Janelle had to take a step back to see his face. When she did, she wanted to take another big step back away from him.

Gideon Wells. As she lived and breathed. She'd imagined him showing up to her store one day to whisk her off her feet, tell her that he had been the one to kiss her that night at the dance so many years ago, and that he'd thought about her every day. She had to get her head out of the clouds.

The tall man had a hard expression on his face until he stared at Janelle. Then it softened. His blue eyes drew her in like the stare that had mystified her so many years ago when she'd dared to look her mystery kisser directly in his eyes before she'd run home. Pretty soon, he started to smile a bit. What power this man had. As soon as she caught his pleasant look, Janelle's heart stuttered.

Maybe he had remembered her. Then reality hit her. What the hell had happened to her no-man rule? How had seeing this god caused her to imagine romantic possibilities? She needed to ground herself, root herself in reality.

Janelle tugged at her sweater. No way could he find her attractive. She dropped her gaze for a millisecond to take inventory of her outfit.

She had on her standard uniform of droopy sweater, well-worn jeans, broken-in sneakers, and a turtleneck. Gideon, on the other hand, looked like sex on a stick in his T-shirt, jeans, sneakers, and a leather jacket.

He had his hair pulled back into a ponytail like Janelle had seen in pictures online. His stare bored a hole through her soul. If he asked her to drop her panties, she might do it, a strange reaction considering she had only heard of him yesterday.

"Um, hi." Janelle's voice broke when she finally addressed him. She had her hands to her hips at first, but thought the stance looked too aggressive and so lowered them to her side. Damn, now she looked like a stiff-armed mannequin. "How can I help you?"

"Yeah, you need a bouquet for a young lady?" Penny came around the counter and stood next to Janelle. "Or maybe you need something for your brother Gunnar?"

Janelle whipped her head around to Penny. Under her breath, she whispered, "How do you know that?"

"Google," Penny replied through her smile to Gideon. "We heard about the shooting yesterday. How awful." She poked Janelle on her side to get her to speak.

"Uh, yeah. Horrible. Hope they catch who did it." Janelle nodded. "Good that you rushed back home. That was very, very—um—sweet."

Penny groaned and lowered her head.

"Thanks." Gideon's deep voice rumbled over Janelle.

Her stomach twitched as soon as she heard him. Yep, definitely a panty-dropper type of voice.

"I'm looking for Janelle Gold." He pointed to Penny. "Is that you?"

Penny started to nod when Janelle pushed her friend away. "I'm Janelle. I own Flowers Galore. Penny Lister is one of my employees." For now, she could say that with some authority.

Penny held her hand up to Gideon. "Hi."

Despite Penny positioning her hand in a way that begged for Gideon to kiss the back of it, he, instead, held it like a gentleman and shook it. She slipped out of his grip and stared at her hand like an oddity.

Penny leaned over to Janelle and whispered, "I'm never washing this hand again."

"Good to know." Janelle patted her friend's back and nudged her back to the counter. Then she turned back to Gideon. "You're looking for me?"

"Yes, my mother said that if I got in a bind at her store to come see you." He moved in closer to Janelle.

She stood her ground. No way would she run away from someone within her own establishment. Plus, once she smelled his musky scent, she wanted to take it in more. Gideon smelled like what a man should smell like. Earthy yet fragrant, like a cherry blossom tree. His aroma mixed well with the flowers in her establishment. Although she didn't want to admit it, he fit.

"Oh, yeah? Who's your mother?" Janelle couldn't imagine who would refer Gideon Wells to see her.

"Elizabeth Sommerville. Queen Elizabeth. You know her?"

Janelle's jaw dropped again. After all the conversations she had shared with Elizabeth, how could she not know that Elizabeth had adopted Gideon and Gunnar Wells? The different races and last names shouldn't have had anything to do with her not knowing. She would have thought she would have heard something about it considering what he did. Then again, Janelle had shut down all conversations about sports with Penny during the game last night. Before then, she hadn't been open to hearing about athletes and sports.

Elizabeth talked about her family, but never mentioned her sons' names or professions. That shouldn't have surprised Janelle. Elizabeth, despite the moniker from the neighborhood residents, had always been down to earth. She talked about the success of her children in their chosen professions like any mom would. So what she had a champion MMA fighter son and now a Super Bowl-winner son? Now that Janelle thought about it, Elizabeth did mention a third son. She wondered what he did for a living.

"I didn't know you're Elizabeth's son." She put out her hand. "Hi."

Gideon held Janelle's hand. Before that touch, Janelle had always wondered why flowers and plants craved the sun. As she held Gideon's hand, she understood the power of radiant heat. His large hand enveloped hers. She could imagine what it would feel like to be held by him, to have him stroke her bare skin with his fingertips, or how he would touch her as they had wild, animalistic sex.

At the last thought, she pulled her hand away from his and crossed her arms over her chest when she felt her nipples hardening.

"Nice to meet you." Gideon cleared his throat. "As you may have heard, my mother is going through a health issue right now, so I'm trying to help out at one of her stores. I'm over at the Pick 'N Clip, but there's an issue with some supplies, and I'm hoping you can help me. Our last shipment got destroyed. I was hoping to buy some of your stock." He smiled.

As Penny screamed, "Yes," Janelle said, "No."

Gideon split his attention between Penny and Janelle but settled on Janelle. He stared at her like he wanted to challenge her. She imagined that behind a menacing face guard on a football helmet, he probably intimidated lots of men. She wouldn't crumble. She hoped her quick response would get him to leave.

Janelle cleared her throat as she glared at her employee. Penny and her big mouth. Then she glared at the man who'd come to her at the worst time in her life. "I'm sorry, Mr. Wells."

"Gideon."

Janelle shifted in her spot. An itchy tickle crept over her shoulders and down her stomach like a weed taking over an abandoned piece of property. "We can't spare any today."

"Janelle, yes, we can. We got that shipment—"

"Sorry we can't help you. Tell your mother hi from me. I hope she gets better." Janelle turned around and walked to the other end of the counter away from Gideon. When she pivoted so that she could see the front door, she expected to see Gideon leaving her store. She noticed he hadn't moved.

"I'm a customer like any other. If I offered to buy every flower in your place for someone special, you would sell to me? As soon as we receive our shipment, I would replace your stock." His tone remained even and smooth.

Janelle had stood toe-to-toe against bankers who had refused to loan her money for her store and hadn't backed down from that challenge. Gideon's determination rivaled hers. She couldn't take giving something up, not today, not now. His offer felt like he wanted to buy her out of the business.

"But you don't know when that'll be, right?" Janelle braced her hands on the counter.

"One, maybe, two days tops." He strolled closer to her.

Penny gasped. Janelle gripped the counter to keep herself steady.

"We have a large order for some hotels down on the strip. They want an assortment of flowers. How about I buy some carnations, daisies, and calla lilies and leave you your roses? I know how important those are right now. Hopefully, that'll hold our store and not put you all in a bind." Gideon lowered his voice.

Cool under pressure. Janelle understood now how Gideon had made quarterback on his team.

Penny clapped her hands. "That's sounds more than fair. I'll go get—"

Janelle held up her hand to halt her overeager friend. "Please understand, Mr. Wells. I can't sell off the bulk of my stock to you. I also have a business to run. If you buy it all, I'll have to shut down." She would leave out the fact that the money she would get from him would be enough to pay off her bills.

She should yield. The angel on her shoulder whispered in her ear that Elizabeth would sell him the flowers. Her head refused to back down. She looked around her modest place and imagined it with empty shelves and cases. The image proved too much for her to bear, even if the situation would be temporary.

"Why not give the order to me so that we can fulfill it? I'll be glad to take that business." This time she smiled.

Chapter 6

Gideon rested his hands on his hips like a gunslinger as he squared off against this statuesque beauty. As a gentleman, he should have accepted Janelle's first response and left. Then she'd turned her back to him and he'd spied her luscious ass under her tent of a sweater. His mother would have smacked him on the back of the head for objectifying this woman, but he couldn't walk away from this fight. Not yet.

"I would like to discuss this even further." He stared into her deep brown eyes.

She looked familiar to him. Maybe because he'd imagined a dream woman matching her appearance. Her cocoa-colored skin had Gideon thinking about stroking her flesh to see if it did feel like velvet. He didn't know much about hair, but he could tell her chestnut-tinted hair in a bun had to go down to her shoulders and had its natural curl.

As soon as he'd touched her hand, his heart had pounded so hard it scared him. Staring down this adversary didn't have him quaking in his shoes. He liked the challenge. The fact that she didn't fold to him made her even more attractive.

"Like I said, I can't lose anything else today." The bun in Janelle's hair gave her an uptight look. The grandma sweater didn't help her cause.

"Did you lose something already?" Gideon lowered his voice so that Penny couldn't hear their conversation.

Janelle blinked.

Gideon took that moment to move in closer. He could stare at her plump bottom lip forever and never get tired of the sight. Even though she didn't look like she wore makeup, her lips carried a healthy pink shade, and they covered a set of straight, white teeth.

"You good-looking guys really aren't used to hearing no from a woman. Or is it because you won some World Series game or something, and you think you own the world?"

"Super Bowl." Penny leaned forward in between Gideon and Janelle.

Janelle waved her hand in the air. "Whatever. As much as I respect Queen Elizabeth, I can't help her this time."

"Good. I'm glad you brought my mother into the equation. This has nothing to do with me and everything to do with her and her business."

A customer walked into the store, but Gideon kept his interest on Janelle.

"Penny, will you help our customer, please?" Janelle spoke to her employee, but like Gideon, she kept her stare directly on him.

"Sure, boss." Penny pivoted and sauntered away.

"Like I was saying, my request has nothing to do with me or who I am or some game. I'm trying to keep her store running until she can get on her feet." Gideon tried to appeal to her sense of compassion, hoping she had some.

If his mother had suggested he go to Janelle for help, she must have a good heart. He had to keep thinking that to keep his cool.

"I told you I can't. It doesn't matter that you're a Bobcat or whatever."

Penny popped her head in between the two of them again. "Wolf."

Janelle glared at her friend, and Penny resumed her work duties with their one customer.

"I'm not a Wolf now. I'm a man." Gideon saw Janelle's eyes widened and she swallowed hard. He hadn't meant for the statement to come out as salaciously as it did. His pulse accelerated when he caught Janelle's reaction. He continued. "I'm a son trying to help his mom. You understand that, right?"

"Yes, I understand, you wild violet."

"What?" He moved in closer.

"You're like a weed that you can't get rid of. You think you have them all killed and they keep coming back." She brought her stare up to his. "You don't give up, do you?"

He nodded. "Now you're starting to understand me, you aloe plant."

This time, she blinked. Before she could ask what he meant, he offered an explanation. "You are able to help. You have the ability to heal, but unless someone is careful enough to break through your thorns, you're only interesting to look at. I don't need all of your essence. I only need a little help to get by. What do you say?"

Janelle dropped her gaze to the floor. "Maybe if—"

"I knew it!"

Janelle peered around Gideon before he turned around. A man wearing a Wolves jersey stretched across his protruding belly pointed to Gideon as he approached him.

"What the hell are you doing here?" The enthusiastic fan shook Gideon's hand.

"Watch your language in front of the ladies, man." Gideon liked being competitive, but he hadn't lost his manners.

The fan glanced at Janelle and Penny. "Oh, sorry. What are you doing here?"

"Helping my family." He glanced at Janelle, hoping she understood his stance.

"Yeah, I heard about your brother. That's rough. Is he going to be all right?" The stranger patted Gideon on the shoulder like he knew him.

"Yes, he'll pull through." Gideon gave him a solid nod.

"Do you mind if I get a picture with you and an autograph? The guys at the office will never believe this." He pulled out his rectangular phone and set it up to take a picture.

Before Gideon could object so that he could focus on Janelle, the customer took the selfie while standing next to Gideon. Then the fan shoved a piece of paper and a pen at him that he snatched off the counter.

"Make it out to Studly Dudley." The fan rubbed his stomach.

"I'll sign it to Dudley." Gideon would do a lot for his fans. He wouldn't sign anything that talked about some guy being a stud, even one that wore Gideon's jersey.

Gideon heard Janelle sighing hard as he signed the crumpled paper. He hadn't meant to disrupt her life. He would have to have a serious conversation with his mother on her friendly resources.

He handed the autograph to Dudley. "Thanks for being a fan." He turned to Janelle. "It was a pleasure to meet you." He saw her blink at his statement. "Thank you for your consideration." He snapped an order form from a pad and grabbed a pen from the counter. "If circumstances change, I'd appreciate it if you would give me a call."

"I have Pick 'N Clip's number." Janelle set her jaw.

"I'm sure you do." From the few glances Gideon threw her way, he watched her staring at his hands as he wrote. He pressed his lips together to keep from smiling.

"So what are you writing down?" She stood on her tiptoes to peer over his hand. She lowered herself once he stopped writing and took a step back.

He folded the paper and handed it to her. "This is my number." Gideon stared at her until she accepted it.

Janelle didn't look at what he'd written. She folded it two more times until she'd formed a ball and shoved it in her pocket.

He couldn't figure this woman out for the life of him. He didn't make it a habit of giving his contact information to anyone. Whenever a woman asked for his number, he would politely decline or give her Dennis's digits. The longer he looked at Janelle's luscious mouth, the more he hoped to God she would call him.

Gideon moved closer to Janelle before departing. "By the way, your swamp hibiscus should have been cut back. If you want it to survive, you need to keep that door closed. Please excuse me." He turned to leave as soon as he heard Janelle gasping.

Gideon would have to thank his mother for referring him to this bitter, angry woman.

Once he got back in his car, it took him no time to arrive back to Pick 'N Clip. Victor rushed to him.

"Well?" His mother's employee peered around him, looking for the needed supplies.

"I went to Flowers Galore."

Victor beamed. He looked like he knew Janelle Gold and her normally generous capacity. So her change in demeanor must have had to do with him. He still couldn't figure out why.

Gideon shook his head. "No go. I asked to buy some flowers and plants from her and she turned me down flat."

Victor, who looked to be on the verge of tears, turned away from Gideon and raised his hands in the air. "Queen Elizabeth is going to kill me. She'll never trust me to run her baby again. This will break her heart." He covered his mouth and looked at Gideon. "Oh, I didn't mean that."

Gideon held up his hand, a usual stance whenever he spoke to Victor. "I know. I'll try other places until we can get another shipment in."

Victor's eyes widened. "Really? You'll do that?"

"For my mother? Of course. We won't let her down."

Victor wrapped his arms around Gideon's shoulders and collapsed into his chest. "I'm so glad you're here."

Gideon liked being home. He wished it could have been under better circumstances.

The front door crashed open. Gideon didn't expect to see Janelle Gold, although a tiny part of him wanted to encounter her again.

Though antagonistic, the natural beauty caught his notice. Even as she glared at him, his heart raced. He couldn't wait to watch her leave to peep at her backside.

"Can I help you?" Gideon moved in front of Victor, blocking her from going any farther into the store.

Janelle breathed heavily as she glared at him. Had she run to his mother's store from hers? Granted, a few blocks separated the two stores. He peered behind her, looked through the front door and didn't notice any new cars in the parking lot. One car rolled on to their lot and parked as he stared through the glass. He peered down at Janelle.

"How did you know?" She jutted her thumb over her shoulder while attempting to catch her breath.

Gideon felt his eyebrows rut together. "Know what? That you would fight me on the flowers?"

Janelle shook her head. A strand of her hair managed to break free from her bun. It waved as she moved around, swaying like a willow in the wind. "No. The hibiscus. How did you know about the plant?"

Queen Elizabeth would have wagged her finger at Gideon for his eye roll, but her question warranted that reaction.

"Why wouldn't you think I would know what that plant was and how to care for it?" He crossed his arms over his chest as he directed his glare at her.

Damn it! Why did she look so familiar? Had he gone to school with her? He would have to look through his yearbooks.

"Because…" Janelle stopped and waved her hands up and down in front of him. "You're you."

"And what does that mean?" Gideon started to feel a slow simmer in the pit of his stomach.

Besides hating hearing assumptions about him and his family, he couldn't stand to be underestimated. He knew in his gut this woman would be insulting him in three, two, one…

"You're a football player." Janelle crossed her arms over her chest to match his look.

Gideon paused before he answered. "I'm not just a football player." He pointed to the floor. "I grew up here. I learned from my mother." He waved his hand all around him. "I learned about all these plants and flowers. I'm not some stupid jock."

Janelle's burned-butter skin tone transformed into a dark crimson shade over her cheeks. "I didn't say—"

"You didn't have to. I got it from your statement. Sorry for interrupting you." He turned to Victor. "Where's the closest greenhouse or nursery?"

"Greenhouse?" Janelle chewed on her bottom lip as she volleyed her gaze between Gideon and Victor.

Gideon faced Janelle. "Yeah. We have to resort to Plan B to fulfill orders."

The reddish hue over her face deepened. Gideon dropped his gaze to the floor for a moment. If he stared at her any longer, he would start to feel guilty, a strange reaction considering he didn't think he had done anything wrong. Seeing Janelle looking so conflicted, he decided he needed to back off from his harsh demeanor. The woman had run to the store to confront him.

"Go into Mom's office and look on her desk to see if you can find a number for an electrician. I'm sure she has one she uses all the time." He pointed to Queen's office.

"Are you sure I should be going through her things?" Victor peered around Gideon to look at Elizabeth's office.

"If she notices anything out of place, I'll say I did it." He nodded toward the room. He brought his attention back to Janelle. She glanced around the store.

"You really don't have a lot of inventory, do you?"

"The flowers got overheated." He removed his jacket and put it behind the counter. "So why are you growing the hibiscus?"

Janelle eased into the store even more. "Why do you want to know?"

Gideon studied her from behind the counter. He switched to quarterback mode a little too easily. He watched her mannerisms, trying to figure her out and wonder how she had become so guarded. He replayed their conversation from her store over in his head.

This woman had scars, demons, past battle wounds. He had to come at her a lot more cautiously than hitting some opposing player.

Instead of talking to her from behind the counter, Gideon strolled around it and stood in front of her. He stared into her eyes. She didn't flinch. That impressed him. She didn't seem in awe of the fact that he had won some game as she had called it. He liked that even more.

"My mother is a very good judge of character," Gideon began. "When she told me I could trust you to help me, I'm sure she suggested it because she knows you're a good person. I want to know more about the woman my mother says is good people."

"Oh." Janelle lowered her arms.

"Also, I want to know about the woman who thinks I'm good-looking."

* * * *

Janelle didn't need to look into a mirror to know that her face had turned the brightest shade of red known to man. Her neck and chest felt hot under her turtleneck, and it had nothing to do with the garment.

She could only be mad at herself for Gideon's comment. She had called him good-looking as a way to insult him. Up close, the man had a disarming appearance that matched his charm. Another man would have kicked her out of his store after she'd treated him so deplorably. Gideon wanted to know more about her. To top it all off, he also knew about plants. No way could he be real.

"Somehow, we started off on the wrong foot." Gideon smiled.

All thoughts escaped from Janelle's head. When she felt her knees shaking, she slammed her legs together, hoping to steady them.

Gideon continued. "When Victor comes back, would you like to go get some coffee somewhere? I would ask you out to dinner, but I'm going to try to get back up to the hospital to see my brother again."

God, Gideon came off as such a gentleman and so genuine, and here she had punished him for circumstances that he hadn't caused. Thelma had left because business had slowed. Janelle had money problems long before Gideon had gotten there. She still couldn't figure out if he had been the one to kiss her. Only one way to find out.

"I, um—" As Janelle started to talk about the contest and coffee, a man walked into the store.

She stared at him for a bit and recognized him as the customer who had been at her store moments ago. Gideon had given the man an autograph and picture, although he'd looked almost embarrassed to do so. What else could he want? How did he know where to find Gideon?

"Holy shit!" The man covered his mouth when he looked at Janelle. "Sorry for the language, ma'am." He turned back to Gideon. "I didn't believe that girl from the other flower place when she said that you were over here."

Great. Janelle would have to remember to kick Penny's ass when she got back to Flowers Galore.

"I'm in town to help my mom." Gideon leaned on the counter.

"Really? That means you'll be here for a while?" the customer asked.

Gideon glanced at Janelle before directing his full energy back to the man in the tight Wolves jersey. "I'm not sure how long."

The customer pumped his meaty fist into the air. "Awesome! I'm telling all my boys about this. For now, I'll get a dozen roses for my girl. No, make that two dozen. Hell, I'll buy the whole stock. I'm here with Gideon Wells!"

Gideon held up his hand. "Wait a minute. Didn't you buy some flowers at Flowers Galore?"

"Nah, man. As soon as that cute redhead told me where to find you, I bolted and came over here. How many times can I say in my lifetime that I bought flowers from a Super Bowl MVP?"

Gideon blinked. "I made MVP?"

"Yeah, didn't you know?"

Janelle shook her head. "Great. Like I didn't have enough problems. Enjoy my business, Mr. Wells. Congrats on making VIP."

"That's MVP, lady," the customer called after her.

"Whatever." She stormed out of the store.

"Wait," Gideon said.

Janelle didn't. Once she hit the cold, she realized that in her haste to confront the man who had approached her on the wrong day, she had also forgotten to grab her coat. She stepped up her strut to a trot all the way back to her store.

Once she returned to Flowers Galore, she opened the door and stared at her friend.

Penny smiled back at Janelle at first. "Did you talk to Gideon? Is he even hotter up close?"

Janelle ground her teeth together and had to take a couple of deep breaths before she spoke. "You and I need to have a talk."

Penny's smile melted and she stood up straight. "What did I do?"

"For one thing, did you open the door where I'm keeping my hibiscus?" Janelle pointed to the back of the store.

"Yeah. I thought I heard a beeping sound coming from inside it. I opened the door to check it. But I know I closed it."

Janelle shook her head. "You didn't."

"Sorry." Penny said it in that annoying, dismissive way teenagers caught doing something they shouldn't respond to their parents or other authority figures.

"And thanks to you, you sent business over to Pick 'N Clip. That customer that was in my store said you told him where to find Gideon."

Penny shrugged. "Yeah. So?"

"So while I was there, he came to see Gideon and wanted to buy as many bouquets of roses that he could. Oh, and he said he would tell all his friends that the Gideon Wells is working there. I am so screwed." Janelle put her hand to her head as she paced around her spot.

"Oh, no."

Janelle didn't acknowledge her friend. Right now, she had to figure out a way to regain some ground.

"Look on the bright side."

Janelle raised her head. "And what's that?"

"There are two great-looking guys here in town now."

Damn. The wrong employee had left her store.

Penny wrapped her arm around Janelle's shoulders. "This could be a win-win for both of you."

Janelle cocked her head as she stared at her delusional friend. "And how's that? He's got fame. He has the championship. No one knows me."

"But you can capitalize on his fame." Penny dug into her back pocket and held up her phone. "Got a shot of the two of you talking. I'll print this and hang it up by the counter. We'll tell every person who comes in that you are close friends with Gideon Wells." She waved her phone around. "And here's the proof."

Janelle stared at the shot. Instead of looking like two business people talking, the way Gideon's head tilted down toward her, and the way she stared at him, it looked more intimate than innocent. In the picture, she stared at him like she wanted to kiss him. Those great eyes of his had her sucked into every word he'd said.

"No." She turned away from the picture. "Don't use that."

Penny looked at the shot before she peered at her friend. "Why not? It's not often we get a celebrity in here. He came here for you. He knew your name. His mother referred him to you. You should use that to your advantage. You think he's not going to use his celebrity status to get customers over there? Of course he is."

"I don't care about what he does. That's his business." Janelle started to head back to her office. "I started this business on my own with the desire to cater to people who love flowers. I'm not going to use someone to get ahead." She swallowed as she thought about her past. Before Penny could ask her anymore probing questions, she continued. "I'm not using this guy to drum up more business. That would be wrong. We'll be fine."

Penny groaned. "You are such an old lady sometimes. You are so not twenty-seven."

"I am a good person." She ducked into her office and sat behind her small desk that wobbled when touched.

Penny's argument had merit, but Janelle couldn't go down that route. Penny reminded her of Ida. The thought of that sent a shiver up Janelle's spine and turned her flesh as cold as her refrigerator holding her arrangements.

Janelle would have to figure out how to gain some customers the honest way…and retain her dignity. Had she actually called Gideon Wells good-looking to his face?

Chapter 7

Gideon visited four different greenhouses, nurseries, and other florists to get enough flowers to restock the store and fulfill orders. By seven that evening, he had sold every flower and arrangement in the store. After Dudley had posted his picture to every social media page he had, customers had come to Pick 'N Clip in droves, including the media.

"Why are you in Virginia Beach at a flower store?" one reporter had asked him.

"Quarterback to florist. Quite a leap," another journalist mused.

"What do you think of the new moniker for you, Gideon? MVP Mama's Boy?" a young man who claimed he came from a top 40 radio station asked with a laugh.

Gideon certainly had been called worst names growing up. Being called a mama's boy didn't bother him as much as the media wanted.

He took a deep breath before speaking. "Ladies and gentleman, I appreciate you all coming out. As you can see, I'm helping out at one of my mother's stores while she's dealing with a medical issue."

"What issue is that, Gideon?" a reporter asked.

Gideon ignored the inquiry and continued with his speech. He raised his hands in the air. "Business was really good today. If you would like to place an order for an arrangement, I'd be more than happy to take it. If you're in need of flowers tonight, I would strongly suggest you checking out Flowers Galore, which is only a few blocks away."

Elizabeth would be proud of Gideon that he broke from his normal competitive self to throw business Janelle's way. After the way Janelle had stomped out of the store, that would be the only thing he would give her.

Gideon leaned against the front counter. "This is the only statement I'll make at this time."

An audible groan rumbled from the crowd. Gideon knew he should have offered more than that. He'd just helped his team win a Super Bowl championship for God's sake. Plus, if he wanted to keep up in this industry, and he did, he would have to put himself out there to the media as well as show some support to his team. He couldn't think about anything else but his family.

Despite his overt brush-off, the reporters, photographers, and DJs all shoved their business cards at Gideon. He tossed each one on top of the counter. His mother would be disappointed if he threw them into the garbage in front of them. He would wait until they all disappeared first.

Besides, before he could do any kind of press, he would have to talk to his coaches and agent. Then he would have to patch things up with Dennis.

Gideon shifted his weight to the side with his injured knee. Yes, he would need to see someone about that. When he could find some alone time, he would handle his personal business.

One by one, people cleared out of the store until the fan who had followed Gideon from Janelle's store remained.

"I'm afraid I don't have any flowers left." Gideon went behind the counter.

"I know. I wanted to tell you something about the woman at the other store." Dudley pressed his belly against the counter and leaned forward.

Although Gideon hated gossip, knowing that he could get better insight into Janelle Gold's life intrigued him. He remained quiet as he stared at the man.

"Her employee told me that she's growing that plant to enter it into some contest. Virginia's Best Plant and Flower show or something like that."

Gideon knew the competition well. His mother had entered it annually and usually won the award for best floral arrangement. Once they'd gotten home, she would give the ribbons to Gideon. At the time, the show hadn't allowed anyone younger than eighteen to enter. They hadn't known that Elizabeth's entries had actually been done by Gideon.

"Why would you think I would be interested in that?" Gideon wiped down the counter.

Dudley shrugged. "I don't know. I figured you're a competitor. I don't know why you're here exactly, but if you really do know about flower arranging and all that stuff, I'd say enter the contest and be a bigger champion in another area. Wouldn't that be a hoot? A Super Bowl quarterback who's also a florist." He laughed.

In the customer's revelry, Gideon ran the idea through his head. Janelle had accused him of being someone who didn't know his way around flowers. Although she denied calling him a dumb jock, he knew what she meant.

She would definitely eat some crow if he showed up to the contest and beat her in her category. Winning would be the ultimate redemption.

"Thanks for the information. I think I have enough on my hands." Gideon moved around the counter and ushered the man out the door.

If he gave a hint to Dudley that he would think about entering the contest, the news would be all over the Internet. In this situation, silence would be golden. He wanted to see the look on Janelle's face when he walked in with an arrangement and a plant that would beat hers in a contest.

"Oh, yeah. Whatever, man. Hey, great meeting you."

Gideon shook his hand as another man approached the door. "Hot damn. Gid the god is here."

More than being called the boy next door or America's Couple when he'd dated Hilary, he hated the fan nickname of Gid the god. It had started in high school and stuck with him through his athletic career no matter how much he'd tried to stop it.

"I was about to close up." Gideon stood at the doorway to stop the shorter man from entering. As he stared at him, he started to recognize him. "Ant? Is that you?"

The young African-American man held Gideon's hand and pulled him in for hug. "Yes, indeed. Can't believe you remembered me. Your brother Guns didn't."

"You were in my same class. Gunnar is older." Gideon would leave out the fact that Ant had annoyed Gunnar…and him.

"What do you mean you're closing early?" Ant managed to slip under Gideon's arm to go into the store. "What is this place?"

"A flower store."

Ant turned around. His halo of hair shaped in a circular Afro framed his face. Gunnar could do a lot with a head of hair like that.

"Pick 'N Clip. This isn't a flag football league?"

Gideon suppressed a laugh before he answered the delusional man. "No, this is my mother's place. I'm running it while she's out."

Ant raised his hands in the air. "I can't get a break. I thought your brother was managing a gym, and that turned out to be a hair salon. And now this."

Gideon suppressed a chuckled as he regarded the diminutive man and his troubles.

"Can't you change the place now that you're here?" Ant placed his hands together in prayer form.

This time, Gideon couldn't help but laugh out loud at Ant's request. "This is not my place to change. Come on. Valentine's Day is coming up.

You want to place an order? Maybe something for your mother?" Gideon pointed to an arrangements book on the counter. "Nothing like getting some flowers sent to the only woman in your life."

"Hey, I have a girlfriend." Ant puffed out his scrawny chest that hadn't changed that much since their high school days.

"I'm sure you do." Gideon smiled, but another chuckle threatened to make his way out of his mouth at any moment.

"Forget you, man." Ant stormed out of the store.

Gideon took that moment to lock the front door. He exhaled. He felt as though he'd been holding his breath in all day.

Victor appeared from the back-room area. "Everyone gone?"

"Everyone and everything." Gideon raised his hands again. "I gave Janelle's place a shout out. I hope that gets her some business."

"Aww, that was nice of you." Victor patted Gideon on his cheek. "Queen Elizabeth raised nothing but gentlemen."

Gideon smiled but kept his mouth clamped shut so he wouldn't say anything disparaging about his younger brother. "Did you get a status update about the rush order? We'll definitely need more flowers. If they can't make a rush shipment, we're going to be taking orders. I have a feeling while I'm here, business will be booming."

"That's a good thing for Queen. I'm sure her medical bills will be high."

"Even if her businesses failed, her medical bills would have been paid for. Between me and my brothers, we would make sure she's taken care of."

For as much as Elizabeth Sommerville had done for Gideon, Gunnar, and Thane, paying for her bypass surgery would be the least they could do for her.

As he looked at Victor, he realized his mother's reach and responsibility. She had employees. She had people depending on her for their lifestyles. Gideon felt a sense of pride to step into his mom's shoes.

"It was a good day today, huh?" Gideon braced his hands on the counter as Victor put money from the register into a bank bag.

"Very good day. Would you mind it terribly if I hung your body from a flagpole in front of the doors to get people to come in here?" Victor giggled.

"I'd mind it a little. It's cold out there." Gideon slipped on his jacket and glanced down at his watch.

Before leaving the store, he called his mother.

"Darling, did you go back up to the hospital?" Elizabeth's smooth voice oozed through the phone.

"No. It got really busy here today." Without saying a word, Gideon pointed to the bank bag and then pointed to himself to see if Victor needed him to drop off today's take at the bank.

Victor shook his head and put on his coat. He flung his purple scarf around his neck. Then he slipped on his red leather gloves. The man loved his colors.

"Are you still at the hospital?" Gideon asked as he opened the door for Victor.

"Uh, no. Gunnar needed some space."

The way his mother made the statement and her tone gave Gideon a niggling feeling of concern. "So are you at your house?"

"Yes, getting dinner ready. Are you coming by?"

"How can I refuse a home-cooked meal from you?" Gideon smiled as he unlocked his car. "See you in a bit."

"Do you want to ask Janelle if she wants to come to dinner?"

That uneasy feeling came across Gideon again. "No. I need to talk to you about her when I get to your place."

After disconnecting the call, Gideon worked on getting the ice off his windshield and Victor's before going to his mother's. He parked in her driveway, thankful not to meet with a ravenous team of paparazzi.

He thought that being in Virginia, he would be able to avoid those trappings. He could only hope that with time, the fervor would die down and he could live a normal life until training time.

Although his mother would encourage him to walk in the house, he felt odd doing so now. He rang her doorbell and waited. A tall, dark-skinned African-American woman answered the door. With her two large Afro puffs on the sides of her head, Gideon couldn't tell her age. She wore a tight T-shirt with the word *Fancy* emblazoned across the front and tight black leggings. Was she someone from the community center or one of his mother's many employees?

The longer he stared at her, the more he noticed something unusual with her face. Although the pound of makeup she'd used around her eye probably hid something sinister, she couldn't disguise the swelling. Gideon felt his pulse racing even though he didn't know this woman, didn't know her story. For all he knew, she could be a friend of Gunnar's, a female MMA fighter. The way she stood so delicately and looked at him like a savior, he had a feeling she hadn't asked for the fight she must have engaged in to get that souvenir.

"Well, well, well. Aren't you a sexy thing?" She nibbled on her bottom lip.

Definitely not a teenager. Then again, nowadays young people said things that he would have gotten punished for had he uttered the same comment at that age.

"Thank you." Gideon peered into the house to give this woman a hint that he wanted to be out of the cold.

"I suppose you want to come inside…of the house I mean." She winked.

"Move aside and let my son into the house." Elizabeth held the woman's waist and eased her off to the side.

Like a teenager, the stranger rolled her eyes and moved away from the door.

Queen, in a crisp, white button-down blouse and black slacks, opened her arms to welcome Gideon.

"Hey." Gideon hugged his mother and gave her a kiss on the cheek.

"Honey, this is Shay. She works at Press 'N Curl. She's staying here until she can get on her feet." His mother put her hand on Shay's shoulder. "Shay, this is my middle child, Gideon Wells."

"Nice to meet you." Gideon put his hand out to her.

"Oh, no. I'm a hugger." Shay threw her arms around Gideon's neck and held him tight enough that he could feel every part of her body. Gideon wished he'd worn all of his football padding.

Being a gentleman, he patted her back and attempted to let her go. Shay held onto him harder.

"Mmm, he even smells good." Shay nuzzled her nose into the crook of his neck and took a deep whiff.

The feeling of air by his neck tickled. Gideon shrugged and tried again to get out of Shay's embrace. She held him tighter. This woman needed to be a tackle or linebacker.

"Let that boy go." Elizabeth cocked her head as she regarded Shay. "Go set the table, please."

"Fine. You know how to ruin a girl's fun." She winked at Gideon before she trotted off to the kitchen.

"She's, um, something." Gideon removed his coat and hung it in the closet. "How long has she been here?"

"Only a few days."

He waited a beat before continuing with his questions about Shay. "Did she slip and fall on the ice? I noticed her cheek looks a little swollen."

Elizabeth held her son's hand. "She has some issues." She smiled. "Don't we all?"

He felt that anger flaming up inside of him again. "Anything I need to do?"

"No," Queen responded quickly. "You know I don't like confrontation. It's been taken care of." She took a deep breath.

He recognized Queen's desire to get off the subject as fast as possible. "Whatever you're cooking smells great. And I skipped lunch, so I am starving."

"Good. It's all done. We can sit down and you can tell me about your day." Elizabeth linked her arm around Gideon's and walked him to the formal dining room.

Gideon stopped by the table. "Not until you tell me about Gunnar."

Elizabeth glanced into the kitchen where Shay moved around getting dishes to set the table. "Later."

Gideon nodded. "Now that I'm home, I think I want to get back into competing."

"What do you mean, darling?" She rested her hand on her hip.

"Flower arranging. I hear the flower show is coming back in town. Have you already entered?" He had a plan to knock Janelle down a peg or two since she assumed he didn't know anything about flowers.

"I haven't. And I really didn't think you would want to do it again with me. How nice. I think it's a great idea." She kissed his cheek. "I've been growing some white roses in the greenhouse at your house. They would make perfect for the arrangement."

He rubbed his hands together. He had a plan for the plant. He would use their beauty to crush the competition. Now he felt like the old Gideon Wells. This flower competition couldn't match the excitement of the Super Bowl, but it would mean something to him. Seeing the shock on Janelle's face would be payment enough.

He faced his mother. "By the way, why did you want me to invite Janelle Gold to dinner?"

"You didn't find her pleasant?" His mother crossed her arms over her chest.

"I know you taught me to never say anything negative about anyone, especially women, so I'll say that I must have caught her on a bad day." Gideon would leave out the fact that the woman had shot laser beams out of her eyes at him, especially when she'd discovered her customer had come to Pick 'N Clip without buying anything at her establishment.

"Really? That doesn't sound like her. Yes, she can be a little guarded when she first meets you. But once she gets to know you, she's very nice. I thought that she could help you at the shop and that you two would get along. She likes flowers. You like flowers. Just seemed…"

The hairs started going up on the back of Gideon's neck. "Oh, no."

"What?" Elizabeth's eyes widened as she regarded her son.

"You're trying to set me up."

Shay chose that moment to walk out of the kitchen. "With who? Me? Is that why you invited me to stay with you, Queen?" She placed the stack of plates, utensils, and napkins onto the table as she stared at Gideon like he would be served as dinner that night.

"No. You need to get your life together before you think about dating anyone again." Elizabeth shook her head at her and then directed her to finish her job. She faced Gideon again. "I wasn't trying to set you up. I figured since you broke up with Hilary and you were in town that maybe you two could, I don't know, get to know each other."

"Mom, this is not like me going to a new school or those dances at the community center that you used to sponsor. I'm a grown man. I can find women on my own." As much as he loved his mother, her intrusions into his life, especially now, still bothered him.

"Yes, you can." Shay placed a plate on the table. She moved around to where Gideon stood and shimmied her body in between him and the table. Her ass brushed against his crotch. "A woman could be right in front of you."

Gideon needed to nip this overly flirtatious behavior from his mother's houseguest in the bud now to cut down on some embarrassment. "Shay, I'm really here for my mother and her business. I would like to make new friends, but I'm not interested in anything else. I hope you understand and respect that." He glanced at his mother in hopes she understood what he'd said.

Shay sucked on her teeth and glared at Gideon and then Elizabeth. "Damn. You sound like your brother. Whatever." She returned to the kitchen.

"You're making friends all over the place, aren't you, son?" Elizabeth smiled and held his hand. "She'll be fine."

"Which one?" The fact that his mother saw something in Janelle to want him to date her had him intrigued again.

Not that Gideon needed much prompting to think about Janelle Gold. She reminded him of a stripped-down version of his mother. Headstrong, stubborn, smart...slightly damaged.

"I'm talking about Shay." Elizabeth leaned close to Gideon and whispered. "Glad you're still thinking about Janelle."

Damn. He couldn't get anything past his mother.

"I hope you're hungry." His mother strolled into the kitchen to get dinner when the doorbell chimed. "Honey, will you get that for me?"

"Are you expecting someone?" He headed to the door. His luck, some overly ambitious reporter would be on the porch ready to pounce.

"No. Maybe it's Eboni," Queen called from the kitchen. "Or Victor. Or—"

Gideon opened the door. "Janelle."

He stared at her for a moment while gripping the door like a bouncer.

After a beat, Gideon and Janelle said at the same time, "What are you doing here?"

She never moved back from him. She kept her stare directly on his eyes. "I thought you said you were going to the hospital."

"Change of plans." He wouldn't go into detail about Gunnar. This woman had given him the cold shoulder for a reason. "How do you know where my mother lives?"

"Who is it?" Elizabeth asked from behind him.

Gideon didn't move or respond to his mother's inquiry until he felt her hand on his shoulder.

"Janelle's here." He took a step back.

"Hi, sweetheart." Elizabeth embraced her. "Don't stand out in the cold. Come on in."

"Thank you." Janelle stepped into the house but kept Gideon in her sights. "To answer your question, Queen Elizabeth invited me over."

Queen wrapped her arm around Janelle's shoulders. "I think her thumb might be greener than yours." She winked at Gideon.

"Gideon came to my store today and mentioned you and your health." Janelle cut her gaze away from him long enough to look at Elizabeth. "I'm glad you invited me so I can check on you myself."

"And no other reason?" Gideon wanted to hear if this stone-cold ice queen had a heart and would perhaps apologize for her actions.

"Do I need a reason to visit with my mentor?" Janelle's glare could cut the thickest pane of glass.

Damn, Gideon liked his women with a backbone, but this one had a body made of titanium. She couldn't be broken.

When she turned back to Elizabeth, she smiled again. "You're looking good as always." She glanced into the dining room.

Elizabeth smiled at Janelle. "I've missed our talks. Take off your coat." She headed Janelle to the dining room. "I was just telling Gideon that he should have asked you here for dinner."

"Really?" Janelle peered over her shoulder. "That's very kind of you."

"It's no trouble at all." Queen pointed to a chair at one side of the table. "You can sit there." Then she pointed to the chair next to it. "Gideon, you sit there."

"Mom, there are four sides to this table. We don't have to sit on top of each other. We can each have a side." He knew what his mother planned.

"I think this setup is better." She rearranged the settings so that she and Shay sat across from Gideon and Janelle. "Okay, let's dig in."

Before starting the meal, Gideon held out a chair for Janelle. His mother would never let him live it down if he didn't treat her respectfully, especially in Elizabeth's home. He helped Janelle move the chair under the table after she sat in it. Then he did the same for Queen and Shay. With the women all seated, he sat down to what he knew would be an interesting dinner.

Elizabeth had prepared a tender pot roast with mashed potatoes, roasted carrots, homemade rolls, and chocolate cake for dessert. He hadn't forgotten that he needed to stay in training condition. With his knee in its current state, he didn't need to add more weight to it. He would eat the dinner but skip dessert.

Throughout dinner, he kept his attention on Janelle. With his mother, Janelle showed herself to be charming and bubbly, almost cute whenever she smiled. When Gideon caught her joyous expression, a warm feeling flooded his body. It started from the pit of his stomach and radiated out through his insides, going up to his head and down to his toes.

To keep from falling for her charms, he reminded himself of how she'd acted in her store earlier. She'd refused to help him without reason. He wouldn't forget that no matter how attractive he found her slender fingers whenever she picked up her glass. Gideon cleared his throat and sat taller.

"Gideon, Janelle has had her store for nearly two years now. Isn't that nice?" Elizabeth pointed her fork toward Janelle. "Like me, she opened it on her own. She hired a competent staff. And she's helped me out a lot at my store. She's great."

Shay snorted. "Selling flowers? Queen, you do that and have two other businesses. How hard could it be to sell some shriveled-up roses?"

Janelle placed her fork down on her plate and regarded Shay. Gideon could almost see the flames coming straight from her eyes. "Actually, it takes a lot of knowhow to sell flowers. Besides selling them, I also do arrangements." She smiled like she wanted to make friends with Shay. "In a lot of ways, you and I are a lot alike."

Shay stopped eating to stare at Janelle. "How's that?"

"You make people look good with different hairstyles. I try to make rooms look good with my plants and arrangements. People feel better after seeing you when you give them the style they want. Flowers make people feel good when they get them. Isn't it always nice to get a surprise bouquet sent to you from a man when you weren't expecting it?"

Shay snickered. "I wouldn't know about that. I guess I don't know guys who are the flower-sending types."

"That's a shame. Every woman should have a relationship where she gets at least one bouquet sent to her for no reason." Janelle carried a wistful expression as she picked up her fork.

"I will agree with that." Gideon stared at Janelle until she connected her gaze to his. Then he looked at his plate of food. He swirled the strings of beef through the brown gravy.

Elizabeth laughed. "I know you believe in that." She dabbed the corners of her mouth. "Out of my three sons, Gideon is the romantic. Back in high school—"

Gideon shook his head. "Mom, don't."

"Don't interrupt me, please."

"Yes, ma'am." He clamped his mouth shut and counted in his head until she told her embarrassing story about him, one of many.

"Like I was saying, Gideon here worked with me at Pick 'N Clip, so he had every kind of flower and plant at his fingertips. I could tell how much he liked a girl by the number of flowers he would give her. First-time courtship, he would give her one flower." She held up her index finger to illustrate her point. "If she was a nice girl, she would get a carnation."

Janelle chuckled but quickly covered her mouth with her hand.

Elizabeth continued. "If she was a, um, popular girl who he'd just met, she would get one red rose."

"Ooh, you are so nasty." Shay gave him a playful hit on his arm. "You know one long-stemmed red rose means you're telling her that's how big your di—"

Queen cut off her employee. "That's enough, Shay."

Shay winked at Gideon and took a healthy chomp from a roll. He had already counted to one hundred in his head and hadn't stopped.

Elizabeth stared at him. "Gideon took this lovely girl to the prom. Not only did this girl get a dozen roses delivered to her at school, he also made her corsage." She covered her mouth to stifle her laughter. "The thing was so huge it weighed the poor girl's wrist down. She could barely pick it up. I think in your prom picture, you had to hold her hand up."

At this point, the other two ladies at the table erupted in laughter.

"It was my first time making a wrist corsage." He straightened his back. "She said she liked it."

"Because she liked you." Queen pointed at him. "At least you treated her like a lady. The gesture was very sweet."

Janelle corralled her laughter for a bit. "Yes. Very sweet." She wiped under her eyes.

"Not bad for a weed, right?" He needed the attention off him for a bit as he turned to Janelle. "What about you? How was your prom?"

The smile slipped down her face. She continued eating while keeping her focus on her food. "I didn't go to my prom."

"Too busy?" Queen took a sip of her water.

When Janelle didn't respond, Shay happily filled in the blanks. "No one asked you?" She shook her head and stared at her with pity in her eyes.

Although he had gotten off on the wrong foot with Janelle, he didn't see her as a woman deserving pity. He definitely didn't understand why no one would have asked her to prom. He couldn't imagine that she looked that much different now than when she attended high school. Her lips and eyes alone had him drawn to her.

To lighten the mood and break up the tension, he spoke. "Congratulations on the shop. I mean that." He nodded. When Janelle brought her attention to him, he continued, "Most new businesses fold within the first few months. Takes a lot of guts to go out on your own, and it takes a lot of knowhow to make it this long." He wiped his mouth and steeled his nerves to be the bigger person here. "And thanks for helping out my mother and being a good business associate to her."

"Your mother has supported me from the very beginning." Janelle shifted and her knee brushed against Gideon's leg.

Although she moved it away quickly, the damage had been done. The one connection had ignited the spark within him. Staring at her luscious mouth fanned the flames.

"Is that why you sent business to my store today?" Janelle allowed a small smile to peek through. "The last three hours that I had my store open, we were flooded with customers. I sold out of everything. So if you did that, I appreciate it."

Gideon studied her face. Janelle had changed from that hard woman who wouldn't allow him to have her surplus flowers to a genuinely appreciative store owner. As soon as he took in a deep breath, he knew fighting against it would be futile. He caught her distinct scent of citrus and vanilla, an odd combination that worked for her. He found it fascinating that she didn't go for a flowery aroma like his mother.

His heart started pounding in rhythm with his knee bouncing. He drummed his fingertips on the table but quickly stopped when he caught his mother's disapproving glare. "We ran out of stock. The right thing to do for customers looking for flowers was to refer them to another location. You're the closest one."

"I appreciate it. It was our best day ever." Janelle faced him for a moment before turning away to stare at Elizabeth. "I'm sorry for how I treated you earlier."

"What happened?" Queen split her attention between Gideon and Janelle.

"Victor called me at the hospital to see if I could help him get more stock. I went over to Janelle's to see if I could get some." Gideon let the story stop there. He wanted to hear what Janelle had to say about the situation.

When she remained quiet, Queen pressed on with her questioning. "Janelle, were you able to offer him some?"

Janelle didn't say anything. She grabbed for her water as though stalling for time. He wouldn't allow her a chance to spin the story in a way that made her come out looking like the victim.

"Had to hit several places to get enough inventory to satisfy your current orders." Gideon turned to Janelle, waiting for her to respond.

"Oh, Lord. You shouldn't have had to do that." Queen made a face like Victor had plopped a heap of compost on her plate. "Why couldn't you offer Gideon any of your inventory?"

Janelle put her fork down and gazed at Elizabeth. "Thelma quit."

Queen put her hand to her chest. "She was amazing. She was responsible for that beautiful butterfly garden at the Norfolk Botanical Garden." She turned to Gideon. "You remember that exhibit there."

Gideon had. The few times he'd been able to take a break in the springtime, he would take his mother to the location so that she could view the colorful gardens. The butterfly garden had been a recent favorite.

Janelle nodded. "I know." She turned to Gideon. "You caught me at a bad time. I shouldn't have taken my frustration out on you when I lost Thelma. I had some other personal things going on at the same time. Everything hit me at once. I am so sorry."

"You're not sorry, dear." Elizabeth smiled sweetly. "You apologize. There's nothing sorry about a young woman who is a business owner and has everything riding on her shoulders."

Gideon felt like a heel, like a weed choking out grass and plants. "I've seen that work at the Botanical Garden. She did a great job." He looked Janelle in her eyes. "I understand why you would be upset if you lost someone like that." He placed his hand on the table next to hers.

He felt the slight heat coming from her delicate fingers. He inched his pinkie toward her and brushed it against her hand. When she'd opened up about her misfortune, he'd felt compelled to comfort her. She certainly hadn't given off the vibe that she needed help. He couldn't ignore the sexual tension between them.

"So you lost an employee." Shay shrugged. She stabbed her fork into a piece of carrot. "If someone like Gideon had approach me, I would give him whatever he wanted." She winked before she licked the tip of the carrot and slid it into her mouth.

Janelle moved her hand away from his. "I have to go." She sprang to her feet and went to the closet to get her coat. "Thank you so much for the meal."

As soon as Janelle stood, Gideon got up as fast as he could. He followed her to the closet where his mother secured Janelle's coat. Janelle slipped one arm into the outerwear but got assistance from Gideon on the other sleeve.

"You have to go so soon?" His mother wiped her mouth with her cloth napkin.

"Yes, I have some things to take care of." Janelle zipped up her coat. "Dinner was great. Thanks again for inviting me."

"Have a good evening, Janelle." Gideon meant that. He'd gotten brief insight into this reserved woman who had likened him to a weed.

Janelle took two steps off the porch before she stopped and turned back to him. "Thanks for understanding. And you're not a weed."

Gideon stepped outside. "Yes, I am." He smiled to let her know he hadn't taken what she'd said to heart. "I'm relentless."

From the way she smiled back, he assumed she understood.

Gideon stepped back in the house and locked the door. The more he thought about Janelle, the wider the silly smile that sprang over his face got. Before he turned around, he made sure to arrest it before his mother could catch him.

When he turned, she said, "She is pretty special, huh? And pretty in general."

"Then maybe you should date her." Gideon strolled back to his chair and finished his dinner.

"I would, but I don't want to cheat on Fred." She furrowed her eyebrows. "Dear, you have something on your face."

Gideon started wiping his cheek and around his lips. "Did I get it?"

"Nope. You're still smiling." She giggled as she ate her dinner.

He sighed. "I actually missed this torture?"

After dinner and dessert, Shay helped clear off the table along with Gideon. Then she retired to the apartment over the garage.

Gideon sat on the couch with his mother. "So what's going on with Gunnar? I noticed you didn't want to talk about it in front of Shay."

Elizabeth held Gideon's hand. "Gunnar is going through some issues. I know a small bit about it, but I had fully expected for him to handle his business by now. Because I knew something about it, he's not very pleased with me."

Gunnar could be pigheaded when he wanted to be. That stubborn streak existed in Gideon as well. Coach Brick and Gideon's agent had been calling him all day. He'd used the excuse of the store being busy to avoid the calls.

"What's going on with you and Janelle?" Queen nudged Gideon's shoulder. "I noticed you had a hard time looking at her during dinner."

"That's because she was sitting next to me. It's a little awkward to turn my head and look at her while she eats." He leaned back on the couch. "Maybe you should have put her across from me so I could stare at her all night."

"Good idea. I'll be sure to do that the next time." She winked.

He shook his head. "You can give up the fight. She called me a weed."

"Marijuana?"

He snickered. "No. Wild violet. It was her way of saying I was persistent."

"You are. When you get it in your head about something, you don't stop until you get it. I remember when you wanted to learn how to dance. You would watch videos and copy the moves you saw until you got them."

"I'm still a better dancer than Gunnar." He stretched his legs out in front of him, mainly to give his knee a rest.

"Darling, turtles are better dancers than your brother. He never wanted to try to learn how to dance. Speaking of trying something new, did you make a doctor's appointment?" Elizabeth stared at Gideon.

"No, ma'am. I was busy today." Now he had another person he could use that excuse with today.

"And I appreciate your hard work in my store." She reached into her pants pocket and pulled out a slip of paper. "That's why I took the liberty of setting you up with an appointment tomorrow."

Gideon felt a stone drop into his belly as he accepted the paper. "Mom, you really didn't have to do this."

"It was no problem. While I was visiting your brother, I went over to the orthopedic wing of the hospital and found a nice doctor who knew you, well, knew of you, and he said he would be happy to check your knee out." She smiled. "Now do you want to play cards?"

"Against you? Not tonight. You're too slick for me." Gideon chuckled. "Funny."

The smile slipped down Gideon's face and he held his mother's hand. "Tell me about you. What's going on?" He pointed to her chest. "How bad is it?"

Queen Elizabeth held her head up and smiled wider than he had ever seen before on her. "I'll be fine, sweetheart. A simple in-and-out surgery. I'll be back on my feet in no time."

Gideon squeezed his mother's hand. "You've never lied to me. Ever." He shook his head. "Please don't start now."

She opened her mouth like she had planned on refuting his claim, then she stopped. "I need bypass surgery. Double, possibly triple. The surgery will be next week. I asked them to postpone it until your brother gets out of the hospital." She nodded and attempted to smile like she needed to reassure him.

"Oh, wow. Are you able to wait that long? I can take care of Gunnar if you need to reschedule your surgery." Gideon had watched his mother during dinner. She hadn't eaten much. Now he understood why she looked so preoccupied.

"Right now I'm fine. Just a little tired sometimes." She got quiet for a moment as her smile slowly disappeared. "The day of my surgery, I can't go to the hospital with makeup or scented lotions. I won't feel like a woman." She put her hand to her chest. "I'll have a scar."

Gideon recognized fear hidden behind his mother's vanity. "Don't worry. Fred will still love you. You should have invited him to dinner instead of trying to fix me up."

His mother patted his leg. "Can't a mother want the best for her son?"

"Of course." He kissed the back of her hand. "I'll be there with you the day of your surgery. And don't worry about the businesses. We'll take care of them for you."

Queen nodded. "I know. I raised good men."

Gideon liked this moment, this quiet time with his mother before all hell broke loose. At that thought, his cell phone rang. He peered down and saw Coach Brick's name across the screen.

"Answer it." Elizabeth patted his knee. "I'm going to go to bed early. I'm a little tired."

"You okay?" Like the gentleman she raised him to be, Gideon stood when his mother did.

She nodded. "Take care of business. I'll be fine." She kissed his cheek and walked up the stairs slower than normal.

Once he knew his mother couldn't hear his conversation, Gideon answered the call. "Coach, how are you?"

"Now you can answer the phone." Irritation and frustration dripped from each word his coach said. Gideon imagined the squatty man getting red faced as he spoke on the phone.

"I've been busy. My brother had gotten shot the night of—"

"I know. I saw it on the news." Brick exhaled. "You close to your house?"

Gideon's stomach twitched. "Maybe thirty minutes away."

"Get here. I'm waiting at the gate for you. This guard won't let me in."

"No, sir! No one gets up to Mr. Wells's place without permission or appointment. Try sneaking past me and I have fifty-thousand volts for your ass."

Gideon heard Pearl through his coach's phone. The woman deserved a raise. No way would that cheerleader have gotten past her.

"Get here quick before this woman fries me."

Gideon grabbed his coat from his mother's closet. "On my way."

Chapter 8

"Holy shit!" Penny screamed that phrase over and over while on the phone with Janelle. "I don't think we've ever sold out of everything."

Janelle agreed with her friend. As she drove home from Queen Elizabeth's house, she recalled how the shelves that held vases of rose bouquets now sat empty. Racks that had greeting cards now resembled bare wire trees. Janelle's baby had remained the only plant in the store. To call today a good day would be an understatement.

"They bought everything." Penny squealed again. "What a great frickin' day!"

"Yeah. Amazing." Janelle knew the reason for her sudden good fortune.

As though reading Janelle's thoughts, Penny said, "Gideon."

Janelle slammed on her brake at a stoplight harder than she'd intended. Hearing Gideon's name had a jarring effect on her.

Penny continued. "It had to be him. I bet he sent folks over. How else could you explain this feeding frenzy?"

Janelle took a deep breath before revealing the truth. "He did send customers our way." She shouldn't have been so hard on him earlier.

"How do you know?" Penny asked.

"I went over to Queen Elizabeth's house for dinner, and he was there."

"Really? You went to her house for a meal, huh?"

Janelle heard the suspicion in Penny's voice. "Yes, I did. He'd told me that he planned on going to the hospital to see Gunnar. I didn't think he would be at her house." Not that she'd minded seeing him again.

He'd looked even better at Queen's house. The soft lighting in her home had given him an approachable appearance. It helped that Elizabeth had treated him like her child and not like some sort of superstar. It also helped that he'd acted like a gentleman, opening doors for her, pulling out her chair at the table, waiting to be seated until after all the women sat. Janelle could get used to that type of behavior from a man.

"So now what?" Penny's question broke Janelle's thoughts.

"What do you mean?" Janelle pulled off from the light. A few more miles and she would be home.

"We have no inventory tomorrow. Were you able to get a rush order?"

Janelle had ducked into her office and tried ordering additional flowers to supply her store. At her first supplier site, she'd hit the submit key after entering her order and got a message that until she resolved her past debt with them, she wouldn't be able to complete her order. She'd encountered that message with two other sites.

Now that she'd had a great sales day, she could pay off some of her debts. That would require depositing the money in the bank, waiting for the funds to post before she could make her payments to these suppliers. She would have nothing to show in the store tomorrow.

Great.

"Uh, no. There were some issues." Janelle couldn't tell her remaining employee about her money woes. "I'll resolve them tomorrow."

"What about the store? We won't have anything to show customers."

Janelle moved her phone to her other ear. "We have samples. We'll have to take orders."

"That's cool for future orders. What about same-day? How are we going to—"

Janelle interrupted her friend. "Tomorrow. All will be fine tomorrow."

Janelle would have to come up with a plan. Today had turned out great. She needed more. To keep her business afloat, her employee paid, and a roof over her head, she would need more than one good day.

Two traffic lights away from her apartment, she thought about Gideon. First, she thought about him as the man who intrigued her. His eyes, his hands, his incredible ass.

Janelle gripped the steering wheel and wrung her hands back and forth. She glanced over at the passenger seat and saw the crumpled paper that contained Gideon's phone number, the one he'd given her. He'd willingly shared his personal number with her.

She took a deep breath. The least she could do would be to call him and thank him again for the additional business and for dinner, especially after the way she'd bolted at the end.

She recalled seeing his large hand on the table next to hers, making her hand look small. She also remembered the molten heat permeating from his body. At the slightest touch, she'd wanted to strip every bit of her clothes from her body. Janelle knew if she'd remained there a minute longer, she would have embarrassed herself. It had been bad enough that she had to admit her failings to him and his mother, her competition.

Janelle started to reach for the paper and stopped. Never had she experienced this level of fear and trepidation. She'd ignored guys like Gideon in high school and college, mainly because they'd paid no attention to her.

She had to stop thinking of herself as that shy girl. Like Queen had said over dinner, Janelle had proven herself by starting her own business and keeping it going. She had shown she had grown over the years. She could call Gideon. Maybe she could ask him if he wanted to do the coffee thing with her. As she reached for the number again, a car horn blaring behind her stopped her.

She looked up and noticed the green light. Janelle pulled off and quickly drove home. There, she parked her car in front of her apartment building but left it running.

Janelle made sure to douse her headlights to not alert Buddy and Althea of her arrival. She needed some alone time to fully concentrate on her conversation with Gideon. Having the elderly couple asking her if she wanted cookies and cocoa would kill the vibe.

She removed her phone from her purse and stared at it for a moment before deciding to dial Gideon's number. She ran scenarios in her head of how Gideon would answer the phone. Would he be cool and smooth like earlier? Or would he be cold because of how she'd treated him? Hell, would the man even answer the phone at all?

She didn't have to ask him out for coffee. She could thank him and see where the conversation went.

Janelle picked up the paper and unfolded it. With shaky hands, she punched in Gideon's number and waited. The phone rang once, then twice. At the third ring, she nearly disconnected the call.

"Hello?"

Gideon's strong voice had a way of rendering Janelle immobile. She balled her free hand into a fist before she spoke. "Uh, hi." *Think like a boss.* "Hello," she said again with a bit more authority. "This is Janelle Gold. You came to my establishment today."

Janelle squeezed her eyes shut. Too much. Now she sounded impersonal, like she wanted to do his taxes.

"And you came to my mother's house for dinner."

She could almost imagine him smiling—no, laughing—at her.

"Did you forget something? Are you okay?"

She turned down the heat in her car. "No, I'm fine, Gideon."

"Good. You dropped the Mr. Wells thing."

"Yeah. Yes." She sat straighter to give herself a boost of confidence. "I'm calling you because I wanted to thank you again for sending business my way. Most business owners don't do that. After the way I treated you this afternoon, I wouldn't have blamed you if you'd totally ignored me and stolen the rest of my business."

"The competitive person in me probably would have done that. But my mother told me that flower store owners were nothing like quarterbacks. She told me how much you all support one another. I'm glad for your sales." His tone remained heavy yet approachable, like Janelle shouldn't be afraid of him. "Does that mean you're going out to celebrate? Maybe you and your boyfriend?"

Janelle knew her head must have burst into a bright white flame. "Really?"

"What?"

"That was so not subtle." She quickly sucked her bottom lip in between her teeth to keep from laughing.

"Ah, so you can take the tackle. Are you seeing someone?" Gideon's voice dipped down so low the sound rumbled the phone.

"Do you always ask people you're doing business with personal questions like that?" Janelle slid her hand over her thigh. "I believe you were asking me about my day."

"Wow. You move faster than a running back." He moaned before he kept speaking. "The only reason I ask is because my mother is trying to use her matchmaking skills on us. It would be great if I could tell her that you're seeing someone else already. So are you?"

"Tell your mother that if she wants to ask me something, she can come to me herself."

"I will. So tell me. Are you seeing someone? I'm asking for myself now."

Janelle's skin tingled. "My store and that swamp hibiscus are the only two things I'm interested in at the moment."

"Good. Good. I'll take that as a no." Gideon sighed. "I didn't mean for that one customer to bail on you and come to Pick 'N Clip."

"I know you didn't." She pressed her thighs together to tamp down the heat. "I would offer you some help with flowers, but I sold everything."

"Not a problem."

For a big-time athlete, she found him so down-to-earth. She expected nothing less from someone raised in Queen Elizabeth's home. Janelle heard some rustling on Gideon's end.

Then he said, "I hate doing business over the phone."

She leaned forward. "Yes?"

"I also don't like the taste of coffee, but I'm willing talk over a couple of mugs of it." He cleared his throat. "I'm heading home. I have to handle something personal very quickly."

She chewed on her lower lip as she waited for what he would say. Then again, she could ask him out for coffee. As she opened her mouth, he continued.

"Would you like to meet for some coffee? You ran out the house before we could offer you some along with dessert."

Janelle pinched her leg to keep from squealing and realized very quickly how that tactic would not work. The intense pain shot right up to her head.

She gritted her teeth before speaking. "I was hoping you would make the offer again."

Penny would be so proud of her. Would a dull woman get asked out for coffee by a hot guy? Even her mother would approve of this man, but for the wrong reason of course. Ida would want Janelle to use Gideon for his money. Not on her life.

Gideon exhaled. "Good. You can come to my house."

"You mean go back to Queen's house?"

"No. My home down at the Oceanfront. I'll leave your name at the gate so that they'll let you in."

Janelle's smile melted into a frown. She never pictured Gideon, Queen Elizabeth's son, to be the type to lure a woman to his place for some drive-by sex.

"No. I can meet you somewhere, but I'm not going to your house." As though Gideon could see her, Janelle sat in her car shaking her head.

"Why not?" Disappointment and surprise filled his voice.

"Because…" Janelle searched for the right words to not insult him and call him a predator.

"Because we just met," he began.

"Yes." Her breathing slowed as he shared his understanding of her feelings.

Gideon continued. "And, although you know my mother and we had dinner at her house and you called my personal cell phone, you don't really know me."

"Exactly." Janelle relaxed back against her seat. Maybe now he'll suggest a nice, brightly lit restaurant to meet.

"Because you don't trust yourself around me?"

Her back stiffened. "What?"

Gideon laughed. "It was a joke."

She heard him cursing under his breath. "I have company with me right now. My meeting should take about an hour. If you want to come over afterward, we can—"

"Mr. Wells—"

He groaned. "Oh, no. We're back to that again."

Janelle balled her free hand into a fist as she spoke to him. "It sounds like what you're proposing is some sort of late-night rendezvous."

Gideon chuckled again. "I think the term you're looking for is booty call. No, I'm not asking for that."

Janelle put her hand to her face when it started to feel hot again. "I don't think it would be appropriate for me to show up this late at your home. We barely know each other."

"Anything before ten at night is not late. I want to be able to have a normal conversation with you without fan interruption or a reporter or two popping up."

"Mr. Wells, I—"

Gideon interrupted her. "I know you love plants and flowers as much as I do. And I know now that you have a good heart."

Janelle heard through the phone what sounded like a knock against a pane of glass.

"One sec," Gideon said away from his mouthpiece. "I have to go. Look, you know who I am. You know where I work. You even know my mother. I promise all I want you to do when you come over is talk about business and have some coffee."

"You are an oleander."

The line went silent.

"You're going to have to explain that one," he said.

"You're good looking but dangerous." Too much of a good thing, in both the plant and with Gideon Wells, spelled disaster.

"Then you, my dear, are a ghost orchid."

Before she could ask him to explain, he expounded. "You are rare. I have never encountered a woman like you." He chuckled. "I like that you talk in flowers and plants."

She smiled. "My mother calls me a geek for doing that."

"You are. So am I," he grumbled. "If I didn't have to get up so early, I could meet you first thing in the morning since it looks like tonight is out." Gideon sighed. "Now that I have your number, I'll call you when I'm available."

"That sounds good."

Good and boring. No way would she get caught up with another man with a separate agenda on his mind. Had she gone to his place and things happened, he wouldn't be around her long. As soon as Queen got better, Gideon would be traveling with his team and forgetting about her.

She tried hiding the deflated sound from her voice, but it came through anyway. "Guess I'll see you tomorrow." Janelle peered into her side mirror and saw a man approaching her car.

Her heart raced as she watched the stranger in dark pants, a dark coat, and a black knit cap pulling something from his pocket as he charged to her door.

"Jesus!" She pressed her hand against her car horn, hoping to grab enough neighbors' attention to witness whatever this psychopath had in mind.

"What's going on? Janelle?" Gideon sounded as frantic as she felt.

As she screamed, a light flashed in her car, then another. She peered off to the side and saw that this stranger held a camera and took several pictures of her.

The momentary flashes caught Janelle off guard. She pulled her hand from the car horn to shield her face from the blinding lights with her free hand while she continued holding her phone in the other. From inside her car, she heard Buddy screaming at the maniac with a strange agenda.

"What's going on out here?" Buddy opened his door and secured his robe around his body. "Hey, get away from her, or I'll bust your head wide open." He turned into his apartment. "Get my bat."

"Calm down. I'm getting a picture of Gid Wells's new side piece," the stranger said.

Janelle turned off her car and had the strength to get out of it. "What did you just say?"

"A source said Gideon Wells rushed home after the game because of his brother. When he gets back, he referred some business to your place. So how long have you two been dating?" The man snapped another picture of her.

Janelle felt like she had fallen into the *Twilight Zone*. "You think Gideon Wells and I are dating? You're crazy." Thank God he didn't mention the fact that she'd had dinner with Gideon and his mother.

Oh, wow. Could she consider their dinner together tonight as their first date? She headed to her apartment. Seeing Buddy made her want to take a detour. She needed to be with people who would keep her safe.

"He kicked out a She-Wolf cheerleader from his home so that he could come to see you." The photographer continued assaulting her with lies as she headed to Buddy's apartment. "Pictures of the two of you at your flower shop are all over the Internet already."

Damn Penny. Janelle would have to fire her, rehire her, then fire her again for this betrayal.

"We're not dating." She ducked into her friends' apartment as Buddy hoisted up his bat and took a swing at the menace.

"Get away from here. Come back, and I won't miss." Buddy stood guard at the door until the creep slinked away.

Buddy closed and locked his door while Althea made sure to secure all the blinds and curtains.

"Dear, what is going on?" Althea wrapped her arms around Janelle's shoulders.

When Janelle went to hug her back, she realized she still had her phone in her hand. "Oh, no." She put the phone to her ear.

"Janelle? Janelle? Where do you live? I'll come over and get whoever is there to leave you alone," Gideon said.

"No, I think you've done enough for one day." She put her hand to her forehead. "My life is completely turned upside down since I've met you. I think having coffee with you would be a mistake." One photographer at her home gave her proof that she didn't need any entanglements with the famous football star. "Good night."

"Janelle, wait. I can help you."

"I don't think you can." Janelle didn't know if she should keep calling him Mr. Wells or Gideon. She disconnected the call before she could make up her mind.

Out of exhaustion, she slumped down into an overstuffed flowered chair in the living room.

"Did I hear that guy right?" Buddy began.

Janelle lifted her head.

"Did he ask you if you're dating Gideon Wells?"

She nodded.

Buddy scratched his head. "Can you get me an autograph?"

"Really?" She flopped back and covered her eyes with her hand.

"Look at what you've done to the poor girl," Althea said. "She's tired. That's okay, honey. You spend the night here. If we see that guy again, we'll call the police."

Janelle wouldn't be able to call the police every day of her life. She would have to do something. No way could she live her life like this. Although, for a fleeting moment, the idea that she could be on Gideon's arm as his main squeeze, or a side piece as that guy had called her, did tickle her. She didn't need this added complication.

Chapter 9

By the time Gideon stepped into his house, he couldn't stand still. He'd parked his car in front of his home instead of in his garage, afraid he would run through a wall. Until Coach Brick closed the front door behind him, he had forgotten he had business to handle.

Hearing Janelle scream had set off the protective nature in him. He had no idea sending business her way would get the media making assumptions.

A side piece. That asshole had called her a side piece. Gideon balled his hands into fists.

"Son, I don't know who you were talking to on the phone, but I could use you with that anger on the field the next time we play." Brick waddled over to the couch in Gideon's living room and took a seat without invitation.

Until Brick sat down, Gideon hadn't noticed his coach had carried in a tall box. Maybe it contained Gideon's stuff that he'd left in his locker when he'd bolted from Pasadena.

Gideon shook his head. "Something personal. I'll handle it."

"You say that a lot." Brick snickered. "You'll handle it. It's not your responsibility to protect the world. You know that, right?"

Gideon didn't need this right now. If he didn't think he would wake his mother up, he would call her and see if she knew where Janelle lived.

Other women, hell, other people would jump at the chance to sit down with him. Gideon would rather that people get to know him before wanting to spend time with him and not because of his career.

A woman had broken into his house, tried to seduce him, claimed that she loved him, and Janelle didn't jump at the chance to be in an intimate space with Gideon. He liked her character. She intrigued him.

"You're here for a reason, right?" Gideon stopped his pacing to address his coach.

"Yes, I am." Brick opened the box and pulled out the iconic silver MVP trophy.

For a moment, the world stopped. Gideon forgot how to breathe. With everything that had happened to his family and the drama surrounding the store, he'd forgotten about his true passion. Winning the Super Bowl meant everything to him. Getting presented with the MVP award showed him what hard work and determination got him.

"I suppose you would like this." Brick handed the award to Gideon.

Gideon held out both his hands and cradled the substantial trophy like a baby. He caught his reflection in the shiny metal. He thought he would see the look of a hopeful boy gazing back at him. In the angular, slender base that held up a football likeness, he saw a man with a dream fulfilled. He'd done it.

He wanted to share this with his family. It would have been wonderful to show it to a woman, his woman. He didn't have that. Maybe not having someone in his life allowed him to be a champion.

Gideon broke his concentration on the award for a moment to peer at his coach. "Thanks." He could only muster that one-word sentiment.

"No use thanking me. You earned it. You worked hard." Brick cocked up a crooked smile at the side of his mouth. "Now for the real reason I came over." He pointed to a chair across from him. "You might want to sit down for this."

"Is it bad?" Gideon asked as he sat on the arm of the chair next to him. He placed his award on the coffee table.

Brick didn't respond right away. He peered down for a moment before returning Gideon's gaze. "Have you talked to your agent?"

Gideon blinked. "No."

"Oh, ignoring his calls too, huh?"

Gideon held up his hand. "Wait. You have to understand. I—"

Brick cut him off. "You're on the injured list until we get proof from our doctor and an independent doc that your knee is okay."

"No." Gideon bolted to his feet. Mistake. His knee took that moment to weaken and Gideon stumbled. "Damn it." He braced his hand on his knee until the pain subsided enough for him to continue his conversation. "It's not as bad as it looks."

Brick blinked. "No? Son, you almost fell to your knees just now from pain."

"You saw me at the game. I ran half a football field for that touchdown." He looked at his gleaming award. "I'm MVP, for Christ sake. You can't do this to me."

"You did this to yourself." Brick shrugged. "You're a quarterback. Be a damn quarterback. Throw the ball. Call the plays. Rally the team. For God's sake, stop trying to be running back and wide receiver."

Gideon shook his head. "This can't be happening. I told you I'm fine."

"But you're not."

Gideon reached into his pocket and pulled out the note his mother had given him. "I have an appointment with a doctor tomorrow. If you want to go with me, you can. I'm sure he'll say there's nothing to be concerned about. I'm fine."

Brick struggled to stand. He strolled over to Gideon. "You're not. You can keep saying that over and over again until you're blue in the face. You and I know the truth." He put his hand on Gideon's shoulder. "The one good thing about this is that the big game is over. You did that. Now you can do the talk-show circuit, write a book, or, hell, join *Dancing with the Stars*. Lots of athletes do that show." He patted Gideon's shoulder.

Still full of anger over this news, he shrugged off his coach's meaty hand. "Am I still on the roster?"

The smile disappeared from Brick's face. "Talk to your agent."

"I'm talking to you, my coach. Tell me something. I want to play. I need to play." Gideon hated the desperation choking every word he'd said.

Not playing meant they could possibly touch his money. He couldn't have that. Not now.

Brick turned to the door. "You're young. It's not the end of the world. Do what the doctor tells you and rest up that knee. I'm sure everything will work out."

Gideon brought his face up. "You're not sure if I'll remain on the team, right?"

Brick took a deep breath before speaking. "Your ring will be mailed to you. You have my number. Keep me in the loop about your condition."

Gideon didn't bother walking the man out the door. Brick left without another word. Dropped a huge bomb like that and retreated without asking how he could help.

As usual, Gideon would have to figure out his fate. He would have to thank his mother for setting up the appointment. Right now, he didn't even know if he still had a team. What would he be now without his life in football?

Gideon went over to the front door and locked it before taking out his phone and calling his agent.

"Gid is god. How are you doing?" Scot Arundelson answered the phone the same way he talked if standing face-to-face with someone.

He screamed every conversation like he wanted everyone to be in on it. It surprised Gideon that his mother approved of this man as his agent.

"A man who talks like that has nothing to hide," Queen Elizabeth said. "I never trust a man who is great at whispering."

"Scot, what the hell is going on? Coach Brick was here and said I'm on the injured list. What gives?" Gideon paced.

"Formality, Gid, my man. The Wolves have to look out for themselves. They have to list you that way to cover their assets." Scot's easy Southern drawl never appealed to Gideon, but the man knew about sports and making great deals.

"Am I cut? Brick said I'm still on the roster."

"You're not cut. You are still a Wolf. However—"

That pause forced Gideon to swallow hard.

Scot continued, "There's nothing that says we can't explore options elsewhere. I mean, you're a Super Bowl-winning MVP quarterback." He released a loud scream. "Other teams would pay out their noses to have that on their roster. As far as I'm concerned, the Wolves made a mistake. You can pretty much write your ticket to go anywhere."

"I want to be a Wolf. I want to stay in Virginia Beach." With his mother's condition and the business, Gideon didn't see himself going anywhere else.

"Gid, don't close off your options. Although I don't think the Wolves will drop you, I do think this is a great opportunity for you to test the waters elsewhere." Scot paused. "It's late and I have a special friend coming by. By the way, great angle to get viewers interested in you."

"Angle? What are you talking about?"

"You and that small-business owner. The picture online is grainy, but she looks cute. You hitting on her shows people that you're approachable."

"Scot, I wasn't hitting on her." Not exactly, Gideon should have added.

Janelle had seen right through his line about her husband or boyfriend. He and Gunnar had used that trick back in high school. Janelle showed she wouldn't be falling for any tired lines, something else that made her appealing.

"Whatever, man. You are trending right now with the hashtag 'Eliza Doolittle'." Scot released a boisterous laugh.

Too bad Gideon didn't get the joke. "Who's that? That's not the shop owner's name."

"I guess you're not a musical-theater geek. That's the name of the female lead in *My Fair Lady*. Yeah, fans like that you're bringing this small-town girl up to your level."

Gideon shook his head. "I have to go. I have an appointment tomorrow to see an orthopedist."

"Good! That's good. Let me know what he says. We'll get through this. Until then, do some talk shows. The two late-night Jimmys keep calling me."

Gideon disconnected the call. He had a lot more to think about than talk shows and his trending pattern. Janelle had been right. Since he'd come to town, he had thrown a monkey wrench into her daily life. He knew how to fix it.

* * * *

Janelle checked her bank account as soon as she got to the office. The cash from her deposits had been credited to her account. The few checks she'd received had not, and the credit card payments slowly trickled into her balance. She, at least, had enough to make one emergency order of roses, baby's breath, and vases.

"The natives are restless." Penny looked almost scared as she walked into Janelle's office. She split her attention between Janelle and the front door. "I've never seen so many people here." She scanned the place. "We still don't have any flowers. What are we going to do?"

Janelle closed her laptop. "Open the store and take orders like I said. That's all we can do. I'm not going to close the store."

"I hope the rush orders come in soon."

So did Janelle. She'd never been in this predicament. It would seem like being sold out of all inventory would be a good problem to have. Not with Valentine's Day right around the corner.

Janelle strolled to the front door. She saw a bevy of people—men, women, children—all with phones aimed at her to take her picture or video. Since her scare last night, she'd started to notice the number of stares she now received.

She unlocked the door and pushed it open. "Welcome to Flowers Galore."

The crowd rushed into the small store only to stop a few feet around Janelle to take her picture.

Janelle sighed and tried smiling through the odd ordeal. "Unfortunately, I'm completely out of inventory right now. I sold out last night."

No one moaned or seemed upset. The crowd continued to stare at her like an oddity.

Trying to keep her composure, Janelle turned to the front counter. "We have a binder filled with different arrangements if you would like to order something special for Valentine's Day. Penny and I would love to accept your order."

No one spoke. A couple of flashes illuminated the room.

Penny eased her way over to Janelle. "This is like *Night of the Living Dead* shit, only they don't want our brains," she whispered through her teeth. "If you had given your boyfriend some flowers, this wouldn't be happening."

Janelle snapped her head around to glare at her best friend. "He's not my boyfriend."

"So where is Gideon Wells?" one customer asked.

"Yeah. Does he come in later for lunch or something?" A woman aimed her sideways phone at Janelle.

"Is he as hot in person as he is on TV?" A thin, young man raised his eyebrows while the crowd around him did the same gesture. He scanned their expressions. "What? I'm gay and he's hot. Don't trip."

Janelle heard a loud *bang* at her back door. "Oh, hell. Now what?" She started for the door and then stopped. She turned to Penny. "Keep the masses entertained. If anyone gets out of hand, call the police."

Janelle had a business to run and these people kept her from doing that. As she stomped toward the door, thoughts ran through her mind at who could be on the other side. Maybe that jerk photographer stood out back, waiting for her to arrive. She grabbed a lead pipe she had in her office before she went to the door. She'd planned on using the pipe to straighten out one of her plants. Guess she would be using it to sort out whoever dared to cross her.

Once at the door, Janelle took a deep breath and pushed it open. "You picked the wrong day to mess with me!"

She stopped in her tracks when she saw the large white delivery truck backed up to her door.

A burly man jumped out of the driver's seat. "Never mind. Someone just came out," he called over the truck.

"Wow. You all are fast. I just placed the order a few minutes ago." She looked at the back rolling door of the truck.

She noticed the name of the company. She knew of the company as one that sold the very top-of-the-line flowers, plants, and other products that she wished she could afford. She hadn't placed an order with them.

"Excuse me. I think you all have made a mistake." Janelle held the pipe down beside her to not look too confrontational. "I didn't order from you all."

The driver unhitched the door and threw it up. Janelle noticed the container looked half full. It also held more than just roses and baby's breath.

The driver worked some controls on the side to lower a platform. "Lady, I was told to come here with this."

"By who?"

He pointed behind him as he got on the platform and raised himself up to the truck.

Janelle turned and dropped her pipe when she saw Gideon Wells coming around the side of the building. He looked better today than he had yesterday. In the morning sun, his blond hair glowed. His eyes looked so bright and blue. In his heather-gray sweater and dark denim jeans, he could have passed for a model. All pornographic thoughts about him filled her head until she had to avert her gaze to keep from blushing too much.

"I was going to go to the front door until the driver said you were out here." He smiled.

The frost that had hardened around her heart as soon as the vultures had descended on her started to melt. "What are you doing here?" She looked into the truck. "And what is this?"

"Victor, the lovely man I work with, has been following some social media story online about you and, well, me too. Someone has already posted that you announced you were out of flowers like we were. I assumed your delivery truck hasn't arrived yet. So instead of taking this full order, I took half and asked the guy to bring the rest here."

"That's very nice of you but—"

Gideon held up his hand. "Hold that thought. I'm not truly altruistic. You did agree to have coffee with me last night. I believe your stipulation was that it couldn't be at my house."

He stood directly in front of her and smiled. She stared at his kissable lips. She wanted to touch them, kiss them, have him kiss her all over her body.

"You can't do that, Mr.—"

Gideon shook his head. "Please do not call me Mr. Wells again. You're making me feel old. I can't be much older than you. I'm twenty-seven."

Janelle smiled. "So am I."

"And I'm not getting any younger." The truck driver lowered himself along with several cases of flowers. "Where do you want these?"

"Please, I really can't—"

"Yes, you can. And I apologize for interrupting you, but you make it hard to not want to stop you from being stubborn." Gideon went to the door. "Will you unlock this so that he can deliver these flowers for you?"

She stood still for a moment, not used to having someone take care of her. After a beat, she went to the door and unlocked it. She propped it open the same way she would if her delivery driver had arrived. She placed a huge rock against it.

Janelle leaned her head into the door. "Penny!"

After some stomping footsteps, her friend showed up to the back door. "Yeah?"

"Show this gentleman where to put this inventory."

Penny looked at the delivery driver and then peered over Janelle's shoulder. "Whoa. Uh, yes, ma'am. You handle your business out here."

When the driver and Penny disappeared, Janelle turned to Gideon. "Thank you for doing this. You didn't have to."

"Yes, I did. I came to town to help my family. I never meant to cause you any distress." He approached her.

She remained in her spot, powerless to do anything else but keep her stare on him.

He continued. "And since you wouldn't meet me for coffee, I had to come here."

"People are talking." She dropped her gaze for a moment. "They think we're dating."

"The paparazzi will make up a story to sell magazines or keep the hits on their Web sites up. I pay no attention to it. Thank goodness, someone in my life does look at that crap. I wouldn't have known that you needed help." Gideon brought his hand up almost like he wanted to touch Janelle's face. He stopped himself and crossed his arms over his chest.

"How's Queen Elizabeth?" Janelle chewed her lower lip.

"Good. Waiting for her surgery date." Gideon took another step closer to her.

She lowered her voice. "And your brother?"

"Released from the hospital and home." He peered up at the store when the driver and Penny appeared again to get the remaining load. "I know you're kind of busy right now, but I would really like to take you to lunch." He paused. "Or maybe dinner."

Her heartbeat sped in her chest until it bounced off her sternum. Janelle snaked her hand to the back of her neck. Even in the cold of February, it felt sweaty and hot.

"I don't think that's a good idea. I have a store full of people who are taking my picture and filming me because of you." She wrapped her sweater around her body and wished she'd worn something different, something more formfitting.

"People are going to talk whether you go out with me or not. Might as well have fun." He smiled.

This time when he took a step closer to her, Janelle peered down. She noticed something around his leg. At first she thought he had one of those gun holsters around his muscled thigh. On closer inspection, she recognized he had on a hinged knee brace.

"Are you hurt?" This time Janelle moved closer to him.

Before Gideon could answer, she heard a clicking sound from behind him. She looked around him and noticed a photographer. Damn. She didn't know Virginia had this many paparazzi in town.

"Don't say anything." Janelle shook her head.

"What?" Gideon's eyebrows drew together.

"Photographer right behind you. I'd better go." She started to pivot when she felt a hand clamp down on hers.

Janelle peered down at her hand first. When she saw Gideon had a hold of it, she took the time to pan up his long arm to his broad shoulder up to his face.

She didn't know what to expect when she arrived at his expression. He looked more surprised than angry. Then he lowered his eyelids. Lust filled his gaze in a millisecond as soon as their stares connected.

"No one has ever looked out for me like that." Gideon pulled her in, wrapped his arm around her waist, and pressed his lips against hers.

Janelle should have been offended. She should have pushed him away, slapped him, called the police. The way he genuinely stared at her and looked so grateful, the thought never entered her mind that he may be using her for publicity. She took his impromptu gesture to mean that Gideon felt grateful that she'd looked out for his interest instead of her own.

Right now, she enjoyed feeling this man against her body. His hard body pressed against hers for what seemed like hours but could only have been a few seconds.

When Gideon sank in deeper, allowing his tongue to part her lips and dive in her mouth, Janelle sobered to the situation, but not to stop him. When he upped the passion on the kiss, it felt familiar. Janelle touched his arm and felt his muscles through his jacket. The memory brought her back ten years ago to when a shy girl had her fantasies realized by a passionate boy at a community-center dance.

Gideon broke from the kiss and stared at Janelle. "I know you, don't I?"

Janelle felt her mouth move but she couldn't say anything. He would call her crazy if she admitted she thought he'd kissed her back in high school. She couldn't admit that his one kiss had forced her to compare every man she dated after to him.

She unlaced her fingers from his and got out of his grip. When she peered around him, she noticed a second photographer had joined the first. Both couldn't erase the smiles from their smug faces.

"You had better go. I'm sure this will end up on some site or tabloid somewhere." Janelle started to retreat into her business.

"Wait. Can we talk?" Gideon started to go after her.

She shook her head. "Thank you for the supplies. Have a good day, Mr. Wells."

As she closed the back door, she heard him say, "Shit."

Exactly.

Chapter 10

As Gideon ascended the stairs in his mother's home, he couldn't get Janelle out of his mind. He shouldn't have kissed her. He couldn't help it. For the last few years of his professional life, everyone around him, except for his immediate family, wanted something from him. Endorsements, a winning season, fame, his money, sex. Gideon had had to look out for himself…until today when an angelic woman had put his needs first.

He got to the top of the stairs and went into Gunnar's old room. Since coming home, his older brother had been hell-bent on leaving.

"Hey, bro." Gideon, who hid his new knee brace under his jeans, leaned against the door jamb.

He didn't want to wear it, but after his appointment that morning, the doctor had insisted. Opting to not have surgery on his ACL, and instead agreeing to months of physical therapy didn't sit well with the doctor. Gideon had to be the rock. Being sidelined for months would prevent him from being that glue.

Gideon hadn't expected Janelle to notice the brace. His heart still melted from her concerned reaction. He couldn't take the worry and judgment from his family. As soon as the delivery driver dropped off all the supplies, Gideon went back to Pick 'N Clip, ducked into the bathroom, and put the brace under his clothing. As long as he could keep his walk straight, he wouldn't alert his family about his newly diagnosed condition.

When Gunnar continued packing, Gideon filled the silence. "Mom hates that you're not talking to her."

"She lied to me." Gunnar shook his head.

When he told Gideon about Eboni's miscarriage from ten years ago, Gideon had to pick his jaw up from the floor. After his initial shock, he brought home some reality to his brother. It had only been the three boys and Queen Elizabeth together for years. Gideon convinced his pigheaded brother that their mother would never do anything to hurt him on purpose. Bottom line, Gunnar needed to make amends with her before her surgery.

When Gunnar agreed, Gideon allowed him some time to be alone with Queen Elizabeth. Plus, he needed the privacy to try and call Dennis again.

The phone rang once, twice, and at the third ring, someone answered.

"Go to hell!" The line disconnected.

As Gideon started to redial Dennis again, his phone rang. He saw on the caller-ID screen that Dennis called him this time.

"Don't hang up on me again." Gideon knew his friend.

"Kiss my ass!" The line disconnected again.

Gideon paced the hallway upstairs. He felt his heart beating in his head. What the hell had made Dennis angry? Had he been put on the injured list too? Did he have months of physical therapy ahead? Was he unsure about his place with the team?

This time, Gideon opted to do a video chat. No way would his dear friend disconnect the call if he saw his face.

Dennis answered. Gideon had only seen the scowl Dennis carried on game day against the opponents. He had his dreads pulled back into a low ponytail. He had his eyebrows knitted together. When he breathed, Dennis looked like a bull about to charge.

"You have got some nerve." Dennis's mouth drew in a tight line.

"I've had a lot stuff going on, Den." Gideon continued pacing when he noticed Dennis had started. "My brother got shot Super Bowl night."

"Yeah, I had to hear about it on the news. You couldn't tell me? I thought we were boys." Dennis pounded his chest with his fist.

"We are. I wasn't thinking about anyone but my family. I had to get home." Gideon lowered his head, took a breath, and connected his stare to his friend before speaking. "My mom needs bypass surgery. It's serious, man."

Dennis stopped pacing, but the grimace remained. "You didn't tell me about that either."

"It's not something you broadcast, you know. Her surgery is this coming Monday."

Gideon's friend's face softened finally. "Tell her I said good luck." He looked off to the side.

Gideon knew Dennis's mother had passed away years ago from breast cancer, another reason not to tell him about Queen Elizabeth.

"Thanks, man." Gideon coughed. "Did you hear the other news?"

"What? You getting married or something?" Dennis pressed his lips together.

"Yeah, right. No. Coach Brick came to see me."

Dennis stilled.

Gideon swiped his hand over his throat. "I'm done. I'm on the injured list. Might as well say I'm off the team."

"That's rough. Guess you shouldn't have run that last play."

Gideon glared at his friend. "Even though it won us the game?"

"Yeah, but look at you. You're a loose cannon. Coach doesn't know what to do with you, which is a problem for me."

"Why's that?"

Dennis remained quiet for a while before he dropped a bomb. "I told Coach and the managers that when I signed on to be a Wolf, it was with the understanding that the team does a lot of running plays. If they support you running key plays, I need to go find a new team." He shrugged. "Bottom line, I told them it was either me or you. I guess they made their decision since I haven't seen Brick or heard from my agent."

"You bastard. You couldn't come talk to me about the plays first? You ran to the coach and managers like a bitch behind my back?" The knife in his back felt like it sliced through his heart as well.

"I'm the bitch? You're the one who made the most important game of our lives all about you. We all have stories we want to tell our kids, Gid."

Gideon had to sit down. The more he paced, the more it sounded like marching. He didn't need to alert his mother and brother. "No matter what you think of me, I never did anything intentionally to hurt you or your career. You waited until I was weak and you buried me. You know, the phone rings on my end too. You could have called me."

Dennis chuckled. "Why? You know it all. You have it handled, right?" He shook his head. "Good luck with rehab." He disconnected the call.

If Gideon didn't need his phone and the contacts in it, he would have thrown it across the room. As soon as he heard the front door slam, he went downstairs. His mother sat on the couch and looked like he had always remembered her. She knitted while watching TV.

He noticed a cup of tea on the end table next to her along with some cookies. Gideon couldn't indulge if he wanted to be able to play next season.

He sat on the chair across from her. "Do you need anything before I go?"

"Yes, darling." Queen Elizabeth put her knitting project down to regard her son. "Aren't you going to thank me?"

Before Gideon could ask what he needed to thank her for, he thought about the day and his whole life. With his mother, anything could be fair game.

"Thank you for providing me with a great home and upbringing."

"Honey, you don't have to go back that far. Try again." She picked up her tea and took a sip.

"Thank you for making that appointment for me." He smiled and hoped that she wouldn't want to delve any deeper in to what the doctor had said.

"So?"

No such luck.

"So I messed up my ACL pretty badly, but not so bad that I have to have surgery. That's the good news." His smile widened.

"But you need it?" she pressed.

"The doctor suggested I get it. But he also said I could heal with physical therapy."

"Good. So how long will you have to wear the brace?" She smiled as she set her cup down.

Gideon peered down. Through his jeans, he saw the outline of the brace around his knee. "Six weeks for now, along with some physical therapy. Then the doctor will check on my progress."

"Good." She nodded. "Go on."

Gideon shrugged. "That's it." He would leave out the fact that the doctor had strongly suggested surgery.

"Isn't there something else you need to thank me for?"

He collapsed back into the chair. "I'm not going to stay here with you. I have a perfectly good home of my own."

Elizabeth picked up her phone and typed something on the screen before she turned it around to him. Gideon sat up and moved in closer. He caught an image of him kissing Janelle behind Flowers Galore.

Gideon knew the photographers had been behind them. Janelle had warned him and he'd heard the telltale sounds of a camera. He didn't care. He'd wanted to kiss Janelle and do so much more with her. He hadn't felt like that since he and Hilary had parted ways.

"You can thank me at any time for getting you two together." Elizabeth laughed.

Gideon stood. He strolled over to his mother and kissed her on her forehead. He connected his gaze to hers before he said, "Thanks, Mom."

"Now are you two having sex yet?" she asked. "I think I have condoms in my purse."

Gideon rolled his eyes as soon as his mother turned her head. "If you don't need anything else, I'm going to head on home. It's been a long, exhausting day."

"Okay, dear."

Gideon got to the door.

Elizabeth stopped him again. "Just remember, dear. A woman needs a lot of foreplay."

"Good-bye, Mom." Gideon opened the door.

"Never use a woman. Do it only if you truly care about her."

He stepped over the threshold. He couldn't get out of this conversation fast enough. "I love you, Mom."

"And please use condoms. Janelle is a lovely woman, but you can never be too careful. I would love to be a grandmother, but only in the right way."

Gideon started to close the door before he said, "I'll see you tomorrow."

"Love you, dear," he heard his mother say before he escaped.

Not weird at all.

Instead of driving home, Gideon went to Flowers Galore. He knew Victor would be fine at Pick 'N Clip. He wanted to be able to catch Janelle. That kiss had meant more than a simple thank you. He'd felt it. He hoped she had also.

Gideon started to pull into the parking lot to her store when he saw a couple of reporters and photographers milling around outside the front door.

Damn.

Luckily, the photographers hadn't seen him in his car going by the business. He went down the street and parked. He would throw the ball into her court and see what happened.

* * * *

At the end of the day, Janelle felt both beat and exhilarated. What a day full of surprises. First, all the customers that had showed up that morning. Then the surprise of the additional supplies courtesy of Gideon. Then that kiss.

She put her fingers to her lips. It had been a long time since she'd had a kiss like that. Could Gideon be that same boy from years ago?

Her office phone rang.

So far, only news outlets and curious customers had called her, asking her questions about Gideon and their relationship. She'd told everyone who asked that she and Gideon happened to be business associates and no more. Then the kiss had happened.

Janelle answered the phone, hoping it would be more business. "Flowers Galore. How can I help you?"

"How were the sales today?"

Janelle's bottom jaw unhinged.

Gideon continued talking. "Was it like yesterday?"

"Uh, yeah. Yes. Lots of sales and orders. I'll be swamped on Valentine's Day." She crossed her legs and leaned back in her chair.

"That's a shame. Valentine's Day should be spent with someone you love, or at least with someone you really like. Is there someone you really like?"

She could almost see him smiling. She heard the happy lilt in is voice. "Your flirting skills are so lame."

He laughed at her.

"Shouldn't you be apologizing?"

"For what?"

"Kissing me like that when you hadn't asked for permission." She drummed her fingers on her desk.

"Good. You didn't mention that you didn't want to be kissed or that you didn't like it."

She gasped and hoped the sound hadn't traveled through the phone. Gideon had made a great point. If she really didn't like him, and if she'd hated the kiss, she would have mentioned that first. She hoped from the way her body had fused against his that he would have known how much she'd enjoyed his lips capturing hers.

Gideon cleared his throat. "I apologize. I must admit, I've always been a bit impulsive."

"I'm not." She crossed her legs. "The next time the impulse strikes you, ask for permission."

"So you want there to be a next time?"

"What I want should be of no concern to you." She twirled a pen around on her desk like a solo version of spin the bottle.

"But I am concerned. Why hasn't a man scooped you up yet, or better yet, married you?"

Janelle leaned forward. Her chair squeaked under her movement. "Like I said, I'm married to my work. Besides, a husband would get angry with me after a while. I wouldn't be able to wear a wedding band while I work. I do have to dig in a lot of dirt every day." She couldn't wear a lot of jewelry while she did her job. She would be too afraid of ruining a precious piece.

"A smart husband would get you a simple band for working."

"Oh, really? And why is that?" She had to hear this reasoning.

"Your husband would know that flowers and plants are your life."

The smile melted as she listened to Gideon.

He continued. "He would know that you would be happy digging in the dirt while you take care of your babies. The plants, I mean. Not actual children. He would get you something simple to wear to work, something you could have under gardener's gloves. But at home, you would wear the biggest ring out there."

"Oh." Janelle couldn't say anything other than that one word.

He sighed. "So will you do dinner with me tonight?"

Janelle opened her mouth but she still couldn't speak. What could she say? Yes, she wanted to have dinner with him, but the thought of cameras following her around scared her?

"Hello?" he said when she didn't respond right away.

"I can't." Janelle shook her head.

"Can't or won't?"

"Shouldn't."

"Ah. I don't like that word. It implies there's some sort of rule that should be followed. What's holding you back?" The curious tone in his voice weaved through his low timbre.

Janelle chewed on her lower lip. She could reveal so much about herself. How her last boyfriend had fled after he'd accomplished his goals. How her mother's idea of a relationship had tainted her view on men. Or how her fledging business made her feel unattractive to men.

Instead, she said, "You are like ivy. You cover everything and take over wherever you grow."

"At least you didn't call me a poison ivy." He released a chuckle. "Just call me a hollyhock."

She smiled. "Are you saying you're like an annual?"

"I just keep coming back."

Janelle couldn't help but laugh.

"See. A man who can make you laugh is one you can trust."

Her laughter stopped. "It's not you I don't trust."

He latched on to that statement faster than she expected. "See. I was right. You don't trust yourself around me."

Penny poked her head into the office. "You ready to go?"

Janelle held up a finger and mouthed the words, *Just one second.*

"I'll even let you pick where we go. My treat though," Gideon said.

Janelle shook her head as she stood. "As tempting as that sounds, I don't think it's a great idea. It's bad enough now that I'm afraid to go home to see who might be there waiting for me."

"Tell me where you live. I'll keep whoever is bothering you away from you." The sternness in his voice came through as powerful as his words.

"I can't ask you to do that. And I definitely can't tell you where I live. One day you'll go back to train and to football. I'll still have nosy reporters and photographers bugging me about you. It'll be very inconvenient."

"Okay. Then come to my house. Stay with me if you want."

Janelle blinked at that offer as she put on her coat. "You barely know me. Why would you make an offer like that?"

"Like I said before, my mother likes you, so you have to be good people. Plus, I feel like I owe it to you for intruding in your life. I have a guesthouse that you could stay in that's away from the main house."

She snickered. "And here I have a small, seven-hundred-square-foot apartment where I can hear my neighbors sneeze."

"I work hard for what I have. I make no apologies for it." His statement made it seem like he'd had to either explain or defend his choices in the past to other people. "Plus, I have my privacy. You can have privacy and security."

Janelle lowered her voice. "Yeah, but for how long?"

She'd felt secure in her last relationship until the rug had been pulled from under her. Gideon could be like all the rest of the men in her past, including the man who'd fathered her…wherever he might be.

"Thanks for the strange but nice offer. I have to go." She slipped on her coat and hung her scarf loosely around her neck. "Thanks for the extra flowers today. I'll pay you back."

"No need." His tone lightened.

"Please, let me pay you." She hoisted her purse and backpack with her laptop on her shoulder before turning off the office lights.

"Dinner would be a great payment."

"A dinner that you would pay for?" She snickered. "How is that paying you back?"

Gideon paused before answering. "Great company would be priceless."

Janelle stood frozen to her spot as she absorbed his words. Good thing she couldn't see him. He could have had her in any way he wanted.

Penny tugged on Janelle's scarf. When Janelle peered at her friend, Penny nodded her head toward the door.

"I have to go. Have a good evening, Mr. Wells."

"Gideon."

Janelle smiled.

"You have a lovely night, Janelle." He disconnected the call.

She stared at her phone as though the man existed inside of it.

"If you want him, call him back." Penny broke Janelle's daydream when she jabbed her with her elbow.

Janelle put the phone in her purse. "Don't be ridiculous. We're two professionals talking."

"Uh-huh. Talking about dinner, husbands and wedding rings, right? Why don't you admit that you like the guy?" Penny opened the door and headed to her car.

Janelle waited a moment at the doorway before she went to her vehicle. She didn't need someone else jumping out of the bushes to scare her with a camera and a probing question.

"Of course I like him. He's nice and has a great knowledge of flowers and plants. He's a good colleague." Janelle unlocked her car and threw her items inside.

"With a great ass." Again, Penny held up her hands and curved her fingers like she'd done when they'd watched the Super Bowl.

"Oh, by the way. No more pictures of me on the Internet, please. I have enough going on in my life without you adding to it." Janelle pointed to her employee and gave her the sternest look she could muster.

In a surrendering move, Penny held up her hands. "Okay, okay. You win. No more hot, steamy pics of you and that sexy-ass Gideon Wells."

"Thank you." Janelle started to take a seat in her car.

"Hey, boss."

Janelle peered over the roof of her car.

"How was that kiss?" Penny pursed her lips and made an obscene kissing sound as she got in her car and started it.

Janelle pointed to her. "You are not my friend," she shouted to her.

The accountant with an office next to her shop slammed his door and locked it.

"Hello, Mr. Sleaston." Janelle waved to the man, who glanced at her and continued to his car with his head down.

Nothing about the man distinguished him from any other average man. He had a medium to slight build. He wore dark clothing, probably meant for him to blend into his surroundings. His black horned-rimmed glasses gave him a bit of character. Otherwise, her business neighbor could best be described as forgettable.

One day, the man would develop a personality and acknowledge her. Until then, she would continue to talk to him like a good neighbor. Small-business owners had to stick together.

Janelle drove home without listening to music. The silence kept her mind uncluttered and centered on Gideon, that body, that smile, those hands, that kiss. Had he done it because he'd felt compelled to kiss her or did he want to manipulate her? She hadn't known him that long, or really at all to know his character.

She didn't want to think about him anymore. Each time she did, her nipples hardened and her pulse raced. She could barely control her breathing.

When Janelle arrived home, she couldn't wait to get in her apartment. She scanned the parking lot to make sure she wouldn't get any surprises. So far, so good. No strangers jumping out from the bushes. No strange flashes from the paparazzi. Maybe the heat had died down already. One big scandal elsewhere could get the vultures to circle other carrion.

Buddy and Althea didn't step out of their apartment when Janelle walked up the steps to her place. Good. She wanted to get some sleep. Lately, though, her dreams even contained Gideon. What did his body look like without any clothes? Good thing no one came to her apartment. Otherwise, they would see that she kept a screensaver of Gideon's popular spinach ad on her home computer.

"Excuse me."

Janelle jumped as soon as she heard a foreign voice at the bottom of the stairs. Every time she watched a horror movie, she wondered why the screaming female character could never get herself together long enough to get away from the maniac. As this stranger started to creep up the steps, she found it difficult to get her key into the lock.

"Stay your ass right there, or I will kick your nuts up to your throat." Janelle's real threat managed to get him to stop.

As he stood midway up the stairs, she got a good look at him. She didn't want to get any closer. He appeared to be about her height, maybe shorter. The white man couldn't have been from around Virginia. His pockmarked face carried a healthy tan. Maybe he did the tanning-salon thing. A black knit cap covered his head, so she couldn't see his hair color or even if he had any hair. His coal-black eyes caused her to shiver.

"I strongly suggest you turn yourself around and go back to wherever it is you came from." She unlocked her dead bolt first. Then she slipped the key into the doorknob.

"I didn't mean to scare you, Janelle." His high-pitched voice seemed in conflict with his menacing expression.

Janelle had expected to hear a man who sounded like he gargled rocks morning, noon, and night. He dressed in a black peacoat with black jeans and combat boots. He looked ready to go into battle or whack someone.

"Are you that same asshole who's been following me around?" She turned the knob and opened her door, ready to get into the sanctuary of her home.

"I'm offended by the label, but, yes. I have been the one taking your photograph." He tried taking a step closer, but Janelle opened her purse and dug in it to retrieve her can of Mace.

He wouldn't be able to tell that she had emptied the can weeks ago when some teenagers had tried to break in to her car over the Christmas holiday.

"Why? I'm no one famous." She kept her hand in her purse as soon as her fingers brushed over the can.

"But your friend is. So how long have the two of you been—"

She stopped him. "I keep telling you and everyone else that Gideon Wells and I are not dating. He runs a flower shop. I own a flower shop. That's our only link."

"I don't know." The photographer scratched his head. "I don't go around kissing my colleagues the way he kissed you earlier today."

Janelle swallowed hard. "I want to be left alone. If you continue to harass me, I'll get a restraining order against you."

The diminutive man shrugged. "Fair enough. You wouldn't be the first person to do that." He started to turn and then stopped and returned his stare. "I'd like to make you an offer. That's the reason I'm here. Give me exclusive details on Gideon Wells, and I'll pay you a hundred thousand dollars."

Hearing the figure choked Janelle so that she stopped breathing entirely. She had never earned that amount of money in a year working any job or with the flower shop. She could pay off her bills and get herself a bigger store, one with a greenhouse.

She shook her head. No. Using men had her mother's MO all over it. Janelle wouldn't go down that route.

"Get out of here. I don't know anything about Gideon. Even if I did, I wouldn't sell him out to you." She placed one foot into her apartment.

"Fine. Five hundred thousand."

Janelle froze. With money like that, she could buy a house. She'd always imagined her own place with a large yard, big enough for her to have great flower beds and a huge vegetable garden.

No, no, no. Accepting the money would mean using Gideon. She liked him. She liked him a lot. She wouldn't use him no matter the amount of money.

"You're crazy." She shook her head. "How do I know you're not lying about the money? You could be saying that to get me to reveal some details and then never pay me."

The man laughed. "You remember the video that came out that showed the R&B diva and her hip-hop mogul husband in the elevator when the diva's sister punched and kicked her brother-in-law repeatedly? I bought that video and paid two million for it. You recall the British actor in all those romantic comedy movies who got caught on surveillance video with a prostitute? That one was a cool mil. I'm a man of my word. If you don't believe me"—he reached into his pocket and pulled out a business card—"go to my site. The testimonials on there are anonymous, but if you contact me, I'll give you the people's contact information to verify my claims."

"That sounds stupid. You give me their information and I can go to some other media outlet to sell that information." Janelle crossed her arms over her chest as she squared off with this shark.

"To use your line, that sounds stupid. For one, the people who gave up the story aren't the real story. No one cares about them. The people care about celebrities and getting their dirt. They want to know why a championship athlete would drop everything to come home. They want to know why he dumped his smoking-hot, A-list star girlfriend and turned down a sexy She-Wolf cheerleader to be with the flower-shop girl."

"I'm a woman. And for the millionth time, we are not together." His inquiries had her thinking. Had he really turned his back on those women? What did she have that they didn't? Couldn't be money.

"Right." He snickered. Then he placed his business card on the step in front of him. "My name is Jules. You can find my contact information on here." He started to leave again, stopped, and turned back to her. "I was going to leave a note on your door about my business proposition, but I found this tacked to it." He placed a red flyer next to his business card.

Janelle didn't need to see it up close to see the large "Eviction Notice" emblazoned across the top.

"Have a good night, Ms. Gold." Jules strolled out of the apartment building.

Like the weight of the world had been placed on her shoulders, Janelle slumped down to the top step. She stared at Jules's business card and the eviction notice. No doubt about it, she would have to stay away from Gideon Wells.

Chapter 11

Days had gone by and Gideon hadn't seen Janelle. Each time he called her, she would say she had too much going on to talk to him. With it now being Valentine's Day, he felt a stronger need to see her.

As usual, Pick 'N Clip had been nonstop busy all day. Gideon had hired temporary delivery drivers to help with deliveries.

"Whew." Victor put his hand to his chest after finishing a transaction. "I cannot wait until this day ends."

"Don't wish your life away, my friend." Gideon patted the man he saw as an uncle on his shoulder.

Although he gave Victor a positive line to keep him going, Gideon couldn't wait until the end of the day too. He had plans. If they worked, he would be a very happy man.

At the close of business, with no inventory on the shelves, Gideon locked the door. "What a day, right?"

"I'm beat." Victor started sweeping the floor while Gideon counted out the register. "You want me to take the deposit to the bank?"

"If you don't mind." Gideon handed him the bag.

"Of course not. It's on my way home." He finished cleaning the floor and put on his jacket. "Any big plans tonight?"

"Hoping so." Gideon smiled. "Hoping not to make a fool of myself."

"I'm sure you won't." Victor wrapped his neck with a red scarf in honor of Valentine's Day. "Whatever you do, I hope you have a great time."

"Thanks. Don't forget. Tomorrow is Mom's surgery. I won't be in at all. You think you'll be all right handling the store on your own?"

Victor rolled his eyes. "Of course. Tell Queen good luck. Good night."

Gideon didn't have a lot of time to waste. He went home as fast as he could, showered, and changed into a nice pair of black slacks, a white knit pullover, and black leather shoes. He wanted to look right for the night.

His phone rang. When he saw the number came from the guard station, he answered it. "Yeah?"

"I have a delivery for you. Do you want them to come through?" Pearl asked. She sounded like a pit bull that wanted to get off the leash to gnaw on a perpetrator's leg.

Gideon had to admire her tenacity. "Is it a flower delivery?"

Pearl answered, "Yes, sir."

He smiled. "Yes, that's fine. Send them up."

Gideon made the final touches to the dining room table to make sure it looked perfect enough for a dinner for two. He checked his gas fireplace and ignited it just as his doorbell chimed.

He smoothed his hands down his shirt and pants before he answered it. He wanted Janelle to be the first person he saw on the other side of the door. His heart did a stutter beat as soon as his gaze connected to hers. She stared back at him, her mouth agape.

She held a vase full of roses in one hand and a clipboard in the other. "Gideon?"

"Good. Right on time." He took a step back to allow her and Penny entrance.

"This huge order came from you?" Janelle held on to the roses as she carefully crept into his home.

"You're too busy to take my calls. You turned me down for coffee several times. I figured this would be the only way I could see you." He stepped closer to her. "And trust me. I do want to see you."

Penny cleared her throat when the sexual tension in the air hung thick and heavy. "There are a lot of flowers to bring in and I have a date for tonight. Do you mind if we get this going?"

"Penny." Janelle nudged her friend with her elbow.

"No, you're right. Please put the flowers wherever there is room, except for the kitchen and dining room." He stared at Janelle intently. "I have plans for those locations."

In a not so quiet whisper, Penny said to Janelle, "And probably the bedroom."

Janelle's face ignited like the fire in the fireplace. "Yes, let me get the flowers so that we can get out of your hair."

Janelle and Penny worked quickly and efficiently, bringing in all ten vases full of roses. When the last vase had been delivered, Gideon gave Penny a five-hundred-dollar tip.

"Have a great time on your date tonight." He smiled at her.

"I will now." Penny jumped up and down as she shoved the cash into her pocket. "And as we agreed…" She gave Gideon a salute and backed out of the room.

"Penny, wait. What are you doing?" Janelle went after her friend.

"Gid here contacted me a few days ago and asked if you had any plans for Valentine's Day." Penny's smile stretched all the way around her head. "I told him no, but you're too hot to sit at home. He agreed." She peered at Gideon and gave him a wink. "So he asked for this order and requested it be the last order delivered for the day. Then he asked for one more thing."

"What's that?" Janelle's voice lowered to a whisper.

Penny pulled the clipboard from her boss's hands. "He asked that I leave you here after the delivery was made, and he would take you home. I thought that was a great idea."

"No, no, no, it's not. Don't leave me here."

Penny's shoulders slumped. "Why not? What do you think will happen?"

Janelle looked over her shoulder at the man who'd planned a whole evening with her, for her. She turned back to Penny. "Don't do this."

"Look. Remember when I told you I had just gotten an order for ten arrangements of roses? Do you know what you said?" Penny took a step out the door. When Janelle didn't answer fast enough, Penny filled in the gap. "You said a woman has to be really lucky to have someone care about her like that."

Janelle rubbed the back of her neck.

"On the way to Gideon's house, all you kept saying was how gorgeous this neighborhood is and, again, how lucky some woman will be to live here and have all these flowers on this special day." Penny put her hand on Janelle's shoulder. "Why can't that lucky woman be you?"

* * * *

Staying in Gideon's house didn't make Janelle nervous because what he could do to her. Janelle knew that Queen Elizabeth had raised gentlemen. Gideon had treated her that way. She didn't feel tempted to gather information on the man to report to Jules. Although she'd picked up his business card, along with her eviction notice, she had no desire to do business with the devil. Janelle didn't think her heart would be able to take getting to know this man and losing him.

Penny stepped out the door. "You will be fine. You have your cell phone. I know where you are if you don't show up to work tomorrow." She leaned forward and put her hand to the side of her mouth in preparation of a whisper. In an even louder voice, she said, "And I put some condoms in your purse." At that point, Penny reached down next to the door and put her backpack and purse in Gideon's home. "Good night. Have a wonderful time. Love you."

"Hate you. Don't"—the door slammed before Janelle could get out her request—"do this." She turned to Gideon. "So here we are."

"Yes." Gideon clapped then rubbed his hands together. "So do you want to have sex now or later?"

Janelle wanted to run as soon as Gideon made his request. When she heard him laughing, she stopped and stared at him.

"I'm kidding." He held up his hand as though showing surrender. "I only want to spend some time with you. I thought this would be the only way to do it. The only downside of my plan is that you had to work to get here." He moved in closer to her.

Janelle felt powerless to move or react.

"I would much rather have you here willingly without you and Penny carrying in ten vases. If you really want to go, I'll take you home." Gideon stared into her eyes.

She started to open her mouth but closed it when she couldn't talk. After clearing her throat, she found the strength to say something. "I feel like you tricked me to get here and manipulated my friend to leave me here. I should go home."

Gideon remained quiet as she contemplated her choices. She could go home and do nothing but wonder why she'd ended up alone on this romantic day. Or she could stay and check out the possibilities.

She scanned down her body. In her standard jeans and oversize sweater, she felt underdressed and dirty. "I can't have dinner with you like this."

Gideon smiled. "I took that into account. Actually, Penny did. She said she would put some items in your bag for you." Gideon strolled over to a side hallway. "If you go down there to the last room on the right, there's a bathroom with a bathtub and shower. Feel free to use either one. Dinner will be a while, so you have time."

"Why are you doing this?" Janelle picked up her bags.

Gideon stared at her for a long while before he framed her face in his hands and placed the softest kiss on her lips. Janelle had to lock her legs back to keep upright or she would have crumbled to the floor in a heap.

When he pulled back from her, he said, "That's why." He took a step off to the side. "Oh, wait. You did say I had to ask for permission the next time I kissed you, right?"

She nodded.

"May I kiss you?"

Unable to speak, she nodded again.

He brushed his lips over hers ever so slowly. With each small breath she took, he offered her sustenance by giving her oxygen through his parted lips. She held on to his arms to give herself some support. The longer he kissed her, the more her knees felt like jelly.

Gideon pulled back from her. "You'll find towels, washcloths, and soap in there as well. See you in a bit."

Janelle nodded before padding down the long hallway to the bedroom. The room looked like it came out of a magazine. Textured beige carpeting met her feet. A king-size bed sat against the wall and covered with a burgundy comforter set. This room also had its own fireplace.

Once inside, she closed the door. She took a couple of steps toward the bathroom, stopped, and returned to the door where she locked it. She didn't need Gideon popping up. Although his joke about having sex had made her blush, it hadn't been a thought that escaped her mind.

The man looked so sexy, and he stared at her like she exuded the same sultriness even when she didn't feel as hot. She managed to find the light in the bathroom.

"Whoa." She scanned the opulent room that had a marble floor and counters, a standalone shower with rocky tile lining the walls and floor. A white Jacuzzi tub sat next to it. As she scanned the room, it all looked new and unused.

She plugged up the tub and filled it with hot water. If she would be dining with a hot, eligible bachelor, she wanted to be relaxed.

Janelle stripped out of her clothes, grabbed a soft, tan bath sheet and washcloth, and submerged herself in the balmy water. Heaven. The stress of the world melted away. Thanks to Gideon's order, she had enough to pay some of her back rent, which had stopped the eviction order. It also kept her from having to call her mother for help. Janelle would rather live in her car than ask Ida Gold for a dime.

After relaxing for a while and the water started to cool down, Janelle finally bathed herself. Before getting out of the water, she ran the jets to see how they felt against her skin. The forceful bubbles bounced off her legs and back. She could only imagine the pleasure she would feel if she parted her thighs and aimed the stream at her core.

She pushed the thought from her head and emptied the tub. Janelle should have known Penny had been up to something. Penny had insisted on carrying Janelle's bag. Once she'd gotten the bag in their delivery van, it had looked packed to the brim.

Janelle opened it and removed her makeup bag first, which sat on top of everything else. As she stared at her reflection in the mirror, she applied some bright red lipstick, the only tube in her makeup kit. Then she put on some eye shadow that gave her a smoky-eye look.

Hair accessories and her combs sat on top of her clothes. Janelle released her naturally curly tresses from her clip, applied some water to it to refresh the curls, and styled it with the clip again. When she noticed how young she looked with it in place, she removed it again and fluffed out her curls, giving herself a wild, uninhibited look.

Janelle dove into the bag again. She caught something red next. She removed it and saw a short, formfitting dress. Janelle had never owned a dress like this. Definitely a part of Penny's collection. She would have to thank her friend. Janelle looked at what she'd worn to the house. No way could she put on those sweaty, dirty clothes that now littered the bathroom floor.

Janelle reached into the bag again to find deodorant and a flowery perfume that Janelle had once said she liked but had never purchased because she couldn't afford it. Okay, she would have to thank Penny for that gift.

At the bottom of the bag, she found a pair of black stockings and black heels. It looked like Penny had neglected to pack undergarments. Where in the world had Penny put Janelle's clean bra and panties? Janelle checked every pocket on the bag, searching for anything, even thong underwear. Nothing.

Janelle growled. "Bitch."

She picked up her cell phone and sent a text to Penny.

"Really? No underwear?"

Penny sent a smiley face emoticon back with the word, *"Oops"* next to it.

Janelle would not put her underwear back on for the same reason she wouldn't be wearing the outfit she'd arrived in to the house.

"Come on, girl. Let's try new things." She sat on a chair at the built-in vanity and slipped on the stockings first.

It felt strange for her to have on stockings but no panties. She tied the wrap dress snugly around her waist and attempted to keep the V of the dress as closed as possible. Janelle didn't want to give Gideon a show. The dress offered no support for her bust. If a cool breeze hit her, she would be exposed in more ways than one.

Janelle packed her clothing and toiletries back into her bag. After a deep breath, she opened the bathroom and then the bedroom door. A fragrant aroma of baked fish and jasmine rice met her as she headed toward the kitchen. She found Gideon behind the counter tending to several pots. He had his back to her when she placed her things down on the floor.

"Thanks for letting me use your bathroom." She came around the counter.

Each time Janelle took a step, a cool breeze swept over her naked sex. *This is so strange.*

"You're very—" Gideon stopped midsentence when he looked at her. He stared at her.

"What?" Janelle smoothed her hand over her head. "Penny put this outfit in the bag. I don't normally dress like this."

"You should. Wow." He started to move closer but stopped. "No, if I get too close, I'll do something stupid. So far, I think I've impressed you, right?"

"You have, but not because of the flowers or this home." She leaned her hand against the bar.

"No? What then?" Gideon pulled the rice off the heat and opened the oven door.

"You know about flowers. And you thought about the little things."

He placed a long, silver pan on top of the stove and closed the oven door. "What do you mean?"

Janelle took a deep breath before she expounded on her thoughts. "You could have been cliché and driven up to my shop in your fancy car and whisked me away to some expensive restaurant. But you didn't. You purchased an insane amount of flowers from me. Thank you very much. And you're cooking me dinner on Valentine's Day."

Gideon placed the dish towel he'd used to remove the hot pan from the oven on the counter. He moved around it and stood in front of Janelle. Before she could speak, he held out his hand.

"Come with me." He smiled.

When the man did that, how in the world could she say no? Janelle took his hand. He led her to a doorway down a small hallway next to the kitchen. After he flicked a light switch on the wall, he showed Janelle a large garage.

The slate-gray floors gleamed and had small silvery flecks throughout. One black car sat on one side, and he had a red-and-black motorcycle parked next to it. In the expansive five-car garage, she had expected to see more. Now that she really studied the car, she didn't see a luxury brand name attached. No Mercedes hood ornament. No BMW logo.

"I live really simply," Gideon began.

He didn't have a million and one cars like she had seen of other NFL stars, but he did have a large house with a multicar garage. Janelle peered up at him to refute his claim.

He smiled. "As far as cars and such." He pointed to his vehicle. "I just drive that because it's reliable. The motorcycle is my toy. I don't need anything else."

She peered around his tidy and organized garage. Tools had been placed carefully in their assigned spots. He kept the floors spotless. Unless Gideon kept his tools clean each time he used them, they all look new.

"Are the tools for show, or do you really do your own yard work?" She crossed her arms over her chest.

When she peered down, she noticed how much the dress pulled down, showing more of her cleavage. As soon as she looked up, she caught Gideon staring at her chest. Even after getting caught, he didn't look sorry for the stare.

"When I'm home and I can, I do my own yard work." He turned off the light and closed the door. "I have to blame or thank my mother for that. Even as small kids, she made us do chores. I always liked working outside." He took her hand as he started to walk down the hallway. "I keep my tools clean to make them last longer."

Janelle barely heard him. She stared at the union of their hands. She didn't want to wake up from this heavenly dream. As soon as her hand brushed against the calluses on his palm, she believed his claim about the strenuous work.

"I've always loved working in the yard." She talked to ease her nerves. Janelle heard her heart pounding in her ears. Her hands even throbbed with each beat. "I like putting my hands in the dirt and feeling the earth. It calms me."

Gideon stopped in his trek and turned to her. "Are you serious?"

She nodded.

"Me too." He squeezed her hand. "My biggest regret about this house is that it didn't have a bigger yard." He went to the other side of the kitchen, down another hallway to a door at the end of it. "That didn't stop me from having one of these." He opened the door and showed off a small-scale greenhouse.

Janelle let go of his hand as she eased into the room to look around. A fancy irrigation system hovered over the four rows of vegetation. Out of habit, or maybe she wanted to be sure he didn't have this place here for show for her, she brushed her hands over the leaves.

"This is awesome." She touched an unopened bud. "I can't believe a guy like you would have something like this."

When she felt a hand surrounding hers, she stopped and pivoted.

"Stop assuming you know me and my type." Gideon didn't carry a grimace or look disappointed when he made the statement.

He wanted her to see all of him, the real man behind the pads and tackles.

She nodded. "I do that a lot. I jump to conclusions very quickly."

"Why is that?"

She shrugged.

"No. You know the reason," he pressed.

Images from her past came flooding back to her all at once. To keep from crying over the more painful memories, she blurted, "I always want to be the one to know when evil is coming."

Gideon's eyes widened. "Evil? That's kind of harsh."

"I'm not trying to say that Satan is around every corner. I've been hurt a lot in my past. I thought if I could figure people out early and let them know that I know they're full of it, I can stop them from crushing my spirits." For now, she would leave out stories of past boyfriends, the girls in school who'd claimed to be her friend but talked about her like a dog around other people, or her cynical mother.

"I hear you." Gideon put his hand to his chest. "Get to know me first before you judge me."

Janelle chuckled. "Deal. It's hard to break habits, you know?"

He stroked his fingers down her bare arm until he held her hand again. "I know. You're talking to a guy who still gets excited before each game and is the first one up Christmas morning."

She laughed. "Funny. So are you giving me the official tour?" Before he started, she noticed a plant in the far corner of the greenhouse. She started to move toward it to get a better look. "What is that one over there? Is that a—"

Gideon held her hand tighter and pulled her back. "Nothing for you to see. Come on. I'll show you around."

Janelle felt an uneasy feeling slithering over her skin. So far, Gideon had come off as an open book. Whatever chapters he wanted hidden, Elizabeth had no problems revealing them. So why hide the one thing that bonded them?

Gideon led her into a large open space near the front door. "This is the living room. By the way, if you like the furniture and decorations, you can thank my mother for that. I can do great flower arranging, but I'm no good with decorating."

She scanned the staid yet tasteful decor that looked perfect for a single man. "Your mom has good taste."

"I'll be sure to tell her that." He paused and then said, "Nope. I won't."

She felt her eyebrows knit together. "Why not?"

Gideon chuckled. It almost sounded like a nervous laugh. "My mother sort of arranged for you and I to meet. She said that we would hit it off." He glanced at her. "I hate to admit to her again that she was right."

Janelle clasped her other hand over his. "It'll be our little secret."

He went down a long hallway and opened the door at the end. She didn't expect to see something like a small apartment attached to his home.

"This is the in-law suite I told you about. I made sure to have this built onto the house so that if I ever have to move my mother or any of my family members in with me, they can feel like they're still independent." He pointed to the small kitchen area. "Kitchen." He pointed to a door next to it. "Bathroom." He moved his hand to the left to another open doorway. "Bedroom." He cleared his throat as he squeezed her hand. "And this is the living room-dining room area."

"Very nice." Janelle peered up at him. "You're very considerate. I think your greenhouse is the only selfish thing you have in here. That and the motorcycle."

"You haven't been in my bedroom yet."

As soon as he said it, Janelle noticed how low his voice had become. He placed his hand on the small of her back and led her out of the suite. The gentle yet commanding touch became far too familiar very quickly. She made sure to stay in step with him so that he wouldn't have to release his hold.

"You were in this spare bedroom already." He opened a door and showed off a simple room decorated in dark cobalt-blue colors. "Every bedroom has its own bathroom and fireplace."

"Is that something you insisted on when the house was built?" Janelle followed alongside him to the base of the stairs.

Gideon nodded. "I like making sure my family and friends are taken care of."

"Yes, but who takes care of you?" Janelle watched his expression turn sullen before he broke his stare to look up the staircase.

"Come on. Let me show you upstairs and then we can eat." He took her on a quick tour of the other spare bedrooms. "As you can see, if you decide to spend the night, I have plenty of rooms for you to stay in, including an apartment." He started to go down the stairs.

"Wait." Janelle stood at the top landing.

Before Gideon turned, she glanced over at a room to the left where the double doors had been left closed.

He took a couple of steps down before returning her gaze. "Yes?"

"Well?" She crossed her arms.

"What?"

His coy act started to grate on her nerves. That didn't stop the man from looking damn sexy.

"After all that talk downstairs, you're not going to show me your bedroom?"

He didn't answer. He smiled as he stared at her. After a steamy silence, he said, "Maybe."

Chapter 12

During dinner, Gideon marveled at the fact that he and Janelle never stopped talking, never had an awkward silence…except when she'd asked him about his bedroom. He couldn't show her. If he'd allowed her in his room, he wouldn't have been able to stop himself from kissing her, touching her, making love to her. Every part of his being wanted that woman in his bed, especially after seeing her in her dress.

He hadn't given Penny any directives on the clothes she would pick out for Janelle. He didn't know what to expect. Until today, every time he'd seen Janelle, she'd outfitted herself in jeans, sneakers, a turtleneck, and a ratty, old sweater. Conversations with her matched her comfortable style.

"This food is delicious." Janelle finished what she had on her plate, stood, and served herself some more.

"Good. I appreciate a woman with a great appetite." He allowed his gaze to drop to her high, firm ass. A moan rattled in his throat before he covered the sound with a cough.

"Would you like some?" she asked.

When she turned around and looked at him quizzically, he realized her offer had nothing to do with her getting naked and riding him as dessert.

"No, thank you." He wiped his mouth. "You enjoy as much as you want." He watched her occupy her seat again as she dove into her tuna steak. "Looking at you, you would never guess that you eat the way you do."

"Fast metabolism." She smiled and wiped her mouth. "Did Queen teach you all how to cook?"

He nodded. "Among other things. Gunnar learned how to make spaghetti and that's it. He didn't want to clutter his mind on learning anything else." He laughed as he remembered his brother's frustration when their mother had tried teaching him how to make pancakes.

"I'll eat toast," Gunnar had proclaimed after burning batch after batch.

"Mom used to tell us a way to a woman's heart is through her stomach. Then she said that women don't eat as much as men do."

Janelle laughed. "That sounds like something Queen would say." She placed her napkin on the table and sat back.

Damn, Gideon wished she hadn't done that. He fought hard not to look down at her chest. He had to crank up the heat because he saw her hard nipples through her shirt. After a while, and after buckets of sweat poured from his head, he realized that maybe her reaction had nothing to do with the chill. Maybe, instead, excitement ran through her body, sexual excitement.

"What happened with Thelma? That was the name of the woman who worked for you, right?" He pushed his plate to the side to give her all his attention.

"She quit." Janelle kept her gaze down to the table. "That's it."

A tickle crept up the back of Gideon's neck. He wouldn't push her. He wanted tonight to go smoothly.

She brought her gaze up to meet his. "She was great. If she would come back, I would hire her all over again." She kept her gaze down to her plate. "But I'll be okay with her gone. Penny has been my best friend for years. It's great to be able to work with someone you know and trust."

"Kind of like being on a football team." With his third erection of the night now subsided, he stood and gathered the dishes. "You have to be able to trust that your teammates will have your back."

The words he'd spoken resonated with him and brought up memories of his last game. If he truly trusted his team, why hadn't he thrown the pass to Dennis? Hell, he would hate to admit to Dennis that he'd been right.

He pushed the thoughts from his mind and piled the dirty dishes next to the sink. When he looked back to the dining room, he found Janelle had moved to one of the kitchen barstools. When she sat, the flap of her dress dropped open, exposing the top of her black stockings.

Before he could think about all of the scintillating ways he could touch her thighs while she kept the stockings on, he turned back to the sink and started rinsing each plate to load into the dishwasher.

"I can understand why you weren't eager to give anything else up that day." Gideon kept his back to Janelle now that his lower half had started to rise again.

Down, boy. Let's get through the night.

"Yeah, that was a bummer. But there's more."

He stopped loading the dishwasher and returned his attention to her.

"You don't remember me, do you?" She gave him a mischievous smile.

"What are you talking about?" He wiped his hands and moved to the bar directly across from her.

"At least I think it was you." She looked down, snickered, and shook her head. "I can't believe I'm going to say this, but I will." She stared him in the eyes before saying, "I think you gave me my first kiss when I was seventeen."

Gideon cocked his head but said nothing. He didn't have the love-'em-and-leave-'em style like Thane, but he hadn't kept his heart and hormones tied up with one woman like Gunnar either. In the few dates he did have in high school, he didn't remember ever dating Janelle. He hadn't even heard of her name until his mother had given him Janelle's card.

"I was a huge nerd back in high school, bigger now than back then." Janelle rested her hands on the bar as she spoke. "I was raised by my maternal grandmother until she passed away when I hit about sixteen. Then I moved in with my mother. My mother, who is the complete opposite of me, kept telling me I needed to get out and meet people. I told her that I wanted to stay home to study. You would think a mother would love hearing that from their child." She shook her head. "Not ol' Ida Gold. She had me at fifteen. I guess she must have thought I was a late bloomer."

Gideon blinked at Janelle's candor but said nothing. He had similar negative thoughts about his biological mother. He would never voice that opinion out loud. He trusted Janelle, but he needed to know her more before he could let the wall come down completely.

"Sorry. I didn't mean to get heavy back there. Anyway, we lived near the Oceanfront Community Center. They would do these youth dances from time to time. She forced me to go to one. I epitomized a wall flower. I found a spot against the wall and stayed there. When they dimmed the lights in the big gym, I thought God had granted me my wish. I moved to a quiet corner next to the bleachers. I was content to hide there for the rest of the night. Then something happened."

Gideon's heart started to pound as he made a slow trek around the bar.

Janelle continued. "I looked up and there was a tall boy standing in front of me. In the darkened corner, I couldn't tell who it was. All I remember is him saying something about lips before he kissed me." She touched her lips as though recalling that moment. "It was the best and most surprising kiss I have ever had...until you kissed me behind my shop. You kissed me in the same way he did so many years ago. After that kiss, something happened in the gym and he ran off. I took that moment to run out of the gym. I walked all the way home, but I have never forgotten about that kiss." She peered up. "So when I saw you in my store the first time, I had in my head that you were the one who had kissed me before. When you didn't remember me, that pissed me off. Again, you didn't deserve that. It was me being—"

Gideon didn't give her a chance to finish her statement. He framed her face in his hands again. "Lips." Then he pressed his lips against hers.

Everything came back to him in that one moment. No wonder she seemed so familiar. He had been the one to kiss her.

He pulled back from her. "After all these years, I can't believe that was you."

Janelle put her hands on his arms and brought them down. "It really was you? You kissed me that night? Why? How?"

"My mother chaperoned those dances. She would make me and my brothers go with her and, like your mother, she would force us to mingle. She wanted us to dance with girls who hadn't come with dates. She would tell us every girl deserves to be treated like a princess."

Janelle stopped smiling. "Oh, so you felt sorry for me?"

He shook his head. "No. I didn't even see you until I looked through the bleachers. I could barely see you in that dark corner. I remember that one of the strobe lights shined across a part of your face." He smoothed the pad of his thumb over her bottom lip. "Your lips. I couldn't resist you, or at least your lips. I was going to ask you to dance, but I couldn't stop staring at your lips. I took that opportunity to kiss you." He chuckled. "Truth be told, you were my first kiss."

That bit of news brought a smile to her face. "So what happened? You ran from me."

"A fight had broken out. My brother had gotten into it with some other kid. I went to break it up. By the time I came back to you to introduce myself and apologize for kissing you without permission, you were gone."

"You are still kissing me without permission." She screwed up her lips to keep from laughing.

"Wait a minute. I asked for your permission for my last kiss. But if you don't remember, I'll ask again." He moved in closer to her, his lips mere inches from hers. "Is it okay if I kiss you now? Would you like that?"

Her breathing increased. He felt her breath feathering over his lips.

Janelle nodded. "Yes."

"Maybe it'll happen again." He backed away from her and went back to the dishwasher.

She growled. "You are an evil, evil man."

"But I made you dinner."

"Which was wonderful."

"And got you over a hundred roses. Would another man do that for you?" When Gideon didn't hear a response, he gazed up and saw Janelle sauntering toward him.

"No." She licked her lips.

"My God. What idiot let you go?" Gideon enjoyed talking to her, discussing plants, and kissing her. He found her charming, funny, and beautiful. What man wouldn't want her?

"Let's not talk about that jerk unless you want to talk about yours."

Gideon added cleanser to the dishwasher, closed the door, which got rid of the barrier between the two of them, and started the cycle.

"Nothing to say really. Our schedules didn't mesh. I live on the East Coast. She lives on the West. Neither of us wanted to move. We were doomed." He approached Janelle. In a lowered voice, he said, "Thank God." He put his arm around her shoulders and led her to his den.

"Oh."

He brought her to a brown, overstuffed couch and encouraged her to take a seat. "I thought we could watch movies or play some board games." He leaned over her body. "You aren't the only nerd here."

That admission made her laugh. "Okay, testing your nerd levels. If we watch a movie, will it be black and white?"

Gideon picked up a remote and called up his movie library on his large-screened TV. "Comedy, drama, or romance? I'm also a bit of a sci-fi junkie."

"Man of my dreams. I'm thinking *Blade Runner*. What do you think?"

Gideon brought up the movie and started it. "I'm thinking this is the best Valentine's Day ever."

He sat down next to her, turned off the lights, wrapped his arm around her shoulders, and pulled her in next to him. Without missing a beat, she wrapped one arm around his waist and she rested her other hand on his chest. She removed her shoes and curled her long legs on the couch.

"By the way, my last serious boyfriend left me after I graduated college. We had spent a night at the Cavalier Hotel as a gift to ourselves. The next morning, he said I didn't fit into his plans." She exhaled like she'd been holding on to that secret for years.

Gideon tightened his hold around her shoulders. "Asshole. Pardon my language."

Janelle settled onto his chest. "No apology necessary."

He propped the leg with his bum knee up on an ottoman.

She gazed up to his face. "Are you okay? I mean your leg and all. Will you be able to—"

He silenced her with a kiss on her forehead. "Let's just watch the movie." He looked down at her. "It'll be fine." If only he believed that.

At the end of the movie, Gideon found Janelle asleep against him. Without jostling her too much, he turned off the TV. Mustering as much strength as he could, he picked her up in his arms. He felt a sharp pain shooting up from his knee to the top of his head. He gritted his teeth for a moment and breathed through the pain. Once it subsided, he took his guest up the stairs to a bedroom far from his room.

He'd thought about putting her in the bedroom downstairs or even in the suite. If she woke up before he did, he didn't want her feeling so far removed from him.

At the top of the landing, he went to a spare bedroom and turned on the overhead light by brushing his elbow against the light switch on the wall. As carefully as he could, he pulled the comforter and sheet down and placed Janelle on the bed.

As soon as her head hit the pillow, she snuggled against it. Gideon's gaze dropped down her body. Her dress had fallen open, exposing her completely shaven sex. Before he could stare at her body any longer, he covered her and extinguished the light.

* * * *

Janelle eased her hand between her legs as soon as Gideon's image filled her head. "Mmm, Gideon." She busied her other hand by cupping her breast through her dress.

He'd been a perfect gentleman all night, catering to her needs, even doing the dishes. If she didn't want him before, now she really did.

She massaged her breast and found her small hand to be a poor substitute for Gideon's large one. As soon as her fingers brushed against her clitoris, she opened her eyes. Janelle peered around the darkened room, trying to get her bearings. She felt next to her, hoping to touch an end table. With all of the spare bedrooms Gideon had, she had no idea where he had placed her.

When she felt a table, she reached for a lamp and found it. It took her no time to find the switch and turn on the light. As soon as her eyes adjusted, she recognized the room as one of the spares upstairs. So Gideon wanted her close. She wanted to be close to him.

Janelle threw the covers off her body and peered down. She still had on her dress…and no panties. She got out of bed and padded to the door. Without thinking, she opened the door and made a sprint over to Gideon's bedroom. She kept her mouth open to take in as much oxygen as she could as she made this bold move.

Before she could reach his door, it opened. Gideon stood on the other side wearing only pajama pants. Janelle stood a couple of feet away from him.

"I want you in my bed now." Gideon didn't move. His massive chest rose and fell with his harried breaths.

Janelle pulled the string that held her dress together and allowed it to fall open, exposing her nude body. "Take me."

Chapter 13

Exposing her body to Gideon felt right. She ached for him. Needed him. Craved him. In sleep, she dreamed of only him, how he would take her, conquer her, make her come. As soon as she'd awakened, she'd sought him to satisfy her deep need. The throbbing between her legs wouldn't stop until he had her, all of her.

Gideon pulled her into his arms. The roughness of his hands brushed against her skin and scratched her so deliciously that it tickled and teased her. She pressed her breasts against his bare chest. Janelle felt his heart beating hard, pounding in the same rhythm as hers. In her mind, it meant that he wanted the same thing she did. Total satisfaction.

As he kissed her, he stepped back into his darkened bedroom. Janelle still wouldn't get the opportunity to see the actual layout. Right now, she didn't care. Her new dress lay in a heap on the floor outside of his bedroom. Her shoes remained in his den downstairs. Only her stockings covered her legs.

She broke from the kiss and started pulling down her stockings.

"Leave them on," he said with a growl.

Janelle smiled. "Yes, sir."

She coasted her hands down his muscular chest to his rippled abs and to the waistband of his pants. Before she could touch him, Gideon grabbed her wrists.

"Let me take care of you." He nudged her back to his California king-sized bed.

She fell back on it and crawled to the center on her elbows.

Gideon covered her body with his. As he cradled the back of her head with his hand, he brushed his lips over hers, almost stealing her breath since she gasped with each pass. She swallowed and slipped her hand behind his head. When she fisted his hair, he captured her mouth.

                    Crystal B. Bright

His tongue sought hers and found it, teased it. She arched her back, needing to feel him on her at all times. The length of him pressed against her stomach. As she reached down to touch him, Gideon arrested her hand again.

"Touch me and it'll be all over with." He cocked a smile at the side of his mouth. "I want this to last."

Janelle did the only thing she could do, nod. He kissed down her body. In a slow and methodical way, he placed his lips over her collarbones from one side to the other as though imprinting her with a sensual necklace.

His massive hand palmed her breast. She'd never thought she had a large chest, a fact her mother loved teasing her about whenever they talked.

Gideon held her like whatever she had suited him. He planted pecks along the center of her body and once he got in between her breasts, he dragged his tongue to one side. As he continued to hold her tit, he kissed her nipple first before swiping his tongue over it.

Janelle sucked air between her teeth and writhed on the bed as he maintained his decadent treatment. He twirled his tongue around her stiff peak, which caused her back to rise off the bed.

"Gideon, oh, God." She whipped her head to the side when he didn't stop.

Once he covered her whole breast with his mouth, she cried out. Janelle kept her grip on his hair while she snatched a handful of his comforter in the other to keep her grounded. None of this seemed real. How could she be in bed with a Super Bowl champion, the nerdy girl who'd hidden behind bleachers in high school and didn't want to be noticed?

Gideon gave her one last lick and kiss before making his way over to her other tit, where he gave it the same salacious treatment, swirling his tongue around it and sucking her until she felt spent. Janelle's body squirmed underneath his as light tingles washed over her. She wrapped her legs around him to keep him in his position. She used her heels to try and push down his pajama bottoms.

Before she could get them over his droolworthy ass, Gideon continued laving her body, creeping his tongue over her ribs then to her stomach. For a man who battled behemoth men on the field each week, he treated her body so tenderly.

Janelle barely noticed when her giant of a man managed to position himself between her thighs. He pressed her legs apart while he caressed her nether lips with his thumbs.

"Gideon. Please, please." Each word came out in a gasp, like her life depended on his next move.

Gideon didn't say a word. He blew his hot breath over her throbbing clit. The light sensation had her sucking air between her gritted teeth.

When he flicked his tongue over her slick, hardened nub, Janelle arched her back and held her breath. No one had ever made her feel this cherished, this desirable, this sexy.

Like he had done it a million times before, he twirled his tongue around her clit. Her legs twitched. Each time she attempted to close her thighs around his head, he gently eased them apart.

When he covered her sex with his mouth and pressed his tongue against her, Janelle jackknifed up from the bed. As she held the back of his head, her body gyrated, grinding her vagina in his mouth. She didn't recognize herself from her reactions. Never had she been this aggressive in bed. Never had she demanded anything for herself sexually.

Janelle kept pumping her hips, thankful that she'd kept herself shaved completely. She felt her body trembling. Her stomach tightened into a ball before contracting into spasms. She didn't want this to happen already. She didn't want to be the first to have an orgasm. At best, she wanted to come with Gideon.

Gideon kept his mouth over her while his skillful tongue touched, teased, and tantalized her. Then he hummed. The vibrations went through her body until she felt like her heart would explode.

Before she could stop herself, Janelle's body froze in its spot as the strong orgasmic wave washed over her.

She reclined and attempted to catch her breath. "I want to taste you."

Gideon pulled off his pants. "Another time. I need to feel you."

He opened a drawer next to the bed. In the dark, Janelle couldn't see what he retrieved. From the telltale sounds of a plastic wrapper being opened, she suspected he pulled out a condom.

While still sitting on the bed, he rolled it on himself with his back to her. Janelle realized that Gideon hadn't allowed her to either touch his penis or even see it.

She touched his back. "I don't care what size you are." She kissed his shoulder. "It'll be great because you're great."

She thought she heard Gideon snickering.

"Thanks, babe. You keep that in mind once I'm in you."

Before he did anything, he turned on the light next to the bed. Then he climbed on top of her. The wild look in his eyes excited her. His blond hair fell forward around his face, giving him more of a primal appearance.

"No matter what, you keep looking at me, okay? Don't stop looking me in my eyes," he said.

Janelle nodded and then cut her gaze down to see what dangled between his legs.

"Hey, look at me." He braced one hand on the mattress next to her head as he reach down between their bodies with the other. "That's it. Right in my eyes." He smoothed the tip of his cock up and down her opening until he finally eased the tip inside.

She squeezed his shoulders. Gideon slid more of his shaft in her channel. As instructed, she kept her stare directly on his eyes. Then she stopped breathing. The girth of him hit her first before she recognized how deep he had gone in her.

"Breathe, babe. Breathe." He gave her quick pecks and held her chin. "Good?"

She managed to take in a deep inhalation. On the exhale, she said, "Big."

He smiled and moved himself in and out of her so slowly, making it seem like he controlled time and space. "You want me to stop?"

Janelle nodded, but her body had other plans. She coiled her legs around his hips and undulated her body under him. "Don't."

His thrusting slowed down.

"Stop." She bit her bottom lip.

"You want to—"

She cut him off. "Don't." Then she wrapped her arms around his body and dug her fingernails into his tough flesh. Her hips never stopped moving.

"We don't have to—"

"Stop." She kissed the side of his face.

The saltiness of his sweat met her lips and tongue. She savored him. Every part of him.

"I don't want to hurt you. If this is too much, we can—"

She held his face in her hands and stared into his eyes. "Don't stop."

His hard member found her spot. With each thrust and curve of his hip, he managed to hit the sensitive zone each time.

She had her head craned back as he slid inside her, stretching her to a painfully good level. When she looked up, she noticed Gideon wince.

"What's wrong?" She placed her hand on the side of his face.

He shook his head. "Good."

He kissed her, allowing her to taste her own juices that still coated his lips. It felt strange to taste herself, experience her level of saltiness. The fact that she knew how he'd obtained her essence curled her toes again.

She stared him in the eyes and noticed him scowl again. "Am I too tight?"

His eyes widened. "Are you kidding me? No such thing." He thrust deep and groaned. "Perfect."

He grumbled, then punched the mattress.

Although Janelle hadn't known him for very long or had even seen him play, she could tell something didn't feel good to him.

"It's your knee, right?" She sought truth in his eyes.

"I'll be fine." He kissed her like he wanted to reassure her.

She didn't believe him. With all of her might, she pushed against his shoulder and managed to roll him onto his side. She moved back to disengage.

"What are you doing?"

Before Janelle answered him, she turned her back to him and pressed her ass against his crotch. "We can do it this way." She looked back at him and smiled. "Easier on your knee."

"Yeah, but I can't see your face and I'll be damned if the first time I get my dream woman in bed, I don't get to see her come." Gideon tried turning Janelle on to her back.

"I hope you were looking up earlier when you were between my legs." She reached behind herself, held his impressive shaft and aimed it at her pussy opening. Before he could protest or push, she ground herself down onto him.

"Christ, you don't play fair." He wrapped his arm underneath her body and held her breast as he swept her top leg over his for better access.

It didn't take Gideon long to get back into the same rhythm. It also didn't take Janelle long to realize how easily they fell into a comfortable pace. She reached back and held his head, a move that prompted him to press his lips against her neck and cheek.

"You have the best ass." He eased the hand he'd been resting on her hip down between her legs.

Janelle's body trembled in anticipation of his touch. He brushed his thumb over her distended clitoris.

"Yes." She curved her head down and nibbled on his strong forearm. "Feels so good."

She moved with Gideon as one unit, back and forth, slow and easy. Sweat covered both of their bodies.

She felt him shaking, a first since they started. He'd been Mr. Control. Her hero. Her savior. She knew he would be breaking soon, because she wanted to…again. Janelle pressed her thighs together to trap his hand and him. Then she gyrated her body more.

"No." Gideon shook his head. "Not like this."

He removed his hand and pulled out of her.

"What are you doing? I was so close." Frustration filled her voice.

He sat up and moved to the edge of the bed. As he held her hand, he pulled Janelle toward him until she figured out he wanted her to stand. When she did, she got to finally see Gideon's full package.

She blinked as she studied the length and thickness of him.

"Come here." He pulled her over to him and helped her onto his lap so that she faced him.

She spread her legs and straddled his. "I won't hurt you if I'm on your lap?"

He shook his head. "I'm fine." He held her waist with one hand and the base of his shaft with the other. "Down. I need you." He stared into her eyes again. "I need you."

As carefully as he had done before, she eased him into her vagina inch by inch until fully seated. Then she wrapped her legs around his waist and gripped his broad shoulders.

With his one hand on her backside, palming it like a football, and his other hand behind her head, he thrust his hips up, hitting her spot again and never disengaging his stare.

The intensity of the moment shook her. She wrapped her mind around the absurdity of the situation by smothering him with kisses. Only then did it seem real.

"I'm-I'm-I'm—" Janelle didn't know when she lost her memory of all vocabulary. With the intensity of the moment, she couldn't form words, sentences, thoughts.

She pressed her forehead against his as he continued filling her, satisfying her. Gideon didn't laugh at her. He nodded. He squeezed her ass cheek.

"Come with me." Not waiting for a response, he captured her mouth and slid his tongue inside.

With his mouth on hers, Janelle had no other recourse than to scream against his lips. Gideon released a long, low moan and shook as he gave her two hard pumps before settling down.

He swept her hair from her face. "Better than I thought." He smiled and kissed every available part of her face.

"I can't believe you carried me upstairs." She reached behind her and patted the knee she'd seen with the brace. "You could have let me sleep on the couch."

Gideon shook his head. "Never. If I didn't think you would have called me a pervert, I would have put you in my bed. But I'm a man. I respect you as a woman. I couldn't sleep knowing what was in the next room. As soon as I heard you opening that door, I got out of bed and prayed with each step I took to my door that you wouldn't ask to go home."

Janelle smiled. "You could have woken me up. For this, I wouldn't have minded." She smoothed his hair from his face. "And you can ask for help." She held onto his shoulders. "I don't mind being on top if you aren't able to—"

He stopped her. "I told you. I'm fine." He removed her from his lap and placed her on the bed. "Sorry for cutting you off. I'm going to clean up."

Gideon disappeared into his en suite bathroom and closed the door.

For a man who seemed to be an open book and have his life documented at every turn, he kept himself closed off to the world. Janelle curled under the comforter. Now that she had him, what the hell would she do next?

Chapter 14

Janelle snuggled down into the firm but comfortable bed. Not any bed. Gideon's bed. Gideon Wells's bed. Gideon Super Bowl Champion Wells in his massive beachside mansion.

She stretched her legs. The sweet soreness between her thighs reminded her of what she'd done last night and earlier that morning. Janelle felt her mouth pull to the side in a self-satisfied smile. She'd had no idea going into Valentine's Day that she would have the night that she did.

Janelle reached over to touch Gideon. For as long as she lived, she would forever remember his hard body, how he handled her, damn near carried her like a rag doll. She liked his control. The more she extended her hand, the more her heart pounded for the wrong reasons.

Nothing. She felt nothing but the mattress. Or had it been the mattress at all? Could she be on a couch? Janelle took a deep breath and inhaled the distinct aroma of roses.

Oh, God, no.

Had Gideon carried her spent body back downstairs to the living room where she and Penny had placed all the arrangements of roses Gideon had ordered? She hadn't felt him carrying her up the stairs to put her to bed when she'd fallen asleep during the movie. After their wild night, she wouldn't have awakened if he had carried her back downstairs.

In her mind, that treatment would be worse than what her ex had done to her. Gideon had used her and thrown her away. She squeezed her eyes shut and curled her legs closer to her body.

"Can't be happening," she whispered to herself.

"You woke up."

Janelle shook when she heard the rumbling voice. Still refusing to open her eyes, she pulled the comforter up to cover her head, a protective move she hadn't done since she used to wear pigtails to school. She wanted to keep the fantasy about her great night with this football hero.

She hoped he didn't want to send her back to home, back to nothing, a failing business, a lonely apartment and a hole in her heart.

She felt a sinking feeling behind her, then a large arm surrounding her waist. Janelle instantly moved to touch him, clutch his arm. She stopped herself. She'd already gotten too deep too quick with her feelings for him. No use getting attached even more.

"You said the next time I should wake you up." Gideon brushed himself behind her.

Janelle felt his hardness against her backside. No way did he carry her out of his bedroom and now wanted sex.

With anger bubbling in her gut, she sat and turned to him. Only then did she notice the sunlight-filled room. As she lay nestled still in Gideon's bed, covered in a pure white comforter with matching white pillows, she noticed rich-red rose petals covering every inch of the bed, the floor and out the door.

She whipped her head around to stare at Gideon, who only looked back at her with a self-satisfied smile. "You did all this?"

"You don't get over a hundred roses and not use the petals." He cupped her face. "I was hoping to surprise you."

"Trust me. You did." She curled back down and kissed him.

Gideon broke from the kiss. "You're shaking. Are you cold?"

Janelle shook her head. A sudden rush of emotions took over her. "No one has ever done something like this for me." She scanned the room.

In the full light of day, she noticed the expansive space. A large standing dresser sat across from the bed. All the oversize furniture reminded her of the man in bed with her. Large, imposing, sturdy.

"I thought—" Janelle stopped. She had to quit lumping all men into one category. That attitude epitomized her mother's mentality. She didn't want to be like Ida Gold. Certainly, Gideon didn't deserve to be categorized with other men.

"What? What were you thinking?" Gideon put his hand on her bare stomach.

"I reached over and I didn't feel you." She kept her head down, afraid to see his expression. "I smelled the roses. I thought you moved me back downstairs." She stole a peek at him.

Gideon's disappointed expression cut deep in her.

She averted her gaze. "I'm sorry. You didn't deserve that. I was burned before. It's hard for me to open up, to trust." When she looked at him again, his face softened. "I hope you understand."

He squeezed a snicker through his nose. "More than you know." He slid his hand back and forth over her stomach. "My mother taught me and my brothers to respect women. I would never let you or any other woman feel inferior or less than."

"I'm glad you said that." She smiled as she looked around the room. "And I'm thrilled you're a romantic." She held his hand. "You should have been honest with me."

He stopped smiling. "When did I lie?"

"Not lie." She peered down his body, specifically his crotch area. "Withheld some information. Why didn't tell me about your, um, assets?"

Gideon worried his eyebrows for a bit until he followed her gaze down his body. When he arrived at the destination, he laughed. "Really? You don't think it would sound a bit cocky, for lack of a better term, to say that I may be well endowed?"

"We could have discussed it first." She crossed her arms over her chest to look indignant. Too bad her body screamed for more of him.

"At what point should I talk about it? Should I have said something during dinner? If I had, I would have sounded like I expected us to have sex, and I didn't. Should I have said something when you came out of the bedroom and we were looking at each other? Or should I have told you when I saw you at your store for the very first time and thought you looked so cute."

Janelle gasped. "You did?" Then she quickly sobered to the moment. "It doesn't matter. You must have thought it would be an issue since you wouldn't show me before we had sex."

He nodded and sat against his massive padded, white leather headboard. He exhaled. "I have been disappointed the last few times I've tried to be intimate with women. I lost my virginity at eighteen when I went away to college. The young lady I was with was also a virgin at the time. Between our inexperience, my eagerness, and my size, it did not make for a good scene. She said she liked it, but we never did it again. Nope. That's not true. We tried it again. After the second time, she called me a freak and broke up with me."

Janelle covered her mouth. "Really? Did you ever hear from her again?"

He nodded. "As soon as I made pro. She called me out of the blue and tried to reminisce about the good old days. I reminded her of the freak comment and didn't hear from her again."

"And with Hilary?"

He glared at her before dropping his stare. "It didn't work out." He reached over to her and held her hand. "I wanted to be with you." He connected his gaze to hers. "I wanted you to want me, regardless of who I am or my size. If this is not what you want, tell me now."

Janelle waited a beat before removing her hand from his. "Okay. Cards on the table. I want to see it."

Gideon blinked. "Okay." He started to push the comforter down when she stopped him.

"Let me drive."

He laughed. "Fine."

She eased the covers down his rippled abdomen and stopped right at his hips. She swallowed before revealing him. His impressive penis lay dormant between his thick thighs. Janelle reached for him. As soon as she touched it, as though she needed to check for its authenticity, he sucked air between his clenched teeth.

* * * *

The more Gideon hung out with Janelle, the more he started to fall for her. He hadn't expected her to bring up his method to avoid telling her about his dick. He thought that if he satisfied her, she would forgive him. Her need to be respected on all levels impressed him.

Now that she wanted to see him, all of him, he had to contain himself. Her first touch broke him. She stroked his shaft, gently at first. Her fingertips danced down the length of him to his thick tip and then back up again to the base where she twirled her fingers in his sandy nest of hair.

"Nice." She never broke her stare from his cock.

Janelle slid down the bed and slithered between his legs as she held him. No way could she miss him getting hard in her hand.

"You don't have to do this." He waved his hand to her.

"I want to."

The first teasing swipe of her tongue over the weeping tip had him thankful she wanted to pleasure him orally. She swirled her tongue around the mushroom-shaped head and then eased her mouth down as far as she could go. Janelle wrapped both hands around him in a staggered fashion and twisted her hands in the opposite direction of each other while her mouth continued coating him.

As a kid, he and his brothers had made that same hand motion on each other's arms and called it giving an Indian burn, a derogatory term their mother made them stop saying as soon as she heard it. When Janelle did that same hand motion on him with her delicate fingers and soft hands, he wanted to scream mercy in a good way.

More than the motion with her mouth and hands, the fact that she kept constant eye contact with him got to him the most. He returned her stare as his breathing increased. Instead of gripping the back of her head, he fisted the comforter around him. He couldn't stop his hips from gyrating, which slid his cock in and out of her mouth.

In response, Janelle tightened her lips around his shaft. Each time he stroked up, she pressed her tongue against the tip. She kept up this technique for what seemed like hours. When she reached down and started massaging his sac, Gideon couldn't hold back.

"So close." He said it as a warning.

Even with him in her mouth, Janelle managed a smile. She bobbed her head up and down faster while her hands seemed to be everywhere at once. He felt her stroking the skin between his asshole and his balls. That had him wanting to climb the walls.

"Can't hold back." Gideon's toes curled.

He felt his legs shaking as he tried hard not to release his load into this goddess's mouth. Then he heard her whisper, "Come."

His muscles tightened as he climaxed, releasing his seed into her awaiting mouth. She swallowed every bit of his essence. When she pulled back, she grazed her teeth over his sensitive tip.

"I'm not delicate. I'm a woman. Treat me like one." She sat up on her knees, leaned forward and kissed him.

The taste of himself didn't turn him off as much as he thought it would. He had done the same to her last night.

"I'm assuming that's the bathroom." She pointed to an open doorway in the corner.

Gideon nodded. "Extra toothbrush and washcloths are in the cabinet. As soon as I get feeling to my legs, I'll join you."

She laughed. Then she glanced at the clock in the room and cursed. "Sorry. I can't believe that's the time. I'm so late for work."

"I'll call Penny for you." He started to reach for his phone next to the bed.

"No. If you do, she'll know I've been here all night."

An eerie feeling crept up the back of Gideon's head. "Is that a problem?"

"With Penny? Yes. She was the one that sent that online gossip site a picture of us. She has a big mouth. I don't want to get anyone's tongue wagging any more than they are now." She scanned the room and then stopped. "My purse and bag are downstairs."

"Good." Gideon hopped out of bed and headed toward her on shaky legs. "You're going to shower and get cleaned up. Then get dressed and I'll take you home." He glanced at the clock. "My mom's surgery is today."

"Oh, wow. Where is it going to be?"

"Virginia Beach General Hospital."

"Take me home so I can change, and I'll go with you."

Gideon shook his head. "You have a business to run. I don't want to interfere with that. But I appreciate the offer."

Janelle held his hand. "I don't want to be there only for you. Elizabeth is important to me. I want to show her my support."

He cupped her cheek. "I appreciate that. Keep your phone handy. I'll keep you updated on her progress."

"But—"

Gideon held Janelle around her waist and guided her to the bathroom. "Shower now. Questions later."

He allowed her to use the shower while he brushed his teeth. He knew if trapped in a small space with her that they would never leave his home. If his mother didn't have surgery that day, he would have proposed that option to Janelle.

As soon as she finished her shower, Gideon jumped in, but not before giving her a kiss as he passed her. By the time he finished his shower, dried himself and got dressed, he found Janelle downstairs in his kitchen wearing the red dress, her sneakers with no socks, and her heavy work jacket.

"Great outfit." Gideon chuckled.

"I can't put on my other clothes. They're dirty." She made a face and shook her head.

"My mom has spent a night or two here, and I believe she left some of her clothes. You want to put them on?" He poured a glass of orange juice and handed it to Janelle.

Without question, she accepted it. She took a sip before she answered. "That's okay. As soon as you drop me off, I'll change." She held up her phone. "I've already called Penny and told her I overslept, which isn't a lie."

"So how would you have explained going to the hospital?"

"Like I said before, Queen Elizabeth has been a great mentor to me."

"And your competitor."

Janelle shook her head. "I don't think of her like that."

"Then you and my mother have a lot in common. She said the same thing about you when she told me to go see you if I needed help."

"Need any help now?" Janelle's voice dipped down low enough to cause his dormant cock to awaken.

He stood next to her as she leaned her back against the counter by the sink. "I could always use a good hand. What about you?" He planted a sweet peck on her forehead. "Need anything?" He kissed the tip of her nose. "Want anything?" He put his hand to her stomach as he kissed her lips.

As his hand traveled down her body, he hoped she still didn't have on any underwear. He couldn't tell while she wore her heavy jacket.

"Gideon, what are you doing?" She held his arm but didn't stop him.

He parted the flap at the bottom half of her dress, exposing her naked pussy. It had only been a few hours, but Gideon had to have her again. He'd tried waiting, seeing if she wanted to see him again. The more he stared at her, the more his body tingled. She'd become a drug that he needed.

"Giving you something to remember me by." As soon as his hand coasted down to the heat between her thighs, she placed her free hand on the counter as though she needed to brace herself. For what he had planned, she had the right idea.

Gideon slipped his middle finger between her slick nether lips. Janelle parted her legs without him asking. Her sneakers squeaked over the tile floor, which made the scene feel juvenile, like they were a couple of teenagers making out in the bathroom. He didn't care. As soon as the aroma of her sex hit him, he couldn't stop.

He kissed her. He slid his tongue into her mouth and eased his middle finger into her hot core. Janelle moaned, and he felt her slick inner walls closing around his digit. He moved his finger in and out of her ever so slowly, attempting to churn her orgasm.

Gideon felt her hips starting to move back and forth. He stopped kissing her long enough to ask, "You like this? You want more?"

Janelle nodded.

He used the heel of his hand to brush again her clit. When she buckled, he wrapped his arm around her.

"Driving me crazy." She removed her hand from the counter and used it to rub his growing erection through his jeans.

"Make that two of us." He nibbled the side of her neck.

"Please. Please. Please." She got up on her tiptoes and tilted her head back.

Before he could introduce a second finger, Janelle's body shivered. She pressed her face against his chest and released a low moan.

"Bag. Bag." She looked up at him with desperation in her eyes.

"You want to leave now?"

Janelle shook her head. "Condoms. In my bag. Please."

Gideon didn't need to hear her plea. He found her backpack and slammed it on the counter. She dove into it, tossing out clothes and makeup until she got to the stash. She pulled out strings of different types of condom wrappers.

"Which one?" she asked as she pulled off her coat and tossed it on the floor.

He found one in a black wrapper that would work. As he pulled the rubber from the package, she worked on undoing his jeans.

With his mother's surgery happening that day, he shouldn't be thinking about sex. After the incredible night they had and what she'd done to him that morning, he couldn't fill his head with anything else.

It didn't help that Janelle had been so thoughtful during their hot session, asking him multiple times about his knee and even offering to get on top of him, ride him until they both came. Right now, he felt no pain.

She managed to undo his pants and push them down his ass. As she reached out to touch him, he stopped her.

"Hands on the counter."

Janelle did as instructed and even lifted her dress to expose her naked ass.

"Christ." He rolled the prophylactic down the length of him.

He held his hard shaft and aimed it at her core. Once he pushed the tip inside, Janelle arched her back.

"Easy." She craned her head back to look at him.

He nodded. "Of course."

Fully seated, he exhaled. The tightness welcomed him, held him hostage inside her constricting channel, and he loved it.

"Oh, God." Janelle pressed her back against his chest. "Feel so good."

Gideon had to almost thank that wayward cheerleader for coming into his home. If it hadn't been for her, he wouldn't have canceled his contract with his cleaning company. Now he didn't have to worry if anyone would be coming over to his home at this very moment. He had Janelle all to himself.

He pumped slowly in her. Each thrust in, she clamped down on him, as though she didn't want him to escape. Gideon snaked his hand in between her body and the counter. To give her the ultimate pleasure, he brushed his thumb over her distended clitoris.

"Yes," Janelle hissed. She reached behind to hold the back of Gideon's head.

She used her other hand to keep herself anchored to the counter.

He wanted to experience more of her, have all of her. He wrapped his free arm around her body and dipped it inside the top of her dress to cup her tit.

"Yes, I'm there." She bit her bottom lip as she pressed her body against his.

"Scream if you need to. Don't hold it in." He gave her clit a playful flicking motion that had her body trembling.

"Don't. Don't. Don't." She shook her head. "Can't stand."

Gideon regarded her statement and pulled out of her long enough to turn her around and place her bare ass on top of the counter. It didn't take her long to reconnect her lips back on to his or for him to insert himself into her center. Both had them gasping for air.

He untied her dress and pushed it open to expose more of her body. Once he did that, he palmed a breast in one hand. He twirled his thumb around her hardened pebble, which got him rewarded with her legs clamped around his hips.

With a curve of his hips, Gideon must have hit her spot. Janelle clutched his shirt with both hands. She stared at him in his eyes until she started to release a scream.

"Come on. Let me hear it." He increased his speed.

The motion had her thrashing her legs. As she came, so did Gideon. He stayed connected to her until he fully unloaded. Out of breath but sated, he brushed his lips over hers before pressing against them hard.

"You are the best cardio ever." He laughed, which prompted her to do the same.

"You aren't so bad yourself." She ran her fingers through his hair.

Gideon took a step back to disengage. "I'll wait for you while you go clean up."

She eased down from the counter with the help of his hands around her waist guiding her down. "No. I want to go home with your scent all over me. I'll shower when I get home. Who knows when this will ever happen to me again?"

He blinked as he ducked into the guest bathroom downstairs. "What are you talking about?" He disposed of the used condom and washed up a little before fastening his pants.

As Janelle tied her dress again, she said, "Are you saying you want to see me again?"

"Are you thinking that I wouldn't want to?"

"Yes."

"Then you're wrong." He held her face and kissed her. "I want to see you again. I want to see where this goes."

She offered a small smile. "Until you go."

A stone plummeted in Gideon's gut. "I'm not going anywhere. I'm a Virginia Beach Wolf, so my home base is here." He would leave out the fact that his tenure on the team remained tentative at this time.

"But when Queen is better, you'll travel. You'll go train." Janelle picked up her coat and covered herself again. "You might meet someone more exciting, like another actress."

Gideon stood toe-to-toe with Janelle. He wanted to make sure she could see the sincerity in his eyes and in every spoken word. "You are worth it. You are good enough. But you didn't need me to tell you that." He put his finger to her chest. "I judge a woman by what's in here."

That statement got her to smile.

"The fact that you're drop-dead gorgeous is a bonus." He winked.

She gave him a playful jab to his stomach.

"Besides, you need me to help find your voice." He patted her backside and put his hand to the small of her back to lead her to the garage.

"Hey, I'm only at a loss for words when I'm about to climax. Otherwise, I have no problem speaking my mind."

He opened the door and watched her go down the stairs to his car. "Really? In our regular conversations, you don't have a problem expressing yourself. I think you've even yelled at me once." Like a gentleman, he held the passenger-side door open for her. He even fastened her seat belt, a move that allowed him a way to kiss her. After he got in on the driver's side, he continued with his assessment. "During sex, you suppress your screams. You worry me because I think you even stop breathing at times. You have to let it out. I don't live in an apartment, condo, or townhouse. Scream all you want."

He started his car and eased out of the garage. By the time he brought his attention back over to Janelle, she shot death rays with her glare.

"You, of all people, are giving me that advice on letting go? Go down Laskin Road and turn on Virginia Beach Boulevard."

"Got it. And what did you mean me of all people? You don't think I express myself?" Gideon thought about her words. Had she never seen him on a football field, leading his team to victory? Did he need to take her with him the next time he volunteered his time at the community center? Or maybe she'd missed hearing him grunt and groan all night long.

"I don't know. Tell me, Gideon. How's your knee?" She pressed her back against the door as she kept her stare on him.

He avoided looking at her. "It's fine."

"It is? So it's fine for a young man to wear a knee brace? It's fine for an athlete like yourself to limp the way you do? And the fact that doing missionary style bothered you is—"

He interrupted her speech. "Okay, it's a little sore after the Super Bowl. Not a big deal." He didn't mean to snap at her but he didn't want to talk about his condition, not with her, not with his coach, and not with his mother. He could handle himself. He always had.

Janelle directed him on how to get to her apartment building. After that, they rode together in silence. Gideon stewed about her intrusive questioning. He had been there for her, both in business and in bed. What more could she want?

He stopped in front of her building. He pulled into a spot and parked. "I want to see you again."

She regarded him for a moment and then slowly shook her head. "No."

When she started to open the door, he held her hand. "How did we go from having the best night and morning ever to you not wanting to see me again?"

"Because you don't need me. You want me." She lowered her head. "It's flattering for a nerdy girl like me to have met a guy like you, and for you to treat me so wonderfully. I will always remember the roses and waking up in a sea of petals." She placed her other hand on top of his. "And the sex." She took a deep breath. "But if you can't share with me everything that's going on in your life, then I'm nothing more than a groupie or something. I know the surface of you but not what makes you tick. I need more. I deserve that."

When she removed her hand to leave, he squeezed her fingers to keep her there. "Why won't you and everyone else believe me when I say there's nothing to worry about?" He put his car in Park and turned his body so that he faced her completely. "My mother adopted me when I was about six or seven years old. Gunnar was a year older than me and already a handful. Thane, my younger brother, was just a baby. Gunnar was going through some things because of what our biological mother did to us as kids, so he acted out. Thane was a sickly baby. I remember Queen Elizabeth taking him to doctor's appointments all the time. Between Gunnar's troubles and Thane's issues, I wanted to be the one thing that my mother didn't have to worry about. I kept quiet. I did my chores. I did everything she asked me to, and I never cried. Between us kids, her businesses, and her lousy ex-husband, my mother had a lot to cry about. I didn't want her to ever have another worry. I still feel that way. When I say I'm fine, I am. I can fix whatever that's going on with me." He kissed the back of her hand. "I like you a lot. I want us to work. You're the first woman I've met in a long time who I trust."

Janelle regarded him for a moment. She leaned forward and planted a sweet kiss on his cheek. When she pulled back, she said, "Must be very lonely on your island." Then she opened the door, not giving Gideon a chance to go around and open it. "If you ever decide that you need a lover and a friend, you know where to find me. Good-bye, Mr. Wells. Thank you for an incredible evening."

Chapter 15

Janelle took the steps up to her apartment by twos until she could get into her place and lock the door behind her. Against her better judgment, she ran to the window that overlooked the parking lot to see Gideon. She watched him look pensive before he pounded his fist on the steering wheel and then backed out of the spot in front of the building. When he drove away, she took it as a sign that he didn't see a future for the two of them.

She had given him several opportunities to open himself up to her. She'd offered to be a friend and confidante. Gideon kept his wall up around his heart.

She hadn't expected him to share a personal story. Knowing what a burden he'd put on himself as a child tugged at her heart. For a moment, as he'd told his story, she'd wanted to apologize to him, tell him it would be okay, hold him even though he would have probably rejected the offer. He probably would have seen it as her feeling sorry for him.

Gideon had made it obvious that he didn't need help. He stood firmly on his own two feet. A man so sure of himself had always appealed to her. If he couldn't open up, what would prevent him from leaving her? She didn't want to go through another situation like she had with her last serious relationship.

As she stood in her living room wearing a borrowed dress and no underwear, she couldn't help but think about that moment where she had been rejected. No time to dwell on the past or her potential future. She had bills to pay and a business to run.

Janelle took another quick shower to remove the smell of sex and, unfortunately, Gideon's heady scent. She hadn't seen any cologne in his bathroom. His natural essence intoxicated her.

She dressed in her standard jeans and T-shirt before she jetted off to her store. As soon as she strolled in with her backpack, Penny jumped on her.

"If you can't get here on time, get here whenever you can." Penny braced her hands on the glass counter, staring down at Janelle and judging her, as Janelle whisked by her.

"I told you, I overslept." Janelle deposited her bag on top of her desk and removed her coat. She hadn't realized Penny had followed her until she turned around and found her friend in her bag.

"Your dress is at home. I'll wash it and get it back to you." Janelle rolled up her sleeves before attending to the customers milling around her store.

"I could care less about the dress. You can keep it if you want. Probably looks better on you anyway." Penny shrugged and continued digging.

"Oh, shit." Janelle snapped her fingers. "I should have packed your shoes. Come by after work and I'll give them to you."

Penny brought her head up and smirked. "Really? As much clothing and shoes we exchange back and forth, you really think I would care about some shoes? Tell me about your date. How did it go?"

Janelle wanted to confess all, tell her how he'd made a delicious dinner, and that they'd watched her favorite movie before she'd fallen asleep. That he'd taken her upstairs, and then the sex…and the fight.

"It was nice," she said. The statement almost sounded like Gideon's standard response.

"Nice? You were in a house with one of *People* magazine's fifty sexiest people and all you have to say is that it was nice?"

"Yep. That's it." She patted Penny on the shoulder and started to head out the doorway.

Penny gasped. "You slut!"

Janelle whipped around. "Keep your voice down. There are customers out there."

"You fucked Gideon Wells?" Penny's mouth hung open.

"What are you talking about? Where would you get that idea?" Janelle had to fight against touching her increasingly hot face. She knew she had to have been the darkest shade of crimson.

"I know exactly the number of condoms I gave you and the types. From what I counted and from what was missing, I'd say that Mr. Wells must hung like a—"

Janelle came back into the room and pushed against Penny. "Stop it. Shut up. We'll talk, but not here. I don't trust anyone."

"Not even me?" Penny shoved the wrappers back into the bag.

Janelle's shoulders slumped down. "Of course I trust you. But the walls have ears. I don't want to draw any more attention to Gideon or me."

"The extra attention on you could get you more customers."

"I told you. I'm not using Gideon or anyone else to get ahead." Janelle took a deep breath and smoothed her hands down her body. "Now let's get back to work."

"Good. The sooner this day is over, the faster I can find out how big your quarterback really is." Penny put her two index fingers up about a half a foot apart, then kept moving them away from each other to illustrate how big Gideon's penis could be.

When Janelle didn't respond, Penny's eyes widened.

"Yes, cannot wait until we close up." Penny swatted Janelle on her ass.

The hit reignited the tingling sensation she had in her clitoris. She still felt as though Gideon stood between her thighs, moving himself back and forth. Why had she let that man go?

She remembered. Pride. She'd been battered once. She couldn't go through it again.

Janelle checked on her hibiscus. Still looked good. Hopefully, it would be good enough for the win.

"Nice. Is that for sale?"

The unfamiliar voice and inquiry forced Janelle to turn around. She saw the paparazzi guy, Jules, behind her.

"What are you doing here?" She tried keeping her voice low to not alert Penny.

Penny asking questions about Janelle's date with Gideon had been bad enough. Janelle didn't want her friend also finding out about this half-a-million-dollar offer standing in front of her.

"Here to buy flowers, of course." He took a step closer to her. "And see if you've changed your mind on my offer."

Even with the fight, Janelle would never betray Gideon. Jules's cigar smoke wafted to her when he moved closer. She sputtered out a cough before answering him.

"Both this plant and I are not for sale." She pointed to the main part of the store. "We have other lovely items that you can buy if you want."

"Are these the same flowers Gideon Wells gave you when you all ran out?"

Janelle's mouth hung open.

"I have spies everywhere, Ms. Gold." He cleared his throat. "Tell you what. I'll up the offer to a cool million. Hell, I paid that to get pictures of that football player getting his dick sucked by a tranny."

A lot of what Jules said offended Janelle. He reminded her right away of how much a gentleman Gideon had been with her.

"The term you should use is transsexual or transvestite. I don't allow crude language in this family establishment. If you only came for a story, you're wasting your time. You need to leave." She pointed to the door.

Jules shook his head and tsked. "You must have great big ones to let a million-dollar offer walk out the door." He turned around to leave, stopped, and came back to her. "Tell you what. You get me the dirt on him getting put on the injured list, and that'll be good enough for me."

"He's what?" Janelle hated to hear something that important about Gideon from a cretin, bottom-feeder like Jules.

"You hadn't heard? ESPN just reported that Gideon Wells has been placed on the injured list, although he's still on the roster. But come on. Everyone knows that you get injured, a team no longer has any use for you."

This time Janelle moved closer to Jules. "But he just won a Super Bowl. He made VIP or something."

Penny poked her head to the back room area. "MVP."

Janelle glared at her intrusive friend.

Penny shrugged. "What? I was walking by and heard you."

As soon as Penny walked away, Jules continued. "Super Bowl, MVP, none of that matters. Football, like your flower shop, is a business. If a plant you have produces no flowers and should, you would toss it or at least not sell it. If your quarterback can't perform, time to put in someone else."

Janelle tried keeping her shocked expression hidden, but she knew she could be read by Jules or anyone else who walked by and saw her. Gideon loved the game as much as he loved flowers. No wonder he didn't want to talk about his injury. Now she felt like an intrusive fool.

"Offer still stands." Jules walked out of the store.

With the two bombs he'd thrown at her—the increase in his payout and what Gideon's injury would mean to his career—she had a lot to consider.

She grabbed her coat and backpack.

"Hey, where are you going?" Penny asked as she rang up a customer.

"Seeing a sick friend."

* * * *

Gideon took a couple of deep breaths in his car to calm himself down. He didn't need his mother seeing him upset at the recent turn of events. Today would be all about her.

Although he'd missed Elizabeth at her house, Gideon had managed to find her in a hospital room getting prepared to go into surgery. Gunnar and Eboni stood by her bed.

"I apologize for being late, Mom." Gideon kissed his mother on her forehead. "Overslept."

If that excuse worked for Janelle, it should work for him.

Janelle. What a strong woman. Other women who had come after him had settled for less. The cheerleader who'd tried to get in his bed hadn't cared that Gideon didn't know her name. Janelle wanted to know what made Gideon tick. She didn't want to be some side piece, as a reporter had once called her. She wanted to matter.

Being away from her for an hour hurt him. His body ached. He wanted to touch her again, feel her soft skin and run his fingers through her curly hair.

When Gideon pulled back from his mother, she stared at him with suspicion in her eyes. Without warning, she blurted, "You had sex this morning."

Gideon glanced at Gunnar and Eboni. Eboni bowed her head but he could see her shoulders shaking and the telltale sounds of giggling. Gunnar stood next to the love of his life with a big grin. It relieved Gideon that his brother and Eboni had managed to repair their damaged relationship and that they would be getting married soon. He glanced down at Eboni's ring for a brief moment before turning back to Elizabeth.

"Mom, have you already been drugged?" Gideon smoothed his hand over his head.

Gunnar shook his head. "Dude, no use denying it. Trust me. The more you do, the more she'll keep at it."

"I can tell you've had sex. Was it with Janelle?" His mother sat up higher in her bed. "Do you really like her?"

"I don't like this conversation. I can tell you that." Gideon took a seat in the corner.

Gunnar laughed. "Admit it and she'll drop it."

Gideon shook his head. "No." He looked at his mother. "Mom, weren't you the one who told us it's impolite to talk about our sex lives in public?"

"I did. But that rule doesn't apply to your mother. So are you two a couple? Is she here with you?"

Gideon buried his face in his hands. "Jesus."

"We're going to leave you two alone for a bit. We'll be back before they take you to the OR." Gunnar kissed his mother's cheek and gave Gideon a pat on his shoulder before leaving the room.

Gideon closed the door for an added layer of protection. "So how are you feeling?"

"I would feel better if I knew that you and Janelle had hit it off."

He rolled his eyes. "You want to prove that you were right."

"Of course, darling." She smiled. "Mama is always right."

Gideon couldn't help but laugh. "Okay, fine. We hit it off. Happy?"

She stared at him. Until then, he hadn't noticed that his mother wore no makeup. She'd always prided herself on being done up, even first thing in the morning. She still looked beautiful.

"No, not happy. You're not happy. What's wrong?"

Gideon started to open his mouth when Elizabeth cut him off.

"Don't you dare say that you're fine." She held her hand out to him. "Come here."

He stood and held his mother's hand while standing next to her bed. "Yes, ma'am."

"I love you."

"I love you, Mom."

"Good. I should have told you this a long time ago. I'm ashamed I haven't." She squeezed his hand. "You can stop being the rock or the glue or whatever it is you think you need to be to keep us all together."

He let a smile creep up his face slowly before he let out a laugh. "Stop kidding around."

"Don't lie to me, Gideon. I know all you boys too well. I recognized it as soon as I brought you home. Gunnar tested me in every way he could. Thane needed me. I'm not going to lie, son. There were days when all hell was breaking loose where I knew you would be okay."

"Exactly. Aren't I always okay?" He squeezed her hand the same way he did with Janelle to reassure her of his health.

Queen Elizabeth slipped her hand out of his. "You would rather make sure none of us worry about you and that you cripple yourself than tell the truth? Gideon, if you need surgery, have it."

He shook his head and paced. "I have to take care of you. I have to look out for the store."

"Stop it." She crossed her arms over my chest. "This is my fault. I've made you feel like if you don't twirl your finger in the air, the world will stop spinning. I am so sorry that for years I leaned on you for support. You have always been the levelheaded one. As the middle child, you have always been the mediator. You don't have to do that anymore."

"Yes, ma'am, I do. You're about to have major surgery. Gunnar is still recovering from a gunshot wound. Thane isn't here. Who is supposed to take care of you?"

When he didn't hear his mother respond, he stopped and stared at her. Tears filled her eyes.

"Who's going to take care of you?" She pulled a tissue sheet from a nearby box and wiped her eyes. "Please don't feel like you have to be strong for me. And I know you love football, but don't kill yourself to keep doing it. That's the reason I pushed you and your brothers to get an education. At least you and Thane listened. Gunnar went off and did his own thing. Schedule the surgery." She broke her stare from him to gaze up at the muted TV mounted in the corner of the room.

A news story flashed across the screen about Gideon being put on the injured list. He didn't want his mother seeing that. He didn't want her to worry.

He took a seat again and braced his elbows on his knees. "It's funny that you're saying this. You're about to have surgery, one you didn't want."

"But one I need. You need this surgery. You need to not feel pain. And you need to be happy. Making sure everyone else is happy is not fulfilling you. I know it isn't." Her voice sounded strong.

"Janelle and I had a fight about this same thing." He didn't want to open up to anyone about this, about her, but he needed to confide in someone. "She said I must be lonely on my island. Then she said that although I want her, I didn't need her. All of that is bullsh—uh, not true."

"Do you understand why she would say that?" Elizabeth stroked Gideon's head.

He thought about his mother's words and what Janelle had said. "I have always been the one to make good decisions."

"You still will. Think about all this and make a good choice. It sounds like you've finally found a woman who likes what you like and will not put up with your mess. You need that. You need someone to keep you grounded." She patted his shoulder.

"Rooted." He chuckled at his lame attempt at a florist joke.

"Hey, we can do rehab together. Won't that be nice?"

He laughed. "Yeah, perfect. We'll be on side-by-side treadmills." He held her hand.

She hadn't lost her warmth. She still felt like she could fight dragons and demons for him and look great at it.

"I've told this to Gunnar. I wanted to tell you in person. If something happens to me—"

Gideon let go of Elizabeth's hand and started pacing again. "Come on. Nothing's going to happen to you."

"Listen."

He stopped moving.

"If something happens to me, I told Gunnar to make sure to keep the family together. He's the oldest. He's matured now. Now that Eboni is back in his life, they'll make a great team. Listen to them." She smiled like she wanted to convince him of this plan.

"So if he's keeping the family together, what am I supposed to do?" For as long as he could remember, Gideon had kept the family solid. Without that function, he didn't see where he fit.

"Son, be happy. If you're happy, the rest will fall into place."

He took a deep breath. A huge weight felt like it had flown off his shoulders. Had he really put that much pressure on himself to ensure everyone's happiness? Christ, he had fucked it up during the Super Bowl.

He needed to talk to Dennis, but his friend's betrayal still made him feel raw. He had to be calm to approach him. With his mother's surgery, and the prospect of him having to go under the knife, he couldn't have a conversation with Dennis with his current mindset. That didn't mean he had to cut ties with everyone. He had to talk to Janelle. The idea of it had his heart pounding harder than ever.

"So, you never answered my question." Elizabeth's voice sounded strong yet playful.

It interrupted Gideon's thoughts. "What's that?"

"Did you and Janelle—"

"Mom!"

Elizabeth laughed. "You and Gunnar are so similar. Your lives would be so much easier if you admitted that I'm right."

He patted his mother's foot. "Fine. You're right. But if you think I'm going to discuss my sex life with you at my age and in this place, you're crazy."

She sighed. "Won't throw your own mother a bone. Will you at least tell me one thing?"

"What is that?"

"Are you happy with her?"

He thought about her. "She's smart. She's ambitious. We have great conversations. And she's funny. Oh, did you know that she was my first kiss?"

Elizabeth blinked. "The little girl you sexually assaulted at the community center dance?"

"Come on. Don't say it like that."

"I can't help it. When you kiss a woman without asking her first, that's assault. Remember I punished you for that." She wagged her finger at him.

"I remember. I couldn't play football for a month, and I had to do my chores and Gunnar and Thane's. So unfair." He hitched up a smile. "But I would do it again, especially now that I know who she is."

"Okay. You remember that when you two get married and have daughters of your own. You'll get knucklehead boys like you trying to approach them. Then what will you do?" She tilted her head in that motherly way.

"Easy. My daughters won't date until they're fifty." He nodded. "Besides, I think you're putting the cart before the horse. Right now, Janelle doesn't want to talk to me."

"Are you sure she said she doesn't want to talk to you, or did she ask you to do something?" She tapped her ear. "You have to listen. It's not enough to hear that a woman is talking. You have to listen to what she says, understand?"

Before he could answer, Gunnar and Eboni returned to the room along with the doctor.

"Time for you to go. Say your good-byes to your family." The surgeon turned to Gideon and Gunnar. "We'll take good care of her." He pointed to a nurse, who'd walked in after him. "Ella will call the reception desk for you all to give you an update. The surgery should last about three hours, if all goes well, which I'm sure it will."

Eboni gave Elizabeth a hug first. She stood back and allowed Gunnar the next embrace. By the time Gideon held his mother, he couldn't talk. What would happen if she didn't make it? Where would they be as a family?

As though hearing his thoughts and picking up on his anxiety, Queen Elizabeth said, "I'll be fine."

He nodded as he pulled back from her. "We'll be waiting in the family area for you, okay?"

Elizabeth nodded.

The orderlies walked into the room. "Oh, shit. Guns and Gideon Wells here in the hospital?"

"Hey, watch your language in front of the ladies." Gideon kept his glare on the star-struck orderly. "That's our mother. Treat her with respect."

He nodded. "Got it." He turned to Elizabeth. "Sorry, ma'am."

Queen reclined on the bed as they wheeled her out of the room. Gideon walked out with her and to the elevator. Once she got inside, he waited outside the doors, staring at her until they closed.

"She'll be okay. She's strong." Gunnar put his arm around Gideon's shoulders.

"She better be. You would suck at making Thanksgiving dinner." Gideon chuckled to lighten the mood.

Until his mother came out of surgery, Gideon would be on pins and needles. Gunnar at least had Eboni to keep him company. He took his phone out of his pocket and stared at Janelle's phone number on the large screen. Later. He would call her once he found out something on his mother's progress during the surgery. Afterward, maybe he could convince her to have dinner with him to discuss everything.

Chapter 16

Janelle took a chance and decided to go up to the hospital where Queen Elizabeth would be for her surgery. After ditching her responsibilities at her store, she'd driven around for an hour, trying to decide if talking to Gideon today would be wise. She hated the way they'd ended their romantic evening.

She headed to the information desk as soon as she walked through the hospital main doors.

"Excuse me," she began to the woman behind the desk. "I'm looking for—" She stopped as soon as her cell phone rang.

Janelle checked to see if the call came from Penny, letting her know of problems at the store. The name that appeared on her screen stopped her heart for a moment. She moved away from the desk to a quieter area of the waiting room.

"Gideon?" She covered her free ear and concentrated on the caller.

"Janelle. Thanks for taking my call." He sounded defeated. "I know we didn't part under the best circumstances this morning."

"No, we didn't." Janelle wanted to talk about that, especially after hearing on the news what troubles Gideon faced right now.

"Do you have any time to break free from work right now? I don't want to have this conversation over the phone."

"Where are you?" She scanned her location to find the elevators.

"At the hospital."

"I know. Where are you in the hospital?"

Silence.

"Are you here?"

Janelle chewed on her lower lip, afraid of what he would say when she answered. "Yes. I'm downstairs."

"Come up to their third floor. I'm in the family waiting area."

She beamed at his invitation. "On my way."

The elevator took too long to arrive. She should have taken the stairs. As soon as the doors opened, she gasped when she saw Gideon standing outside the doors. He smiled as soon as he saw her.

"Thanks for coming."

Only hours ago, she had allowed this man to caress her in a way she hadn't been touched before. Now she didn't know how to greet him. Should she hug him? Shake his hand? Kiss him?

Before she could continue thinking about the possibilities, Gideon took the responsibility away from her and planted a sweet kiss on her lips. Janelle felt all warm inside, a smoldering heat that started at her toes and rose up through her body like a creeping ivy to the top of her head. Then he held her hand.

"I was going to go to the cafeteria. Care to join me?" He didn't move until she responded.

"Yes. I would like that." She turned to the elevator but felt resistance from Gideon's firm grip. She turned back to him.

"Before we go, I'd like to introduce you to some people." He carried a slight smile as he led her to the family waiting area.

Janelle followed him while nervous energy fluttered through her chest. He gripped her hand tighter as he walked.

Gideon stopped in front of a couple seated in the center of the room. The man looked like Gideon except he had a crew cut. He had the same sparkling blue eyes, same determined jaw, and same muscular build. Despite the similarities, Janelle didn't feel the same way seeing him like she did with Gideon. Gideon had something special.

The African-American woman who sat next to the man had short, black hair styled with minicurls. She held the man's hand like his life depended on it. If Janelle had been a betting type of woman, she would guess that Gideon had brought Janelle over to meet his brother. Since Janelle knew Elizabeth didn't have any daughters, she assumed the woman had to be his brother's girlfriend, or rather, his fiancée judging by the huge rock on her left hand ring finger.

"Gunnar," Gideon began.

The big man stood. He looked to be a couple of inches taller than Gideon.

"This is Janelle Gold. She owns Flowers Galore near Mom's place." Gideon turned to Janelle. He stared at her for a moment before he finished her introductions. "She's a good friend of mine who keeps me in line."

Janelle chuckled a little at that description. She guessed Gideon didn't mind a woman who spoke her mind.

Gideon continued. "Janelle, this is my older brother, Gunnar."

Gunnar extended his hand. "Nice to meet you." He offered a polite smile.

Janelle knew that had to be difficult for him to do considering the circumstance. "Very nice to meet you. I saw the story on the news about the shooting. Glad you're okay."

Gunnar nodded. "Thanks. I'm blessed to be here."

To lighten the mood, Janelle mentioned the men's mother. "Queen Elizabeth is very special. From the first day I opened, she supported me."

"Nice to hear. You'll have to come see her when she can have visitors." Gunnar's deep voice didn't match Gideon's.

Janelle didn't feel the same pulse-pounding feeling when Gunnar spoke like she did when Gideon said anything. She squeezed his hand tighter.

"Janelle, this is my fiancée, Eboni Danielson." Gunnar helped Eboni to her feet. "Eboni, Janelle Gold." He leaned over and whispered something in her ear.

Whatever he said, Eboni giggled and gave him a teasing slap on his arm.

"Very nice to meet you. I work for Queen at her hair salon." Eboni peered up at Janelle. "Pretty hair. How long have you been natural?"

"Since college. About seven years." On instinct, Janelle touched her hair that she had styled in a topknot bun.

"If you ever want it styled, come on to Press 'N Curl." Eboni wrapped her arm around Gunnar's waist. "He can do wonders with natural hair."

Gunnar kissed her forehead. It shouldn't have surprised Janelle to hear that this big man, the MMA fighter she had heard about, knew how to style hair. Gideon had a great knowledge of all types of foliage.

"Are you guys sure you don't want to come down to the cafeteria?" Gideon asked.

Gunnar shook his head. "I want to be here in case there's another update." He put his hand to his stomach. "Besides, I don't have much of an appetite right now." He glanced down at Eboni. "Babe?"

"No, I'm fine. I'll stay right here with you." She patted his chest. "Very nice meeting you, Janelle." She looked at Janelle and Gideon. "Maybe once Queen is back home we can all do dinner sometime."

Janelle didn't want to get too far ahead of herself. Right now, she didn't know where she and Gideon stood with each other.

Gideon answered for her. "I think that would be great."

Janelle didn't refute his statement. She returned her attention to Gunnar and Eboni. "It was very nice to meet you two."

"Nice meeting you." Gunnar patted Gideon on his shoulder. "Go straight to the cafeteria. Don't get diverted anywhere else." He winked.

"Good thing you're injured." Gideon shook his head as he went back out to the hallway to the elevator.

He pressed the Down button on the elevator and waited next to her.

She scanned around him. It didn't take long for people passing by them to notice him and point. "People are looking at us."

He leaned down close to her. "You know how I handle that?"

The elevator dinged and the doors opened.

After he stepped inside and pulled her behind him, he said, "I keep my concentration on the person I'm with."

Once the door closed, Janelle continued with her questions. "You aren't afraid that they'll take a picture of us and put it out for the world to see?"

He shrugged. "I learned a long time ago that more than half of the stuff published about me is not true."

"Even about your knee and being put on the injured list?"

Gideon glared at her. Janelle swallowed hard but returned his stare with a lethal one of her own. When the doors opened, he continued holding her hand. He led her to the cafeteria area.

He placed a tray on the rails in front of Janelle and allowed her to get her food first. He followed after filling his plate with a large salad, a couple of sandwiches, and a large bottle of water. She started to feel guilty getting a chili dog and fries until she saw Gideon's massive plate of food.

He found them a table at the far corner of the room. She froze when she saw him praying before he ate his food. She hadn't seen a lot of people, especially men, doing that nowadays. She couldn't hide her smile.

"Didn't know you were really religious like that. It's nice." She shook some pepper onto her fries before dipping one into a pool of ketchup.

"To be honest, I haven't prayed before a meal in a while. Today, I asked God for a favor." He picked through his undressed salad. Before taking a bite, he continued unburdening himself. "Before I called you, the OR nurse let us know that Mom is doing okay. They're halfway through surgery. I'm hoping she'll make it the rest of the way."

"We're all thinking about her and praying for her." Janelle put her hand on top of Gideon's, which seemed to calm him.

He took a deep breath before he smiled and ate a forkful of his salad. "I normally don't like eating in public. I'm a homebody."

"Really? I'm kind of surprised to hear you say that. I would have thought you would be one of those guys who likes to go out to clubs and stuff."

He snickered. "Me? Do I look like the dancing, bottle-service type of guy?"

"No. But you don't look like you would be happy being holed up in your house either."

He shrugged. "I partied enough in college. I don't need that life anymore. Now I value my privacy. I love playing football. It's what I've always wanted to do since I was a kid. The money is great. I like the fact that I can be a leader."

"You could have gone into the military if you wanted to lead." She took a bite of her hot dog and followed it with some water when the bland flavor hit her throat. Damn hospital food.

"Tried. Mom freaked out when I told her I wanted to go into the Marines. She cried for days. It killed me. So I told her I'd changed my mind and I played all through high school and college. I got offers from several teams all over. I decided to pick a team close to home."

Janelle stared at the man across from her. She'd had no idea about Gideon's protective nature.

"It's true." He wiped his hands and glanced around their seating area before he continued. "A couple of weeks before the Super Bowl, I hurt my knee. I didn't tell anyone. I thought with enough ice and rest before the game, I would be fine. I wasn't. Word got out about it, and the other team came right for me. They tried taking me out."

She dropped her fry and covered her mouth. "This is why I can't watch football. I can't imagine people purposefully being cruel to one another. It's barbaric."

"Then you definitely don't want to follow my older brother in his sport. He's an MMA fighter. His matches can get pretty brutal."

She shook her head. "So what happened with you?"

"I saw a doctor after I got home. He said I didn't tear my ACL, which is a good thing. But I banged it up pretty badly. He recommended surgery. I opted to go for a knee brace." He finished off his salad.

"You need the surgery. That's the only way you're going to get better." She kept her voice low. She'd learned since Gideon had come into her life that everyone around them had the potential to overhear him and run to the media.

"Now you sound like a mother." He picked up one of his large sandwiches and took a hefty bite.

"I knew Queen Elizabeth was a wise woman. You should listen to her."

"I did when she told me to go see you if I needed help." He smiled. "Best advice ever."

She laughed until she noticed him getting serious again.

"I have a hard time asking for help. I don't like doing it." He shook his head.

"Why?" She dipped another fry in ketchup and ate it. At least they'd fried the fries and not baked them. She liked her greasy foods whenever she could indulge in them.

"I never want to be perceived as weak. When you're a kid and you get passed around from one home to another because no one really wants you, that chips away at your soul a little. You start to feel like you're worthless. I hated that feeling. So once I got with Queen, I made sure to always be self-reliant. I wanted people to need me. I never wanted to need anyone." He dropped his food and held Janelle's hand. "I need you."

Her heart thudded under her ribcage. "Oh, wow." She'd longed to hear those words from someone. To hear them from Gideon Wells made her feel like she could slay dragons.

"I'd like another chance to have a proper date." He curved her hand around and kissed the back of it. "No tricks. No stunts. Just me and you. Would you like that?"

Janelle nodded. "Sounds lovely. Will it be at your house again?"

He shook his head. "It doesn't have to be. Understand that when I go out in public, I'm usually hounded by fans. I was kind of hoping for some quality alone time with you, but I'm trying not to be so controlling." To punctuate that idea, he smiled. "I'm trying to relax."

"Good. Then I'll plan it." She rubbed her hands together.

"Really?" He picked up his sandwich and took another bite.

"You don't think I can arrange a good date, do you?" She gave him a suspicious glare.

"I don't know how you can top a hundred roses and a gourmet meal cooked by yours truly." He moved in closer to her, lowered his head, and whispered, "Then there's that other thing we did."

Janelle giggled and put her hand to the side of his face. "That other thing was really nice."

He held his hand up like a Boy Scout. "I promise. I'll be on my best behavior. I couldn't control myself last night."

"Or this morning."

"I'll do better next time. I don't want you thinking I only want you for one thing. Well, two things."

She felt her eyebrows coming together. "What's the second thing?"

"That award-winning hibiscus you're growing."

That got a big laugh from her. "It hasn't won yet. When it wins, you can have it."

"Really? What else comes with that?"

Her eyes widened. "I need to sweeten the deal more?"

"You never accept the first offer. Besides, I know there's more you want to give, right?"

Janelle licked her lips and parted them to respond when a flurry of flashbulbs stopped her. She turned to find diners in the cafeteria had their phones aimed at her and Gideon without shame. She put her hand up to block the sudden lights and cover her face.

"Hell. Excuse my language." Gideon sat back. "I wish that guy would just leave me alone."

Janelle lowered her hand and looked into the sea of people who suddenly turned their attentions to them. In the middle of the group sat Jules. All the sudden, she felt like a snake had slithered around her body and wrapped around her neck to choke her.

From what Gideon had said, sounded like this nuisance had been following Gideon around for a while. Had Janelle led Jules to Gideon?

She turned to Gideon. "I shouldn't have come here. You alone would have been fine. With me it's now a story." She started to stand when he held her hand.

"They would have done this anyway. Finish your meal. If you want to wait with me to see what happens with my mom, I would like that. Or you can—"

"Suddenly, I'm not that hungry." She put a balled up napkin over her food. "Thanks for lunch. Let me know what happens to your mother."

"And the date?"

Unable to answer, she shook her head as she darted out of the cafeteria area. The only way she could keep Gideon happy and maintain her integrity would be to stay away from him. Now she felt like her slimy ex who'd dumped her after a wonderful evening.

* * * *

Gideon sat beside his mother's hospital bed. Although he faced her, stared at her motionless body while she slept, his mind remained on Janelle. He'd seen the pure fear in her eyes when the diners in the cafeteria had photographed them. He'd gotten used to it after all these years. He knew it would be a lot to ask of her to accept the pitfalls that came with being with him. He had hoped she would.

Gunnar stretched as he sat on the couch that doubled as a bed. Eboni rested her head on his chest and had her legs curled up next to her. Gunnar squeezed his fiancée and reclined his head back.

Gideon took that opportunity to get up from the chair and make his way to the drowsy duo. He tapped Gunnar on his shoulder. "Hey, take Eboni home and you two get some sleep," he said in a whisper.

Gunnar shook his head and slowly opened his eyes. "No way, man. I'll stay here all night with you."

"No use for both of us to stay. Mom will sleep all night. Victor said he'll run the flower shop while I'm gone. One of you should be at the hair salon. Go home." He patted his brother's knee. "I don't have anyone to go home to." He didn't mean to get morose.

Unlike his big brother, he wouldn't be lucky in love. Not this time around.

"Where's Janelle? Did she leave?" Gunnar asked.

Gideon nodded. Instead of telling him the full truth, he said, "She does have her own business to run. You two go. I'll be fine here."

"Are you sure?" Gunnar held Eboni closer.

Gideon nodded. "You're still not a hundred percent. You've got to take care of yourself. I'll go home whenever one of you comes back tomorrow."

Gunnar stood slowly and helped Eboni to her feet.

"Where are we going?" Eboni leaned against her man, still with her eyes closed.

"Home. Mom's house." Gunnar kissed her forehead as they headed to the door.

"Is she okay?" Eboni opened her eyes and peered over at Queen Elizabeth in repose.

"Surgery went great. She's sleeping. Hopefully they'll remove the intubation tube tomorrow." Gideon walked his brother and his future sister-in-law to the door. "I'll stay. You two go and get some sleep."

Eboni, while still holding Gunnar's hand, strolled over to Gideon, got up on her tiptoes and kissed his cheek. "Thanks so much, Gideon. Had I told Gunny that we should go because he's still not all the way healed, he wouldn't have done it."

"Hey, I listen to you." Gunnar pulled Eboni close to him.

"See you tomorrow." Eboni waved to Gideon before leaving with Gunnar.

Gideon stood by his mother's bed and stared at her. She'd made it through this surgery. If she could do that, he shouldn't have a problem with having his knee repaired. The idea of going under that knife didn't bother him. He worried about his place on the team. He worried about his job.

The door opened again and a nurse stepped through to get his mother's stats. She turned to Gideon. "She's doing great. Blood pressure is normal. Heart rate is fine. Her oxygen is a little low, but that's normal."

Gideon nodded, not sure how to respond.

"I can bring you blankets, sheets, and pillows."

"That would be great." He grinned because he didn't want to show this stranger his worry.

The nurse walked out of the room and within a couple of minutes came back with an armful of pillows and linens. "There's a community refrigerator down the hall. If you need ice cream, please help yourself. There's also an ice machine and water dispenser if you need some water. And coffee and tea stations all around the floor. Is there anything I can get for you, Mr. Wells?"

He shook his head. "I'm fine. Thanks." He accepted the items she carried and tossed them on the couch where Gunnar and Eboni had been.

"If you need anything, or if your mother needs anything, hit the Call button. We'll be in and out all night checking her stats, so I hope you're a heavy sleeper."

"I doubt I'll do a lot of sleeping, but thanks for the warning."

When the nurse left the dimly lit room, Gideon sat on the couch and leaned his head back. Instead of torturing himself wondering about Janelle, he pulled out his phone. He didn't want to talk in case the noise woke up his mother. He didn't know if he could use the phone in the room. Although he hated it, he decided to send her a text message.

"Get home OK?"

At one in the morning, he doubted Janelle would be awake. He mainly sent the message so that she knew she stayed on his mind.

When he didn't get a response, he transformed the couch to a bed and placed a sheet down first. He put the pillows at one end so that he could face his mother. Then he removed his shoes and sat at the same time his phone alerted him of a new message.

He sprang from the couch, which sent a sharp pain from his knee up to his head. He winced before picking up the phone.

"Got home fine. Thank you. How's Queen?" read the reply.

Gideon couldn't help but smile that she had responded and asked about his mother. *"Out of surgery. Resting."* He sent the message and then thought about something. He quickly added, *"I'm here alone. Very quiet here. Come on up."*

He waited for a reply. He stared at his phone for over five minutes before he got a response.

"Don't think that's a good idea. Sleep."

"Shit." Gideon peered up and hoped his mother hadn't heard that.

"Goodnight." The final message she sent came quickly after her rejection.

He could do nothing but relent. *"Good night. Still holding you to that date."*

No reply came.

Anger built inside of Gideon the more he thought about Janelle and the whole situation. He would never be classified as a quitter. Never in his life. He didn't think Janelle would hightail it and run when she didn't like the situation. He needed to do what he always did—come up with a plan of attack. He couldn't let this woman go.

Chapter 17

The knock that sounded on Janelle's door so early in the morning didn't give her an easy feeling. Only being behind one month on her rent, she didn't think her landlord had made a trip to her home. Gideon had sent a very thoughtful, if not late text, so it could be him. After she looked through the peephole, she wished Bigfoot or an alien stood on the other side.

"I know you're up. I saw you looking through the peephole." Ida's voice carried through the door into Janelle's tiny apartment.

Janelle took a deep breath, smoothed her hand over her oversized T-shirt that doubled as her pajamas, and opened the door. "Good morning to you too, Mom."

Ida stormed into the apartment and closed the door. "Why aren't you dressed?"

"Why are you here? I've never known you to get up so early?" Janelle looked at her watch.

Hell, she needed to get ready for work. Her plants and flowers wouldn't care that she'd had a long night, tossing and turning and thinking about the man who she'd turned her back on, but with good reason. He had too much going on with his career and family. She didn't need to add to his worry.

"I'm here because of this." Ida turned her phone around so that it faced Janelle.

A grainy picture of Janelle and Gideon sitting together in the hospital cafeteria populated the large screen. She remembered that moment quite well. At the time, she'd wanted to kiss him. She liked the intimacy they had created. Then it had all been ruined.

"So?" Janelle turned her back on her mother and headed to the kitchen. A conversation like this this early in the morning required coffee, and lots of it.

"So? Are you two dating?" Her mother threw her phone on the counter and planted her fist on her hip, her usual stance.

"What we are is none of your business." She popped a small premeasured cup into her coffeemaker.

The familiar hissing calmed her a bit until round two began.

"None of my business? Don't think you're too grown for me to put you over my knee and spank that ass."

Janelle cocked her head. "Mom, what is it that you want? You have never cared about what man I have in my life. Why start now?"

"Oh, so you are admitting he's a part of your life? You two are dating? Or are you just having sex?" She punctuated the salacious question by dragging her skinny, pink tongue over her lips.

"Don't be crude. It's too early for that." Janelle rubbed her eyes with the heels of her hands.

"I may be crude, as you call it, but I'm a realist. And I know how much that man is worth."

The turn of this conversation raised the hairs on the back of Janelle's neck. "His money is his money. None of that is my concern or business."

"Maybe it should be." Ida strolled across the kitchen to Janelle. "Maybe you stop taking your birth control pills or skip getting the shot or give up the patch for a while and let him give you a full-money guarantee." She rubbed her hand over Janelle's stomach.

The touch alone made her lurch. "You're disgusting. If you think I would ever do that to him or any man, you're mistaken. If that's all you came over to discuss, you can leave. I have to get ready for work, and you are holding me up."

"Oh, I am?"

"Yes. You see some stupid pictures on the Internet and read some dumb stories, and you think that all that should lead to something. It doesn't. He's running a flower business just like me. We talk about business." She didn't lie. They had discussed flowers. She would leave out the part where he'd covered her in thousands of rose petals and given her some of the best toe-curling orgasms she'd ever had.

Ida moved back to the end of the bar to retrieve her phone and purse. She dropped her gaze down long enough to notice something. She picked up an item Janelle couldn't see at first. When her mother slammed the red notice on the counter, Janelle's throat became dry.

"Looks like you might need a little help. That man is there for the taking. Use him. Make him pay your bills."

"Get out. I don't know why I keep letting you in my life when all you do is bring me down. I love you, Mom. I don't like you right now."

Ida snickered. "Fine. Be all high and mighty. Everybody uses everybody. Don't think this millionaire is any different. He's just like every other man out there." She opened the door in time to be greeted by an older deliveryman with dark hair and streaks of gray on both sides of his head.

He nearly jumped when Ida squealed. He held a tall, gold box with a bow on the top. "Looking for Janelle Gold."

"I'll take that." Ida snatched the box.

"Mom!" Janelle attempted to get the package from her mother while not embarrassing herself in front of the deliveryman. She signed for the package. "Um, let me see if I have some money in my purse." She knew she didn't, but she wouldn't let this man or her mother know that.

"No need." He bowed and walked away.

As soon as Janelle closed the door, she heard her mother reading the card attached to the box. "Trying to win you back from A to Z."

Janelle snatched the card from her mother.

"Guess you are seeing him for more than just business."

Even though her mother had tainted the message, Janelle read the card for herself. She tried hiding her happiness, even though the message seemed cryptic. She opened the box and understood what it meant.

"I've never seen a plant like that." Ida tilted her head like a confused puppy. "Is that a rose?"

Janelle shook her head, knowing full well what Gideon had sent her. "It's an amaryllis." She touched the red petals. "Beautiful."

"Don't wait. You've got an eviction notice and you're not getting any younger." Ida smacked Janelle on her backside, gave her a wink as though Janelle had agreed with her heinous plan, and walked out of her apartment.

For a short while, Janelle sat in her quiet apartment, listening to the quiet drip of coffee going into her single-serve cup, and staring at this beautiful plant with its deep, rich, red petals. She guessed from his card that he would be sending her twenty-five more arrangements. She couldn't wait.

* * * *

"Wake up, lazy bones." Gideon felt a hard punch to his shoulder right after he heard the statement.

When he opened his eyes, he saw Gunnar standing between him and their mother. "Is Mom awake yet?" He sat up. The pain in his neck forced him to keep his head still for a moment before he could twist it back and forth.

"I'm awake, darling." Elizabeth sounded like a shell of herself. She whispered instead of talking with her full voice.

Gideon stood and went to her bed. "You look good."

She laughed. "I taught you boys to never lie."

Gideon beamed. "I'm not. You already look healthier." He held her hand.

"And you look horrible. Did you sleep here all night?"

"Yes, ma'am, I did."

"You didn't have to do that, sweetie." She squeezed his hand. "I don't want to keep you away from other obligations."

"The store is fine. I talked to Victor earlier." He'd made sure his friend had made that special delivery that morning. Gideon hoped Janelle liked it.

"I wasn't talking about the store. Janelle. Did she stay with you here?"

He shook his head. "No, ma'am. She got freaked out by some fans taking pictures of us."

Gunnar whistled. "Tough break. I don't get it as bad as you and Thane. No one cares about us MMA fighters unless we go out with a porn star. That makes the news."

"I'm sure you're not going to let her get away, right?" Queen asked.

"No, ma'am."

"Good. Now go home and shower. No woman wants to be with a man who slept in his clothes all night."

Gideon kissed his mother's forehead. "Love you." He headed to the door. "I'll come back later."

"Get some sleep. Hopefully, they'll move me out of intensive care." She blew a kiss to Gideon.

He barely remembered how he got home, working on adrenaline and hope. He strolled to his greenhouse first. Before he could get any sleep, he had to tend to his beauty. The white roses he'd grown for the upcoming contest wouldn't be impressive on their own. Yes, he had cultivated them to have large flowers. In this day and age, he couldn't win on that alone.

Gideon picked up a small pitcher of water and dropped a couple of drops of inky-black food coloring in it. After a good swirling, he poured some into the soil. As he stared at the flowers, he wondered what Janelle would think.

Suddenly, his thoughts went to her being covered in rose petals. His body tingled. He missed her more than he thought he would. If he could get her to his home, he could protect her there. Her need to be independent and self-sufficient drew him to her. That didn't mean he wouldn't try to capture her attention again.

Before he could be any good to her, he had to handle some business. He called his mother's flower shop first.

"Good morning. Pick 'N Clip. Victor speaking. How can I help you?" Victor's voice sounded as light as a spring day.

"Good morning, my friend. How is everything?" Gideon held on to the staircase post, hesitant to take that first step up the stairs. He found if he could get used to the pain first, he could settle in to it a lot easier.

"Gid—uh, I mean, good morning, customer."

Not subtle at all.

"Bunch of customers in there now?" Gideon asked.

"Yes."

Gideon could tell Victor kept his answer short to keep the customers at bay.

"Reporters and photographers in there?"

"Absolutely."

Gideon took a deep breath. He should have been an accountant like his mother wanted. He might have had a better love life. "Did you get that arrangement delivered for me?"

"Of course. We handle all deliveries promptly. We enjoy seeing the recipient of our arrangements smiling and happy to get them."

Gideon's belly filled with a smoldering heat as he imagined Janelle smiling over the flower arrangement. "Good. I'm glad she liked them. Mom is doing great. Came out of surgery like a trouper."

"Good to hear. I'll visit later."

Gideon heard some rustling on the other end before Victor returned to the call.

"I've been at the hospital all night. I need to get a couple of hours of sleep before I come in. Can you hold the fort down for a bit longer?"

"Sure."

"I've secured some help for you. You won't be doing it alone."

Victor exhaled. "Thank goodness."

"I hired someone to help with the deliveries until I can get back there." Gideon still had to decide if getting the operation on his knee right now would help or hurt his career. "Did you get the other special deliveries made up for me?"

Victor giggled. "I did. She will be surprised." The scratches on the other end sounded like Victor put the phone to his chest for a moment or covered the mouthpiece. "It's getting a little crazy in here. Business is good."

"I know. Good for my mom. I won't hold you up. Talk to you later."

"Okay, bye, Gideon." As Victor disconnected the call, Gideon heard through the phone, "Uh, no. I wasn't talking to Gideon Wells. Gideon is a very popular name in Virginia."

Gideon continued working on business. He hit another speed-dial number as he stood by the staircase. He called his agent next. "Scot, what's the word on the street?" Gideon took the stairs slowly to keep his concentration on his agent's words.

Scot sighed. *Not good.*

"I know you're not a social-media type of guy, but have you seen what's out there about you?" Scot asked through an obvious speakerphone.

Gideon hated talking to the man that way. He imagined Scot stood in his office full of sports memorabilia, putting balls into a cup or one of those contraptions that pops the ball back to him if he managed to make the shot.

"I've been a little busy lately. Fill me in." Gideon kept the grunting from the mouthpiece as he kept his trek up the steps.

"I think I've managed to squash the mama's-boy moniker. I put out pictures of your mom. People think she's hot. They don't blame you for dropping everything to be by her side."

Gideon froze in his spot. "Don't disrespect my mother. She's not a commodity in my career."

"Calm down, Gid, my man. I said that's been squashed. Besides, I reminded folks that your MMA brother was shot, which is the real reason you went home. Ah, yes!"

Gideon heard the sound of a ball going into a cup. Damn. He hated being right, especially now when he needed his agent's full attention. "What else?" He turned to his bedroom.

He hated cleaning the rose petals from his room. They reminded him of Janelle. Her scent and the aroma of the roses still lingered in the air. He took in a deep breath as he switched his phone to speaker and set it on the nightstand.

"Did you really kick a She-Wolf out of your bedroom?" With Scot's Southern drawl, he always sounded like he wanted to burst into laughter after every statement.

"What does that have to do with anything?" Gideon pulled off his shirt and sat on the edge of the bed to remove his shoes.

"She first tried lying and saying you two had sex and now she's pregnant with your love child."

Gideon sprang to his feet. The sharp pain in his knee didn't keep him from reacting. "She what? I never touched her."

"I know. The world knows now. After I called her on her bullshit story and demanded a pregnancy test, she quickly recanted and said she only said it to try to save your reputation. After she said that, she put out a video."

"Of what? Me kicking her out of my house and calling the police? That's all I did." He remembered when she'd taken the phone from the bookshelf behind him.

He also remembered the time and extra expense he'd taken to ensure she hadn't bugged the rest of his house. He'd hired a security firm to sweep his home. They hadn't found any recording devices. He couldn't imagine what else she could have recorded.

"No, I wished she had posted that. It would further feed into your Gentleman Gideon persona."

"It's not an act. I am a—"

Scot cut him off. "She posted a video of you barely being able to climb your own stairs right after the game."

Shit.

Gideon sat on his bed.

"Shortly after she posted that video, I get a call from the Wolf's head office asking to review your current contract. Then they put some pressure on the team's doctor about your physical right before the game. That's when you were put on the injured list."

Gideon covered his face with his hand and thought about the implications that his team, his coaches, the world saw him as weak, broken, damaged. He'd never wanted that perception, one that reminded him of his childhood, the kid no one wanted.

"You could have told me this the last time we talked." Gideon gritted his teeth until his agent answered him.

"I didn't want to worry you. I thought I could smooth it all over." Scot grunted. Gideon guessed he'd missed a shot.

"It was a rough game." Gideon stood and undid his pants. A hot shower would cool his nerves. "Of course I'm going to have some aches and pains. Did you see the guys on the Sharks team? Every one of their guys wanted to take my head off. I held up through the game."

"I know. I reminded folks about that. I also talked about the fact that no one had to carry you off the field. And most importantly, you still have your good looks."

Gideon snickered. "Yes, that's the most important thing." Now he felt like a piece of meat. Then again, he hadn't picked Scot because he came off as a humanitarian. The man knew the business and how to get results. "Any truth to the rumor that they're deciding between me and Dennis?"

"The team's camp is being quiet about that. I can't get Dennis's people to talk. You have a contract, buddy. They can't just cut you out. If they do"—Scot cleared his voice—"I have a contingency plan."

Gideon dropped his underwear. If he was about to be screwed, he should be prepared. "What's that?" He removed his knee brace and threw the strappy device on his bed.

"I've been talking to the folks with the Coyotes."

Gideon froze on his way to the bathroom. "As in the Portland, Oregon Coyotes?"

"Yes. They've been interested in you since you were a Tar Heel. They're willing to make a lucrative offer."

"I need to stay here in Virginia, at least a team on the East Coast. My brother and mother, they need me." Gideon could hear his mother in his ear screaming to stop playing the glue that kept the family together. His decision had more to do with how far he could be from Janelle. He couldn't admit that to Scot.

"Dude, I can hire a full-time live-in nurse for your mother and brother if you want. Don't say no to these opportunities. They may not come around again, and you're not that young."

"I'm twenty-seven."

"Walk like it."

Asshole.

"Work on the Wolves. Talk to you later." Gideon disconnected the call and stomped to the bathroom.

As soon as the water flowed through the showerhead, he ducked under the icy-cold stream. He didn't care. The water would warm up. His team would keep him. Janelle would come back to him. Something in his life had to work.

After his shower, Gideon wrapped a towel around his waist and went back to his bedroom, water droplets still dripping down his body. He picked up his phone and dialed the one person he wanted.

"Flowers Galore. Janelle speaking."

"Don't hang up." Gideon kept his feet planted on the floor to give himself some stability. "Are you alone?"

Chapter 18

Janelle hadn't expected to hear Gideon's voice. Business had been steady that morning, keeping her busy enough to keep him out of her thoughts, but not completely. She kept envisioning his incredible eyes. Her body retained the memory of how he'd touched her. Hearing his voice released the waterworks between her legs.

"Um, let me check on that for you," she said as a way to get away from Penny and the customers in the store. She ducked into her office and closed the door behind her. "Hi."

"Hey."

She heard him release a long sigh.

"I had to hear your voice," Gideon said.

She grinned. "So you do need me."

He laughed. "Every Batman has to have his Robin."

"Am I Robin in this scenario?" She sat behind her desk and crossed her legs.

"You would look better in the tights," he said.

"I don't know. I've seen you in your football uniform. You don't do too badly in your little pants."

He released a loud laugh that forced her to laugh with him. "How are you doing?"

She nodded. "Good. No, that's not true. I'm not good. I'm conflicted."

"You don't have to be. My house is safe. It has a guard shack and photographers can't get past them."

Janelle thought about going back to Gideon's house. For such a large space, she felt safe there. It might have more to do with the man who'd slept beside her than the structure itself. She did like his home.

If she stayed around him, Jules would be able to build a bigger story. Gideon didn't deserve that.

"How's your mom? Are you still at the hospital?" She had to get on another topic or this discussion would drive her crazy.

"She woke up this morning. They took her breathing tube out. She looked good. I never thought I would say this, but she's getting color back in her skin. I didn't realize how much color she'd lost from her heart issue until the bypass surgery."

Janelle breathed a sigh of relief. "Wonderful. Can she have visitors? I'd like to see her today."

"I think she can, but no flowers for now."

"I understand. Penny and I can—"

"I want to see you. I didn't mean to cut you off."

She swallowed hard.

He continued. "It's insane for us to not see each other, unless you don't want to see me."

She ran her hand over her head when sweat formed on it. "What I want and what should happen are two different things. I don't want to ruin your reputation."

"With who?"

"Your fans. Your team. Your image."

Again, he released a large belly laugh. "You let me worry about that. Tell me what you want."

She opened her mouth but nothing came from it.

"You want to see me?" he asked again.

"Yes," she finally said once she'd mustered enough strength.

"Good. That takes care of—"

"But I can't."

"You can." Gideon's voice had an edge that almost pushed her to acquiesce.

"You don't understand. I can't."

"Did you like the plant?"

Janelle's heart pounded when she thought of it. "It's beautiful. You didn't have to do that."

"So let me do the math. You like the plant, right?"

She tried suppressing a smile but couldn't. "Right."

"And you like me." His voice dipped down.

"You're okay." She snickered.

"Ah, okay. I'll take that. By the way, I just got out of the shower and I'm only wearing a towel. Is that doing anything for you?"

Heat rose from her chest to her face. "You do not play fair."

"It's the gift of a good quarterback. Know your opponent's weaknesses."

"You think your wet body is my weak spot?" She chewed on the inside of her cheek.

"I'm still waiting to explore all the spots you have that make you weak."

She rubbed the back of her neck. "How's your knee? Did you set up an appointment yet to have the surgery?"

Silence.

"Not yet. But we can talk about that if you come over to my house tonight." His enticing offer almost had her buckling. "Thank you for the plant."

"Oh, no you don't. You are not blowing me off again."

She almost imagined him pacing in his bedroom as he spoke to her. "I have to get back to work."

"Janelle, give us a chance." His tone didn't sound pleading. He made it sound like a demand.

She thought about his request. She thought about a lot of things. Her financial situation. Her love life. Her business. If she asked her mother, Gideon Wells could solve all of her problems. Janelle didn't want to be that woman.

"Tell your mother hi from me. I have to go." She disconnected the call.

Before she could resume her work, she had to collect herself. She had to think about what she'd done. She had a smart, compassionate, sexy man who wanted her, needed her, craved her as much as she ached for him, and she'd not only turned down his offer to go to his mansion, she'd cut him out of her life completely.

Anyone else, particularly man-hungry Penny and her money-hungry mother, would call her crazy. The longer she thought about it, it did seem ludicrous to reject him when he had done nothing but have a profession that made him easily recognizable and popular.

She stood from her desk and opened the door. When Penny nearly fell into the office, Janelle knew what her wayward friend had been doing.

"Oh, hey." Penny straightened herself up and plastered a fake smile on her face. "Awful long call in there."

"Did you need the phone?" She held up the cordless phone.

"No. I was curious about you and who you were talking to. Was it Gideon?"

Janelle glared at her friend. She handed her the phone. "I'll take care of these customers."

Penny stepped in front of Janelle to block her path. "Really? I thought we were friends. We always talk about our men with each other."

"If there was anything to tell you, I would." Janelle stepped around Penny. "Let's get back to work."

The less she said about Gideon Wells to anyone, the less likely she would see him aligned with her. The additional people she had in her store every day didn't always equate to new business. She caught quite a number of people there to take her picture like some zoo oddity.

At the end of the day, she and Penny cleaned the place in companionable silence. After she placed an order for more supplies, now a daily occurrence, she put on her coat and grabbed her bag.

She picked up an envelope from her desk and handed it to Penny. "Here's your pay."

"Cool. I love this day." Penny smelled the envelope as though she could sniff out the money. "Want to spend your money? There's a bar with our names written all over it."

Janelle shook her head. "Not tonight. Feeling beat. Maybe another time."

Penny stuffed her check into her purse. "Suit yourself. I'll see you tomorrow."

Janelle sat in her car and allowed it to warm up a bit before she drove home. The extra business had allowed her to get caught up on her bills. She still owed her landlord rent for a month, but at least she didn't owe him for four months like before.

When she pulled up to her home, she noticed right away a trail of potted plants going up the stairs to her apartment. She got out of her car and picked up the first potted plant. She didn't have to look at the card identifying it as a yarrow plant.

Janelle plucked the card from the holder and read it. *"Y. Why all the plants? To see you smile."* She peered up the stairs and saw that at least two plants sat on each step. "Oh, my."

She grabbed another plant and headed to the top. Once she got into her home, she placed the two plants by her front window. She went back down the steps to the bottom and grabbed three more. If she could have carried more, she would have. When she got them all into her home, she would read each funny card. Right now, in the freezing cold, she wanted to get her new babies into the warmth of her apartment.

She made a few more trips down the stairs until she got the last ones inside. She closed her door and quickly made herself a cup of coffee. While it brewed, she arranged her plants in alphabetical order. She'd gotten the plant starting with the letter A before she'd left for work.

As she identified each plant, she figured out what Gideon had done. When she found the begonia, she knew that was the next in the series. In that card, he wrote, *"B—Beautiful like you."*

Calla lily came next. *"C—Crazy for us to fight this feeling."*

Each card had something endearing, funny or sexy. After half an hour, she had all the plants arranged and cards read. No man had ever tried so hard to get her attention, to get her. A knock sounded on her door.

Janelle looked at her spread and realized that Gideon had only gone up to Y. The Z plant must be on the other side of the door. She opened the door and had two surprises. Gideon stood on the other side holding a zinnia plant, a card, and a bag of food that smelled so good her stomach started to growl.

"Delivery for Janelle Gold. May I bring it in?" Gideon's smile weakened Janelle's knees.

"How can I say no?" She stepped to the side.

* * * *

Gideon had hoped Janelle wouldn't take his plant and food and simply sent him on his way. As soon as he stepped into her apartment, he saw how she'd displayed the other twenty-five plants. She'd put them in a semicircle under her large window. He placed the zinnia plant he carried next to the yarrow.

"Wait. I didn't get to read the card for that one." Janelle pointed to the plant on the floor.

"No card on it. I have the last card." He held it up to her. When she seemed reluctant to accept it, he said, "You read, and I'll set up dinner for us."

She took the card. He strolled toward the open kitchen. He stopped in his trek to wrap his arm around her waist and kiss her.

He pulled back from her and stared into her eyes. "I've wanted to do that for the last couple of days."

To steady herself, she held his arms. "Glad to oblige."

Gideon went into the galley-type kitchen with a breakfast bar on one side and a counter on the other. The fact that it had a bar and not a wall kept the space from feeling too cramped. Definitely not like the kitchen at his house, but he liked that. The kitchen and the whole apartment reminded him of the place he'd lived when he attended college. He'd shared a small apartment off campus with three other guys, Dennis being one of them. How times had changed.

As he opened each cabinet, looking for plates and cups, he discovered a little about Janelle. She only had four sets of plates, saucers, cups, and bowls. They all matched and looked very expensive. Another cabinet hit a few old school metal lunch boxes. One box had *Peanuts* characters with Charlie Brown and Snoopy on several sides. The one with Wonder Woman had him laughing.

"What's so funny?" She strolled to him as she carried the card he'd given her.

"Wonder Woman?" He pointed to it and brought down two plates.

"What can I say? She was an inspiration to me as a kid. A woman who can protect men and women. What little girl doesn't want that for herself?" She took the plates from him and placed them on the counter. "But those two weren't my favorite." She opened a cabinet above it. She picked up a pastel-colored metal lunch box and handed it to him like a mother handing over her baby. "Holly Hobbie. I loved this one." She pointed to various pictures on the small, metal case. "If you notice, almost every picture has little Holly with flowers or a plant or trees."

Gideon stared at the little lunch box. He looked at the image of the small girl in profile holding flowers she'd plucked from a meadow. He ran his hand over the top and felt the raised image under his fingertips.

"I remember having this same lunch box as a kid." Janelle didn't remove her stare from it as she spoke. "After my grandmother died and I moved in with my mother, it got lost in one of the moves. It was like losing my best friend. I remember crying so hard, which is crazy." She looked up at him. "It's a stupid lunch box, right? I wasn't a little kid anymore. I was sixteen at the time. My mom said that I needed to grow up. Stop holding on to things."

"So if you lost it, how is it that you have it here?" He held up the box and shook it, letting the plastic and metal handle jiggle.

"A lovely little place called eBay. The first bit of money I earned, I bid on it. I couldn't believe I won it." She smiled at her gain. "I remember camping out by our mailbox every day until it came, because I knew if my mother saw it, she would laugh at me or try to throw it away again. In my mind, I imagine that this is the box I had as a kid. Someone found it in the trash or at one of the places we lived, saved it, and put it up for sale." She brushed her hand over the metal. "I saved it."

"Gives you hope that your childhood wasn't lost or a mistake." He understood her need to mine something good out of something so horrific.

He also now understood her need to hold on to things. Although she'd claimed when he'd asked her for some of her inventory the first time they met that her refusal had to do with losing an employee that day, he now knew the truth. Janelle couldn't take any kind of loss…period. When you had nothing, you learned to hold on to everything. Knowing her struggle made her even more endearing.

She wiped her face and took a couple of steps back from him. "I bet you looked up to Superman, right?"

Gideon shook his head and handed her back her precious find.

"Batman? Regular guy with a great utility belt." Janelle returned the lunch box to its resting place and closed the door on her past.

"Nope." He reached in to the bag and pulled out each container.

"Who?"

"Underdog."

She shook her head. "Should have figured. That or Mighty Mouse." She strolled to a doorway in between the living room and kitchen area. "Would you mind if I took a quick shower? I feel like I have fertilizer and dirt all over me."

He fought the urge to invite himself into the shower with her. "Of course not. I know you just got home from work. And you had to carry all of these plants up to your place."

"That's right. You owe me big for that." She peeled off her sweater.

He came around the counter toward her. "I'll definitely pay you back."

She continued backing into her bedroom. "Make yourself comfortable. I won't be long."

"So no help getting to those hard-to-reach places?" He removed his jacket and put it on the back of one of the barstools.

"Cute. I think I'll be fine." She stopped moving and put her hand to his chest. "Trust me. I'll be much more responsive on a full stomach. Then we can talk."

Gideon regarded her for a moment and then nodded. "Yes, talk."

Janelle disappeared through a door on the side of the living room. She didn't close the main door, but she did close the bathroom door, evident from the telltale clicking sound. Did she lock the door?

Probably best she did that. After seeing her, Gideon wanted to strip down and hop into the shower with her.

Down, boy. Easy.

He returned to the kitchen and placed all the containers on the counter in front of the plates. He caught the smell of fresh coffee before he noticed that she'd made herself a cup. He placed the mug on the counter by a plate and poured himself a cup. He also grabbed a couple of glasses and filled them with ice and water. With what he'd brought for dinner, he didn't know if she would be able to handle the heat.

By the time he finished dressing the area with folded napkins and utensils, he heard the shower stop. He allowed his imagination to wander. Janelle would be drying off her delicious body, moving the towel down over her curves.

"How are you doing in there?" He needed to fill the space with some chatter to keep his thoughts off Janelle and her body.

"Getting dressed," she said from her room. "Be there in a minute."

Gideon took the opportunity to take in his surroundings. The modest apartment had hardwood floors throughout except in the kitchen. Tan tile covered that floor. One dark brown couch sat against the wall. Besides her newly acquired plants, she'd decorated the home with paintings and photographs of flowers.

"I know it's not like your place."

He turned around when he heard her voice. Now dressed in black leggings and a formfitting T-shirt, she still looked good enough to eat. She took her hair down from its bun and allowed her wild curls to dance over her head. She'd covered her lips with a pink lipstick. Thick gray socks covered her feet.

"No, it's better." He approached her.

"Don't tease me." She made her way to the breakfast bar.

"I'm not. This place feels cozy, like a hug. My house is huge for a couple of reasons. For one, that's what the home owners association required." He pulled the chair out for her before she sat. "The second reason is because I'm hoping to one day get married and fill it with a boatload of kids."

"Really?"

He sat down across from her. "Yes. What about you? You want kids?"

"Of course." She put her hand to her stomach. "I'd like to think I will be a better mother than my own." She dropped her gaze for a moment. "Sorry. Didn't mean to bring in a heavy topic."

"No, I like it when you're real." He stared at her for a moment before looking over at what he'd brought. "I hope you're into Indian food."

"I've never had it, but I'm willing to try anything."

"Good, because I actually brought Mexican."

She gave his arm a playful slap. "You are so wrong. I thought I smelled cilantro."

"I have nachos and cheese along with some salsa. I have tamales, chicken with chorizo, refried beans, rice, guacamole. I brought a buffet of food."

"Good. I'm starving." She rubbed her stomach.

"I'll serve." He spooned beans and rice onto their plates, then placed a chicken taco on each plate. "Start with that first."

Gideon thought he had a voracious appetite. He watched Janelle. She finished off her plate of food and went in for seconds, getting the grilled chicken and chorizo in her next round. Her satisfied moans let him know his dinner pick had hit her spot.

With her formal dinner done, Janelle started on the nachos. "I can't believe you're here in my home."

"Why?" He picked up a chip and ate it plain. The taste brought him back to the days of working in a Mexican restaurant to help pay for additional expenses while in college. "I wasn't kidding when I said I wanted to see you. So tell me why you didn't want to see me. What are you protecting me from?"

She shoveled another salsa-filled chip in her mouth, probably to stall for time. She made sure to chew it completely before she answered. "I go on the Internet all the time. There are pictures of us everywhere. They're saying such nasty things about you."

"See, that's the problem. Stop reading the stuff you see on social media. It'll drive you crazy. It'll make you angry." He brushed his thumb over her cheek. "I don't want to see this face angry. Like I said before, I could care less what people say about me. The only people I care about are my family and you."

"But they keep coming to my store and asking me questions."

He shook his head. "Don't answer them. Eventually, they'll leave. They'll make up stories anyway, even if you tell them the truth."

"And what's the truth?"

He put his fork down and regarded her seriously. "That you're truly, deeply, achingly in love with me."

She could barely contain the food in her mouth through her laughter. "Stop it. You're going to make me choke."

"I'll save you."

"Speaking of saving. How did you and your brothers get with Queen Elizabeth? I know you said you were adopted when you were about seven."

He hadn't really talked about that with anyone outside of the family. "Our biological mother was a bad drug addict. I was old enough to remember the funny-looking glass pipes that littered our trailer. There were people that were in and out of our home all the time." Recalling those moments, Gideon could almost feel the roaches crawling on his skin again. He swiped his hand down his arm before continuing. "Once Thane was born, Child Protective Services came to the house and took all of us. I have no idea who my father is, although once I made pro, lots of men tried reaching me to tell me they'd had sex with my mother. Not an awkward conversation at all to have with a perfect stranger. Anyway, the three of us got bounced from one foster home to another. Sometimes, the three of us were together. Sometimes, we got separated. Queen took the three of us in her home as a foster mother at first." He smiled to himself. "I remember the moment she took the three of us upstairs in her home and pointed out our individual rooms. We had never had a room of our own. We always shared bed in a room that we shared with someone else or shared a couch or slept on the floor somewhere. With her, we had our own rooms with our own beds. The house was warm in the winter and cool in the summer, and not the other way around. And she could cook. Man, my mom is great in the kitchen."

"Sounds idyllic." Janelle dipped a chip into the cheese mixture and then the salsa before taking a bite.

"It was. I count my lucky stars every time I think about where I could be had I stayed with my birth mother. I would probably be in jail or a junkie or dead."

"Have you heard or seen from her?"

Gideon shook his head. "Last I heard, she died of an overdose when I was a senior in high school. I believe it. I never did any digging, and I would never disrespect my mother now to try and find any information on her. It doesn't matter. I'm where I need to be." He picked up his coffee and took a sip. "What about you? You're tight-lipped about your family." He scanned the living room area. "I don't even see pictures of them on the wall."

"Not much to tell." She kept her gaze down. "That I know of, I'm an only child. My mother had me when she was fifteen years old. Unlike your birth mother, mine wasn't a junkie. She rolled with a bunch of older kids, including the rumored twenty-five-year-old pervert who knocked her up before skipping town."

Gideon blinked. "Wow. Heavy. So you never knew your dad?"

"Not really. I saw pictures of him."

"Your mother had pictures of him?"

She shook her head. "No. She told me his name. I Googled him and found him on the sex offender registry for Virginia. Yes, he's currently doing time for taking inappropriate liberties with a minor. It made me sick. I look up his information from time to time to see if he's out of jail. Otherwise, I don't care to know him."

"And your mother?"

She let out a sarcastic laugh. "She's busy trying to be my best friend. She thinks it's cool to only be fifteen years apart. She gives me such horrible advice on life and men." She waited a beat before she continued.

"She's one of the reasons why I want to stay away from you. You are amazing. You shouldn't get wrapped up in me and my screwed-up family."

"Hey." He framed her small face in his hands. "I'm a big boy, and a pretty good judge of character. You let me take care of any issues that come my way. As long as you like me, that's all that matters."

She turned her head and kissed the palm. "I do like you. A lot." She touched his knee.

Not wanting her to feel his knee brace he had hidden under his pants, he held her.

"Did you make an appointment to have the surgery?" she asked.

Gideon couldn't lie to her. "No. Playing football is all I really have. It's what I want to do. I can't have that ruined, and if I have this surgery I'll have to be out of commission for months."

She sighed and got out of her chair. She stood between his legs. "You remember when you said you wanted children?"

Gideon nodded. "Are you offering to start now?"

She grinned at his lighthearted joke and then became somber again. "Think about your house full of children, all running around you, and you barely able to walk or keep up with them. Imagine not being able to hold them." She held his shoulders.

"You are amazing, you know that?" He watched her blink at his statement.

"Why do you say that?"

"You are so open when you talk to me. But during sex, you barely make a sound." He watched her face flush to a bright shade of pink.

Janelle tried stepping back, but Gideon caught her around her waist and pulled her forward. "You are so strange."

"No, I'm not. Men want to know that they're fully satisfying their partners in bed. If you keep it all bottled up"—he kissed her neck—"I won't know if what I'm doing is turning you on."

"Trust me. You definitely turn me on."

"I do?" He slipped his hands up the back of her shirt. "Are you sure?"

She nodded. "I'd like to show you. But you have to do one thing for me." She pulled on his hand and guided him toward her bedroom.

"What's that?"

Once inside of her bedroom, she went to a tall dresser and opened the top drawer. She pulled out a long, black scarf. "You have to trust me."

Chapter 19

Janelle had had no plans to ever sleep with Gideon again, although every cell and molecule in her body had begged her to amend her thinking. Seeing him again and listening to him and touching him had her changing her tune.

"What's the scarf for?" Gideon peered down at her hands before returning his stare to her eyes.

"Let's call it a trust exercise." She approached the big man, who looked even more massive in her small bedroom.

Only a couple of feet separated his head from her low ceiling. If he spread his arms apart, he probably could touch the walls on either end.

Her home embarrassed her compared to Gideon's palatial estate. His bedroom had been decorated in all white, from the walls to the linens. He had several bedrooms and bathrooms and even an in-law suite. She barely had room to add a litter pan for a cat. Then she remembered his story about his childhood. He had been in homes worse than her tiny apartment.

Janelle touched his muscular chest over his pullover sweater. He didn't have to flex for her to feel his muscles. She licked her lips as she brought her hand to his small pebbled nipple. Using the tip of her finger, she circled it. Under her manipulation, it became harder. She listened to his breathing becoming heavy.

Gideon eased his hand behind her head to bring her forward. When he pressed his lips against hers, her body tingled from her scalp to the soles of her feet. She felt the need to remove all of her clothing so that her bare skin could rub against his. First, she needed to get him naked.

She stepped back long enough to remove his top over his head, or high enough so that he could finish the job. With his bare chest in front of her, she pressed against him. She sought his nipple with one hand. She kissed the other and then licked it.

He growled and wrapped his arm around her waist. She felt so secure in his arms, like nothing mattered outside of her home. He made her feel important and sexy.

As soon as she felt him reaching under her shirt to remove it, she backed up. "I'm the one driving here."

"That means I don't get to touch you?"

The longer she looked at him, the more she wanted to buckle. "Not yet. I want you to relax your need to control everything."

He leaned his head down. In a lowered voice, he said, "You're asking for a lot."

She nodded.

"If I'm going to be giving up something, I expect you do to the same." He swept her hair over her ear and whispered. "I want you to scream." To ignite the spark, he licked the shell of her ear and then nibbled her fleshy lobe.

"Oh, God." She put her hand to his chest again in an attempt to push him back.

Instead, she eased it around to his back and held him in place. She felt his heart pounding as she touched his back. He started kissing down her neck. Her body felt like he had doused her with gasoline and set her body aflame.

"Wait. Wait." Janelle attempted to catch her breath. "I need you to sit on the bed."

Gideon peered down. "Little difficult to do in my current state."

She started to look down to see what he meant. Before she could do so, he took her hand and held it against the front of his jeans. His impressive erection pressed against his zipper and the tip nearly peeked over the button closure.

"Jesus." To give him some relief, and to take another look at his penis, she unbuttoned his jeans and slowly eased down the zipper.

Janelle hooked her thumbs on the sides of his jeans and his briefs, and pushed them down his legs. As she crouched down in front of him, his hard cock waved in her face. She got his jeans down around his ankles.

"Now sit on the bed." She nudged him back so that he landed on her platform bed.

Janelle dropped to her knees to free him of his shoes and jeans. She finally got to see his knee brace. "Do you need to leave this on?" She rested her hand on his knee.

"No." He ripped the Velcro straps apart and freed himself from the orthopedic cage. He tossed the device on the floor. "Okay, you have me naked. Now what will you do to me?"

She crawled on the bed and moved behind him. She removed the scarf she had hanging around her neck. "Remember, you trust me."

"I'm trying."

"Close your eyes." She waited a beat before she covered his eyes and tied the silky fabric around his head. "Now lie down."

Gideon did so. "You'd better be joining me soon or this blindfold is coming off."

"No. Don't." She kissed him. "I hope you like this." Janelle crawled out of bed.

"Where are you going?" He reached his hand up like he wanted to touch her.

"I'm getting undressed." She pulled her shirt over her head and removed her bra.

"No fair. I want to see that." He started to take off his blindfold when she stopped him.

"Hey, no peeking. You promised you would do this."

"Okay." He lowered his hand. "I hope you know you're the only woman I have ever let do this to me."

"Really? None of your previous girlfriends wanted to blindfold you or tie you down?" She removed her pants and panties.

"You aren't going to tie me down, are you?" A bit of worry laced his voice.

"Would you let me?" She tiptoed to her adjoining bathroom and looked around for lotion or baby oil.

"You really are pushing it, aren't you?"

Unable to find oil, she went with her vanilla-scented lotion. When she returned to the bedroom, she straddled his body. "I don't want to tie you down. Just keep you blindfolded so that you don't know what's coming."

Gideon put his hands on Janelle's thighs. "I have condoms in my wallet."

She leaned forward and put her mouth by his ear. "Don't worry. I'll protect us both."

He wrapped his arms around her in her prone position. While down on his body, she kissed the side of his face. His goatee scratched against her skin.

When she felt him trying to turn her over onto her back, she wriggled out of his grip and sat. "Relax."

"How am I supposed to do that when you—"

The first dollop of lotion that hit Gideon's chest silenced him for a moment. His body stiffened under hers. When she rubbed the creamy lotion into his flesh, she felt his body loosening. He exhaled and rested his hands on her thighs.

"Smells like a cake or cookies." He took in a deep breath.

"It's my lotion. You like it?"

"Do I like you rubbing my body? Of course. Do I like smelling like a bakery? Not so much." He chuckled.

"Hey, are you saying I smelling like a pastry?" Before he could answer, Janelle reached down and held Gideon's sac.

He gritted his teeth and arched his back. "You smell and feel so good."

"Good answer." She continued massaging him until he sat and wrapped his arms around her.

"You are torturing me, you know that, right? I couldn't watch you undress. You're limiting my touch. And now you're making me so hard I can't think straight because all my blood is rushing to my lower half."

"I thought you liked a little teasing." She raked her fingers through his blond hair.

"Teasing is one thing. Tormenting me is something else. But two can play that game." He lowered his head and found her breast.

"Oh, yes." She held the back of his head as he licked her nipple.

When he sucked her whole breast into his mouth, Janelle felt powerless to do anything but fold to his will. She shouldn't have been surprised when he massaged her other breast. Taking away his sight didn't lessen his need or his ability to find her hot spots.

"Wait. Stop." She kissed the side of his face. "Back." She tried pushing him down again.

"What are you doing now?" He kept his hands on her thighs and slid them up to her core.

Janelle sat taller and opened the drawer next to her bed. She'd stored the condoms Penny had packed in her bag on Valentine's Day in there. She grabbed one in the black wrapper. When she opened it, a smile crept across Gideon's face.

"That's it, babe. Come on."

She rolled the condom onto him. Before he could object, she held the base of his shaft and hovered herself over him. Janelle braced her hand on his chest as she impaled herself ever so slowly. "Oh, yes."

He squeezed her thighs as she settled on him. "I should be on top."

"No. Let me satisfy you. Let me cater to you." Janelle closed her eyes. "See if you like this little trick I learned."

Without moving her body, she squeezed her inner vaginal muscles around his shaft. She tightened her walls, held it for a beat, and then released him.

"Where in the world did you learn to do that?" Gideon leaned his head back and gripped her thighs tighter. "That feels incredible."

"Thank God for Kegel exercises." She braced one hand on his chest.

Gradually, she began to rotate her hips on him while still clamping her muscles around him. When she felt him pulling her back and forth and raising and lowering his hips to thrust deeper, she ground her hips down harder on him.

"I can't take this." He removed one hand and ripped off the blindfold.

Janelle didn't care at this point. She wanted to stare into his eyes. They looked almost black with a small silvery-blue ring around them. With the barrier between them gone, she took his hand and placed it on her breast. Her hard nipple brushed against his palm, and her throbbing heart pounded against her chest.

He slid his hand off her thigh and brought it up to her back. With very little effort, he eased her down so that she lay against his massive chest.

The nerd and the football player. Who would have imagined this pairing?

"Talk to me." Gideon's deep voice rumbled in his chest and vibrated Janelle's body. "Tell me how it feels."

She started to open her mouth but stopped herself. She crushed her lips against his as he held her around her waist. After she parted her lips, he took no time to snake his tongue into her mouth. In such a short amount of time, he'd managed to infuse himself into her life, into her routine. She wanted more of him but didn't know how to express herself. Growing up with the type of mother she had, she didn't have to say anything. Before Janelle could complain about the cold temperatures, Ida had already proclaimed her displeasure.

Plants and flowers never talked back to her, although she talked enough for a whole forest as she tended to them. She could complain about a bad day to them or lament about a horrible relationship. They didn't judge her. Instead, they flourished. They flowered. They gave her life.

"Tell me how you feel." Gideon continued thrusting in her. "So good."

"Good." She nodded like a broken bobblehead doll.

"More. Tell me more. What do you want?" He kissed the side of her neck.

She froze. Having him kiss her in that spot, continue to massage her tit, and fill her completely with his cock, she finally succumbed to her hidden desires.

Janelle grasped at words in her head and blurted whatever came in her mind. "Beautiful man."

"Keep going." The thrusting increased in speed.

"Big hands." She brought her mouth down beside his ear. "Great eyes."

"You are my bleeding heart flower. Sexy, seductive, enticing." He held her tighter.

His compliment wove its way around her heart. She brought her face up to stare into his eyes. "No one has made me feel as special as you."

Gideon released his hold on her chest, sat, and swung his legs around the side of the bed. In this new position, she wrapped her legs around his waist but never stopped moving.

"Ixora." The name of the flower popped out of her mouth as fast as it entered her head.

"What?"

"Ixora. Ixora. Ixora." Sweat poured down her back. "Jasmine plant." She kissed the side of his face. "Supposed to renew passions." She held the sides of his face as she stared into his eyes. "Oh, God, yes! Yes! Yes! Ixora!" Her chest opened as she screamed each word.

Never before had she felt so free. She clamped her thighs around him and her body trembled as the orgasm took over her senses. Before she could settle back down, Gideon drove himself deeper into her core.

He surprised her with his sheer strength and determination when he stood with her still connected to him. He carried her to a waist-high dresser and placed her on top, toppling over bottles of perfume and a small mirror.

"Your knee."

He stopped her worry with a simple kiss. Gideon erased all doubt with his incredible stamina, stroking her so lovingly that he coaxed another climax from her, one that had him joining with her.

"Christ, I want this every day, every hour." He captured her lips in a soul-stirring kiss.

When he broke from it, Janelle couldn't help but scream her excitement again. She clawed his back until her body could settle down and her heart had stopped racing.

"I knew you could do it." He brushed her hair back from her face. "I knew you could open up that voice box of yours and tell me how you feel." He swept his thumb over her throat before bending over to kiss it.

"I've been quiet for far too long." She ran her fingers through his shaggy hair. "It felt good to let it all out like that. Now I understand why you football players scream at each other."

"I am a little jealous though." His face went serious.

Janelle's heart stopped for a moment. "Why?"

"Here you finally express yourself, and you scream out a plant's name."

She laughed as she hugged him. "That was strange. I know. I don't know where that came from. I thought about the sexiest plant out there that reminded me of you, and that was the first thing that popped in my head."

"You're going to have to teach me about that flower." He smiled as he pressed his forehead against hers. "I've never heard of it."

"Anytime. And I promise the next time we do it, I'll only call out your name."

Gideon kissed her. "Don't tease me." He pulled back from her and held her waist. "Since you exposed a little of yourself, I think I should."

Janelle put her hand on his heart. "No, you don't have to."

He held her hand against his chest. "I love football. I love playing the sport and pushing myself. But the main reason I do it is for the money. It sounds bad, but it's not what you think." He brushed his long thumbs along her sides.

She wanted to laugh from the tickling sensation, but she bit her lip to keep from doing it.

"I told you how broke my family was when I was a kid."

Janelle nodded but kept silent as he shared his life.

Gideon continued. "I was determined, even at a young age, to have some sort of financial security for not only me, but for my family also. That's another reason I wanted to go into the military. I figured the benefits would help my mom if something happened with me."

"But Queen has, what, four or five businesses?" She relaxed her legs from around his body but continued staring in his eyes.

"She has three."

"With three businesses, I would think she would be fine."

He shook his head. "It wasn't enough for me. I wanted to be sure. I needed to save as much as I could to give her the most secure lifestyle possible, because she gave that to us as kids. I wanted to make sure that if one or all of her businesses suddenly failed, she still wouldn't have to worry about money."

Janelle cupped his cheek. "You are a very good son, and an excellent man."

Gideon smiled.

"But at what expense are you doing this for your family? They wouldn't want you to hurt like this." She ran her fingers through his hair. "I don't want to see you in pain."

He smiled wider at that admission. "You don't?"

She shook her head.

"I'm going to tell you something that I haven't even told my family yet." He shifted in his spot like he wanted to ground himself. "There's a chance I might go to another team because of this injury and what I did during the Super Bowl."

"What did you do?" She hoped she would be able to understand whatever he'd done considering she never watched football.

"Instead of letting one of my teammates run the final crucial play that would have guaranteed us the win, I ended up running it. At the time, I didn't see the move as being selfish. The more time goes by, the more I understand why my teammate and friend is mad at me. I made a mistake. It got us the win, but I ruined a great relationship. I caused distrust among my team. And I hurt myself further by doing it. In the end, even making MVP and having a Super Bowl win under my belt, it wasn't worth it. The only great thing that's happened to me since is that I got to meet you." After purging so much, Gideon took a deep breath and connected his stare to Janelle's. "I've decided to go on and have the surgery. If the Wolves kick me out because of it, so be it. My agent said there's another team interested in me."

"Awesome." She beamed. "Who is it?"

"The Coyotes."

Janelle felt her eyebrows knit together. Not being that familiar with all NFL team names, she didn't know what city hosted that team.

"They're out of Portland, Oregon," Gideon said.

"Portland?" She tried keeping her face neutral, but how she truly felt showed through to Gideon.

"I know. It would mean I would have to move. But they're offering me more money than what the Wolves paid me. My family would be set."

"Is your family asking you to do this? Do they need you to be the breadwinner?" She placed both hands on his chest and leaned back. "Thinking about them is admirable, but everyone is an adult. They all have highly successful careers. The burden to keep everyone in the lifestyles they've become accustomed should not be on your shoulders. At some point, you have to look out for yourself."

He snickered. "Now you really sound like my mother."

She smiled. "She's right." Even though her heart broke inside at the thought of Gideon possibly leaving, she had to think of him. "Whenever you plan your surgery, I would like to go there to support you."

"You'll hold my hand the entire time?" He slipped his hands down from her waist to her backside.

"If that's what you want."

"Oh, now we're getting to what I want. I would love for you to scream out the names of each of the plants I got for you."

She rubbed her legs against his ass. "Sounds like fun. I would love to show you my—"

A hard pounding sounded at her door before she could finish her statement. "Virginia Beach Police. Open the door."

Chapter 20

Gideon eased himself out of Janelle as soon as the pounding sounded on her front door. "What the hell?" He looked around for his pants. "Why would the police be here?"

Janelle shrugged as she planted her feet on the floor. He had hoped after such an incredible lovemaking session that he could hold her and talk. Like in football, things changed on a dime.

"Oh, no." Janelle went into her bathroom and slipped on a cotton robe that looked to be two sizes too big for her.

Considering she hid her naked body underneath the hunter-green cover-up, he wanted to tell her to wear something else.

"It could be my neighbors downstairs. They're elderly. I hope nothing has happened to either of them." She ran to her bedroom door and then stopped. She turned and put her hands on Gideon's chest as he followed her. "You stay here."

"Why? If something's going on, I want to be there for you." As a man, he didn't feel right hiding out from potential danger.

"I know. Look at us. I don't want the police running to the tabloids."

He shook his head. "I could care less about that. I'm concerned about you."

The knocking sounded again.

"Please, just wait here, okay?" She nodded and backed out of the room.

Gideon would wait in her bedroom for a short while to appease her, but he wouldn't stay silent or hidden for long. In his mind, Janelle now belonged to him, in his heart and soul. He would do anything to protect her. Standing by and waiting for something to happen seemed like a strange way to react.

He stood close to the bedroom door and listened intently after Janelle opened the door.

"Is there a problem, officers?" Janelle asked.

Her voice sounded fragile. Gideon chalked it up to the distance she stood from the bedroom. He couldn't help but think how scared she must be. He hadn't met her neighbors from downstairs, but she acted as though they meant the world to her, probably more than her own mother.

He couldn't hear everything the officers said except for the words *concern* and *help*.

Gideon disposed of the used condom still attached to him and slipped on his jeans. He moved closer to the door.

"Who called?" Janelle asked.

He could no longer take hearing only a part of the conversation. He marched out of the bedroom. One officer put his hand on top of his gun until he took a good look at Gideon.

"Are you Gideon Wells?" the tall, thin policeman asked.

"I am. Is there a problem?" Gideon stood next to Janelle and put his arm around her waist.

"You didn't have to come out here." She crossed her arms over her chest. "I'm fine."

The second officer said, "We received a call from a neighbor that they heard screaming up here. They said the woman had been accosted before. Was there an issue?"

They stared at Gideon longer than they regarded Janelle.

"As you can see, there's nothing going on here." Had he been wearing a shirt and shoes, and if she had on any clothing, that statement might be plausible.

"So where did the screaming come from?" The thin man crossed his arms over his chest.

Gideon took that time to adopt his mother's teachings to never talk about intimate details about a woman with other people.

"It's not what you think. We—"

Janelle put her hand on top of his arm. "I'm fine. Not too long ago, some crazed photographer hid somewhere in the parking lot and jumped out as soon as I came home. It scared me, but I was okay."

"Did the same thing happen tonight?" The second officer took a couple of steps toward the window and peered out of it. Thanks to the rows of potted plants, he couldn't get too close.

"No." She shook her head.

"So what happened?"

Gideon sighed. "Is this really necessary? She said she's fine."

"Why are you getting defensive, Mr. Wells?" The officer moved away from the window and stood next to his partner.

Gideon had to harness his growing anger. He couldn't tell if these cops wanted him to spill juicy details of their sex life or they didn't understand why a man and a woman, partially dressed, would have been screaming only moments before. Could they be that thick or that opportunistic?

"Please." Janelle held up her hand. "No one is getting defensive. We were having a nice night in. I got excited and screamed out of happiness, not distress. Really, I'm fine." She pointed to Gideon. "He's fine. Thank you for responding so quickly. Honestly, there's nothing to report."

The police stared at the duo for a while. Then the first officer glared at Janelle. "Anything else going on here that we need to know about? Any money exchanging hands?"

Flames filled Gideon's vision. "You son-of-a—"

By gripping his arms, she stopped him from charging the lawman. "Stop." She turned to the police. "I'm a business owner. I own a flower shop called Flowers Galore. His mother owns another flower store, and we're friends. That's how we know each other."

"My apologies. I have to ask considering the circumstances. We didn't want another Ray Rice situation where someone in authority could have done something and didn't." He gazed at Gideon. "We'll need to see both of your IDs and write a report."

"Why? We're both telling you nothing happened." Gideon felt the hairs on the back of his neck rising.

For one thing, he never wanted to be compared to a man who beat on a woman, a woman he claimed to love, a woman who had borne his child. A man wouldn't do something so deplorable. When Officer Asshole had implied that Janelle worked as a prostitute, Gideon had wanted to rip the man's head off his thin shoulders.

Janelle patted Gideon's arm. "Of course. Not a problem." She headed to her purse on the kitchen counter.

"I'll go into your bag." One cop grabbed Janelle's purse before she could get to it.

"Um, sure. I understand." She nodded and closed her robe around her neck.

From the way her face turned dark red, Gideon knew this bothered her as much as it did him. To get her alone again, he would have to calm down and comply. "My wallet is in my back pocket. Would you like for me to get it, or do you want to?" He held his hands up with his fingers splayed.

"You can get it, Mr. Wells. Just turn around when you pull it out."

He did so begrudgingly, then handed the first officer his Virginia state license. Who knew sex would turn into an inquisition?

After identifications had been verified and they'd documented their statements, the police left, but not before the shorter, heavier one of the two asked for a picture.

"You interrupted our evening, accused my girlfriend of being a prostitute, and treated us like criminals. Forgive me if I don't join you in a selfie." He held the door open for them and slammed it after they left the apartment. "Can you believe that guy?"

Janelle said nothing as she disappeared into her bedroom.

Gideon had to lighten the mood. "You can blame me. I told you to let it out. I didn't know it would scare your neighbors."

He didn't expect to see Janelle carrying his shirt, socks, and shoes.

"Thank you for the plants and dinner. But I think you should go." She looked at him in his eyes before dropping her gaze.

"Okay. I'll go." He took the items from her. "But you're coming with me. Get dressed and pack a bag."

She shook her head. "No. Those cops are going to run to a news outlet and tell them what happened here. I'm ruining your career."

He dropped his items and held her arms to make her look him in the eyes. "You've done nothing but make me the happiest man during a time I thought would be the worst time of my life. Between my mother and brother and—" He stopped before rehashing the news about his knee and his future with his team.

"What?" She brought her gaze up to his.

Looking into her soft brown eyes, he couldn't lie to her. "I'm my happiest when I'm with you. Don't you feel the same way?"

She returned his stare without answering for a while before she turned her head. "Please go home."

"I'm not running away. Not from those cops and not from you. If I leave, I want you to come with me."

She shook her head.

"I can protect you in my home. We can finish talking."

She took a deep breath. "Before you, I didn't need protection. I didn't have people wanting my picture because of who I was sleeping with. I was a simple flower store owner with a dream."

"I'm also a man with a dream. Why can't we do this together so we can support one another? Why are you so afraid?"

She wriggled out of his grip. "This isn't my life. Cameras and questions and police."

"Those are all temporary. As soon as the game hype dies down, it'll all go away."

"Yeah, then start up again when you go train. Then you'll leave. And I'm here. My business is here. I'll stay."

He sighed. "Rooted."

She paced. Each time she stole a peek at him, she averted her gaze like the look would turn her into stone.

Gideon watched the fear etch across her face but didn't know how to erase it. "Please come to my house so we can talk."

"Why can't we talk here?"

"Privacy. If your neighbors hear us talking passionately—"

"Arguing."

"Talking with enthusiasm, I'm afraid they'll call the police on us again." He took a step closer to her, and she took two steps back, almost into a corner.

With the shadow covering a portion of her face, she reminded him so much of that nervous young girl hiding by a set of bleachers so many years ago.

"No sex."

Janelle blinked.

"Tonight. No sex tonight. We'll talk. When you get sleepy, you can sleep in a spare bedroom."

Janelle remained pensive as though tumbling the possibilities over in her mind. She shook her head again. "I need time to think. You have a lot going on in your life. Maybe adding me to it is one complication you don't need."

Gideon regarded her for a moment in silence. "Okay." He picked up his belongings from the floor and slipped them back on while she watched him. Now dressed, he picked up his jacket and put that on while he stared at her. Before leaving, he approached her. "Do not think for one second that me leaving means I've given up on you, on us. I haven't. If I have to fill your whole apartment with flowers and turn it to a greenhouse for you to see what you mean to me, I will. I can't do anything about the paparazzi following me. I have the house that I have for privacy, not flash. I know what I want. I know what I like." He held her small face in his hands. "Don't be so afraid."

She remained silent while a single tear rolled down her cheek. "Take that same advice, okay?"

He knew exactly what she meant. His knee. Maybe to prove something to her he would have to prove something to himself. "Will you still go with me when I have my surgery? I'll need all the support I can get."

Janelle didn't answer. She kept her stare to the floor.

Before leaving, he had to kiss her. When he did, he saw fireworks in his head as he always did. It made him wonder if she experienced the same thing. Did she see a future with him like he saw with her?

He pulled back from her and ached to tell her what had been plaguing his heart for a while. He loved her. With her fear and this dismissal, he couldn't take the rejection. Once he made himself whole, he could try to get her again.

Going home to an empty house felt worse than ever before. He'd found someone. She completed him in every way. Yet he stood alone.

After a night of tossing and turning, Gideon went to the hospital before going to his mother's flower shop. He found her awake and eating lunch.

"Darling." Her breathy salutation had a different connotation now that she'd gone through surgery.

"Are you doing your breathing exercises?" He picked up the tubular contraption that the doctor had told her to use throughout the day to strengthen her lungs and prevent pneumonia.

"I'm fine, dear."

He heard the line he'd so famously used for the last few years, since starting professional football. Gideon sat down next to her bed. "When are you getting discharged?"

"If all goes well, maybe in the next couple of days." She pushed her tray away and adjusted her bed to recline a bit more.

"Good. When you're discharged, you're coming home with me."

His mother blinked and raised her head again. "We've discussed this. I'm going back to my home."

He shook his head. "No. You can't go up the stairs, and you have no bedrooms downstairs. I have a whole suite where you can stay. I'll hire a nurse who can stay there."

"Oh, so that's what it is. You want some at-home entertainment at my expense." She giggled.

"No. I've decided to have the knee surgery." He kept his gaze down to the floor. "It's for the best. It'll take half of a year or more to heal, but it'll be fine." When he didn't hear a response from his mother, he looked up.

"What happened with you and Janelle?"

He stood. "Nothing." He gave Elizabeth a kiss on her forehead. "Absolutely nothing."

Queen took his hand before he could go. "I've never known you to quit anything."

"I'm not quitting. You were right. I need the surgery. So I'll get it done and stay at home. You'll be there with me. Like you said. We can rehab together." He tried putting on a brave face, but his insides crumbled. "My surgery is in a couple of days. Gunnar and Eboni will bring you back to my house."

"Son—"

"If you'll excuse me, I have some details to take care of before I have surgery." He strolled out of the room when he couldn't take seeing the look of concern on his mother's face.

He found a quiet room at the hospital meant for doctor and family consultations. He closed the door and dialed his agent first.

"Gid is god. How are you?" Scot sounded like he talked to Gideon from the back of a yacht.

Gideon heard a ship's air horn and seagulls squawking in the background. "I'm having the surgery for my ACL. I'll be laid up for a while. I can't take the pain."

His agent didn't need to know what type of pain he meant.

"Oh, wow. Heavy. Do the Wolves know?"

Gideon marched in place. "That'll be my next call."

"Good. You haven't called them. Don't."

He felt his brows rut together. "Why not?"

"Let me work some magic with the Coyotes first before they get wind of you having this surgery. I don't want the Wolves tainting your image before you get an offer. Is that what you want? Do you still want to play football?"

At this point, Gideon had nothing left. "Yeah. Sure. Sounds good."

"Awesome. They're willing to offer you twice what the Wolves gave you, and that already was the highest deal in pro football history. You'll be making money hand over fist."

Gideon sighed. "Yep, sounds like what I want." He disconnected the call.

He had somewhere to go. What he had to do couldn't be done over the phone.

Gideon drove to Chesapeake to an area close to the North Carolina state line. Off the main road and down a two-mile stretch on a paved road surrounded by woods sat a large house. A black, high fence circled the property. As he looked through the fencing, he saw a trail of expensive cars parked along the circular aggregate driveway. He saw a black Bentley and knew the owner of the house would be home.

Gideon pressed the call button on the box at the gate. He peered up at the camera. After a beat, a voice came out over the speaker.

"Dennis the Menace is not signing autographs."

Gideon couldn't mistake his friend's voice or the anger in his tone. "Come on, Dennis. We need to talk."

He didn't hear anything through the box. Had Dennis dismissed him completely? Gideon started to back up his car to leave when the gate started to open. He waited for it to open completely before driving through and parking behind the row of expensive rides.

He got out of the car with one battle down. Whether Dennis would allow him into his home would be a different story.

Gideon got up to the front door and raised his finger to ring the bell. Before he could touch it, the door opened. Dennis stood on the other side wearing a red tank top, black track pants, and his own line of sneakers that gave the Michael Jordan sneakers a run for their money in popularity.

"You got a lot of nerve coming up here." Dennis shook his head as he stood in the doorway.

"Can I come in?" Gideon waited for a response.

After a terse thirty-second stare down, Dennis took a step to the side.

"Thanks, man." Gideon walked in but didn't remove his jacket. Knowing Dennis, he wouldn't allow him to stay very long.

Gideon heard loud voices coming from the game room area of Dennis's house. Unless Dennis had rearranged the place, Gideon remembered the layout.

"Still having your weekly poker games?" Gideon stared at Dennis and hoped his friend saw that he didn't mind that an invitation to the games hadn't been extended to him.

"Let's cut the small talk." Dennis waved his hand back and forth between them. "What's on your mind? Make it quick. I've got a good hand going."

Damn, Dennis wouldn't be making this easy.

"Fine. Was hoping we could sit down like friends to talk again, but since that's off the table, I'll say it here. My ACL is bad. I got it checked after the game not too long ago."

Dennis snickered. "Dude, you're not telling me anything I didn't already know. You don't call the kind of play that you called unless you're hurting." He headed to the door. "If that's all you have to say, you can bounce so I can get back to my friends."

Gideon took a deep breath. "I'm having surgery to repair it. I'll be out for a while."

Dennis rested his hand on the doorknob but didn't move. Gideon watched him standing with his back to him. He noticed the boisterous conversations from the other room had stopped. When he turned, he saw a group of about five men standing behind him. A couple had cigars in their mouths and the others held bottles of beer.

Gideon didn't recognize any of them. No one came from their team. These must be Dennis's childhood friends.

"Den, this dude bothering you?" a tall Asian man asked.

Gideon didn't need a fight, but he would if he had to if it came down to it.

Dennis turned around. He stared at Gideon for a beat before he turned his attention to his posse. "Nah, it's cool. Hey, y'all go on without me. I'll be down in a minute."

Dennis waited for his friends to vacate the area before he walked by Gideon. "Come on to my office."

Gideon knew the location of the office but followed Dennis. When he entered it, the place looked exactly like he remembered it, full of memorabilia from Dennis's sports accomplishments from childhood on up to his professional career. He saw an empty pedestal sitting next to his desk.

"That's the spot where my MVP trophy should have been, but you got that." Dennis plopped down in a chair behind his desk like he had called this meeting.

Gideon sat in a chair in front of the desk. If Dennis wanted to treat him like this, he wouldn't be here for very long. "Look, I know you're pissed at me for what I did at the Super Bowl."

"Damn right. I thought we were boys."

"We are. I thought I knew what was best for the team. I was wrong. I'm used to thinking I can take care of everything around me. I should have listened to you."

Dennis regarded him for a while before he snickered. "What? Do you think you're going to die under the knife or something? Why are you doing all this confessing now?"

"Because I realize that by not being open, I'm losing a lot of important people in my life. I have to be honest." With each word Gideon spoke, he felt lighter.

"Okay. So since you're feeling so honest, tell me. What do you think about me leaving the team if you stay?"

Gideon didn't pause in his answer. "You're a fast man. You can rally the team together. And you're smart."

"You're not telling me anything I don't already know."

"But you don't think things through. You're a hothead. That attitude will get you in trouble." Gideon sat taller. He wanted to prepare himself if Dennis kicked him out of the house. "What we have as friends, well, as teammates, is gold. We know how to read each other. That kind of chemistry is hard to build."

"Chemistry? It's not rocket science. It's game play." Dennis rocked in his chair. "Good to know how you really feel. I guess you'll see from your couch the next time I play."

Gideon smiled. "I guess I will."

"So with this surgery, are you nervous?"

"Little bit, but the thought of not being able to run around with my kids later on in life scares me more." Janelle's words had hit home for him. Too bad she wouldn't know her effect on him.

"Kids? Are you trying to tell me something? Did you decide to take Candy up on her offer?"

"Who?"

"The cheerleader. You know." Dennis nodded and gave Gideon a knowing look.

"No, man. I—"

"Because I told her that you would like it if she surprised you at your house."

Gideon felt a thud to his gut like he'd been stabbed. "You sent that woman to my home?"

"Yeah." He clapped his hands and laughed. "You're welcome."

"She convinced the guard at the gate and my cleaning staff to let her in. She was naked in my bed."

"Really?" Dennis rubbed his hands together like Gideon would be telling him a perverted bedtime story.

"She had her phone recording everything when I kicked her out of my house. I told you she is not my type. Why would you send her to my house?"

"You looked a little wound up. I thought you would like some relaxation."

"It's not my thing to use women like that. It's degrading." Gideon shook his head. "I may have given out your phone number to fans, but I would never tell them where you live or how to get to you." As he stared at Dennis, he got the full picture of his life. "I don't know why I'm surprised about you with the cheerleader or your decision with the team. I have always had your back, even at the expense of my health."

"What the fuck are you talking about? I ran that shitty play you called." Dennis pointed at Gideon. "I ran it and you ran for the touchdown. Gid is fucking god." He snickered.

Gideon struggled to his feet. "When you're done with your pity party, one day sit down and look at that final play. Don't look at me this time. Look at your damn self."

"What's that supposed to mean?" Dennis didn't stand.

Gideon had a feeling that as soon as he left, Dennis would be cuing up the video in his office to check out what he meant. "Put yourself in the quarterback's position and you decide if you would have thrown the ball." He remembered the play and recalled Dennis showboating to the crowd before he'd acknowledged Gideon. By that time, Gideon had started off in a run for the final play of the night. "Good luck with everything. I truly mean that."

Dennis stood. "So what happens now?"

"I'm going to have my surgery and then take some time to figure things out." Gideon shook Dennis's hand and pulled him in for a half hug. "Remember. Think before you act, okay?"

"Whatever, man. I got this."

Gideon nodded. He had a lot to think about.

Chapter 21

The last couple of days had Janelle feeling down. She'd missed Gideon but felt her decision to break ties with him would be beneficial to him in the long run. Too bad her heart suffered for it.

After getting dressed, watering her forest of plants, and forgoing breakfast for the second day in a row, she threw on her coat, grabbed her purse, and headed to the door. On the kitchen counter sat Gideon's watch. He'd left it his last night at her apartment. She should have called him to let him know or at least gone to his business to give it back.

As she brushed her fingertips over the pricey jewelry, she didn't think about selling it to save herself, save her business. She slipped the watch onto her wrist. Even after closing the clasp, it dangled off her hand. It reminded her of Gideon's size.

For such a nice piece, why hadn't he contacted her to get it back? Why hadn't he come to see her?

Janelle shoved the watch into her pocket. If she truly wanted Gideon out of her life, if she wanted closure, she had to purge him. The plants could stay. She had to give him back his timepiece.

She opened the door and started to head out when she stopped in her tracks. She gasped when she saw her landlord standing on the other side. She had no idea the man woke up early enough to make a trip to her apartment.

"Mr. Norwood, good morning. I was just heading out to work." Janelle kept up a pleasant demeanor to not set off his short fuse.

The man could be pleasant until you messed with his money.

"I want you out in thirty days." He jutted his thumb over his shoulder to indicate that he wanted her out on the streets by St. Patrick's Day.

"Why? I'm only one month behind on rent, and I promise I'll catch that up when I pay for next month's rent." She closed her door and locked it.

"The police were here for you. I don't like trouble." The older man shook his head hard enough that the few springs of hair on top of his head waved back and forth.

She shook her head. "No, no. It was all a misunderstanding. Nothing happened. No tickets. No arrests. No charges. Buddy and Althea thought they heard something, but it was nothing."

"I don't care. I want you out in a month." He shoved an eviction notice at her, careless if she caught it or not. Then he waddled downstairs.

"You've always wanted to get rid of me." She didn't bother looking at the paper. She'd seen the warnings. "You found your excuse."

He hit the sidewalk and ducked out of her view. She heard a car starting and pulling out of the parking lot.

Janelle took the steps down slowly, hoping that at her pace she could somehow reverse time. By the time she stopped next to Buddy and Althea's door, it opened like the elderly couple had waited for her to get to them.

She glanced over to their doorway. In their standard uniform of tattered robes and bedroom slippers, they stared at her like disappointed parents.

Parents. Hell, if her mother caught wind of this, she would tell Janelle that she'd told her so, and quickly follow that up with an invitation to not stay with her.

"You can stay with us if you need to." Althea spoke first.

"Ah, so you know. News travels fast." Janelle put the eviction notice in her purse.

She started to tell them that their hasty call to the police had pushed Norwood to kick her out. The way they looked at her now with so much remorse and regret in their eyes, she didn't need to further twist the knife. They had called to protect her. At least someone had looked out for her.

"I think if Norwood finds me living with you all, he'll kick you out. I couldn't live with that." Janelle smiled despite the rough news handed to her before she'd even had a cup of coffee.

"It's so cold outside. Where will you go?" Buddy asked. His voice cracked as he spoke.

To prevent herself from crumbling, she headed to her car. "I have family." Not any family she could rely on to help her. "And I have friends." She hoped Penny would help her. "I'll be fine."

"So sorry about all of this, dear. We thought you were in trouble."

Janelle offered a sweet smile. "Thanks for looking out for me. I appreciate it."

Too bad their overprotective nature had forced her out of her home. She had to push that idea out of her thoughts and head to work.

She arrived to the flower shop and had to blink several times when she saw Penny already there. All air escaped her lungs when she saw her talking to Jules.

Janelle parked and jumped out of her vehicle. "Unless you're here to buy flowers, you have no business here."

Penny glared at Janelle before ducking into Flowers Galore. What the hell? Janelle didn't understand that reaction.

"I'm having a harmless conversation with your associate. You may want to have one with her now." He strolled away from the door. "But I won't be far. If you need me, give me a call."

"Don't bet on it." Janelle stormed inside her business. "What did he say to you?"

Penny barely looked at Janelle as she put her personal items away and cleaned up the store.

"Hey." Janelle grabbed Penny's arm. "What's going on?"

Penny jerked her arm from Janelle's grip. "I don't know, friend. You tell me."

"What is it?"

"I thought we were best friends." Penny crossed her arms.

"We are. What did that asshole tell you?"

"He didn't have to tell me anything. The world knows your business before I do. Why didn't you tell me you're seeing Gideon Wells?"

Janelle opened her mouth to refute the statement when Penny cut her off.

"Don't you dare lie to me and tell me you two aren't an item, because there are pictures of you to together, and he was at your place a couple of nights ago."

"Wait. You're the one who left me at his home."

"Yes, I knew about that night. You never told me what you two did. You certainly kept quiet on the fact that the cops showed up to your place while he was there."

"How do you know that?" Janelle put her hand to her chest, hoping to still her racing heart.

"It's all over the Internet. Or have you been too busy with your new man to even notice what's going on in the real world?" She continued to glare at Janelle until she moved around the counter. "I suppose you're going to tell me you didn't know that your man is going under the knife and that he might get traded, right?"

Janelle felt light-headed. "I haven't seen or talked to him in a couple of days."

"Rumors are going around about him that he slapped a quote-unquote mystery woman around, and that's why he's getting traded."

"That's all a lie."

"Since you two are both being so tight-lipped, the media is free to make up stories. People like me tend to believe them since no one is saying anything." She cocked her head. "So what do you say? You want to talk?"

Janelle put her hand over her pocket and rubbed Gideon's watch. "Yes." She ran out of the store and looked around the parking lot.

She found Jules sitting in a dark gray sedan rental parked at the far corner of the lot. She ran up to his car while he busied himself by snapping pictures of her during her trek.

Janelle knocked on the driver side window and waited for him to power it down before she spoke. "An interview. I want to do an interview with you."

Jules didn't act surprised. His smug smile spread even farther across his face. "How about today?"

She peered down at her outfit. "I want to change first."

"Good."

Yes, it would be good. She would make this all right for Gideon.

* * * *

Gideon drummed his thumbs over his thighs as he waited for his name to be called for the surgery. As he sat in the hospital waiting room, he didn't care if the other patients stared at him and Gunnar. The nerves that riddled his body came from not hearing from Janelle or seeing her.

He glanced at his phone to see if he had missed any calls or messages.

"Dude, you have your phone set on the loudest ring and most obnoxious alarm if you get a text." Gunnar put the magazine down on his thigh and huffed as he stared at Gideon. "Haven't you heard the saying about a watched pot never boiling?"

Gideon shook his head. "I know she's going to call." He glanced at his brother. "She is so warm and giving. Even from the smallest things, she's always thinking about me."

The memory of their last night together where she'd climbed on top of him and given him the best sex of his life remained etched in his brain. He could never forget that woman. Yet it seemed like she could push him out of her mind and heart so easily.

"If she was thinking of you, she would have called. Better yet, she would be here." Gunnar's tough-love advice didn't appeal to Gideon.

The door to the waiting room opened. Gideon glanced at it but slumped down when an elderly couple strolled through it.

"Damn." Gideon glanced at his bare wrist.

"Where's your watch, man, the one Mom gave you when you made pro?"

Gideon didn't want to answer. He'd left it at Janelle's place after she'd asked him to leave. At first, he'd chalked up his absentminded mistake to the chaos of the evening. It had been a while since he'd been confronted by law enforcement. Not since his teenage years. Then he knew what he'd done hadn't been an accident. He wanted her to contact him. He knew she would. Each day she hadn't, he figured she must have kept the watch, sold it, or thrown it away.

If she kept it, Gideon hoped she wore it and remembered him like he would always remember her every time he smelled vanilla or oranges.

"Are you sure Eboni is okay at the house with Mom?" Gideon asked.

Had he known their mother would get released that day, he would have postponed his surgery. Too bad his mother hated that plan and had insisted he go through with it.

"Eboni will be fine. She said she's used to caring for people, and she loves Mom as much as we do." Gunnar put his hand on Gideon's shoulder. "Don't worry about Mom. Don't worry about Eboni. Hell, don't even worry about me." He pointed to Gideon's chest. "You worry about you this time."

"I keep getting that advice." Gideon kept his stare on the waiting-room door.

"Learn to take it and we'll stop telling you to do it." Gunnar chuckled as he pulled Gideon in for a hug. "Did you call Thane?"

Gideon nodded. "Woke him up this morning."

"Good." Gunnar went back to reading his magazine. "Mom just had major heart surgery and you're having knee surgery, and he's not even here. Bastard."

Gideon glanced at the people around them. He nudged Gunnar's leg when he noticed a few of them listening in on their conversation. Gunnar scanned the other people and went back to his magazine.

"You've had relationships with other women before. What makes this one so special?" Gunnar shrugged but kept his stare on the sports magazine he held.

"She talked in plants and flowers." Gideon smiled when he remembered all the names she'd called him, both in anger and in lust.

"So she's a nerd like you." Gunnar laughed.

"She's headstrong."

"Stubborn. Like you. I'm starting to see a pattern here." Gunnar smiled and broke his concentration from his reading material to glance at Gideon.

"She looked out for me." Gideon's heart pounded as he remembered the time she'd alerted him to a nosy photographer.

"Then where is she?" Gunnar tossed his magazine to the side.

"Are you saying when you and your girl had problems that she remained by your side?"

Gunnar nodded. "Yeah, as a matter of fact, she did. Even when I wouldn't talk to her, she came and saw me every day, bugging the hell out of me until I realized how much I love—" He stopped midsentence and stared at Gideon. "You love Janelle, don't you?"

Gideon stared at the wall ahead of him and said nothing.

Gunnar couldn't keep quiet. "If you really dig this woman, tell her before it's too late."

"Mr. Wells," a nurse called from a doorway.

"Here." Gideon handed Gunnar his phone.

"I'll be waiting out here for you." His brother patted him on the back before he walked through the doorway.

"How are you feeling this morning?" the nurse asked as she led him down a wide hallway.

"Nervous." Gideon's nerves had nothing to do with the procedure.

What if Janelle didn't care about him at all?

"Don't worry. The doctor is the best and the surgery won't take too long. Before you know it, you'll be running up and down the football field again."

Gideon nodded, but his head and heart remained on Janelle.

Chapter 22

At the end of the workday, Janelle stared at the clock on the wall across from the sales counter. Her insides felt like they all vibrated at different intervals.

"You want me to lock up?" Penny touched Janelle's shoulder.

The connection shocked Janelle so much that she gasped and jumped.

"Whoa. What is your deal?" Penny took a step back.

"Sorry. I've got a lot on my mind." Janelle put her hand to her head before turning to her friend. "I need your help."

Penny crossed her arms over her chest and cocked her head. "Really? That's a first. You didn't need me before when—"

Janelle grabbed her friend's shoulders and stared into her eyes. "Penny, please."

Penny's expression became somber. "Oh, okay. Let me lock up and we can go to my place and talk."

Janelle shook her head. "We can't leave. Not yet."

"Why not?"

Janelle released a long sigh. "I'm talking to that photographer who's been following me around for weeks."

Penny's eyes went wide. "Are you serious?"

"I want to clear Gideon's name. He doesn't deserve all the bad press he's been getting. It isn't fair." Janelle went to the front door of her store and locked it. Then she turned off the Open sign.

"It may not be fair, but it's the life of a celebrity. Tabloids make stuff up all the time." Penny shrugged. "I don't know if you should have agreed to talk to that guy. You know he can twist your words around. If you say that all you and Gideon did was play cards and he beat you at poker, that jerk will probably lop off the tail end of your statement to say that Gideon beat you."

Janelle paced the floor. "I hadn't thought of that."

"Did you sign a contract or anything?"

Janelle remained quiet.

Penny rolled her head back. "Christ, you did. Do you have it?"

Janelle darted to the office and pulled it from her purse. "Here it is." She handed it to Penny.

Penny started reading it until it looked like her eyes would pop out of her head again. "A million? This guy agreed to pay you a cool million for spilling the dirt on Gideon? Way to go." She held up her hand to give Janelle a high five.

The whole thing now felt like a betrayal. She shouldn't have made the deal. She should have gone to the hospital to be with him during his surgery. She had promised him she would be there.

"That was the other reason why I did it." Janelle took a deep breath before facing her friend. "I'm having money problems."

Penny blinked. "What are you talking about? My checks are always good."

Janelle nodded. "Yes, because I do without paying myself sometimes to pay you. It's the real reason Thelma quit. She saw a disconnection notice from the power company and she paid it for me. She didn't want to be a burden on me. Having Gideon in town has been a blessing in a lot of ways to me. I've managed to keep my business afloat. I've paid some of my bills. But I'm in trouble, and I don't know what else to do. I'm getting evicted from my apartment."

"What? Why?" Penny moved in closer to Janelle.

Janelle needed that personal connection right now. "It's a long story, but part of it has to do with me being behind on my rent."

"Girl, why didn't you tell me all this before? You can move in with me." Penny put her hand on Janelle's shoulder.

Janelle cocked her head. "You live in an apartment smaller than mine that's located above your parents' garage. How is that going to work?"

"We could make it work. I'm your friend." She held up the papers. "Reading this, it looks like you're going to have to do this interview. Has he already given you the money?"

Janelle nodded. "Wired it right to my account. I can't believe I have all that money. I don't even want to spend it."

"Don't. Let me finish reading this contract. I think I have a plan. Is that guy coming here?"

"In an hour. I have another outfit to change into."

"Where are you doing the interview? Out here or in your office?"

Janelle shrugged. "He didn't say."

"Good. Let's take advantage of this. I think I know of a way for you to keep the money free and clear and get your intended message out."

Penny continued reading the contract when Janelle wrapped her arms around her friend and hugged her harder than she'd ever had.

"I love you. Thank you for always sticking by me and never judging me."

Penny hugged her back. "Of course. You're my girl. We have to stick together."

"When all this is over, I'll tell you all about Gideon and how wonderful and thoughtful he is."

Janelle headed to her office.

"And the fact that he's hung like an elephant?"

That statement stopped Janelle in her tracks. She turned to Penny.

"It's the word on the street." Penny winked and kept reading.

"You concentrate on a plan and stop thinking about my man's penis." Janelle laughed a little as she ducked into her office.

Her man. She hoped after this stunt, she could repair what she'd broken with Gideon. She hoped he still wanted her as much as she wanted him.

* * * *

Gideon slowly opened his eyes. Soft light met his gaze as he took a deep breath. He felt oxygen tubes in his nostrils, giving him additional air. After a couple of long blinks, he spotted a nurse hustling by him to get to another patient in the expansive room.

"I see you're awake now, Mr. Wells."

Gideon turned his head toward the sound of the voice and saw another nurse standing by his bed. She smiled almost like she needed to reassure him he would be okay.

"Am I about to go into surgery now?" he asked.

"No, sir. You're all done." The nurse gazed down to his right leg.

Gideon hadn't even thought about taking inventory of his body. He lifted his head and saw the bandages around his knee along with a compression sock. Right now, he didn't feel a thing. He knew later the pain would come and hard. Then he would have to go through arduous months of rehabilitation. The pain and punishment would keep his mind off Janelle.

"We'll take you to a room to rest up a bit more, and then you'll be discharged." The nurse started unplugging his IVs from the wall sockets and unlocking the wheels on his bed.

"Is my brother still here?" He couldn't imagine that Gunnar would have gone anywhere unless something had happened to their mother.

"Waiting for you in the room." She pushed him down the hallway until she reached a room at the end. With careful precision, she got his bed into the room and against the wall without hitting anything.

"Hey, big guy." Gunnar stood and patted Gideon on the shoulder. "How are you feeling?"

"No pain right now." Gideon smiled. "None physically."

"Hope I can help repair your heart."

The female voice he heard sounded familiar. He knew it didn't come from Janelle. Whenever she spoke, his heart drummed a wild beat. It didn't sound like the nurse who had moved him to the room.

Gideon turned his head and had to blink a number of times to register the view. "Hilary?"

The blonde bombshell smiled. "In the flesh and here for you, dear." She leaned over for a kiss.

Gideon had enough strength and the wherewithal to turn his head so that her lips landed on his cheek. "What are you doing here in Virginia?"

She peered up at Gunnar, who stood on the other side of the bed. "Maybe we can talk a little later without the crowds."

The nurse plugged everything back in and checked Gideon's vital signs before leaving the room and closing the door behind her.

"Okay, the nurse is gone. Why are you here?" Gideon asked again with a little more bass to his voice.

She tucked her hair behind her ear and glanced at Gunnar again. "Do you mind giving us a little privacy?"

"No." Gideon grabbed his brother's wrist. "Anything you can say to me, you can say in front of him. He's family. Last I checked, we weren't a couple anymore."

Hilary pursed her lips and cleared her throat. "I'm here as a favor to Scot." She looked at her nails like this whole conversation bored her.

"Scot? What does he have to do with you being here?" Gideon found the controller for the bed and lifted his head a bit more.

"He told me that to get people interested in you again, I should show up and be by your side during this difficult time. It's perfect. You're hurt. You've gone through this surgery, which could drastically affect your career. And I'm here to nurse you back to health. Besides, if the Portland Coyotes see that you have more ties to the West Coast than the East, they'll be inclined to sign you." She put her hand to his chest. "Then maybe we can start over. Pick up where we left off."

Gideon had to shake his head a few times while he digested her words. "Where we left off was me finding out that Scot was the one who'd sent you to me in the first place so that we could date and become a couple, and me finding out that you were never really interested in me."

Hilary rolled her eyes. "That's the business part of show business, baby. If you didn't talk so much about plants and flowers all the time, we probably could have lasted a bit longer."

Gunnar snickered. Until then, Gideon had forgotten his brother stood in the room with them.

"I apologize for boring you. I promise I won't do that anymore." Gideon felt his face go tight the longer he looked at her.

Hilary smiled, showing off her expensive dental work. "See, that's the spirit."

"I don't suppose you have some movie about to come out soon, do you?"

She beamed even more. "As a matter of fact, I do. Not Oscar gold but it could be a blockbuster at least."

"Good. I'm happy for you. I really am. But if you think you're going to walk out of this hospital with me, holding my hand or pushing my wheelchair while a bunch of photographers snap the shot, you're crazy." Gideon pressed the Nurse Call button as he watched his ex-girlfriend's smile turn into a scowl. "We've been broken up for months. I've moved on. I'm sure you have also. I have no reason or desire to use you for some publicity. That's your deal, not mine. Had I known then that the only reason you wanted to be with me was to up your star status, I would have steered clear of you. I've met someone."

She snorted. "Who? The flower girl? What does she have that I don't have? I can get you into A-list parties. You could have the best of everything."

"With her, I have the best of everything." Gideon had hoped her face would be the first one he would see after his surgery.

Hilary snatched up her purse. "Fine. I hate Virginia anyway. J.T. warned me this was not a happening town."

"J.T.?" Gunnar asked.

"Justin Timberlake. Duh." She rolled her eyes. "Good luck wherever you go."

Before Gideon could respond, she stormed out of the room.

Gunnar put his hand on Gideon's shoulder. "Let me get this straight. Your agent set you up with an actress to be your girlfriend?"

"Didn't find out until I heard her talking about me over the phone one day. I knew she wasn't into the football thing. I didn't realize she also wasn't into me." Breaking up with Hilary had been hard. Rebuilding his shattered ego had proved to be even more difficult.

"Wow. No wonder you didn't want Mom setting you up." Gunnar rubbed his hand over his eyes.

"Yeah. I don't want to experience another woman using me." Gideon shook his head.

"Did you get the impression that Janelle wanted to use you? She didn't come off that way to me."

Before Gideon could answer, a nurse appeared at his door. "Are you okay, Mr. Wells?"

"I think I'm ready to go now." Gideon wanted to be home. The shock of seeing Hilary had reminded him that his heart mattered.

"Yes, sir. I'll see if the doctor has prepared your discharge orders yet." She disappeared down the hall.

"What the hell is that?" Gunnar picked up the remote and turned up the TV volume.

Gideon had to blink a few times to focus. Once he did, he caught Janelle's image on TV.

"An exclusive interview with the modern-day Eliza Doolittle herself will be posted on the ZMT celebrity tabloid site sometime today," a news anchor said with a big smile across his face. "Reports say she'll reveal secrets about her tryst with none other than Super Bowl MVP, Gideon Wells."

Gideon felt his blood boil as he watched the telecast. "Can't be."

Gunnar squeezed Gideon's shoulder. "Shit, man."

"Supposedly, she'll talk about how they met, his football career, and if there are wedding bells in their future. I know this station will be watching out for that interview. We'll feature clips as soon as they become available. In other news—"

Gunnar turned off the TV. "That's got to be bullshit. She wouldn't do that to you, would she?"

Gideon rubbed his wrist where his cherished watch used to be. "I don't know."

If she had betrayed him, he would be done. No more love. He could take a lot. The pain of having his heart broken again would drain him.

Chapter 23

Janelle paced in her apartment while Penny sat at the kitchen counter with Janelle's laptop in front of her. Janelle had hoped after all she'd done, her plan would work.

"Well?" She wrung her hands together.

"The jerk's video is out." Penny looked up from the computer. "As we thought, he did a hatchet job on it."

Janelle put her hand to her head and groaned. "I knew I shouldn't have done it. I shut my business down all day today because of this. I knew I would get more questions than sales. If Gideon or his family sees his video, they're going to hate me."

"Not after I do this." Penny did a couple of clicks on the laptop. "Done."

Janelle ran to Penny and peered over her shoulder. "Are you sure my original video will go as viral as Jules's? I want the truth to be out there."

"It should. Every time I posted a picture of you and Gideon, they took off. I have a lot of friends on social media." She smiled.

"And you don't think this guy has a leg to stand on to sue me?" Janelle chewed her lower lip.

"The one good thing about watching all of those episodes of *Judge Judy* and *Law & Order*—"

"Along with having parents who are both attorneys."

"Yeah, and that. I learned a lot about loopholes. This guy is good, but if he tries to sue you, we can throw it back in his face that he has in his contract about editing your content. It's a good thing we hid that camera in the office while you did the interview." Penny tapped her temple.

"It's a great thing for me that I have a really, really smart friend. My ride-or-die chick." Janelle hugged her from behind.

Penny leaned her head toward Janelle. "Now call your man, or better yet, go see him."

"I won't be able to get by the guard at the gate." Janelle shook her head. "He probably won't want to see me."

"Won't know unless you ask." Penny held up Janelle's phone.

Janelle paused before accepting the phone from her friend. "Although I've shared with you everything that's happened between me and Gideon these past few weeks, I'll need to make this a private conversation."

Penny held up her hands in surrender. "Fine. Be that way. I'll be out here after you're done talking. I'll be the one with the two glasses of wine." She nudged Janelle toward her bedroom.

Janelle paced in her room for a moment. Her video hadn't been out long enough for Gideon to know what she had done. The other video had been out all day. It had gained legs and been picked up by several media outlets. Janelle had become famous for all the wrong reasons.

She took a deep breath and dialed Gideon's number, hoping beyond hope that he hadn't changed his number.

The phone rang once. Janelle's heart pounded as her pacing slowed. It rang a second time. Sweat covered her hands despite her having to lower the temperature in her apartment to save on her electric bill. On the third ring, she knew he wouldn't answer. She would leave him a voice-mail message and hope he would listen to it one day. Before the fourth ring, she heard a *click*.

A heavy sigh sounded after the *click*. Janelle sat on her bed and waited for the screaming to commence.

"Hello?" She decided to start the conversation when no one else spoke.

"You have some nerve calling me." Gideon sounded tired but reserved.

"I know you're angry." She kept her speaking voice low and stretched out her words, hoping to lower the tension between them. "Please let me explain. I didn't tell Jules anything about your family or your football career. He asked and I avoided the subjects."

"That's not how it looks. I watched a snippet of the video." Gideon growled.

Janelle didn't know if his growling came from anger or pain since he'd had his surgery. "How are you doing? How's your knee?"

"Oh, no. You are not going to jump off topic with me. If you truly cared about me, you would have done what you promised and showed up to the hospital," he said. "I guess you had better things to do, like that interview." He cursed, but quickly apologized. "I will never learn my lesson. I will always be the one with his heart on his sleeve."

"Gideon, please. I want you to listen to me. That guy lied to me. He edited the video so it looked like I said things that I didn't. He made it seem like I was angry with you, and I'm not. I asked you to stay away from me because I was trying to protect you. I thought the media would leave you alone if we weren't together, but I was wrong, and I hated being away from you." She balled her free hand into a fist. "You probably won't believe me, but I'm going to say this anyway. I love you. I love you so much. It hurt me to ask you to leave. I was so afraid that if you went to that other team, you would pick up and leave and I would be here."

"Rooted," he whispered.

"With my store." She wiped under her nose. "I know you hate me. I understand. I really thought I was doing a good thing for you because it angered me so much to read all those lies about you. People were saying you hit that cheerleader and that you assaulted me, and I knew that wasn't true. They were calling you a coward, and I know the man who is so strong and so brave who would never back down from a fight. All I wanted to do was let the world know the man I know, the man I fell in love with. The man who has my heart forever."

He remained quiet. Janelle hoped Gideon hadn't disconnected the call.

"Penny actually had a good idea." Janelle sniffed.

"Yeah? What was that?"

She breathed a sigh of relief after hearing his voice. "She suggested I hide a camera while I did the interview and post the full interview after this guy posted his so that everyone can see the truth. I don't hate you. I never meant to hurt you. I mean it when I say I love you."

Before anyone spoke, Janelle heard a knock at her door.

"I'll get it!" Penny called from the other room.

"Never, ever talk to these tabloid guys." Gideon sniffed. "Unless it's Oprah or Barbara Walters, everyone in the media lies. They have to in order to sell themselves."

She smiled through her tears. "Good to know."

"We can talk about it more if you want to come—"

Penny appeared in the doorway, looking as white as a snow-covered orchid. "Janelle, something bad has happened."

"Gideon, hold on." Janelle stood.

"What? What's going on there?" Worry filled Gideon's voice.

"It's the flower shop. There's been an accident."

Janelle put her hand to her stomach while keeping the phone pressed to her ear. "What?"

"The police are here. They said there was a fire." Penny shook her head. "Everything is gone."

Janelle remained frozen in her spot as though her muscles had stopped working. She dropped the phone from her ear as she stared at her friend. "No."

"We, uh, have to go." Penny put her arm around Janelle's shoulders. "I'll drive."

* * * *

Gideon grumbled as he hobbled toward the garage. He'd never expected to hear from Janelle after what she'd done. After she'd explained her reasoning behind it, he could understand what she'd thought.

Then, in the blink of an eye, everything changed. He thought he'd heard someone say the word "fire" before the call ended. He'd tried calling her back but got nothing. Now he needed to see her.

When he'd gotten home from the hospital, Gunnar had set him up in the spare bedroom downstairs. It took a while for him to dress himself. He'd taken some drugs for the pain, which left him feeling a bit woozy. The white compression stocking around his knee hid the bandages underneath and prevented him from seeing the full swelling around his leg.

"Eboni and I were about to head out since Mom is sleeping now." Gunnar stood in the doorway. "What do you think you're doing?"

Gideon slipped on some bedroom slippers since he couldn't bend his knee to put on anything with laces. "I need to go."

"No. You need to rest. You had surgery earlier today and you're on a lot of medication." Gunnar put his hands on Gideon's shoulders and tried easing him back to bed.

Gideon held onto Gunnar's arm as he hopped to prevent going down on the bed. "No, I have to go. Janelle called me."

Gunnar dropped his hold and shook his head. "You talked to her? Did she apologize for selling you out? She's got some nerve calling you after she—"

Gideon cut off his brother. "I think her store burned down. I have to go and make sure she's okay."

"You can't leave." Gunnar went to the closet. "Not with those shoes. Mom won't let you out of the house with slippers on." Gunnar helped him switch his gym shorts to track pants and then got down on the floor to put on Gideon's sneakers. "I remember helping you get dressed as a kid. Who knew I would still have to do that now?" He laughed.

"You're hilarious." Gideon slipped on his jacket. "Come on. We have to go."

Gunnar handed Gideon the cane he needed to help him get around. As soon as they hit the front door, Eboni appeared.

"I thought we were going back home." She split her attention between the two men.

"Gideon thinks Janelle's store was burned down." Gunnar put on his coat.

"For what she did to Gideon, I wouldn't be surprised. Fans are loyal." She crossed her arms over her chest.

"Do me a favor." Gideon put on his coat, a feat with the cane. "Janelle said she uploaded the full, uncut interview. Will you find it and look at it for me? Tell me if the two match."

"Sure." Eboni nodded.

"I'll be back as soon as I can. Call me if anything happens here." Gunnar kissed his fiancée. He helped Gideon to his Hummer and drove as quickly as he could to Flowers Galore.

Gideon remained quiet the entire ride there until a few blocks away from her store, when he caught the sight of red, twirling fire-engine lights.

"Oh, no." He sat taller and pressed his hand against the dashboard as though trying to push the Hummer to go faster.

When he arrived at the scene, Gideon took in the full damage. The entire strip mall where Flowers Galore sat in the center now looked like a black kindling. Smoke from the smoldering ashes wafted in the air.

Gunnar barely parked the truck before Gideon opened the door.

"Hold on, man. Let me help you or you're going to fuck up your knee." Gunnar jumped out his side and raced over to the other to help Gideon, who had managed to get his good foot down to the ground already.

He staggered over to the scene that had been blocked off by police and fire trucks. "Janelle! Janelle!" He scanned the area.

A small crowd had formed around the fire along with news crews. When he called for her, the attention turned to him.

"You've got to be kidding. It's Gideon Wells." Someone pointed to him as he continued searching the crowd.

He finally spotted her talking to a few firemen off to the side. He headed toward her when a man blocked his path. Gideon peered down and saw Dudley, the fan he had met his first day working in his mother's shop.

"Good to see you again, man." Dudley tried shaking Gideon's hand.

Gideon moved around him. "I've got something to do."

"No worries. That bitch got what she deserved."

The statement stopped him cold. Gideon turned around. "What did you say?" He stumbled back to Dudley, who did his own dance backward.

"Did you call her a bitch?" He fisted the fan's shirt. "Did you have anything to do with this fire?"

"Whoa. No, man. I swear. I saw she did an unflattering interview about you. I wouldn't be surprised if a bunch of Wolf fans burned down her place. You can't talk about Gid the god."

Gideon let him go. "Unbelievable. That was her life. You shouldn't be happy about someone destroying a life." He turned away from Dudley.

"Why not? She tried to destroy yours."

Gideon ignored him. He continued on to Janelle. As soon as she looked up and connected her gaze to his, she broke down and sobbed hard.

"Sir, you can't cross the line." The officer held his hand up to stop Gideon.

He had a mission. Get to Janelle. He pushed past him and got to her. Janelle collapsed on to Gideon and cried into his chest. He held her and didn't talk. He allowed her to grieve the loss of her business.

"It's all gone," she said against his chest. "I was turning it all around, and now it's all gone."

"Do you know what happened?" he asked. "Was it a fan that was angry about the interview? Was it Jules because you released the other video?"

Janelle pulled back from him and peered up. Her red eyes displayed her grief and anger. "Sleaston."

He shook his head. "Who's that?"

She pointed to the area where the end unit would have been in the shopping area. "He was the accountant who had an office there. He was having financial problems. He stole from his clients. He was arrested for embezzlement and he decided to burn the evidence."

"Good. So they know who did it and this guy can be prosecuted." Gideon brushed his thumb over her cheek.

Janelle shook her head. "He was in his office. He'd already shot himself after he set the fire. They found his remains." She stared at the shell that used to be her store. "My swamp hibiscus. No one will ever see it. It's gone. It's all gone." She covered her eyes with her hand.

"Are you done here with the police and fire department?" Gideon looked at the men and women in uniform behind her.

Janelle nodded. "I don't think there's anything else I can do. They're chalking it up as arson. I'll have to get a formal report from them to give to my insurance company. Until then, I have nothing."

"Come on home with me." He held her hand.

"What? You want me to come to your house?"

"You need me." He squeezed her hand. "I need you. I love you."

She nodded and wrapped her arm around his waist as he led her to Gunnar's truck. When Gideon spotted Gunnar by the truck, he continued on his trek.

"She's coming home with me."

Gunnar said nothing. He opened the back door and helped her inside. Then he helped Gideon get in on the passenger side before taking them both back to his home.

The inside of the vehicle remained quiet all the way to the house. Once there, Gunnar helped Gideon out of the truck first before they both attended to Janelle. With his cane in one hand and his arm around his woman, he guided her into his house.

Eboni met the trio at the door. "Wow. You all smell like smoke."

Gideon hadn't realized the smell until she pointed it out. They had taken on the foul aroma of the charred-up remains of Janelle's shop.

"I'm in the same bedroom where you took your bath. Go in there and I'll meet you in a few minutes." Gideon kissed her forehead before she padded down the hall. Then he turned to Eboni. "Did you find anything?"

She smiled. "I can tell she really loves you."

Gideon's heart swelled in his chest before he heard anything else.

Eboni continued. "She recorded the whole interview. That guy she dealt with was a weasel. He chopped up everything she said. She talked about you like a woman in love with a man." She wrapped her arms around Gunnar's waist. "She spoke about you like how I would talk about Gunnar. It was pretty incredible. I'm glad she posted it. It's a shame what happened with her business."

Gideon nodded. "Thanks for doing that for me." He looked at Gunnar. "Thanks for taking me to the scene. I owe you both big-time."

Gunnar waved his hand. "That's what families do." He peered down at Eboni. "We're going to head home. Call me if you need me. I'll be back in the morning to help the two of you."

"Thanks, man." Gunnar escorted them out and locked the door.

He went to the bedroom. He didn't expect to see Janelle sitting on the side of his bed looking so broken. She hadn't taken off a stitch of her clothing or her shoes.

"You want to take a bath?" he asked.

She shook her head. "I'm so tired."

Gideon understood what she meant. He pulled back the comforter on the bed. "Take off your shoes."

She kicked them off. Without prompting, she removed her pants and her coat. She left her T-shirt on. Before getting into bed, she undid

Gideon's pants and pulled them down his legs. When she got to his knee bandages, she stared at them and a new wave of tears flooded her eyes.

"I'm okay."

Janelle peered up at him.

"No, I really am this time. I'm not saying it to make you feel better. The surgery went well. I'll have to do a lot of rehab, but I'm ready." Gideon smiled to let her know he would be okay.

She helped him sit on the bed. Once he did, she removed his pants and his shoes. "What do you need for your knee?"

He stared at her.

"Does it need to be elevated? Do you need pain medication?"

He nodded. "Elevated would be great."

Gideon positioned himself on one side of the bed and allowed Janelle to put pillows under his right knee.

"Good?" She looked at her handiwork.

He nodded. "Now come to bed." She slipped under the covers and nestled next to him.

"Thank you." She wrapped her arm around his waist and held him.

Gideon had more to thank her for than she thought. She complemented him in every way. He had to ensure that she would remain in his life forever.

Chapter 24

Janelle woke up to find Gideon gone from the bed. How a man with a bum knee could manage to move around unnoticed baffled her. Had she truly been that out of it? The memories of her former business came flooding back into her head. She'd lost it all. In losing it all, she'd gained her man again.

She slipped out of bed and strolled to the bathroom. Before she could do anything else, she had to get the smoky smell from her hair and body. She started the shower, stripped, and ducked into it.

After the shower, she realized very quickly that she didn't have any clean clothes with her. She'd left the scene of the crime to Gideon's home. She opened a closet door and found it filled with Gideon's clothes. He knew he would be living in this room for a while. She found an oversize sweatshirt and put it on. It came down to her knees like a dress, not even a minidress. So that her feet wouldn't get cold, she put on her sneakers.

She opened the door and tiptoed out into the open area.

"Come over here, darling."

The sound of Queen Elizabeth's voice startled her. She hadn't expected to see the matriarch sitting like royalty in the living room while clutching a heart-shaped pillow to her chest. Janelle walked into the room and sat on the sofa that faced Elizabeth. She didn't want to be in swinging range of her if the woman wanted to hit her.

"How are you feeling?" Janelle asked.

"Getting stronger each day. Coughing is hard." She patted the pillow. "That's why I have this." She took a deep breath before she spoke. "Gideon told me about your store. I'm so, so sorry."

Janelle mustered a smile and nodded. "Thank you. It's the worst feeling in the world to see your dreams go up in smoke."

Queen shook her head. "No, darling. The worst feeling is losing a loved one. You can rebuild."

"I had a very special plant in there. I was going to enter it into the upcoming plant show." She slipped her feet out of her shoes and curled her legs onto the couch.

"You will come back stronger than ever. I know that. In the meantime, I do have some questions for you." Elizabeth coughed in the lightest way she could. When she settled down, she addressed Janelle again. "What did you hope to accomplish by doing your interview?"

Janelle had known she would be questioned about it. "I read all of these horrible things online about Gideon. I wanted to set the record straight. If it wasn't for Penny giving me a great backup plan, people would still think he'd done all those bad things." She found her voice to keep talking about Gideon. "Queen, I love your son. You may think I have a strange way of showing it, but I do love him. He understands me. I hope he knows that I truly understand him. I used to be the woman content to hide in the shadows." She shook her head. "No more. Now I want nothing more than to shout to the world about how much I love him. Hopefully, he feels the same about me."

"I do."

Janelle turned and saw Gideon standing behind her. She stood and ran to him.

"Easy. Don't tackle me." He smiled.

"I would never hurt you. Not ever again." She hugged him and gave him a long kiss. She only broke from him when she heard Queen clearing her throat.

"Dear, I think you forgot to put something on underneath your shirt." Elizabeth pointed to her.

Janelle peered down and found that the back of her sweatshirt had risen above her backside. She brought her hands down and tugged on the garment. "Sorry."

"No apologies necessary. I know you came here with the clothes on your back."

"That's why I want to make a few offers to you." Gideon led Janelle back to the couch and sat her down. "I was talking to Mom about my duties at Pick 'N Clip. With the surgery and my rehabilitation, I won't be able to be there as much as I want to help out. Until your store gets rebuilt, we would like to offer you a job as manager. What do you think?"

Janelle smiled. "I would love it. I already miss being around flowers."

"Good. We already hired Penny. She's there driving Victor crazy right now," Queen said.

Janelle laughed. "She is an acquired taste."

Gideon held Janelle's hand. "I talked to Penny for a while this morning. She shared with me some disturbing news. Baby, why didn't you tell me you were getting evicted?"

Janelle blinked. She would have to fire, rehire, and fire Penny again for breaching her trust. "I didn't want you to know. It happened the morning after the whole police incident. The landlord saw me as a liability. I never want people to feel like they have to take care of me."

"Hmm, sounds like someone else I know." Queen nodded toward Gideon.

"Yes, Janelle and I have deep stubborn streaks." He stared at Janelle. "That's why Penny is going to your apartment right now to pack everything for you and ship it all here. You're moving in with me."

She started to open her mouth when Gideon cut her off.

"No objections. I can't have the woman I love living on the streets." He kissed the back of her hand. "Now you need to come with me so I can show you this last thing." He rose to his feet with the help of his cane and led her to his greenhouse. "You remember when you were here and I showed you my greenhouse? At the time, you noticed something in the corner that I wouldn't let you see."

"I remember."

He held her hand and led her to the corner. There sat a white rose bush that had something special about it. The roses all had a gradient black-to-white color scheme. Janelle reached out and touched the petals.

"I was going to enter it in the plant show. I was going to call it Janelle's Rose after you." Gideon put his hand to the back of her neck and rubbed his thumb across the base.

"They're beautiful." She put her nose into one open bud and took a deep sniff. "So sweet. How did you get them to be black at the bottom?"

"Black food coloring in the water."

"Too bad it's not organic. I wish something like this actually grew in nature."

"If you think that's weird, take a look in that center flower." Gideon pointed to the biggest flower in the arrangement.

Janelle looked at it and noticed something shiny in the center. At first, she thought that extra water had landed on the plant. On closer inspection, she saw that her assessment didn't hold water either. She covered her mouth and took a couple of steps back.

Gideon reached into the flower and pulled out an exquisite engagement ring. "If I could get down on one knee, I would. Since I can't, I'll do the best I can." He held her hand and stared into her eyes. "Janelle, you are the woman I need in my life. You're strong, smart, beautiful, and have the same love of plants that I have. Make me the happiest man in the world by marrying me."

Janelle's constricted throat prevented her from speaking. She simply nodded.

Gideon slipped the ring on her finger. He framed her face and kissed her so passionately, Janelle felt her body trembling.

"Let's tell Queen the great news." Janelle took Gideon's hand and pulled him back out to the living room.

"Easy. I can't run. Not just yet." Gideon laughed.

Queen had turned the TV on and left it on Gideon's go-to station, ESPN. It seemed Dennis had called a press conference.

"Is that your teammate?" Janelle asked.

"Yeah. This ought to be good." Gideon stood behind his mother as he watched the TV.

"The Wolves' quarterback, Gideon Wells, had surgery on his ACL. I don't know about the coaches and managers, but I can tell you"—Dennis paused before he continued speaking—"I will not play another game as a Virginia Beach Wolf without Gideon Wells."

Gideon blinked at that news.

"Gideon is the heart and soul of this team. Even hurt, that man ran a play during the Super Bowl because I wasn't there for him. I looked away at a moment when he had a chance to throw me the ball. He had to pick up my slack. He truly is the MVP."

Gideon nodded. "I didn't expect him to say that."

Janelle put her hand to the side of Gideon's face and kissed him.

"The stellar team of Gid the god and Dennis the Menace may still hold strong for Virginia Beach," the sports analyst said.

"It was awfully nice of Dennis to say that, huh, Mom?"

Queen didn't answer.

"Mom?" Gideon touched her shoulder and she slumped down. "Call nine-one-one!" He dropped his cane and hobbled over to his mother as best he could. "Mom, talk to me. Mom!"

Janelle found her cell phone and called for an ambulance. She couldn't go from having the best day of her life to potentially losing her mentor.

* * * *

Gunnar paced in the waiting room at the hospital. Gideon knew his brother must have worn holes in the carpeting by now.

"Tell me again what happened." Gunnar kept moving even as he spoke.

"She was fine. She was up talking to both of us. Janelle and I went to my greenhouse. When we came out, she wasn't responding. It happened that fast." Gideon almost felt guilty leaving her alone for even that short while.

Her doctor appeared in the room. He pulled Gideon, Gunnar, Janelle, and Eboni into a consultation room.

"What's going on?" Gideon started in on the questioning first.

"It looks like your mother had a stroke. It's not uncommon for heart patients, even after surgery. With her vitals all being so strong while she was here, we didn't think she would have a stroke after being discharged. We're going to hold her here until she stabilizes."

"What can we do?" Janelle asked. She hated feeling helpless.

"Be here for her. Offer her love and support. If you're religious, pray for her." The doctor headed to the door.

"Is it that bad?" Eboni covered her mouth.

"It may not be. But she's not young. She just had major surgery. It's touch and go right now."

"Thanks. Whatever you can do for her, do it. No matter the cost. Save her." Gideon shook the doctor's hand.

When he left the room, Gideon remained silent.

"She'll be fine." Eboni firmed up a smile even though tears streamed down her face. "She's so strong."

"Yes, she is." Janelle held Eboni's hand.

"And you know she wouldn't miss two weddings." Eboni held up Janelle's hand. "Beautiful ring."

Janelle looked back at Gideon. "From a great man who made me a better woman." She held Gideon's hands. "I love you."

Gideon wrapped his arm around her. "I love you."

With all the love in the room, it had to be enough to save Queen Elizabeth. Janelle's love had certainly saved him.

Meet the Author

Crystal Bright graduated with a B.A. from Old Dominion University with a major in Creative Writing, a minor in Communications, and an emphasis on Public Relations. She earned her M.A. from Seton Hill University in Writing Popular Fiction. She is a member of Romance Writers of America. For more information about Crystal and her writing, please visit her website at www.CrystalBrightWriter.com. You can also find her on Facebook at https://www.facebook.com/crystal.bright.397, or follow her on twitter: https://twitter.com/CrystalBBright.

Don't miss the first book in Cyristal B. Bright's Mama's Boys series!

The Look of Love

You can't fight love…

There's only one thing MMA fighter Gunnar Wells is more devoted to than his career, and that's his mother, "Queen" Elizabeth. An elegant African American woman who adopted Gunnar and his two white brothers, Elizabeth was there when they needed her, and they'll do anything for her. For Gunnar, that means running her hair salon when she suddenly falls ill. And if that's not awkward enough for the champion fighter, he'll have to work alongside Eboni Danielson, the other love of his life. The one he left behind to pursue his dream. The one he's never forgotten…

Between the salon and her volunteer work, Eboni keeps busy to keep her mind off the man who broke her heart. So when Gunnar shows up again, she does her best to stay cool—on the outside. But the more she watches Gunnar step up and help out, the less she can deny her feelings. Soon Gunnar is doing everything he can to convince Eboni to give him a fighting chance. Can she trust him again—even when old secrets and new dangers come between them once more?

On sale now!
http://www.kensingtonbooks.com/book.aspx/31356

Chapter 1

The adrenaline coursing through Gunnar Wells's body needed some release. The muscles in his arms and thighs tightened, ready for activity, for combat. A good workout would ease his tensions. Tonight, his mixed martial arts match would have to do.

He paced the cramped dressing room that smelled like rose petals and bleach, too dainty and too clean for what he had to do. The delicate aroma and the rough sport he would be engaging in soon reminded him of his mother, always a lady in demeanor and look, but a tough taskmaster.

A smile tugged at the corner of his mouth before he could arrest it and pull it back down to a scowl. He needed to keep his mind on his match. Staying away from his childhood home helped keep him on track.

A mural of the famous Welcome to Las Vegas sign painted on the locker-room wall snagged his attention for a brief moment. The blue, red, and white neon sign full of diverse geometric shapes attracted tourists every day. Gunnar saw the city as a place to start another part of his life. He didn't need a reminder of the location he'd made his home for the past ten years.

The Silver Streak Hotel and Casino spared no expense in keeping both the crowds and the performers entertained. Gunnar had heard that hosting these mixed martial arts matches had afforded the hotel enough funds to add a new wing to the hotel with another two hundred hotel rooms. He guessed beating a man to a bloody pulp meant good business.

Gunnar tilted his head from one side to the other to stretch his neck and help clear his head. Even with the door closed to his dressing room, the sounds from the audience in the main arena area filtered through the walls.

With each chant of "Guns" from the crowd, Gunnar's heart pounded harder and harder until both the chant and his heartbeat became one.

"Guns! Guns!"

Thump! Thump!

He swiped the back of his hand over his sweaty forehead. The tape on his hand scraped across his skin, leaving a tingling sensation in its wake. Gunnar glanced at the tape to make sure he hadn't ruined its integrity. After doing this sport for so many years, he found that every little thing mattered. A loose binding on his fist would distract him. Like a hunter, he needed to keep his focus.

For his match against a fairly established mixed martial artist like himself, he didn't feel unnerved. In his ten-year professional career, he'd battled absolute monsters. Being six-foot-three and two hundred forty pounds, he fit in the behemoth category. Like his mama always taught him, it's not the dog in the fight; it's the fight in the dog.

Gunnar attempted to push thoughts of his mother from his mind. He couldn't help but think about her and his brothers before each match. One brutal fight could leave him broken, destroyed, or dead. After all his family had done to support him, he couldn't let them down. He fought for them as much as he fought for himself and his career.

Truly the only woman who had ever understood him, thinking of her would only turn him into mush. For what he had to do in a few minutes, he needed to be on his game, an animal. He needed to be Gunnar "Guns" Wells, the heavyweight International Ultimate Fighting champion that the spectators loved to hate. Or maybe they hated to love him since he hadn't lost a match since starting the sport.

As he marched in his bare feet, he closed his eyes and envisioned the entire match, a calming technique he'd employed for years thanks to his yoga-loving mother. He stomped on the thin carpet that covered the concrete flooring. The hardness reminded him that nothing came easy to him, and it shouldn't. Only hard work would get him the rewards he wanted. Fighting afforded him the lifestyle he'd only dreamed of as a youth. If only he could have shared the success with someone.

"No negative thoughts. No negative thoughts." Gunnar talked to himself a lot to get into the headspace needed for his match.

As usual, he'd made sure to clear out his locker room before his match. No one disturbed him or retrieved him until he got called to the ring. After each winning match, he did the same ritual. He called his mother and then his two brothers, Gideon and Thane. All three of them understood the mentality it took for him to psych himself up to perform.

His brothers, as professional athletes themselves, had their own pregame rituals. Their mother proved to be a bit harder to train. She would call to wish Gunnar luck every now and then, probably when she thought his opponent looked too gruesome or menacing. She'd gotten better lately about letting him have his space.

After this match, he really had think about going to visit her. It'd been far too long since he'd been down to Virginia Beach and seen his mama. As soon as the thought entered his mind, his gut wrenched like he'd already been kicked in it by his opponent. The usual cold sweat he would get anytime he ventured close to the East Coast covered the back of his neck and back.

Although his mother would welcome him back home, not everyone would. Time and distance hadn't cleared Gunnar's mind of his past mistakes. He had a feeling some other people he'd left wouldn't be as open to his appearance.

Gunnar squeezed his eyes shut and stopped moving, stopped marching. He allowed the moment to be real for him, this fight, his job. He squeezed his taped hands, allowing the tightness of the adhesive to stretch over his achy knuckles.

He gazed down when a sharp pain struck a nerve in his wrist. He shook his hands to relieve the ache. The discomfort would be temporary. Security would last forever.

A two-rap knock sounded on the door before his trainer, Chuck Wilhelm, poked his shaved head into the locker room. Gunnar's insides twitched as soon as he saw the man. He knew what the next step would be. Showtime.

On instinct, Gunnar raised his hands, readying them to have them outfitted with his trademark black gloves with an eye embroidered on the backs of each. He already had his hair pulled back into a ponytail, something Chuck hated.

"Shave it all off," his trainer would tell Gunnar.

"What? And look like you? No way." Gunnar never thought his shoulder-length hair caused him a problem, especially since he never lost a fight because of it.

As Chuck approached him, Gunnar noticed his trainer carrying a cell phone.

"Call." Chuck held up the phone.

Gunnar shook his head. "You know the rule. No calls. No interviews. Just fighting." He picked up a plain black T-shirt and slipped it over his head.

"It's Mama." Chuck smirked.

"What?" Gunnar stopped moving.

"Queen Elizabeth." Chuck snorted. "Still don't understand how a big, blond dude has a black mother who calls herself Queen Elizabeth."

Gunnar didn't answer Chuck's standard question. He'd heard that comment about his relationship with his adoptive mother since she'd taken him and his brothers into her home.

Gunnar snatched the phone from Chuck's hand and turned his back to him. "Mama, how are you?"

To anyone else, Gunnar would have bitten their heads off and yelled about calling him before his fight. For the woman who had given him more chances than he deserved and a better life, she'd more than earned his respect.

"Darling," his mother said her standard opening that she gave to everyone. "How are you?"

As much as he didn't want to, Gunnar couldn't help but smile. She'd done it. With her smooth delivery and tone, she turned his insides to pudding. "Kind of a strange time to call to ask me how I'm doing, don't you think? I have my match starting in a few minutes. Chuck is getting me ready." He turned back to Chuck and held up one hand so that his trainer could slip on at least one glove.

"Oh, you have that thing tonight, don't you?" Her enunciation of each word further solidified her Queen Elizabeth nickname.

This time Gunnar did laugh out loud. "You can call it work, Ma."

"Good luck at *work* tonight." Elizabeth coughed.

The way she coughed raised the hairs on the back of his head. A standard Queen Elizabeth cough consisted of something that sounded like a slight puff of air through her always richly painted lips. She would usually follow what she considered an impolite expression with an apology. This time, she said nothing.

"Ma, what's wrong?" Gunnar squeezed his now-gloved hand into a fist.

"Why do you always assume the worst? You, out of all of my boys, are the most pessimistic, and I don't--"

"Don't start with me on that. You know--"

"Did you just interrupt me?"

His mother's stern tone came through clear on the small cell phone.

"I apologize." Gunnar had violated rule number one from his mother. Always hear a person's complete thought without interrupting. He certainly wouldn't want someone to cut him off midsentence.

"That's better. I think you hanging around those, um, those--"

"Coworkers," he added.

Elizabeth released an exasperated sigh. "You've done this fisticuffs thing long enough. I think it's time for you to come home."

Gunnar blinked. In all the years he'd done MMA, his mother had never asked him to quit and come home. Goose bumps sprang over his arms and crept up to his neck to the top of his head. He swallowed hard as he digested every word in her request. Then he heard a high-pitched beeping noise in succession…like in a hospital. A stone dropped in his gut.

"What's that sound?" Gunnar grounded himself to one spot. "Where are you? Are you in a hospital?"

"Guns, you've got to go." Chuck grabbed Gunnar's other hand.

The hold forced Gunnar to brace the phone against his ear using his shoulder. "One second." Gunnar didn't care about the match or Chuck. He needed to know what Elizabeth had neglected to share at the start of the call. "Ma, what's going on with you?"

"I know you have to go. We can talk later." Her voice cracked a little.

Gunnar's heart snapped. "Ma, don't hang up."

"You will be disqualified if you don't get out to the ring now." Chuck pulled on Gunnar's arm.

Gunnar snatched his limb out of his trainer's grip. "One damn minute!" he snapped at Chuck.

"We will talk later. Go do your fighting thing."

Her light voice made Gunnar imagine his gorgeous mother smiling. He couldn't smile. At the moment, his chest felt like every opponent he'd fought in his lifetime sat on it and constricted his air. He couldn't get out from under the weight. Right now, with his mother across the country, an arena full of people waiting for him, a ravenous opponent in the ring, and his impatient trainer, Gunnar found obstacles everywhere he turned.

Gunnar heard another woman's voice in the background.

"Queen, you cannot be on the phone."

"Who is that? Is that a nurse?" Gunnar scratched his head.

His mother cleared her throat. "No, it's not."

Gunnar heard some shuffling on the other end of the line.

"You need to get your rest. You can make your calls tomorrow before your tests."

Gunnar strained to hear this stranger's voice through the phone. It sounded a little familiar, but he couldn't place it.

"I love you." Elizabeth made a kissing sound through the phone before it disconnected.

Not content with ending the conversation that way, Gunnar tried redialing his mother. As he'd suspected, the number went to the reception desk at Virginia Beach General Hospital. After demanding to get transferred to Elizabeth Sommerville's room, he waited through several rings before disconnecting the call. Then he tried calling her cell phone. The call went straight to her voice mail.

He tried calling the hospital again. Once he got the main desk representative again, he asked about his mother. At the word cardiology, he nearly dropped to his knees. How could a woman who opened her home to three strangers have anything wrong with her heart?

After being transferred to the nurses' station, Gunnar unleashed a verbal assault. "I need to speak with a patient on your floor." Before she could ask for a name, he spouted, "Elizabeth Sommerville. Get her."

"Okay, please hold, sir."

Listening to the easy-listening jazz that played when the nurse placed him on hold didn't help to calm his nerves. Gunnar marched back and forth this time.

"Guns, you *have* to go." Chuck held the doorknob. He must have thought better of his decision to touch Gunnar again.

"One second." Gunnar held up his finger.

The music stopped. "Sir, Ms. Sommerville's daughter has requested no more calls for this evening. You can call again in the morning after eight."

Gunnar felt like flames engulfed his body. "Daughter? My mother doesn't have a daughter. She has three sons, and I'm one of them."

"Sir, I'm sorry. Your mother concurred with the young woman in the room with her, and we did just give her medication to help her sleep. Please give her a call in the morning when she wakes up." The nurse kept her voice even and authoritative, and before Gunnar could keep up his argument, she disconnected the call.

"Keep trying to call her." Gunnar shoved the phone at his trainer before cursing.

He hadn't even found out why his mother had to go to the hospital. Had she had a heart attack or a stroke? Every scenario he thought about had him grinding his teeth in anger.

"You have got to go." Chuck opened the door to usher him through.

A wave of chants flooded the room. The support should have been like a warm blanket around his body. Instead, Gunnar likened the shouts to spectators in a coliseum waiting to watch a hapless gladiator get mauled by a lion. Little did they know, he had enough fire in his belly to crush a lion, a tiger, and a whole damn safari.

"Something is going on with my mother. I'm fine just walking away right now. Just hop on a plane and go all the way back to Virginia." Gunnar put his fists to his hips and glared at Chuck to get across his intent.

The idea of going back to Virginia brought a layer of cold sweat that dripped from his head. He chewed the inside of his cheek, a habit he hadn't done since childhood when he'd prayed in his head that the foster father he'd had before getting with Queen Elizabeth wouldn't come home drunk with his own need to fight…anyone. Gunnar had left Virginia for a reason. Returning to it would stir up more questions and problems than what he faced in the ring.

Chuck held his hand up as a way to calm Gunnar, but Gunnar couldn't be reasoned with, calmed, or reassured until he either spoke to his mother or, better yet, saw her.

"Tell you what. I'll keep trying her. After your fight, you can talk to her again." Chuck placed Gunnar's heavyweight championship belt on Gunnar's shoulder.

Gunnar nodded. "Get her on the phone after the fight." He adjusted the heavy metal belt on the thick black leather backing.

Without another word, Gunnar stormed out of the door and headed to the octagon. The cheers from the audience roared in the large auditorium. He kept his stare directed on the lit ring. Fans grabbed at Gunnar's shirt and his arms as he stormed to the middle. He paid no attention to them.

The closer he got to the ring, the more his surroundings got smaller until his competitor became the only thing he saw at the end of his tunnel vision. He stepped into the ring and didn't bother stomping around like Tony "The Shark" Palombo. With it being a championship match, Gunnar handed his belt to the referee.

He didn't like the entertaining part of doing MMA. He just wanted to fight. Right now, he had a lot of aggression to get out of his system.

Gunnar broke his attention away from Tony for a moment to check Chuck. From the side of the ring, Chuck held up his phone to Gunnar and shook his head.

Gunnar wanted to race to the side and scream at his trainer to keep trying to get his mother. Why the hell was she in the hospital? Why wasn't that the first thing she'd said to him? Whatever afflicted her, it scared her enough to want him to come home. That fact consumed his thoughts more than anything else. He attempted to look at Chuck again when Tony got in his view.

"You're going down!" Tony screamed and stood an inch from Gunnar's nose.

Gunnar gritted his teeth. Right now, this hefty man sporting a Mohawk and tattoos covering the vast real estate of his enormous, chestnut-colored body stood in between him talking to his mother.

Gunnar removed his T-shirt and tossed it to Chuck. The screams heightened, especially from the women. He didn't pay attention to them. He had a job to do. He kept women out of his personal life so as not to get diverted from his goals, a decision that haunted him since jumping on a Greyhound bus ten years ago.

The referee spouted the rules and regulations that Gunnar ignored. The sounds in the arena blurred into one muted hum. His laser focus remained on Tony, directly on his eyes. He called this feeling right before he threw his first punch the glaze.

Chuck had once told Gunnar at the beginning of his career that every time he would start to fight, he got this glazed-over look in his eyes like he couldn't see anything else but the opponent in the ring with him.

A single sweat droplet rolled down between his shoulder blades. He planted his feet on the hard mat as he shoved his black mouth guard over his teeth. He tasted nothing but the bitter plastic. The palms of his hands itched in anticipation of what would happen. He had a job to do.

As soon as the match started, Tony surprised Gunnar by landing a solid punch to his left eye. A whole fireworks display lit up in Gunnar's head with the contact. He didn't even notice the pain. The man did carry some power behind his punch. Gunnar had something on him that even Tony didn't have--a purpose.

As soon as Gunnar filled his head with images of his mother in a hospital bed with tubes coming from her nose and wires attached to her fingers and hand, a volcano erupted inside of him that he couldn't contain or control.

Gunnar gave Tony a roundhouse kick to his head. The contact of the hit against his foot stung. That first strike sent an adrenaline rush through his body that gave him the needed boost for the next move.

When the big man hit the mat, Gunnar leapt on top of him and pounded his fists in his opponents face and head repeatedly. He heard nothing. Crimson shaded his gaze. He felt Tony's tree-trunk thighs attempt to hook him under his arms to bring him down. Instead, Gunnar moved down to the mat, cradled Tony's head in the crook of his elbow and framed the top of his head with his other arm.

Gunnar squeezed and clamped his legs around Tony's waist to keep the man still. Whenever Tony moved, Gunnar tightened his arms and legs around Tony's neck and body.

For every match, Gunnar kept his mind focused on winning, on his next move. Now, his mind clouded over with thoughts of his mother. What would he and his brothers do if something happened to her?

Until he felt the referee tapping his shoulder, Gunnar didn't realize that he had rendered Tony unconscious. He blinked and peered down at the person in his arms. Tony's blood dripped from his forehead and nose and onto Gunnar's arm.

"He tapped out, son. Release him." The referee grabbed Gunnar's arm and attempted to uncoil his hold on the limp body. "Stop fighting."

Gunnar blinked and unraveled himself from Tony. He sprang to his feet and gazed down at his handiwork. Tony's body lay motionless, curled in an unnatural position like a discarded marionette, as his trainers and handlers attempted to revive him.

Gunnar wanted to run from the ring, leave his belt, and get on a plane. He had to wait until Tony's trainers revived him. In that time, he paced in the ring, waiting for his moment.

Once Tony rose to his feet, the referee raised Gunnar's hand as the winner. A bit of relief washed over him. He'd finished work, and in record time. Now he had to go.

"Did you get her?" Gunnar asked as he climbed out of the ring and headed back to the dressing room.

He ignored the interviewers who shoved microphones into his face right after the match. From their grunts and groans, he knew they hated his silence.

"Are you kidding? You just did that match in about seven minutes. I barely had time to breathe let alone make calls for you." Chuck ran alongside of Gunnar.

"Guns! Guns! Just a quick question." An interviewer tried stopping Gunnar's trek by stepping into his path. "That match seemed too easy for you. Are you ready for Seamus Flannery, the second-ranked contender?"

Gunnar didn't answer. He stepped around the suited man and continued to his dressing room. If he didn't have another man's blood on him, he would have just thrown on some shoes and caught the next red-eye flight.

"You can't just blow off journalists." Chuck slammed the dressing-room door behind the two of them. "They can make or break your career."

"They haven't so far." Gunnar stripped. "You talk for me. I'm going to Virginia."

"Virginia? You can't go right now. You need to start training for your match with Seamus." Chuck started pacing.

Gunnar couldn't think about how Chuck felt. As much as he loved his career, Gunnar loved his family even more. With the threat of losing his mother, he would brave going back home to be with her.

Until he saw his mother and could see that he'd overreacted to whatever he'd heard on the phone, he wouldn't be able to rest. Then he would find out what woman had posed as his sister.

"What am I supposed to say as far as booking your next match?" Chuck asked.

Naked, Gunnar stood in the doorway leading to the bathroom to take a quick shower. "Tell them I'm going home."

* * * *

Eboni Danielson stirred awake with a throbbing pain in her neck thanks to sleeping in a steel and barely padded hospital chair. She should have slept on the couch, but she'd wanted to be as close to her friend as possible. She blinked to get a sleeping Queen Elizabeth into focus.

Yesterday morning, when Elizabeth had fainted in Press 'N Curl, the hair salon Elizabeth owned where Eboni worked, Eboni had wasted no time getting her friend and mentor to the hospital. Ever the diva, Elizabeth had refused to go until her hair had been styled and her nails had received a fresh coat of deep red polish.

Elizabeth looked like she'd redone her makeup sometime during the night. Her light brown skin glowed, especially with the morning sunlight streaming through the hospital-room window. Bright red lipstick covered her lips. Even her fake eyelashes looked like they had been curled.

As a child, Eboni and her girlfriends had all wanted to grow up to be just like Miss Queen Elizabeth. Not only did the woman always look amazing and have the best clothes and cool shoes, she owned not one, not even two, but three businesses.

The hair salon, more than her flower shop and the clothing boutique, had the most customers in Eboni's eyes, and the most buzz. Although she didn't plan to work in a hair salon for the rest of her life, Eboni definitely wanted to be close to the woman who could guide her into being a success in business.

The morning Queen fainted, Eboni had planned on talking to her about doing a fund-raiser to help renovate the community center. Kids with nothing to do had a tendency of finding dangerous activities to pick up from other wayward souls. Eboni didn't know how, but she knew she had to break the cycle.

A nurse walked into the room. "Ms. Sommerville, time to get your vitals." She opened the blinds and allowed the February sun to stream through them. The morning rays reflected off the gleaming-white snow that covered the ground.

Eboni wrapped her camel-colored dress coat around her body. The businesslike apparel didn't give her a cozy feeling like the poncho her grandmother had made for her. Appearances meant everything for Eboni.

Eboni remembered being a child and watching her grandmother knit the whole thing. She couldn't wait until she got to a size to wear it. Of course, her grandmother made the garment large anticipating that Eboni would never lose that baby weight that plagued her for most of her youth.

She'd changed. Times had changed. Eboni had to give up childhood fantasies, including finding that one true love. Seeing Elizabeth in a hospital bed made everything real.

"Do you have to wake her now?" Eboni rubbed her eyes. "She just got to sleep."

The nurse glanced down at Elizabeth's face and chuckled. "Is she going to an opera later? When did she put on all this makeup?"

"*She* can hear everything you're saying." Elizabeth opened her eyes and glared at the nurse before cutting her gaze over to Eboni.

"Darling, you didn't have to sleep in that awful chair." She shook her head.

"I didn't want to leave you alone." Eboni stretched her arms over her head attempting to relieve some of the ache in her neck. "Besides, I would have slept on the floor if I had to."

Elizabeth smiled, showing off an impressive set of straight, white teeth. "You're silly. The staff here would have taken care of me just fine." She finally turned her smile to the nurse who had already placed a black cuff around her arm and pumped away to get her blood pressure.

As the nurse allowed the blood pressure cuff to hiss out the air she'd pumped into it, she said, "A very loud and angry man called the desk for you last night." She removed the stethoscope from her ears. "He claimed that this woman is not your daughter." She glanced at Eboni.

Eboni swallowed but continued returning the nurse's stare, hoping to convince her of the lie Queen had told. Eboni hadn't corrected her. In a lot of ways, she did feel like she belonged in Queen's family.

"That's ridiculous," Queen said when she no longer had a thermometer in her mouth. "This beautiful young woman is as much as my child as my sons are."

Eboni smiled. She stood from her chair and held her friend's hand. The warmth of it as well as Elizabeth's words hugged her heart.

"Did you already pick your breakfast items today?" The nurse held up a menu.

"Yes. The lovely woman from food services got my order about an hour ago."

The nurse nodded and exited the room, partially closing the door behind herself.

Eboni felt her eyebrows draw together. "I don't remember hearing anyone coming into the room."

"Because you were out cold." Elizabeth placed her soft palm against Eboni's cheek and then brought it down to cover Eboni's hand. "You will need to go home at some point today to shower and get some real sleep."

Eboni shook her head. "Until the doctors tell me what's going on, I'm not leaving."

"Oh, honey, I know what it is. Back in my day, we called it having the vapors. I just got a little overwhelmed with work and had a little fainting spell. That's it." Queen removed her hand from Eboni's and turned her face away like she wanted to watch something on TV.

Eboni knew better. "I know Virginia is the South, but we're not that far south. I don't believe in this vapors nonsense. Something's going on with you, and I'm not leaving until I know what it is."

Elizabeth shook her head. "Stubborn. You're just like Gunnar."

At the mention of his name, Eboni became quiet. Like when he'd walked away from her ten years ago to pursue his fighting dream, Eboni's heart stilled again.

She'd thought she and Gunnar would have a future together. Her being African American hadn't stopped him from pursuing her, not that Eboni thought it would. If he didn't have a problem with his adoptive mother being black, she knew he would date outside of his race.

Eboni had been surprised the day he'd given her the critical ultimatum--go with him while he trained as an ultimate fighter, or break up with him and stay home. It had broken her heart to turn down his offer, but she couldn't leave. Not just yet.

"You talked to Gunnar?" Eboni backed up to her chair.

"I called him last night before his thing." Queen huffed. "I told him he should stop that stuff and come on home."

Eboni collapsed in the chair. "You told him to come home? Why?" Would the man who'd had no problems running from her ten years ago come home because his mother asked him to?

"Darling, while I'm a touch incapacitated, I'm going to need someone to run the businesses."

At that bit of news, Eboni's spine crumpled enough for her to melt her back into the chair. "I thought you would let me run Press 'N Curl."

"You are running Press 'N Curl. Gunnar will do what I do there." Elizabeth waved her hand as though this aspect meant very little to her.

"So he'll have his nails and hair done?" She winked at Elizabeth. The little bit of levity helped her not think of Gunnar.

Elizabeth gasped. "I do more than just have my hair and nails done."

"I know."

"Don't forget eyebrow waxing." Elizabeth winked.

Eboni laughed. Queen Elizabeth wouldn't be a success if she'd been an absentee owner. The woman defined hands-on. When a stylist didn't show, she had no problem taking their clients.

"What in the world am I going to do without you at the shop?"

"You'll be fine, and Gunnar will be fine in my spot." Elizabeth nodded. "I'll eventually have to bring my sons in to the businesses. I was just hoping it would happen later than sooner." She sighed. "Besides, all three have signed power-of-attorney forms for the businesses in case something happens to me."

It made sense to have Elizabeth's sons to acquire the three businesses when something happened to her. Eboni just hoped Gunnar would stay away from her while she worked.

"Speaking of bad timing." Eboni made sure to make eye contact with Elizabeth. "Before you, um, caught the vapors, I was going to propose that we do a fund-raiser for the Oceanfront Community Center. You know that in my free time I volunteer there."

"I know. That's why you haven't dated in forever and a day." Queen wagged her finger at Eboni.

Eboni sighed and ignored Elizabeth's comment about her sad personal life. "Anyway, besides volunteering, I've donated all of my tips to the center too. But it's not enough. You know business at the salon has dropped lately."

Elizabeth's expression changed to a forlorn one. "I know. I've tried drumming up more customers."

Eboni held up her hand. "We all appreciate your efforts. That's probably what landed you here." She patted Elizabeth's shoulder. "If the center doesn't get more money just for operating costs, they're going to have to close, and at-risk kids will take a wrong turn."

Queen Elizabeth regarded her for a moment before a broad smile lit up her face. "That's what I love about you." She sat up higher in her hospital bed. "Other people would have asked me for money. Hell, my own family has asked me for money just to go to Vegas. Not you. Not my girl. You want to *raise* the money."

Eboni's heart beat stronger. "I learned from the best. Working with you, I know that only hard work will get me what I want."

"You're right. You know I'm in for anything to help out that center. I know that after your mother passed, that place--"

"And your shop," Eboni interjected.

"Helped you growing up." She patted the mattress beside her. "Right now, I'm a little stuck. This is something that needs to happen soon, right?"

Eboni nodded. When a distressed expression crossed Elizabeth's face, Eboni had a change of heart. "Look, don't worry about it. I'll figure something out. I shouldn't have said anything." She waved her hands and backed up.

"If I wasn't out of action, I would love to help you." Elizabeth's eyes lit up. "I'm hoping Gunnar comes to town. If he does, he can help. Wouldn't it be great for you to see him again?"

Eboni swallowed hard. Did she want to see the man who'd been her first love? She wanted to hate him. He'd had a goal like she had when they'd severed their relationship. She and Gunnar had stubborn streaks as long as the universe.

Before she could answer, the hospital room door burst open. Encompassing the entire frame stood Gunnar. He had his dirty-blond hair pulled back into a ponytail. His crystal-blue eyes drew her attention to his strong face. His jaw looked like it had been chiseled from stone. He looked beautiful and scary all at once, especially with the addition of a black eye.

Eboni couldn't look in his face. She refused to watch any of his matches, but she imagined that his current hard expression matched what he would look like before each of his fights.

Her gaze volleyed between his full, very kissable lips and his barrel-sized chest. The more she stared at him, the more her heart accelerated. This man had given her the deepest heartache she'd ever had. Within a millisecond, she found herself still wanting him. She could kick herself for being so stupid now.

Eboni didn't remember Gunnar being that immense. Seeing him again made her want to stand up to him like one of his opponents. He'd caused her to cry more than she cared to admit. The hell she would allow him to make her feel less than her best. If confronted, she would let him know that.

"Ma, what's going on with you, and who's this daughter you said you have now?" Gunnar's voice boomed throughout the room, and probably all down the hall as well.

Guess the man came for a fight. She wouldn't back down.